THE LITTEL TALE OF WINTERING

By Richard Easter

This edition first published in Great Britain in 2022 by The Vivid Press.
thevividpress.co.uk

This paperback ISBN; 978-1-9162169-8-3

Also by Richard Easter
The Snow Trilogy;
The General Theory Of Haunting
The Gentle Art Of Forgetting
The Littel Tale Of Wintering

Cover Stories *(8 Classic Songs Remixed As Short Stories)*

Don't You Want Me? *(Anna Leeding Mystery Number One, 1981)*

"He scatters the snow like birds flying down,
and its descent is like locusts alighting.
The eye is dazzled by the beauty of its whiteness,
and the mind is amazed as it falls.
He pours frost over the earth like salt,
and icicles form like pointed thorns.
The cold north wind blows,
and ice freezes on the water;
it settles on every pool of water,
and the water puts it on like a breastplate."

- Ecclesiasticus 43.13-33

"Look, register, understand, and retain. Some truths can hide in plain sight if you don't look at them just so."

- Mrs Kerstmann.

INTRODUCTION

I'll start proceedings with these three statements.

First, thank you. Books are useless unless read, so you've just given this one its purpose.

Second, every story is made by two authors; the writer and the reader, which means we're in this together now. Writers fill the pages but readers draw the pictures, therefore everyone's novel is different even though the words are the same. So I sincerely hope you enjoy the tale you're now part of.

Third, this book can be read in one of two ways; as a totally rational and explainable series of events, *or* through a lens of magical thinking, where the fantastical is possible. Either way works whichever reader you decide to be, realist or fabulist.

To business, then; soon you'll meet the residents of an English village called Littel Wade. But before that, we must go back a few hundred years to its cold, stupid birth, because I believe to truly understand the present we must know the past. As you'll discover, context is everything.

R.E. 2022

PROLOGUE;

21st DECEMBER 1533
24th DECEMBER 2019

PROLOGUE (1)
DECEMBER 21st, 1533, SOMEWHERE IN DORSET, ENGLAND

"This is ridiculous. Now where am I? Exactly?"

Thomas Cromwell, Henry VIII's Surveyor Of The King's Woods, Chancellor of the Exchequer and more, glowered out of his carriage window at hunched, snow cloaked trees. It would soon be sundown, the hearths of his London home were over one hundred miles east and he was stuck in deepest and imminently darkest Dorset. "Does *anyone* know where we are?" he whined again. *Because I don't*, he thought, *In fact, I don't even know why I am here at all.*

Two days ago the king had charged Cromwell to find a location for a garrison near Dorchester. It was an unusual request which left Thomas suspicious of Henry's motives. Being this far from power made him nervous since the court were constantly jockeying for favour. Anyone who left the immediate vicinity (or even left the *room* at times) could find themselves frozen out. And now Cromwell was literally frozen out, which made him extremely worried.

He banged on the carriage roof.

"*Coach-mannnnn*," he bellowed again. "I asked where I am."

There was an impatient snapping of reins from above, the vehicle stumbled to a halt and its driver clambered down. The man looked like cold itself made flesh; a sallow, extremely unattractive proposition.

"Yes, sir, chancellor, sir, yes?"

Obsequiousness does not excuse stupidity, Thomas thought.

A couple of the soldiers escorting him lazily rode back to see what the problem was.

"Ah, sir, it's Dorset, sir," said one, pleased with himself.

"Oh, I know that," Thomas hissed."But what I specifically wish to know is where in Dorset am I?"

"Ah, well, there's the problem. I have reconsidered my route and may have made a wrong turn a mile or four southwards." The coachman pointed back down the track."I now believe Dorchester is…that-a-way, no more than ten mile. If the mares don't tarry, we'll be there just after sundown."

"Wonderful."Cromwell leaned out of the window. "Oh, what's that on your neck?" he asked with a concerned expression.

The driver felt around his neck with both hands.

"I don't know, sir."

"It's your head. Enjoy it while you can. Now make haste."

*

Eventually another road appeared, heading south. As fresh snow began to fall, the carriage stopped. Thomas saw a few shacks in the distance and battered on the roof once again.

"*Coach-mannnn!* What now?"

"Dip in the road, sir. Looks quite deep, iced up. I could try to lead the horses in, but if we get stuck or worse still the axle breaks, we're going no-where for a long time."

The thought made Cromwell shiver and not just from the cold. He could *pretend* to have investigated the land but Henry had spies everywhere. This moronic driver might even be a theatre-class actor who reported back to the king. Thomas couldn't take that risk.

"There's no way to pass? Through the fields, perhaps?"

There was a noise from above which could have been coughing or laughing.

"Fields are about three feet lower than the track, sir. Topped up with snow. No chance."

Cromwell smacked his fist against the door in frustration and clambered from the carriage. The soldiers trotted back.

"We have to pass. Could I ride with one of you through that dip in the road?"

The soldiers examined the frozen hole.

"We could, but the ice might make the mares slip. Or if it's too deep, they could get caught in the mud underneath, then fall. We've been given strict instructions to protect your person, sir. If we go over, you could be crushed by the horse, sir. Not nice being crushed by a horse. My cousin got crushed by a horse. Broke his eyes."

"Broke his *eyes*?"

"Both of them. Cracked like walnuts. He had very brittle eyes, my cousin. Terrible affair."

Cromwell paced through the snow and tried not to scream. "Then we cross on foot! I have to examine the lie of the land for myself. The king has ordered it!"

Because the king is treating me like a bobolyne, he thought. *There are no end of people that could have carried out this mission, but yet he chose* me. *And that is a big worry.*

Cromwell strode toward the dip's icy surface and gingerly placed one foot upon it. The ice held.

I have to show leadership, since any one of these idiots could be recording every move for the king to mock me with later.

He tentatively took another step.

"The ice holds!" He beckoned to his three gawping companions. "Come, let us…" At that point, the ice decided not to hold any more. Cromwell fell through, flailed, but had no choice than to head forward. A few sodden steps further and he'd reached the other side. Now a frozen, shivering mess, Thomas looked toward the huts, from which what appeared to be an ambulatory bundle of rags approached.

The chancellor attempted to sound authoritative."You there. I am Thomas Cromwell and I represent the king. What is the name of this place?"

The rags shrugged. He could now see they covered a woman of indeterminate age.

"Name? No *name*, sir." She seemed amused by the very idea. "So what brings you here? I see that this is a foreign land to you, just as a smile is a foreign language to your face. It does not hurt to smile, sir."

"It does if smiling results in painful, drawn out execution."

The woman laughed. "Oh, sir, you do have a fine sense of humour."

"Oh, I do. So if this place does not have a name, then what is yours?"

The woman told him her name but he could barely make it out, lost in Dorset's rolling vowels and tapping consonants.

"No matter, woman, no matter, your name is of no consequence, much like where you live. I am not surprised. I have regretfully found somewhere so uninviting one even has to even do a pathetic little wade to get in."

The coachman laughed. "Perhaps that's what it should be called, sir!" He tittered. "You've just named it! We should call it Little Wade. A good name, a right name, wouldn't you say?"

Cromwell had to admit the man was right. And he liked the responsibility for naming something. Despite himself, the minister laughed.

"Indeed! It is a good name for a place full of nothing and no-body that one must wade through ice to visit. Where none should wish to live, that removes all traces of a smile." He warmed to his theme. "A place even

God himself would become stuck! I curse it! Make all regret their choice of home and never smile forthwith! Yes, Little Wade it shall be. Let us be the first true noble men to set foot in *Little Wade*, where no man shall ever smile again!"

Cromwell strode back to the carriage and his place in history. The ragged woman shouted after him, "I fear you have cursed this cold place to sadness, sir! Cursed it to sadness!"

*

So that is why Little Wade earned itself such a curious name, but I'll defer the reason for the unusual spelling *Littel* until later.

Although we must leave Thomas Cromwell in his frozen torment for now, we'll meet him twice more in the course of this tale, and each time a truth will be revealed.

Although of course that rather depends on how one defines *truth*.

Come, onward.

PROLOGUE (2) / THE MARRYMAN FOREST, LITTEL WADE, 24TH DECEMBER 2019

It is exactly 177,511 days after Thomas Cromwell literally fell into a place *he* called Little Wade, but we'll know as *Littel* Wade. However, before we visit the village we must first head to a forest just outside its boundary.

*

Dressed in camouflage gear, Gregory Underbore crept between birch trees and gorse. Frozen ground is full of traps for an unwary hunter; the cracks and snaps of fallen branches and icy puddles are loud enough in daytime, but at one thirty a.m. even Greg's shallow breathing was a cacophony.

Occasionally a pair of tawny owls called out to one another from deep inside the woods. Gregory knew the tawny's *t-wit t-woo* cry was actually two birds; a female called *k-wick,* then the male responded; *hoo-hoo*. He'd learned the forest's many languages because this place was his training ground.

Greg was sixteen, a gangly boy with few friends who'd left school in June with poor qualifications and no intention of taking education any further. Besides, his mother wanted him to get a job, any job, because, as she'd explained often and loudly, "The bills don't pay themselves."

But Gregory's dream career lay in the army, and to that end he read military histories, ran every day, watched endless war documentaries… and hunted.

He held a crossbow at his side

Mother sneered at his army fixation as she sneered at most things, but didn't know about these nocturnal trips. Nobody did, because the weapon in his hand could get him into a lot of trouble. Crossbows are banned to under eighteens in the UK, and Greg had also illegally converted this one to a lethal draw weight. Then there was his presence and intention in the forest; hunting is forbidden in Britain except on private land with the owner's permission, which he obviously didn't have. So at this moment Gregory Underbore was breaking at least four laws simultaneously, and this wasn't the first time he'd crossed the line.

Despite his young age he was already known to the police; vandalism, theft and affray were just three of the offences they knew about. He'd been cautioned, fined and given a referral order already, so being caught here in the forest would earn him a more serious punishment.

But Greg couldn't help himself. The hunt was addictive.

He stilled, watched as his breath became cloud and then heard a distant shuffling as *something* picked its way through the undergrowth.

October has a Hunter's Moon, November, Beaver, and in December, tonight's shimmering Cold Moon, which briefly illuminated a patch of grey between two trees.

Greg's eyes widened as he realised the grey was a Roe deer. Roe can become nocturnal if regularly disturbed during the day, and a nearby B-road had forced Marryman Forest's deer into becoming night foragers.

A tuft of fur on this one's rump identified her as female. She daintily nipped at leaves and occasionally raised her head to check the surroundings. Greg felt his heartbeat quicken. He'd never killed a deer, since they were protected by law. That alone would make this moment so much more satisfying.

As Greg raised the crossbow his hands shivered with excitement. A head shot would ensure a quick, merciful death, then he'd remove the bolt, take a photo and cover the corpse with vegetation. Underbore would be long gone before the body was found or the forest's other residents disposed of it in their own way.

Greg focused on three elements; the sight, trigger and doe's head. He stopped breathing, since even the slightest movement could ruin his aim.

Everything froze.

Gregory Underbore waited to squeeze the trigger.

The doe unknowingly waited to meet her maker.

At that moment, a tawny called out again; *K-wick!*

The deer raised her head, span, and rushed away. Greg fired, but the bolt missed by a heartbeat and he heard it slam into a tree. His prey crashed away through the awakened forest as wings flapped all around like sarcastic applause. The doe ran full pelt in the opposite direction.

"Fuck *fuckfuckfuck*," Greg whispered, the habit of silence too ingrained to break.

*

But then he saw something, and that something is this story.

*

7

Twenty minutes later, Greg stumbled home. Hyperventilating, eyes wild, trousers wet with urine and jacket caked with vomit, he slammed his door and collapsed against the hallway wall.

"Hello?" Greg's mother screeched from inside her bedroom. "Gregory? What's going on?"

"In the forest…" he managed, then fainted away.

BOOK ONE;
DECEMBER 21st, 2022

1/ LITTEL WADE, DORSET, DECEMBER 21st, 2022

489 years after a freezing Cromwell named it, Littel Wade had grown in size if not fame, a wallflower hiding on a B-road ten miles from Dorchester. Nestled in patchwork fields and islands of dense forest, the village keeps itself to itself.

Littel Wade has gifted the world no famous sons nor daughters, and its understated prettiness isn't enough to attract visitors lost on their way somewhere else. Usually they're heading a few miles south to Cerne Abbas, well-known for a chalk giant carved into a nearby hill. The boggle eyed colossus wields a massive club but one's eyes are drawn to something of similar shape below it. Therefore, any competition between Littel Wade and an aroused behemoth was never going to be a fair fight.

Nothing much has ever happened there.

Until now.

*

So let's go high into the winter solstice sky to fly with curlews, blackbirds, and robins.

From up here the village looks like a tree, with the High Street as its trunk and many smaller branches jutting off. At one end stands St Nicholas' Church, surrounded by a sprawling graveyard and its many residents.

There, see, carved in the many headstones;

Mary Gortoney, Sleeping now in the arms of angels 1834 - 1842

William Fillirish 1807 - 1872 Husband of Victoria, Father to Edina & Ada.

Patience Marryman, nee Dawn, beloved by Francis, with the stars now, iterum, 1774- 1809

These three and others will return to join our story in time, but for now let's leave them at rest.

Look down; there's a Co-op, newsagents, butchers, fish and chip shop, fruit and veg, a tiny primary school next to an even smaller post office…

all the usual suspects. At the far end, a garage and small playing field. The main supporters for any rare sporting events are trees and they never take sides.

There's just one road in and out, so bread and milk are hoarded at the first sight of a snowflake. In past harsh winters, Littel Wade was cut off for days but the villagers didn't care. Generally they don't care for the rest of the world anyway, so a snow barrier might even be considered welcome.

Today is literally the start of winter but you wouldn't know Christmas was coming. You might see a dull twinkle of festive lights in one or two windows, but there are no civic decorations nor decorated tree in a square. There is no square.

Whatever the month there is a curious stillness to Littel Wade. In August insects buzz without enthusiasm, in December birds speed past without a further glance. The earth beneath them is hard, cold and frozen. Some might say many of the people here are the same.

But as we swoop, the clouds part and sunlight breaks through for a moment. An angel's ladder spreads across the land, then…what *is* that?

A *flash-flash* from within a clearing in the nearby forest.

It is the glint of sun on…something.

That something is why we are here.

It's possible that something should not exist.

But as the curtain of clouds draw together again, *whatever-it-is* flashes once more and reality wobbles for a second.

2/ LITTEL WADE / 7:45 a.m. 21st DECEMBER 2022

Up, up again into Littel Wade's cloud cover we go, and there, tumbling in the wind, raindrops crystallise into spires, shards, spikes, scaffolds.

A single snowflake grows within the droplets. Heavier now, it falls, reaches the border between cloud and air, rides high and low pressures, then plunges to feel earth for itself.

Some perspective; a snowflake's falling rush is illusory, since we only see its journey's closing moments. In fact most take around forty-five minutes to travel from cloud to earth, jostling with their millions of frozen brothers and sisters. But today this one flake has the sky to itself. As we fall alongside our view takes in a large swathe of Dorset, but soon Littel Wade will focus.

In time, Dawn Street near St Nicholas' Church becomes the obvious landing ground. It touches down on the driveway of number nine, stays whole for a heartbeat then melts away, unnoticed by anyone except us.

The snowflake is gone but we're still here. Come.

3/ DAWN STREET, LITTEL WADE, 8:15 a.m.

Dawn Street comprises just eighteen houses, but long ago only one great hall stood here, home to the once-wealthy Dawn family. Their fortunes fell in the mid-nineteenth century and their hall followed a few decades after. The only signs the Dawns were ever here are the name of this street and a few graves in St Nicholas'. All things pass.

Number nine is a semi detached with driveway and small, bare front garden.

Come inside with me. Don't worry, we're invisible.

Step over the old sleeping labrador on his dirty blanket by the front door, through the thin hallway then into the kitchen, where Peter Piper eats breakfast and stares out at his little back garden.

Before we meet him properly, I must answer the obvious question. Because like Littel Wade, Peter Piper has a perfectly reasonable explanation for such a peculiar name and therefore I shall get it out of the way before we proceed.

Like most parents-to-be, Julie and Anthony Piper had struggled with naming their child. They'd discarded old and dead relatives' names, because, well, they sounded old and dead. Then, in the bleakest of bleak winters, the baby decided, *OK, I'm ready to come and visit.* But as I've pointed out, Littel Wade and snow don't mix well and on that freezing day, it arrived with a vengeance. On January the eighth a monsoon of flakes fell; a god-send for the village children but a nightmare for Julie Piper. The snow was lovely, dark and deep, so no-one was prepared to risk moving a woman in labour *on a tractor* to a maternity ward over ten miles away.

Then the power went out.

"Just like old days," laughed locals in the Anchor pub by candle-light. In Dawn Street, candles were also lit, Anthony Piper boiled pans of hot water and fetched towels as Julie lay with a local midwife between her legs.

"*Breathe*," offered the midwife, who couldn't offer much else since there was no gas, air, nor pethidine; just Anthony and snow, which flittered about the window as if trying to see what the excitement was all about.

"I *am* breathing," moaned Julie. "Look, I'm breathing, uuuh, uuuh, uuuh, see, oh goodness, it hurts, oh…my…goodness!"

"You're not breathing properly," scolded the midwife.

"How…am…I..supposed…to…breathe…*properly*…?"

"In a rhythm, but slowly. Say a nursery rhyme or something out loud, but just stop breathing *so much*."

So Julie said the first thing that came into her head.

"Peter Piper picked a peck of pickled pepper," she strained. "Peter… Piper…uh…picked a…peck of…uh…pickled pepper…Peter…Piper… Peter…Piper…"

After two freezing hours in a blackout by candle-light, a boy was born. So by virtue of his unusual birth there was only one name he could possibly be given; Peter Piper, of course.

Yes, Julie and Anthony knew few people are named for a tongue twister, and they wondered what it might lead to when he was old enough for school and beyond, but Peter Piper just felt *right*.

So now you know.

That was almost seventeen years ago, so let's return to Peter in his kitchen on the morning of 21st December, 2022.

*

He gazed out at his tiny, bare back garden, large green eyes fixed to a spot just by the rear fence. Peter's red hair had gifted him pale skin, so in contrast his mouth appeared darker, almost as if wearing lipstick. This combination meant well-meaning adults often mistook him for a girl when he was at primary school then that androgyny caused problems from a few bullies at Dorchester High, but less so at Sixth Form. The further up the educational tiers one climbed, the more the idiots seemed to drop away.

College had broken up last Friday and Christmas was just four days hence, but like the rest of Littel Wade, number nine Dawn Street seemed in no mood to celebrate. Yes, every December the first (by mum's decree thus now family tradition) a raggedy plastic Christmas tree was pulled from the loft then stood in the living room. But with each passing year the tree seemed to diminish. When Peter was little it glistened and sparkled. Now the blinking lights looked like sighs.

There'd been a lot of sighs over the last three years. Covid-19 had crept into everyone's lives and put the planet under house arrest. Millions lost their lives and millions more their businesses, savings, mental health and education. Peter didn't know how he'd managed to pass so many GCSE's but often thought he'd had no choice. School and study were a very welcome distraction.

Ironically, Littel Wade hadn't changed much during the pandemic. Its people were already emotionally locked down. And like those medieval villages who'd self-isolated during the Great Plague, Littel Wade mainly escaped infection by virtue of physical and spiritual geography. Three villagers had died of Covid throughout the entire dreadful time, pensioners who'd contracted the virus whilst away in hospital. The other inhabitants had been more than happy to Stay At Home, Protect The NHS and Save Lives. It wasn't even an imposition but their preferred way of life.

There would never be a good time to have a pandemic but for Peter, 2020 was the worst window for its arrival. But what is, *is*, and can't be negotiated with.

The kitchen clock ticked on and as always, his eyes were drawn to a framed montage of family photos.

Tick, mum & dad on their wedding day.

Tock, Peter as a baby.

Tick, Peter as a toddler.

Tock, mum, proud, in her police uniform.

Tick, Peter starting school.

Tock, Peter and his grandparents, both now gone.

Photographs are reassuring because they're immutable. The past is like that; once an event is over, it's fixed and can't be tinkered with, for good or bad.

Two miles away, Peter's father Anthony also sat, stared, and thought.

4/ ANTHONY PIPER, OUTSIDE LITTEL WADE / 8:15 a.m.

Anthony Piper sat in his Vauxhall Astra on a lay-by two miles from Dawn Street.

Anthony, or Tony to his friends, is tall and gangly with a lined, handsome face topped with a wiry mass of black hair, greyed at the temples.

For ten years until 2020, Tony had worked at the four star C&H Hotel in Dorchester as a Front Of House Manager. But then the virus had settled over the world, lockdowns began and social distancing became law. As pubs and restaurants closed and travelling long distances became illegal, hospitality and holiday industries were decimated. Bookings at the C&H dried up, weddings, anniversary and birthday parties were cancelled and corporate events disappeared. As shareholders drew up their financial drawbridges, jobs disappeared too. The rich made sure they stayed rich whilst expendable numbers like Anthony Piper were thrown in the way. Britain introduced a furlough scheme which paid 80% of a worker's original monthly earnings but like so many others, the Piper family had lived on the very edge of their means before Covid. During it, they dropped off that edge.

So Tony became an Uber Driver.

As infections and death rates climbed, he wore a face mask and put up plastic sheeting between front seats and rear. He kept two disinfectant sprays at his side like a cowboy would holster his guns. The idea of sitting at home doing nothing and waiting for the viral storm to pass was untenable to both his financial and mental states. Like a shark, if Anthony Piper stopped moving he would drop to the bottom of a dark ocean and stay there until his time came.

Taxi driving during a pandemic was as frightening as it sounds. There weren't many customers to begin with, but soon Tony found himself having daily verbal battles with righteous passengers who refused to mask up and spouted theories a friend of a friend had seen somewhere in the paranoid outposts of the internet. But journeys were mainly conducted in silence, which allowed Tony to be mentally elsewhere as another area of his brain dealt with driving. He preferred night work because with pubs shut, passengers were often silent *and* sober.

Anthony liked that just fine.

Then at the end of a working night he'd sometimes find himself parked in this particular lay-by. Tony never planned to come, but one part of him was drawn here while another screamed to take a different route.

He rarely did.

So by the first grey of morning his Astra would slip into this lay-by and as its engine died Anthony would also become still. The temperature inside dropped but he never seemed to notice. An observer would be forgiven for thinking he'd died at the wheel were it not for the tiny puffs of condensation he exhaled.

Tony always stared at one specific point in the tree-line. On these early mornings much of Dorset's nocturnal wildlife still went about their business; tawny owls flashed among trees and Roe occasionally stepped from the forest, but Piper's eyes never wavered.

As his breath fogged the windscreen and he could no longer see the trees, their hold over him loosened. Anthony would become aware of the cold and glance around the car's interior as if discovering it for the first time.

Then he would remember what was in the car's boot.

He'd shiver and pull away, but *it* remained there in the darkness, just a few feet behind him.

And so today, once again, Tony had returned to this spot where he stared, waited, and wondered if this were finally the time to take out what he kept hidden.

5/ PETER PIPER, 8:15 a.m.

Unaware his father gazed into another distance, Peter's eyes remained fixed on the back garden. Even as a small child, he'd often disappeared into these reveries. Mum and dad laughingly called them his "Peter ponder" moments.

*

There was movement to the left in Peter's peripheral vision. He glanced over and saw mum framed in the kitchen doorway wearing her police uniform. For the briefest of moments Julie Piper looked pale and tired but then, as if a switch had been flicked, her face brightened and she seemed to cut from black and white to full colour. "Morning, pondery, you're off in a world of your own again, I see," she smiled."Where *do* you go to, my lovely?"

"Just, you know…" He offered.

"Well, I don't, that's why I asked." Julie looked up at the kitchen clock. "God, I am running *so* late this morning. My lift'll be here any minute." Peter looked his mother up and down. She was in her mid thirties, slim, brunette and blessed with a smile that could blast through even the greyest days. From old photos Peter knew she hadn't changed much since her teenage years.

"Got any plans for today?" She switched on the kettle.

"Nope."

"Good. That's as it should be. Holidays are for doing nothing. That's kind-of the whole point of them. I didn't hear dad come in, did I?"

"Not yet, no."

"So what were you thinking about? You were miles and *miles* away."

"Just Christmas."

"*Just* Christmas? I don't think the words ' just' and 'Christmas' should ever be used together. Barely out of short trousers and yet so cynical already," she giggled.

"No, I mean…" Peter gestured to the cold world outside. "Does Christmas seem different to you? I don't feel as…what's the word, "Christmassy" as I used to."

"Ah, well, there's this thing called *growing up*, you see." Mum wistfully looked out at their boxy, bare back garden. "I bet when you were very little that seemed like a jungle. Now it's just a tiny patch of space. Same goes with Christmas, and I agree with you. When I was younger the trees seemed greener, the snow, er, snowier, the tinsel more…tinselly, is that a word?"

"It should be."

"Yes, it should. But then time rubs all the magic off the edges. Wait, are you mourning your childhood? Already?" She grabbed his cheek with her thumb and forefinger then pinched. "You're just a baby!"

"Ow, stop it."

"Never. You'll always be my baby, even when you're in your fifties. That's how it works. But don't worry about Christmas, that feeling will come back, no matter what this world throws at you. Christmas always comes back."

Peter smiled and mum craned round to look down the hallway. "Dad stays out too long on these night shifts. What time did he leave yesterday?"

"About ten, wasn't it?"

"Too long. How many times have I told him? That's too long. Nights screw you up, trust me. Promise me you'll never get a job that involves working nights. And especially one that means working nights *and* dealing with people who drain the life out of you."

"Bad at work at the moment?"

She nodded, sadly. "Ah-ha. But I'm a police officer and, 'Bad at work,' is pretty much the job description." She poured herself a cup of tea, but then from outside came the sound of a car horn. "Not even time for a cuppa and so quickly, here we go again," she sighed, put on her hat and jacket, took a deep breath then smiled widely at her son. "But I'm lucky. Nothing bad happens in here. You make everything tinselly, all year round. Have a good day, but don't forget your jobs. Come and see me off?"

Peter followed his mother up their thin hallway. She opened the door and there as always, was a police Ford Mondeo in its distinctive yellow and blue livery. Peter recognised the driver, who waved his way. Mum opened the car door, leaned in, then popped back up with a loudhailer.

"I *lo-o-ooo-ove* you!" she crackled, laughed and got into the vehicle.

Peter quickly disappeared back inside before the neighbours came to their windows, his normally pale face flushed with embarrassment.

*

Peter had two chores to do this morning. First, the daily walk with Benji, his eleven year old labrador. Second, visiting Marsh The Butchers to pick up this year's Christmas turkey. He pulled on wellingtons, parka, then a blue snowflake-patterned scarf mum knitted him a few years back.

"Walk?" Peter said. That one word is all it takes for any dog. Benji came bounding in, sat and waited to be dressed in his lead. This formality is like a soldier receiving a medal. The dog somehow seems to puff up as if being bestowed an honour which they richly deserve.

Peter opened the door and opted to head up the High Street. Along the way, he passed shops and saw people that had been part of his life since he was born. We should see them too. They're important.

6/ THE HIGH STREET, LITTEL WADE, 8:30 a.m.

The sky had shed its grey but still wasn't frozen enough for snow. There was no morning frost, either. Frost prepares the ground like an undercoat for snow, but not today. A chill wind pushed past villagers like it had somewhere very important to go with no time to get there.

Peter and Benji passed the Candy Box sweetshop; inside, little more than a vintage glass cabinet full of confectionary opposite a wall full of faded village notices. Amongst them, an old comic poster of Superman from even before he became a movie star. Things do *not* change in Littel Wade. All day, every day, owner Mr Julian Farr lurked in shadows behind the counter. No-one knew how old Julian was. He could have been a very well preserved one hundred and fifty or a dilapidated seventy. Greasy thin hair hung over large red ears, while Karloffian winged eyebrows fanned out to his temples. Mr Farr's default expression was *grimace,* which everyone agreed was totally unsuited to a purveyor of treats.

Moving on, Peter passed the imaginatively titled *Fruit And Vegetable Shop* where its proprietor Mrs Joyce Bramell sat and stared amongst her produce like an old, tired harvest queen.

Peter waved.

As Mrs B's right hand flapped like a broken windscreen wiper in return, her left twirled in a grey bracken of hair. Joyce seemed like a child who'd woken up trapped in a pensioner's body. Her voice was composed of sighs, as if speaking was both too much effort and a source of great sadness.

"Hello, Mrs Bramell," one might say, "chilly morning, isn't it?" one might add.

"*Sighhhhh*, yes, *siiiggghhh*, hellloooo, *yessss*, *siggggh,*" she'd reply in the language of a depressed serpent.

Peter walked on past the laundrette (called simply "Laundrette" naturally) where slack jawed villagers had bagged their seats. The Laundrette Show was very popular and always had the same plot, in which a group of clothes drowned whilst engaged in a wrestling match. The geriatric owner Mrs Newman sat in a back room and watched the customers watch their linen. There was no need for her to be there since the machines were automatic but despite her permanent scowl, she seemed to enjoy studying the wildlife.

Onward, past the Co-op.

Peter risked a furtive glance at the nearest checkout but it was occupied by Renee, the sixty-something manager. That was a shame. Peter could always find one excuse or another to visit the Co-op if Phoebe was on duty.

Past the newsagent, called, rather stridently and without the definite article, NEWSAGENT. Mr Nelson was in there somewhere, another husk of a person who spent his days tut-tutting at salacious celebrity magazines which he read cover to cover just to annoy himself.

Past the post office (called, yes, POST OFFICE), butchers, (BUTCHER), Mr Davies' Garage, (DAVIES' GARAGE) and Littel Wade Primary School, (LITTEL WADE PRIMARY SCHOOL).

Peter had gone there of course, a tiny building with three classrooms, playground, and a draughty little hall which doubled as both school canteen and theatre. But on the last day of winter term that dull hall became a place of magic because just before last bell, Santa Claus came. In those first few innocent years at primary, his appearance was about as close to genuine hysteria the children ever came.

"You'll never guess who's come to see you!" the headmaster would bellow, cue for Peter and his friends to shriek, "Father Christmas!"

"That's right!" the head confirmed, "and here…He… IS!"

In the unforgiving light of a sixteen year old's memory, Peter could now picture the scene as it actually happened, rather than how his six year old self perceived it. At first from side stage came a desperate rustling of thick red curtains, as *someone* tried to find their way through. After a seeming eternity of pulling and angry muttering this person would stagger through and inevitably trip on the folds. Then HE was there, bigger than life itself.

The one, *the* only…Rewarder Of Nice, Chastener Of Naughty, live and direct from The North Pole…

Yes, Father Christmas is *in* the building.

Six year old Peter was reduced to a series of nonsense words, like a true believer speaking in tongues. "*Gah de-fah-de-Father-de-Chris-ga-de-Chris-fa-gah-de!*"

Santa's costume was made of cheap red material with frayed white cuffs and wonky collar. If he'd gone near a naked flame, Father Christmas would have gone up like a Roman Candle soaked in petrol. Luckily there was never any fire around, so the awful image of a napalmed St. Nick remained thankfully unfulfilled. Santa's hat kept slipping over his eyes so he was constantly pushing it up with a gardening-gloved hand. Keeping the gardening theme going he wore wellington boots, but not even black ones.

Green.

Then there was the beard, a sorry piece of cotton wool held up by elastic and hope; actually less a beard and more a flat white cat hanging on for dear life. But through sheer force of will and true faith, little Peter airbrushed such inconvenient details from reality.

By the time Peter was eight virtually his entire year had realised Father Christmas was obviously Ted Hamnett the school caretaker. Hamnett never spoke to the kids but was always in the distance doing important things. But on this special day, despite green wellingtons and dead white cat, he went about his role with gusto.

Ho's were *Ho'd* frequently and with relish. A most merriest of Christmases was offered to every child, along with a small wrapped item from a large black bin bag. More than anything else, Peter thought the bin bag should have brought the whole house of cards tumbling down, but he'd managed to see past it. The gifts were always a toy plane for the boys, plastic hair set for the girls. *Stereotype* is not a pejorative term in Littel Wade, but rather an acceptable lifestyle choice. After the dispersal of presents, Santa would take a seat on stage and read three poems; Clement Clarke-Moore's "*A Visit From St Nicholas,*" e.e.cummings' "*Little Tree,*" and Robert Frost's "*Stopping By Woods On A Snowy Evening.*" Year in, year out, always those three verses. Therefore generations of Littel Wade children associated Santa Claus with poetry, which Peter believed was possibly Mr Hamnett's greatest gift to the kids, because the actual presents were shabby.

And so Peter's faith in Father Christmas began to wobble, shift, and finally disintegrate. This is perhaps the first and most important lesson most children learn. Along with the death of a pet, the fading of Santa Claus is harsh proof things that seem permanent can simply disappear. Sometimes this awful truth takes time to make itself known, at others, the realisation happens in moments. Some grieve for Santa and look for him at Christmas for the rest of their lives. Others shrug and move on, only then find to their horror they had no idea what grief *really* is.

Peter could see into the school hall and just for a moment he pictured himself bouncing on its wooden floor as Mr Hamnett alchemised beard, wellingtons, and bin bag into magic. He stood on the spot while Benji waited, aware his friend, although still and silent, was busy. Eventually Peter re-inhabited himself.

"Come on Benji, this way, I think." Peter walked with purpose toward the tree line. "Let's go to Marryman Forest."

7/ THE MARRYMAN FOREST, LITTEL WADE, 09:00

Leave Littel Wade, head south toward Cerne Abbas and one is quickly surrounded by trees stretched over the thin road like an honour guard. There are no street lights, so even in the height of summer the road remains shadow-dappled. Sudden bends jump out at unwary drivers, and even the locals, who know every curve, treat it with respect. Only a fool would put their foot down on this nameless stretch, which starts in Dorchester as a river would, wide and free flowing, before thinning and becoming a tiny tributary of the A352.

*

Once in a while Peter would cycle out of Littel Wade and ride down that winding road. When a vehicle approached he'd pull over, wait for it to pass then resume his journey. The drivers might have wondered why this teenager's expression was so fixed and purposeful.

After twenty minutes he'd stop and stand in a very specific part of the woodland.

Peter was unaware his dad also made a lonely pilgrimage to this very place. Both father and son stared at a spot in the tree-line, and neither ventured close to it. As magnets can attract and repel each other, this particular location drew Peter then pushed him away at the last moment.

He never planned to come, but just as a bird feels it is time to migrate, he sometimes had an instinctual need to mount his bike and go south. Then, just like Anthony Piper, Peter would lose all track of time here. Eventually a screeching bird or passing car might pull him from his reflections and he'd robotically climb back onto his bike and head home.

Anthony timed his early morning visits for when Peter was in bed, or just getting up. Peter timed his for when dad slept after a night's driving. Neither knew nor suspected they were two sides of the same coin. If they had, this would have been a very different story.

*

The woodlands around Littel Wade have no official names but over time locals have given them titles. One might walk in Magpie Grove, go bird watching at Major's Farm (there'd been no farm on the spot for hundreds of years, let alone a major) have illicit meetings within Teller's Wood and so on. The etymology of many of these names has been lost over time but all have theories, rumours and fables attached, as is right and proper. We mythologise our surroundings to feel part of greater, older legends, rather than just people passing through.

The name "Marryman Forest" appears on no maps, but ask any local where it is and they'll know. The forest was gifted to Lord Robert Marryman by Charles The First and in 1810, Francis, the third Lord Marryman, built an opulent hall here. His once great building is now in ruins, proof entropy always wins eventually. In the end, the hall was there, then it wasn't. That is the way of things; they are, then they are not, and debating the whys and hows becomes academic after a while.

When things are *not*, they are *not*.

Well, most of the time.

*

Peter looked up at the branches which almost blocked Dorset's ash-grey sky. Spring robes the trees, winter undresses them, and he appreciated both states. You couldn't have one without the other. He shut his eyes for a moment, breathed in the chill air, let it bloom inside him.

One of humanity's most curious talents is the strange ability to know when someone else is nearby. The Japanese call it *dairokkan,* a sixth sense that pings like a sonar when we're being watched or someone quietly enters a room. It can be dismissed as coincidence or a placebo effect, but at that moment Peter knew he had company in the same way he knew the air was cold. It was simply a fact.

His eyes snapped open and he turned on the spot.

"Hello?"

The trees regarded him.

"Hello?" Peter felt a little silly shouting at the woods. "Is anyone there?"

Silence.

When things are not, they are not.

Then, some fifty yards behind him came the unmistakable *c-crack* of someone walking over a felled branch. That was followed by further snaps and swishes as something approached. Peter knew what deer, rabbits and foxes sounded like but none made these sounds. “Hello?” he repeated.

“Peter Piper?” Someone spoke from behind the trees with a voice that crackled like dead leaves underfoot.

8/ NUMBER NINE DAWN STREET, LITTEL WADE 09:00

Eyes red from tiredness and more, Anthony Piper stumbled into his home. He'd left last night at ten and started his first job by quarter past. As things slowly returned to "normal" after the pandemic, the night shift was busy and financially rewarding. People were out drinking again, which made him the designated choice. And in this week before Christmas party-goers were going at it with a vengeance. The jobs dropped off around two in the morning but would pick up again with hungover customers heading to the train station, too fragile to drive themselves.

"Anyone home?"

As expected there was no answer, so Anthony picked up the post, padded through to the kitchen, flicked on the kettle and looked through their mail.

Bill.

Bill.

Bill.

Tony knew the phrase, "There are only two constants in life, death and taxes," but he added bills to that list. They never stopped, so he never stopped either, constantly running to stand still. Julie once saw him scowling over the mail and laughed, "Cheer up! Even bills seem quite cute when they're addressed to Dawn Street. You know, here comes the dawn, everything's not so bad, the night's gone again."

"Do you *ever* see the dark cloud rather than the silver lining?" he'd laughed.

"Oh, I see the cloud all right, but choose to ignore it. And dawn is such an…anticipatory word, don't you think?"

"Yes, yes, yes." He'd moaned.

Julie's maiden name was Dawn, so sharing it with the name of their street was a source of great amusement to her. "I'm *so* supposed to be here," she'd sighed when they'd first viewed the house. "Come on, it's a sign. Dawn Street? I fear a messy divorce may be on the cards if we don't make an offer."

They'd made one almost as soon as they got back to their rented flat in Lower Burton. Julie had considered looking into her family tree to discover if she was in some way related to the "Dorset Dawns" who gave the street its name, but the trail quickly went cold and she lost interest.

Tony threw the bills back onto the table and shuffled upstairs, to sleep and hopefully not to dream. The bedcovers were askew, so he pulled them into a semblance of order then shut his blackout curtains to hide both daylight and the entire world. Julie had left a handwritten note taped to the wall above their bed.

Welcome home! Four sleeps to Xmas! Get some rest, see you later xxx.

Exhausted, Tony collapsed into bed and willed sleep to come, but it didn't, not for a long time. After a while he drifted off into a deep slumber mercifully free of dreams of forests and cold, wicked Christmas nights.

9/ THE MARRYMAN FOREST, LITTEL WADE, 9:10 a.m.

Peter spun toward the sound of the voice and saw a woman leaning on her cane regarding him.

"Hello, Peter Piper. I thought it was you."

"Hello, Mrs Kerstmann," Peter replied, relieved.

Mrs Kerstmann was one of those old ladies whom it's easy to imagine young. Some pensioners look like they were born gnarled and exhausted babies. But in attitude if not appearance, Mrs K. was more like a twenty-something who'd put on a seventy-something disguise then couldn't quite pull off the decrepitude. Yes, she used a cane, and yes, she was bent and slow, but one always felt she'd throw the stick to one side and suddenly perform a giggling forward roll like Gene Wilder in "Willy Wonka & The Chocolate Factory." In fact, Mrs Kerstmann's expression often had a touch of the young Wilder about it; puckish, ready for fun, no, ready for *mischief.*

She lived and worked in "Kerstmann & Son," a scrapyard at the edge of Teller's Wood. Although *scrapyard* is an unfair description. At first glance it boasted a fair crop of crap; old farmyard equipment, strange rusted skeletons whose original purpose had long been lost, odd cogs, wheels and springs that suggested Ted Hughes' Iron Man had found somewhere new to disassemble. But the yard's full title was, *"Kerstmann & Son; Curious, Puzzling, Old, Unwanted, Lovely & Hopeful Artefacts Passing Through.*" Peter read that sign every time he passed and had committed it to memory. He thought it sounded like a Dorset Haiku. *Curious, Puzzling and Old* made complete sense for a place like Kerstmann's, who was herself all three. But the next three words were a strange combination; *Unwanted, Lovely & Hopeful*. The idea an object could be *Hopeful* felt slightly sad, as if twisted bike frames, strange copper mechanisms and steamer trunks were lined up like workhouse waifs waiting for a rich visitor to whisk them away somewhere warm and safe. And then there was *Passing Through,* which cast Kerstmann's as merely a way point on their journey to somewhere better. It was an orphanage of artefacts.

"You look like you've seen a ghost," she said.

"Oh, I just thought I was alone."

"You're never alone in a forest, particularly *this* one. Ah, and there goes today's *waldeinsamkeit*," she muttered, then poked around the ground. "I always dream of finding some Burgundy truffles, but the trees aren't as conducive round this part of the woods."

"Burgundy truffles?" Peter had never heard the term.

"Mm." She didn't look up from her search. "Most people like the summer variety, but Burgundies have a stronger taste and are worth more." Finally she turned back to him. "You'd be surprised what's hiding away that can be quite, quite wonderful if you know how to look."

"Don't you mean where to look?"

"I know what I mean." She jabbed her cane back into the duff and sighed. Mrs Kerstmann had owned the scrapyard for many years before Peter was born. A local oddity, yes, but certainly no hermit, as she was often found in one of Littel Wade's two pubs or pushing a trolley around the Co-op. But despite her familiarity, nobody really knew much about the woman. There'd never been a *Mr* Kerstmann, which led to predictable village gossip about which side of the congregation she sat on. And despite his presence on the yard's sign, no-one had ever seen her son. Like Bigfoot or the Loch Ness Monster there'd been unsubstantiated sightings but no photographic proof. Like snow, Mrs Kerstmann appeared in a surprise flurry when least expected, then melted away. But despite her private nature she was liked in the village thanks to an unmistakable aura of kindness and eyes that twinkled with curiosity. People who are *interested* are always *interesting* and it seemed Mrs K. was interested in everything and everybody.

She looked up at the tree canopy. "Cold enough for snow, but that doesn't mean any pain to a pig." She was full of these strange aphorisms that appeared to have deep meaning until you thought about them for more than a few seconds.

She stopped and tilted her head in thought. "Ah yes, Christmas is coming. So how are you? Be honest, it always helps."

"I'm OK."

She gave him a little smile. "Good." Mrs K. looked Peter in the eyes and seemed to make a decision. "So…might you possibly be what my grandmother called, 'The wrong end of a split hair'?"

He didn't know what she meant and his expression must have given that fact away.

"By which I mean do you currently have free time?"

"Oh, yes, I suppose I do."

"Excellent! Then I have a business proposition. A chance to earn some ready cash in the last days before Christmas. I need a little help at the yard, and it seems our paths have crossed at what might be an opportune moment for both parties. Might you be up for it? £10 an hour?"

Peter didn't need much more persuading.

"That would be great."

"Oh yes it will be," she agreed and spun her cane like Fred Astaire. "Because it involves treasure, Mr Piper, treasure."

10/ HIGH STREET, LITTEL WADE, 9:20 a.m.

Phoebe Clarke trudged along the same route Peter had taken only an hour or so before. She glanced over at The Candy Box, saw Mr Farr frowning in the window and thought;

You really don't make your shop enticing in any way.

Phoebe shuddered when she saw the way tiny pinpricks of light in his eyes followed her movement. She considered raising her middle finger but there was no point, since she knew her very presence offended him, just as it did for many others in grey, staid, Littel Wade.

Phoebe had turned eighteen in March and lived in the middle of Dawn Street, so had known Peter Piper all his life.

They were *street friends* and nothing more, an informal relationship that could be picked up any time then just as easily dropped for months with no harm. They were also both outsiders, which always has its own emotional attraction.

They both attended Dorchester Sixth Form, where Phoebe was working to study history at university if her A-Levels permitted. After that she intended to become a quirky TV historian, so, at the age of fourteen she'd cultivated a memorable look. Phoebe's new image drew outraged gasps from the villagers since overnight she'd become the only Goth within at least an eight mile radius.

It had all started when she'd heard *Love Will Tear Us Apart* and gone searching for Joy Division on YouTube. Three hours later she'd become fully embedded in Goth music and fashion. It was like she'd been waiting for a certain aesthetic all her life then found out it had been there all along. Goth had risen out of the ashes of punk but was darker and more theatrical, so a gathering of Goths might resemble a party hosted by Dracula, Morticia Addams and Theda Bara. Phoebe threw herself headfirst into the scene, despite the Goth *scene* in Littel Wade numbering just one; herself. Blind with eyeliner, dumb with black lipstick, haughty with blusher, she walked the village like she owned it. Today, however, Phoebe had turned down the Hammer Horror dial, since she was off to work.

She examined the sky for any hint of snow but the clouds stayed shut and sulky. Phoebe felt shut and sulky this morning, too.

Oh dad, she thought, bitterly. *What a screw up. No Christmas last year, none this year. Thanks.*

She passed The Fruit And Vegetable Shop, where Mrs Bramell vacantly stared and twined hair between her fingers.

Next door was Mr Spencer's Fish & Chip Shop. At this hour it sold sausage rolls, hot pastries and awful coffee. Like Mr Farr at The Candy Box, Mr Frederick Spencer was also unfeasibly old. After midday, he'd pop a paper hat onto his speckled bald head and pull on a white coat which gave him the appearance of a deranged surgeon who only operated on fish. But at breakfast Mr Spencer glumly wore a tight waistcoat with "BARISTA" on the back. Phoebe thought he may have mugged a Starbucks employee for it. Although his handwritten sign offered *Latte Cappuccino, Espresso* and *Flat White*, the reality was everything came from instant coffee jars and a kettle. For example, *Flat White* simply meant the cup was overflowing with milk.

Although a hot sausage roll seemed tempting on such a cold morning, Phoebe passed by.

As she approached the Co-op supermarket, her posture slipped. It was difficult to keep one's head held high when the next eight hours involved stacking shelves, cleaning floors and manning till number one. Phoebe couldn't help herself. Every time she came within a fifty yard radius of the store, she'd bark four syllables like geographically triggered Tourette's; "*Fuh. Kin. Co. Op.*"

Renee the manager stood outside draining a cigarette. Imagine if Marilyn Monroe hadn't died but remained married to Arthur Miller, become colour blind, smoked forty a day, had make up and hair done by a stylist with delirium tremens, and then really let herself go. She'd joined the supermarket three months before Phoebe and subscribed to the "New Broom" management theory; come in, sweep away the old order then use your new broom to hit everyone else over the head with.

Renee pointedly tapped her chunky gold-plated watch. "What time do you call this?" Phoebe looked at St Nicholas' clock. "Nine twenty-four. That's six minutes before I start work. Oh, morning!" she added brightly, since she knew positivity always wound Renee up something rotten.

"You'll be turning up at…er…" Phoebe could almost hear the cogs of her boss' mind screech. "…Nine…twenty-nine and…fifty-nine seconds next. I won't have it!" For visual punctuation, Renee threw down her cigarette butt and ground it out with a red high heel. At that moment she looked like Olivia Newton John at the climax of *Grease*, but only if Sandy had melted then wandered into a funhouse hall of mirrors.

In her peripheral vision, Phoebe became aware school caretaker Mr Hamnett stood at the bus stop opposite watching them. This wasn't the first time she'd seen him hanging around the supermarket, and he always appeared to be studying her. Hamnett was in his early sixties but had always seemed much older, a pensioner-in-waiting all his life. He kept fine white hair beneath a flat cap, had thin eyes and equally narrow lips perpetually curved on the edge of a smile. She always thought he had something of a Dorset Clint Eastwood about him.

Oh Christ, not again, that's creepy, she thought, but then the 4A bus arrived and he was obscured.

"Ahem," Renee coughed, pointedly. "Over here, please." She took in Phoebe's crimped hair, eyeliner, leather jacket and lace gloves. "I thought I told you customers don't like…all *that*. And your hair is just too much." Phoebe stared at her boss' dyed blonde apocalypse but thought better of making any comparisons.

"Ahem, *'She hath more hair than wit and more faults than hairs'…* Shakespeare, you know," Renee added, pleased with herself. She had an infuriating habit of quoting prose and poetry in an attempt to appear superior.

"I'll put it up."

"You will. And take that punk rocker leather jacket off."

"Yes, ma'am."

"Good."

Phoebe glanced back toward the bus stop. Even though the 4A had left, Mr Hamnett still squinted over at her.

He didn't get on, she wondered. *Who waits at a bus stop then ignores the very thing they're waiting for? And why's he so interested in me?*

She shivered a little, sighed, then entered the store.

"Toilet roll needs restocking on six, " Renee called after her.

"Ah, the glamour," Phoebe whispered.

I really *hate this place,* she thought. *But while Littel Wade might be the death of me, it might also be my ticket out of here.*

Phoebe Clarke had a plan.

11/ HIGH STREET, LITTEL WADE, 9:45 a.m.

Peter and Benji made their way back home, each excited in their own way. Benji because he was a dog and that is their default setting, Peter because this morning's walk had been very constructive.

Twenty minutes ago Mrs Kerstmann had made him an offer he couldn't refuse:

"My emporium has fallen a little on the chaotic side of late, for which I take full responsibility," she'd frowned. "So I'm offering you the position of General Ship-Shaperer, Official Squaring-Away Operative, Mess Negater."

"I'm sorry, what?" Peter had asked.

"I apologise. Occasionally I suffer from a tendency to over egg the verbal pudding. There I go again, in fact. What I mean is, I just need someone to tidy up, move boxes, put things on shelves, a lick of paint here and there...basically I'd like to be able to wake up on Christmas morning and not see a scrapyard. Yes, I'm well aware *scrapyard* is what locals call it, but my sign says it all; *"Kerstmann & Son; Curious, Puzzling..."*

Peter completed the phrase; "*Old, Unwanted, Lovely & Hopeful Artefacts Passing Through.*" Mrs Kerstmann's eyes had widened and she'd delightedly clapped her hands. "Correct! I knew you were the right fella for the job. So, the clock is ticking and Father Time does not drag his heels. Can you make a start this afternoon?"

"Yes, that'll be fine."

She stuck out an old hand, with nails painted red and a wrist that tinkled with bangles and bracelets. Peter shook it, deal done.

"Right, see you at one?"

"OK."

As Peter and Benji walked away and Mrs K. watched them disappear into the forest, a curious smile flickered across her lips.

*

Peter tied Benji up outside N. MARSH, BUTCHERS, then pushed open the door as a laughing bell *ting-a-linged* above his head. It was the happiest part of the whole experience.

Norman Marsh was busy with a cleaver, the meat version of piscine Mr Spencer. While Spencer angrily fried cod like it had insulted his mother, Marsh dismembered a variety of animals as if they'd committed atrocities too awful to speak of. If you were a detective who also happened to be a sheep, this would be a major crime scene.

Mr Marsh looked up. “Mmm-mm,” he managed, then gave the bare minimum of a smile. He looked like an English Butcher from Central Casting since, along with his faintly blooded apron, he also wore a straw hat perched above a face that resembled an embarrassed beetroot.

“Morning,” said Peter. “Ah, is our turkey ready? ‘Cos…”

“Mmm.” Marsh pulled up a huge bag complete with paper tag which read, “TURKEY PIPER.”

Turkey Piper, Peter thought. *That sounds like a hideous addition to “The Twelve Days Of Christmas.”*

“Here it is. All paid up. Giblets are in a bag inside it.”

“Nice.”

The bird was way bigger than Peter’s small family needed, but mum always subscribed to Scrooge’s maxim; one should always go for the biggest bird in the shop if one possibly could, and so the tradition was upheld.

The bell *ting-a-ling’d* again as Mrs Florence Underbore and her son Gregory stalked in. Mother Underbore and progeny were both tall, lanky specimens; him in combat fatigues, her in fatigued faux fur. Mrs Underbore resembled an ambulatory broom; stick thin with a mass of thick, dirt-brown spiky hair on top. In a certain light Florence could easily be mistaken for the evil and uglier twin of Olive Oyl.

Almost as soon as they entered Gregory turned to his mother and stuttered, “Oh, I, er, I , er, forgot my fags.”

“Then run back and get your ‘*fags*’ Gregory,” Florence sighed without looking in her son’s direction. Greg quickly walked away and the door shut behind him with yet another inappropriately jolly *ting-a-ling.*

She stared at Peter for slightly too long to be comfortable then her puckered lips formed a reluctant smile.

“Peter,” she said, almost too quietly to be heard.

“Morning Mrs Underbore.”

“Morn Mss Undabrrr,” Mr Marsh managed.

“How are you today, Peter?”

“Oh, I’m OK. Just, you know, picking up the turkey.”

“Good.”

Have I missed something? He thought. *The Underbores always make me feel like I once made a terrible faux pas in their company and never apologised, or something.*

Florence continued to stare as if he were some exotic animal.

"So I'd better get this back, you know, to the fridge."

"Yes, you should," she murmured. "I hope you enjoy it."

"Thank you."

Peter left, somehow aware that Mrs Underbore continued to gaze at his back. Mother and son had always been odd, but lately their behaviour had become palpably weirder.

When was *that exactly?* Peter wondered as Benji sniffed about the bag *...I can't put my finger on it, but they've definitely become stranger. But stranger to me or to everyone?*

He had no real interest in pursuing the thought. The Underbore's eccentricities were just another weird sideshow in Littel Wade.

Peter headed back down the High Street and risked a glance into the Co-op where Phoebe Clarke stared blankly from till number one. He tapped on the window. Phoebe turned and smiled.

"Hello Piper," she mouthed through the glass. She'd never once called him "Peter," always simply, "Piper".

"Hello," he mouthed back, raised his eyebrows, gave a questioning thumbs up and added, "You OK?"

Phoebe rolled her eyes and waved her hands about the shop to say, *Here? In all this? What do you think?*

Peter frowned in sympathy. She mimed putting on a noose, went cross-eyed then held up a finger, *wait*, and wrote on a piece of paper;

PLEASE KILL ME.

He shook his head, *nope*.

She wrote again. YOU'RE NO FUN.

He shrugged, *nope*.

Phoebe's pen went to work once more; COME FIND ME LATER?

Peter's heart jumped into fifth gear but he kept his expression neutral. Phoebe raised her eyebrows, *well?*

He held two thumbs up.

At that moment, Renee appeared and proceeded to give her employee a loud lesson in retail. The boss's fag-yellow bouffant shook with fury, clearly as angry as its owner. For a second Phoebe managed to lock eyes with Peter and in that moment her expression clearly said; CAN YOU BELIEVE THIS SHIT?

Peter managed to avoid laughing out loud and walked on. Wrapped up in the window-drama he was unaware Gregory Underbore stood in a shop door up the street. Greg wrung his hands, hopped from foot to foot, and looked like someone who had something to do but didn't have the nerve to carry it out.

12/ NUMBER NINE, DAWN STREET, LITTEL WADE, 10:00

Peter's phone was an embarrassingly outdated Nokia and source of much amusement to the Sixth Form techies but he didn't care.

"OK, good morning, but bad news," trilled mum's voicemail. "I know I've only just left but it's already looking like a bit of a later one for me, which I am *titanically* pissed off about, but what can I do? I've already called dad, I really hope he has his phone on mute and I didn't wake him up, or I am firmly in the doghouse. But you know what dad's like, he never picks up his messages, so I'm relying on you. Don't bother making me any tea, I'll get something here if it looks like things are getting silly, which they always are. This is what happens when you sign up to fight crime and chaos in Dorchester and of course the utter *anarchy* of Martinstown and Bradford Peverell. Love you, *mwah mwah mwah*." Peter heard mum titter as she ended the call, then he pocketed the phone and headed home.

*

Peter gingerly pushed open the door, which creaked at exactly the same spot as it had done for years. There'd been talk of oiling it, but mum had vetoed the idea, saying, "It's the little creaks and whispers that make a home. It's just the house saying hello."

Everybody liked the idea of their house greeting them, so the door remained un-oiled and chatty.

Peter crept into the kitchen and listened for the tell-tale sound of dad snoring upstairs, but all was silent. That was a good sign; when dad descended into the deepest of sleeps, his snoring sputtered out and was replaced with slow, contented breathing. Peter couldn't afford to take any risks so carefully opened the fridge, quietly placed the turkey inside then took off his shoes and mounted the stairs, taking care to miss out the fourth, seventh and tenth, which would also happily creak hello if given the chance. Peter slipped into his bedroom across from where dad slept and opened the wardrobe. If Mrs Kerstmann's Big Clean Up was as filthy as he suspected, he'd need some expendable clothes.

That was the problem.

Peter's wardrobe didn't offer much choice at the best of times, let alone when he needed to possibly sacrifice some items.

He flicked through and mentally put together a work outfit that might be able to take a bit of extra punishment. Then he reached into the upper shelf where hats, gloves and scarfs lay in a jumble.

There was the tiniest flash of silver between the accessories. Peter tried to tear his gaze from the sparkle but couldn't, so pushed clothing over the sparkling object until *whatever-it-was* became obscured again. Then he fell back onto his tiny bed and didn't care how loud the springs grated and groaned in welcome.

*

Anthony Piper lay in bed not ten metres away. Julie had blu-tacked a Post-It note to their bedside table, with a simple biro cartoon of her smiling face in a paper crown with the words, "WE NEED CHRISTMAS CRACKERS! DON'T FORGET LIKE LAST YEAR! YOU HAVE BEEN WARNED!" But Tony's thoughts were elsewhere and he hadn't seemed to have spotted the message.

He'd heard Peter come home despite his son's attempts at stealth. *My house is a tell-tale,* he thought, and not for the first time, *but I ignored the tale it told.*

Sleep had come fitfully as always, but rarely kept him in its folds for long. Yes, the building whispered and chattered but he was used to that. Tony knew *he* was the problem, he was the one who drove sleep away when most needed. As dreams gathered, a guilty part of his mind fought them off, screaming *You don't deserve to sleep!* And that voice would shake him awake, sometimes shouting, but always crying.

The fatigue was unbearable, a tiredness not just of body and mind but soul. There are many things we can avoid if we really put our minds to them, but sleep isn't on that list.

And when Anthony finally dreamed, the images were often intolerable. *Things* tapped from the boot of his car, forests marched toward him like Birnam. Most of all he was trapped in this house. Tony would pound at unmoving doors and scream for help but none ever came.

He didn't want to sleep but feared waking up. Neither state gave him peace. Tony Piper could no longer hold on, he was in free fall and gravity cannot be bargained with.

So this morning, as every morning, Anthony lay in bed with fists pressed against his mouth, trying to stop his moans from flying into the world where people may hear them.

And if they did, they would ask *why*.

And if people asked *why*, then Anthony Piper would have to confront a terrible lie.

13/ KERSTMANN'S YARD, 1:10 p.m.

"Right, as God once said, where on earth to start?" Mrs Kerstmann surveyed her little kingdom and sighed. "I do have an awful, buggerationally excessive lot of crap, don't I?"

"I wouldn't say that," Peter offered. Benji had already begun his important job of sniffing each and every object in the vicinity.

"No, you wouldn't say that because you are unfailingly polite and a credit to your family. But *I* can say that because my curiosity often gets the better of me. There are items here that have stood in exactly the same position for years, lovely and hopeful, as the sign helpfully points out."

She looked over at the sign where,*"Kerstmann & Son; Curious, Puzzling, Old, Unwanted, Lovely & Hopeful Artefacts Passing Through*" were picked out in cracked gold paint. "You know, I can't even remember when I put that up. Or even if it was me that did. That's memory for you. As one gets older it splinters like that paint. I sometimes look at old photographs and wonder if it was the event I remember or just the picture. But every memory is precious, don't you think? Even the bad ones." She shot him a kind smile. "Because you learn from those, don't you? And if you don't, well, you're a moron. Too many people treat experience as something ephemeral, ha, *passing through*, but experience, for good or ill, is what makes us. And every item here has a story even if it can't always tell us what that was."

She gestured about the yard. "There is a system, although one might be forgiven for thinking the scrap giant blew his nose and this is what landed. Over there…" Mrs K. pointed at an area to her left, "…is what I call the Ferrous Wing." Farmyard equipment, carcasses of vehicles, skeletons of engines and other odd pieces of rusted machinery stood ready for a buyer that would probably never come. "They're not all iron obviously, but I like saying the word *ferrous*, so that's what it is."

Peter wandered over as she spoke. "What are they?"

"Oh, stuff I liberated from local farmers, things that caught my eye at auction, items I just found lying about. *One man's junk is another man's jewel* is my motto. Well, it isn't, but not a bad justification, I suppose. My house, well, my office-cum-living space, is where I keep the Art Wing."

Mrs K. lived in a bungalow which had been extended and expanded with no care for the original aesthetic. It looked like a random selection of Lego blocks fitted together by a distracted child. Squares and rectangles in a variety of colours jutted out from what must have been the original building. She'd clearly used up whatever paint was immediately to hand as each new "wing" was added. As if to prove the point, pots of emulsion were stacked against the walls. Mrs Kerstmann caught Peter looking and laughed. "I am aware that my home is somewhat of a smörgåsbord of styles. Like owner, like house, that's what I say. Actually, again, I don't. I said it for the first time just then, but the thought is still valid."

Two chipped Doric columns stood either side of what could have been the front door, but since there were a few entrances dotted about the various walls, Peter couldn't be sure.

Stone gargoyles peered from the roof along with dragons, animals, tiles and faces. While three different weather vanes jostled to catch the wind, a curious half-crescent, half-cross lightning rod waited to usher a storm's electrical fury to ground.

"Art Wing is rather a catch-all term but I mean paintings, toys, books, jewellery, the kind of objects that pop up on the Antiques Roadshow, I hope. Most of it from auctions or charity shops, some just dropped into my lap, as it were. I'll show you soon enough. Those items really do have stories, many of which I know and some of which I will tell, when the mood takes me."

She pulled a pipe from one of her many pockets and began to fill it. "Do you mind? It's a terrible habit, but everything good is bad these days. Or is it everything bad is good? Both, probably. Things change so fast, I can't keep up."

A thought occurred to Peter. "What did you do before all this?"

"Before?" The word seemed to amuse her. "I always did 'this.' Collecting, redistributing, archiving, recording, it's what we Kerstmanns do, going back…well, I don't even know how long it goes back. As long as people tired of things they once thought were important, I suppose. All this frippery meant something to somebody once upon a time,now it just needs to find another somebody, that's all. A bit like all of us, really."

She pointed to another section with her cane. "Over there, that's what I call The Impracticals; items that don't really fit anywhere else." Under a large gazebo several naked mannequins gesticulated to each other, possibly asking *we are nude and lost and how did* that *happen*? They were surrounded by stacks of dead televisions and three pianos in varying states of disrepair. The tableau looked like an album cover from a long forgotten '80s synth-pop band.

"Of course, there are other objects still to be archived properly," Mrs Kerstmann airily indicated yet more boxes piled around the property. "Alas, I have more coming in than going out but do I care? What do you think?"

"No."

"No indeed!" She chuckled. "To me, this is a place of wonder."

"Me too."

"I thought so, which is why I've hired you. But even Xanadu needed a spring clean once in a while and Kubla Khan here has better things to do. So, where to start?" Mrs K. peered about the yard with thin, accusing eyes. "Ah! Those untidy swines!" she threw open a crate to reveal many tools wrapped around each other like a monkey puzzle. "So, you need to unpick these, then box them up separately. Any questions?"

Peter thought, *This is going to take forever.* "Nope, I'll get onto it."

"You'll certainly be earning your £5 an hour." Mrs Kerstmann walked away.

"Sorry, er, five?"

She turned and giggled. "First rule of business. Try to get a bargain. No, I was joking, it's £10. Go on then, those tools won't sort themselves."

For a moment the clouds parted, sunshine shouldered through and its rays sparkled against *something* hidden under tarpaulin way across the yard. Busy in the toolbox, Peter didn't notice the gleam.

Not yet, anyway.

14/ KERSTMANN'S YARD, 3:30 p.m.

The sun was setting and by 3:59 p.m. it would give way to nightfall. Peter had moved on to sand rust from radiator pipes. He was surrounded by the naked mannequins, some of whom appeared to watch him rather intently.

Probably the most fun they've had in years, he thought. *But they really need to get a few jumpers on, they'll catch a death out here.*

It had become bitterly cold and Peter was fantasising about an extremely deep, exceedingly warm bath.

Just for a moment another thin ray of sunlight swept across the yard, then struck something metallic which flashed brightly in return. Mrs K. had many wonderful objects out here but none sparkled. They were *lovely and hopeful*, *curious* and *puzzling*, but none could be described as sparkly.

Intrigued, Peter walked toward a dark tarpaulin-covered hulk by the fence. A gap in the tarp had allowed the sun's last rays to glint against something underneath. Peter lifted the cover and saw a length of chrome tubing along a wooden side. The wood had once been painted red but was now faded and cracked so only flashes of the original fire engine colour remained. A door was cut into the side complete with a tiny verdigris covered copper handle and hinges. As Peter dragged the tarp away further he saw the object in its entirety.

What the hell? He thought. *She has a* sleigh. *How does Mrs Kerstmann have a sleigh? Mind you, she has all kinds of odd stuff in every nook and cranny, so why am I surprised by this? It's just a sleigh.*

The vehicle's front curved up like the bow of a boat. Sturdy yet rusted iron runners ran under its body and they too curled like a genie's shoes. Peter looked inside and saw silver rings where reins were surely once threaded. The sleigh's polished wood floor had somehow kept its sheen, as if it had been fitted only that morning. Peter stroked the smooth surface, amazed wood left outside like this hadn't rotted, cracked or grown dull with age. At the rear was a wooden bench, equally rich and vibrant.

He pulled the door handle but the mechanism inside wouldn't budge, so clambered over and stood on the deck of this improbable, wonderful sleigh.

The rest of Mrs K's outdoor treasures were battered and bruised by weather and age but this seemed remarkably preserved.

He rubbed a finger along its length.

The paint has almost disappeared as you'd expect from something this old. He thought. *The runners, the handle and hinges are aged and rusted yet body, floor and chrome are almost new. Perhaps they're later additions. Yeah, someone got some manky old metal bits and fitted them to a well-kept shell.*

That explanation satisfied Peter for approximately two seconds until he thought about it properly.

No. What, someone got hold of a relatively new sleigh then screwed rusty old crap onto it? That's like buying a new car and fitting a cracked windscreen. It's mad.

The word *mad* bounced about his head for a while.

Mrs K. is a bit *eccentric. It's possible she had some old runners and bolted them onto this,because that's the kind of thing she does. I mean, look at her house.*

He glanced back at his employer's home, with its random architectural styles, multiple doors and dazzle ship lines.

I wouldn't put it past her. She obviously likes to tinker.

At that moment as if on cue, one of the doors opened to reveal the silhouette of Mrs Kerstmann. "*Peee-terrr*, I've boiled the kettle. Cup of tea? Coffee?" she shouted.

"Tea would be nice. White, two sugars."

"Two sugars? You live dangerously, young man. Gosh, it's got very dark very quick. Mind you, it's the shortest day of the year, so…Bear with me…As someone or other once said, let there be light!"

At that, the yard lit up from many spotlights mounted on poles and hiding in corners.

"Good, isn't it, my lightshow?" She made her way toward him. "Tea and two sugars for the sweet tooth coming right up. Oh, so you found the sleigh then?"

"Yes. Where did it come from?"

"No idea."

"But you must know where…"

She held up a hand to stop him mid flow. "You asked where it came from and my honest answer is I don't know. The real question is where did I *get* it, and that I can answer. You know George Johnson?"

"From the post office?"

"That's the one."

George Johnson was one of the few older people in the village who'd had any kind of *joie de vivre* about him. He'd run the tiny post office and despite being in his eighties delivered mail rain or shine, with a seemingly permanent smile which suggested he was a man happy in his employment. But Covid-19 had taken him in 2020 and George had died alone in Dorset County Hospital.

“A good man,” she said wistfully, “who died a bad death. I suppose there’s no such thing as a good death really, but that virus…Who dies with nobody to hold their hand? No-one around except strangers in masks and visors? But the skinny man with the scythe comes for everybody, doesn’t he?” She put a caring hand on Peter’s shoulder. “And we can’t bargain with him, so that’s almost that. I wish it wasn’t, but if wishes were kisses it would be Valentine’s Day every day for me. So George died, bless him, and his family came from London to sell off his land and possessions. As you can see, I really can’t help myself, so went to the auction and picked up a few things. He had…ephemera scattered all about his property on the edge of Farthing Forest, you know?”

Peter nodded.

“So I went poking around, as is my wont. And at the very legal limit of his land, keeled over in a ditch, there was this.” Mrs K. tapped the side of the sleigh. “George’s family didn’t even know it was there, but I made an offer, hired a few strong men and a truck then liberated it. Now I don’t really know what to do next. Beautiful, though, right?”

“It is. Would you like me to spruce it up a bit?”

For a moment Mrs Kerstmann looked extremely pleased but quickly hid that expression under one of thoughtfulness.

“I think that would be a very good idea. I might even sell it on to a department store or film company. Let’s face it, Christmas comes once a year but it’s guaranteed, and I bet there'd be a few people who’d love to drag this out come yuletide. Yes, excellent. You are officially on sleigh duty as of now. I’m sure I have some suitable red paint…” She shot him a side glance. “Unless you think another colour would be better?”

“No, no, it has to be red.”

“Yes, I agree. Let me go and find some. You can make a start, but the solstice has somewhat crept up on us, so I don’t expect you to do much more today. Perhaps a little undercoat, no more.”

“OK.”

“I’m so glad you spotted it. Things like this don’t deserve to be hidden away, do they? There are too many things in Littel Wade that are hidden, far too many for my liking.”

Peter was about to ask what that meant, but Mrs K. turned and left.

15/ KERSTMANN'S YARD, 5 p.m.

After giving the sleigh a first coat Peter decided that was enough for today. The temperature had dropped to where puddles start to consider icing up and despite the gloves his fingers were no longer fit for purpose. Peter put down his brush, stretched and yawned. Hot fish and chips seemed an even better idea now. He went to sit down on the bench at the rear of the sleigh, but then spotted two black metal hinges screwed deep into the wood.

Oh, so this opens, then.

Peter attempted to pull up the bench top but it refused to move. Intrigued, he felt along the edge and discovered a small latch.

This isn't just a seat. It's a storage box. But storing what?

He pushed the latch left, right, then backwards. With a satisfying *click*, Peter heard the mechanism unlock and the bench/box was open. At first he thought it was empty, then saw something rectangular inside. Peter picked up the object and studied it in the artificial light.

How long has this *been in there, waiting? Am I the first to see it in*...He looked again, carefully. *Years? How many? And what is it?*

That was the big question, really.

What is it?

16/ DAWN STREET, LITTEL WADE, 5:30 p.m.

As Peter examined his strange find, Gregory Underbore sloped into Dawn Street. He glanced about with the darting movements of a bird, wary any residents might be watching.

While camouflage gear obscured him in the forest, here on a village street it achieved the reverse. The wrong clothes in the wrong situation are a beacon for attention. Greg was almost glowing with guilt but then again, he was right to feel uneasy. There was much about his life the law would find interesting.

His illegal crossbow was now hidden beneath a pile of rubbish in the garden shed, but that didn't stop him carrying another weapon; under his jacket was a fifteen inch serrated "Rambo" survival knife. Greg kept the blade simply because it made him feel ready. However, if anyone discovered its presence he would be in a lot of trouble.

Possibly detention kind of trouble.

Probably never joining the army kind of trouble.

He felt his heart pound faster and heavier. If he were spotted, then this plan could go very wrong.

Greg's purpose here was in his pocket.

Now, just do it now, he thought wildly. *Do it, do it.*

He was about to step into number nine's driveway when Anthony Piper stepped out with a bin bag. Gregory managed to stumble sidewards and carry on along Dawn Street as if he had somewhere to go, aware his forehead was wet with sweat in spite of the cold.

Fuckfuckfuck. I fucked up. Again. I always fuck up.

17/ KERSTMANN'S YARD, 5:15 p.m.

"I had no idea the sleigh's bench was also a box." Mrs Kerstmann examined Peter's find. She'd been just as surprised to discover its secret catch and hinges. "Almost like they're supposed to be out of sight," was her verdict, "I wonder why?"

They brought the object back to her higgledy piggledy house. This was the first time Peter had stepped inside and it didn't disappoint.

If a museum, art gallery, second hand emporium, shop, auction house and multiple family homes got together to brainstorm a space and nobody compromised, the end result would look like this. Time held no sway here; Georgian sideboards jostled with sixties bubble sofas. Seventies wallpaper gave way to William Morris designs, which then surrendered to painted brick. Framed photographs and paintings scattered their way down the walls like Tetris blocks. Peter tried to spot Mrs Kerstmann in any of them, but while some of the women bore a resemblance, he couldn't be one hundred percent sure.

This place is a tip, he thought.

Shelves stoically supported stacks of faded maps, cracked globes, shabby books and statuettes. Display cabinets burst with creepy taxidermy and off-putting toys from bygone, clearly deranged eras. Peter was particularly alarmed by a figure made of a monkey's body, clown's face and duck's flippers. The fact it also reclined in what appeared to be a gaily painted coffin just added to the unease.

But generally Kerstmann's rooms were full of wonders which surely all had tales to tell, just as she'd promised. Yet more mannequins modelled exotic period attire and Peter just *knew* the clothes weren't modern replicas. They'd once been worn by owners long gone, whose presence could almost be felt in the room.

"Test me." Mrs K. said.

"Huh?"

"I know what you're thinking. Same as everyone, 'This place is a tip.' Am I right?"

"Well, no, it's lovely, I was just…"

"Liar. That's fine. If there were no order, it *would* be a tip, but as my mum used to say, 'Every glove has a hand to warm itself.'"

"Shouldn't that be, 'Every hand has a glove to warm itself?'"

"Depends on your perspective." She closed her eyes, turned and faced the wall. "See, I'm not cheating. Pick a thing, anything, I don't care. I'll tell you exactly where it is. Go on."

Peter studied the cavalcade of chaos. In one of many corners was one of many chairs. Wedged underneath was a box marked "CIGARS / ROBUSTO" and behind that, a large architect's compass.

"Compass?"

She waved a hand dismissively. "I'll need more than that, Peter Piper. I have fourteen various compasses in this property. A little more detail please."

"Silver…"

"Oh, well *that's* narrowed it down," she tutted and he pressed on. "It has a black ring on the top and thin metal grooves like, er, fish scales on one of the arms."

"Easy. It's under the grey wash American Oak chair, behind a box of Cohiba Robusto size cigars. Correct?"

He whistled.

"Your tuneful exhalation suggests I am. But I didn't need confirmation. Again."

Peter looked around once more, determined to catch her out. Then he spotted something she'd surely never place.

"Cat collar."

"Oh, *please*. I have twenty two at present."

He looked harder. "Ruby coloured stones set round a green collar."

Mrs K. held a finger aloft in triumph. "That particular feline necklace is on the very top shelf to my right, at *its* extreme left, next to a copy of *The Grand Grimoire* by del Rabina, and in front of…wait…a…first edition of *The House At Pooh Corner* by A.A. Milne, 1928. If you want further clarification, the bookend is Dante in galvanised plaster produced by Paul Mori, 1915. The other bookend in the set features Beatrice, and she stands on top of a cupboard by the yellow door, complete with a 1971 Action Man in scuba gear sitting by her, gazing up adoringly, as he should. Do I pass?"

"Bloody hell."

"Language." She swivelled back to face him and smiled. "That wasn't an exercise in showing off, although it did feel extremely satisfying. It was a lesson, Peter. And what did you learn?"

"Er… you know where everything is?"

"No, that is a by-product. The lesson is simple; look. But not just look, any fool can look. In fact, the world is full of fools who look but don't see. The key is to look, register, understand and retain. Even apparent chaos can be made to fall in line if one simply follows that rule. Some truths can hide in plain sight if you don't look at them *just so*. Seemingly irrelevant facts become extremely important once you know their context, but unless you look, register, understand and retain they will remain irrelevant. To you, at least. Or to put it another way, start at the edges and work your way in."

I think I've just been told something that has absolutely nothing to do with a cat collar, Peter thought. *But what, I have no idea.*

"Which brings us to this strange little thing…"

She held up Peter's find from the sleigh. "What is it?"

"A book."

"Very good Peter, you have looked and registered it's a book. I'm not being sarcastic. That's the first step. Things are not always what they seem and we must guard against assumption. But I think we can both agree this *is* a book. It has a cover, spine and pages, ergo…"

The book was around one foot in length, half in width and a couple of inches thick, bound in deep red leather. Like the sleigh's wood it too remained remarkably well preserved.

"Very well, first principles, from the good condition, what can we deduce?"

"It hasn't been in there very long?"

"That would be a fair assumption, yes. I purchased the sleigh from poor George's estate last year. However his family had no record of when he bought it, no receipt, invoice, nothing they could find. So we have no way of knowing how long it sat tipped into that ditch, hidden by bushes."

"Bushes?"

"Mmm, did I not say? The sleigh wasn't obvious, even up close. I mentioned it was at the edge of his legal property, so the possibility remains even *George* didn't know he had it. So if it wasn't George's, whose was it? And how did it get there? Let's state the obvious, it helps. On what medium do sleighs travel?"

"Snow, generally."

"Correct. There are Stone Boats in America and Australia that travel on flat earth, but my sleigh's runners resemble the prow of a ship, which implies they were built to cut through snow. Something that big and heavy also needs a *lot* of the white stuff to move. The last time we had a major fall was 2017, remember?"

Peter did. The drifts had been knee deep in places and Littel Wade was cut off for a day or two.

"So George could have purchased it then, but I really can't imagine him investing in a *sleigh*, then having it delivered during a snow storm, then leaving the poor thing crashed in a ditch. No, I believe my sleigh had been there longer than that. So let's go back…the time before was…" She looked up and to the left, searched her memory, "…gosh, at least fifteen, twenty years ago."

"It snowed heavily when I was born. Littel Wade was cut off then, too."

"Ah yes, 2005, of course. But that's still assuming George used snow to pull it to that spot…or had it shoved off the back of a low loader into a ditch for whatever mad reason. But of course if we're talking about age, we have to consider this…" She held up the book. "But let's hold that thought for a moment. The truth is, we simply don't know how long our sleigh may have sat in that ditch. And George might not have even *owned* that area of land when it crashed. It could have already been there for decades, centuries, even."

"But if it had been outside for years the wood would have rotted."

"Mm, not always, there are treatments. But the iron runners are spectacularly rusted, which suggests a long exposure to the elements. As you might have noticed, I am a connoisseur of rust. Unless, of course the runners are original and newer wood was replaced later. You know, I only spotted the sleigh because light caught metal through the foliage."

"Same here, but inside your tarpaulin."

"Mm, so the old girl obviously likes to make herself known once in a while. Right, now let's have a look at this odd book. The box you found it in would have protected it to a degree, but leather is organic and no matter how well treated, it will crack and rot over time if not treated with respect. This binding shows no sign of that. Which brings us, as it must, to the contents.As you rightly pointed out, this is where things get a little strange…But I suspect only a *little,* though. Everything has an explanation and sadly I believe this may be disappointingly mundane."

She opened the book and peered down at its entries.

"So, Peter, look, register, understand and retain. What do we think?"

18/ THE HIGH STREET, LITTEL WADE, 5:45 p.m.

With the sleigh's strange book in a carrier bag, £35.50 burning a hole in his pocket and a grumbling stomach, Peter stepped into The Fish And Chip Shop where Mr Spencer was in full flow behind his bubbling friers.

"Evening," said Peter. "May I have…"

Mr Spencer made no eye contact but simply held up his palm like a traffic policeman; WAIT.

Then he waved the tops of his fingers in a beckoning gesture; GO.

"Right, one family special. Oh, and a saveloy, and…a large battered sausage. Large curry sauce. And please may I have some batter bits on the chips?"

Mr Spencer nodded and uttered his only words of the exchange. "£15.50." Then he held out a hand which slowly closed over Peter's money like an oily Venus Fly Trap.

"Thank you," said Peter and mentally added, *It's the personal service that* really *makes a meal.*

*

As he approached St Nicholas' Peter felt a tap on his left shoulder. He looked, then Phoebe appeared at his right.

"That trick's ancient," she giggled. "I can't believe you fell for it."

"Well," Peter shrugged, "I'm not six years old, which was the last time someone did it to me."

She pursed her lips and did a moue. "Ooh, sarcasm, Piper, *nice*. Isn't it lucky I saw you pass just as I left work?"

"Is it?"

"Mm. Because my fish and chip radar is pinging rather loudly." She looked pointedly at his brown paper bag. "Sorry to ask, but could I have a chip or two? I haven't had a thing since lunch."

Peter thought, *You could ask me for anything and the answer would always be yes.*

"Help yourself." He pointed to a bench outside St Nicholas'. "Table for two?"

The teenagers ate in silence for a while as the church bell tolled six p.m. Phoebe peered into the bag and gasped at how much food Peter had bought. "Christ, Piper, where did you get the money for all that?"

Peter explained the day's trajectory and handed her his peculiar discovery.

"Mrs K. told me to take it, see if I could work out what's what. It's old. It's odd."

"Ooh, old, odd things are my favourite," Phoebe cooed.

She turned the book in her hands and examined its red leather binding. "This was inside a *sleigh*? Really? Who has a sleigh?"

"Mrs Kerstmann, apparently."

"Doesn't surprise me. I only went to her place once, I must have been about ten, I think. Dad took me. It was weird, but you know, good weird. I do good weird, as you can tell."

"Hadn't noticed."

She laughed and flicked through the book. Some of the off-white pages were blank, others had just a few entries, but more were full, top to bottom.

"What's this?" she whispered to herself. "It's not in alphabetical order, bit haphazard."

Peter watched her study the contents. He hadn't really seen Phoebe in historian mode before.

"Are these names? No. Yes. Kind of."

On the first page, in faded black ink copperplate;

T Acorn
Ball

A Acree
Penny

P Baker
Paper

P Dawn
Orange

Underneath were more entries; odd words like *Green Hat* and *Hart Hoop* . On the left side, the pattern was repeated throughout;

M Gortoney
Book

W Fillirish
Hoop

But on the right, alongside the words were handwritten red X's;

H Ash Tin X

L Beer Pencil X

I Cooper Bat X

P Dent Ball X

"What's with the red X's?"
"You tell me."
She continued to flick through. "Every single entry on the right has a red X next to it." Phoebe turned the pages back and forth. "Way fewer entries on the left hand sides."

She tapped her black nails against the book and bit her lip. "OK; it's obviously a ledger, but what for?"

"Mrs Kerstmann thought it was a ledger too."

Phoebe shook her head. "No. It can't be a ledger. If it was, it's almost useless. No dates, no addresses, no PAID/ UNPAID entries. This wouldn't help any business stay on track with what was going out and coming in."

She turned to the last page. "Same handwriting throughout. Mmm, this, Piper, this has what my dad calls *Piquing Power*. I am officially piqued. You said the sleigh was on George Johnson's land, right?"

"That's where Mrs K. found it, yes."

"I wonder if this book was his? But if so, why lock it away? And didn't you say the sleigh was in a *ditch*?" Phoebe examined the book's spine. "Hold on, have you seen this?" She pointed to some raised bumps. "See? It was embossed but the letters have lost their relief. You can still just about make them out if you turn it in the light."

Peter squinted and read what she was referring to. "Oh yeah. D..O..something…R…S…something…is that a T?"

"Dorset, Piper. It says Dorset. So this is some kind of totally useless ledger for Dorset. Would you mind if I took this home? Did a bit of research?"

"Of course not. You're more qualified than I am." Peter looked into his brown paper bag. "I'd better get all this back home. It'll need to go in the oven, I think."

"Come on then."

Phoebe looked up at the black velvet Dorset sky. "Clouds have all gone, the buggers. No chance of snow tonight. Only stars."

"*Only* stars?"

She giggled and held up her hands in surrender. "Yes, only those billion year old burning balls which made everything. *Only* those." She blew a kiss upwards. "Sorry, stars. Did you know, back in the day, some ancients thought stars were pinpricks in a huge black cloth, others thought they were souls. Lovely," she added wistfully.

"Souls?"

"Mmm. You'd better get going. That cod's not going to eat itself. What are you doing tomorrow? Want to meet up?"

Peter's heart rate jumped a notch.

"I'm back at Kerstmann's for midday, but other than that, nothing."

She held up the book. "OK, come to mine for ten and we'll discuss. No earlier, please, I'll be asleep." She linked arms with him and they headed back to Dawn Street.

BOOK TWO
22nd DECEMBER 2022

19/ DORCHESTER TO LITTEL WADE, 7:00 a.m.

Anthony Piper gunned his Vauxhall down the dark snaking roads that led from the busy pre-Christmas streets of Dorchester back to the empty, un-festive lanes of Littel Wade. Although his headlamps were on full beam, Tony knew if another car were coming towards him at a similar speed, the lights wouldn't give much warning.

He didn't really care.

Tony hated these evenings, mornings, days, hours, and minutes. But his only alternative was to sit and think and that was no alternative at all. So once again he'd driven the streets and been summoned by his phone to pick up every kind of person, at all stages from polite sobriety to confrontational inebriation. He was respectful to the girls who spoke a little too loudly and giggled a fraction too wildly. He'd tell them to be careful and watch themselves, but knew these evenings were the exact opposite of "being careful."They were supposed to be wild and unpredictable, the same as all young people expect to be at that age.

But youth doesn't make you bulletproof, he'd thought many times. *You're not even close. Believing nothing bad could ever happen was no more effective than crossing your fingers. Bad happens. Bad is out there, and it* will *find you.*

Sometimes he would stop at a certain point on his journey home. Once there, as you have already seen, he would shut down, stare and go somewhere else deep within. During those trancelike times, he would try not to think about what he'd carefully placed in the boot, but oh, how it called to him.

Tonight he kept his foot down.

A single flake of snow wheeled out of the blackness, shone in his headlights then burst against the windscreen.

What?

For a moment, what seemed to be a figure was caught in the strobe of tree and headlamp, frozen as if in a flash of lightning. Anthony only saw the forest-cloaked shape for an instant, as he, she, or it looked in his direction then folded back into the night.

Tony gasped in shock and reflexively slammed on his brakes. Thankfully no other vehicles were oncoming as the car shimmied and slid for another thirty yards before stopping on a verge where its engine whirred and ticked as if out of breath.

Anthony craned round to the spot where he'd thought *something* had watched him.

Nothing there, he thought. *Nothing and nobody, just trees, dark, light and the Marryman Forest.* As he inhaled deeply and pulled away one thought looped in his mind;

If you'd crashed, would that have been a bad thing? Bad happens. Oh, you know bad happens. But would me crashing have been a bad thing?

*

Deep in the undergrowth, Gregory Underbore had no idea Anthony Piper was driving the car which had passed him, just as Tony had no clue the dark figure was Greg.

That was probably for the best.

20/ NUMBER NINE DAWN STREET, MORNING.

Peter's sleeping mind replayed a dream he'd had many times, one that was always made of three interchangeable scenes.

Today the dream began with distorted noise outside his bedroom window which literally shook the glass with rage. Whether produced by human, animal or machine, Peter didn't know, but eventually the sound always swirled into *somebody* or *something* unknown, shifting from human, to growl, to pulsing rumble then finally a bird screeching into the distance.

Then the dream jump-cut to another act where Peter had his ear to a wall, listening to what sounded like snakes screaming. They hissed from the other side, harsh *sssssibillllllances* punctuated by rattles and spits. Peter didn't understand the reptiles' language, but their intent was clear. He knew fangs were bared as the creatures struck at each other over and over again.

This was followed by a sharp change in tone.

Peter was suddenly in Littel Wade High Street. Instantaneous translocation happens a lot in dreams, one of the clues you are sleeping, but at first, this scene always felt real.

It was Christmas Eve in the village, but not one he recognised, since trees glowed from every window and festive lights flickered. Even sleeping, Peter knew he'd layered a version of Bedford Falls over his own home and half expected Jimmy Stewart to run past shouting, "Merry Christmas!" But instead, Mr Farr, Mr Spencer and Mrs Bramell were handing out sweets to passing children, truly an indication this was a fantasy. Alongside them Mr Hamnett was dressed as Santa, but with no sign of wellington boots, cotton wool beard or black bin liner for presents. No, *this* costume would have made St. Nick proud.

Then as the church bells chimed seven p.m. (and it was always that time) snow began to fall like fine static and people looked up with a communal gasp as if a long lost friend had returned.

The fall became faster, thicker.

Soon the villagers were reduced to snowman shapes and shops became blurred pencil outlines. Peter stared in wonder as this happened, like he were watching a Great Draftsman erase reality in order to start again. Everything was in motion. The buildings were made of still-falling flakes, so they shimmered and wobbled.

Across the road, snow clumped together then rolled itself into spheres and cylinders. Detail and definition emerged from these crude blocks to reveal the outline of a person.

Peter always woke up just as that snow-human shape started to walk toward him, and every time discovered he'd grasped his pillow like a life preserver. Only once his breathing slowed and reality truly returned could he trust himself to go downstairs.

Peter stared at himself in the mirror, rubbed his eyes and prepared to pretend both the world and himself were normal.

*

"Ah, here he is," Julie Piper turned and raised a mug to her son. "Morning!"

Anthony was busying himself frying an egg.

"*Both* of you at breakfast?" Peter raised his eyebrows in mock surprise. "Well, I haven't seen that since 2016, I think."

"Cheeky," Julie laughed. "It does happen. We can't be blamed if you're too lazy to get up and see. Sleep well?"

"Well, I slept," Peter replied, a running joke in the Piper household.

"Good. Now; shifts, God, and Dorchester willing, I should be back for about six to enjoy the monosyllabic grunts of my favourite lads over dinner."

"We don't grunt," Tony grunted, monosyllabically.

"Ooh, someone's moody today," Julie winked at her son. "He's so easy to wind up, and it's so much fun doing it."

"Bugger off."

"Bugger off? What year is this? 1975?"

"I wouldn't mind an egg if you could knock one up, dad." Peter wandered over and peered into the pan. "Maybe not incinerated, though."

"Bloody hell, is everyone on my case?"

"I'm just saying that Michelin Star won't win itself."

Julie laughed. "Jokes now? And this early? Oh, talking of which, Tone, Christmas crackers. We didn't have any last year did we?"

"Oh, not this again," dad rolled his eyes.

"Turkey without bad jokes and paper crowns doesn't taste the same. So, in your travels, pick up a box. I've left you a reminder upstairs."

"Yes, yes, I saw it…" Tony sighed.

"And yet still we have none. Tut tut." She peered out of the window into their little back yard. "And we still don't have snow. I think there should be a law that it snows at Christmas."

"Well, aren't you the law, mum?"

"I uphold it, I don't make it," she scanned the sky. "I think if I were given three wishes, one would be for snow in the week before and after Christmas. And proper drifty stuff, like when you were born."

"Peter, do you want toast with this egg or naked?" Tony asked.

"Toast please."

Julie tapped her fingernails on the work surface and continued to look at the clouds. "You know, I'm glad it snowed that day and I'm glad you were born here. It makes our house even more special. Not ideal at the time, but looking back, lying in a ward with loads of screaming women wouldn't have been as magical. A power cut, blizzard, the village snowed in…It should have been a nightmare, but it felt right."

"You're poetic this morning," Tony mumbled.

"I try to be poetic every morning," She turned back to the kitchen. "'Cos it's just…I spend my days working on a horrible planet for the most part, so I'd just like to wake up in December and see the world looking like Narnia. Not much to ask, really." She clipped on her police tie, walked over to her husband, went on tiptoes and gave him a little kiss on the lips. "Shouldn't you be in bed? You must be knackered."

"I am. Christmas parties…they give me a lot to tidy up."

"I bet. Must be awful seeing all those people having a good time and only being able to watch."

"It's OK, just tiring. You do more tidying up than I do."

"I do, to be honest." She sighed and shook her head. "I attended a hit and run on Monmouth Road yesterday, twelve year old boy knocked off his bike. Stolen car, driver just puts his foot down and leaves him by the kerb. Who does that?" Julie looked simultaneously upset and very angry. "So four days before Christmas I had to find his parents and tell them their son was in ICU. It's horrible knowing when you knock on a door you're there to break someone's heart. *Four days before Christmas*." Her expression hardened. "And that driver's probably out there, not even thinking about it, just getting on with his life." She threw up her hands. "Ah, you know what? I'm not going to let the scumbags get to me, they don't deserve my energy."

Julie stood, grabbed a tinsel garland from over the kitchen window and wrapped it round her neck like a feather boa. "How much do I wish I could wear this to work? Julie Piper; Christmas Copper."

"Suits you," said Peter.

"Everything suits me."

From the road came a *beep-beep-beep.* Julie reluctantly removed the tinsel and hung it round her son's shoulders. "Suits you," she said.

"Everything suits me," he replied, drolly. She went to the front door and waved out. "One minute!"

"Must be so nice getting a lift every day," muttered Tony. She looked at him with an eyebrow raised. "What do you mean by that?"

"Just what I said. Must be nice having company. Talking about work, having a laugh."

She frowned and put a hand on her hip. "Oh yeah, work's *such* a laugh. It's just a lift, why are you being so shirty?"

Peter looked between his parents. He'd heard them argue of course, but never in his company. They clearly believed arguing out of their child's sight but not hearing somehow didn't count.

"I'm not being…" he put on a whiny voice. "*Shirty, Julie.* I'm just saying you get a lot of lifts."

"What, do you want me to get the bus?" Peter took the tinsel off since its twinkly presence suddenly felt inappropriate. "Or shall I use Peter's bicycle?"

"You could drive yourself."

"Or I could take up the kind offer of a lift, which I do."

"Very kind offers. Very kind."

"What?"

"Just saying."

"Oh, you know what? Go and have a sleep. Hopefully you'll wake up in a better mood and less unreasonable. Now I'm off to work, which, as I've just pointed out, is no fun at all. I rather hoped this place was a haven from all that, so *cheers,* Tony. Thanks for a shitty breakfast."

Peter's mouth opened at that. He'd never heard his mum swear at dad in that way before.

"Sorry for swearing," Julie said pointedly to her son but not her husband. She kissed Peter on the top of the head. "Hope to be back earlier, as long as he's stopped being such an arse."

Tony pushed past his wife and clumped upstairs with heavy footfalls. Mum looked up toward the sound. "Very mature. Have a good day, Peter. Love you."

"And you love dad too, don't you?"

Her shoulders slumped. "Of course I do. The stupid, moaning, paranoid bloody idiot." Julie kissed Peter on the forehead. "Ta-ta, darling."

She strode down the hall and slammed the door. There was the rumble of an engine and then the house fell into a sulky silence.

21/ PHOEBE'S HOUSE, 5, DAWN STREET, 10 a.m.

Peter stood in Phoebe's porch, knocked, then stamped his feet to stay warm. In just the few yards walk between their homes, December cold had still managed to get under his skin.

Phoebe's mum Pam answered, wrapped snugly in a pink dressing gown with her hair in an untidy ponytail. Pam looked just like her daughter except blonde and with much less make-up. Unsurprisingly, she sounded like her, too.

"Oh, hello, stranger. Madame Morticia said you'd be knocking for ten and…" Pam looked up at a hallway clock, "…ta-dah, you are truly Peter Punctual."

"I try to be."

"How are you?"

"I'm fine."

"OK, good."

Pam waved him indoors. A studio photograph of Phoebe's little family hung in the hallway. It showed Pam and her husband Bill flanking their six-year-old daughter, who wore a proud semi-toothless grin. This picture always amused Peter, since the naive expression on Phoebe's young face was one he never saw these days.

Pam saw him look. "Her majesty still *hates* that, which is exactly why I will never take it down."

Peter laughed, then asked, "Is Bill around?"

Pam's shoulders heaved for a moment and she visibly gulped. "No, he's not right now."

"Oh, I…"

"No, it's fine, he's OK, he's just not here, er, today."

Peter read the signals and let it drop.

Pam composed herself and shouted up the thin staircase. "Phoebe Clarke, please don't pretend you didn't hear the door. Your guest is here, on time, as requested."

"Send him up," ordered a muffled, haughty voice from above.

"*Send him up*," mocked Pam in a posh accent. "Would her ladyship also like some tea and scones?"

"Whaaaat?"

"Oh, I'm so proud of your command of English."

"*Whaaat*?"

Phoebe's mum sighed. "Do you have a girlfriend, Peter?"

"Er, no." He blushed and hoped she wouldn't ask too many questions. He'd dated precisely zero girls, which had been noticed with barely concealed raised eyebrows at both school and now sixth form. It wasn't for lack of trying, but the opposite sex seemed to view him as a friend rather than a catch, which was frustrating on many levels.

"Well, watch and learn, Peter, watch and learn." She indicated Phoebe's room. "That is what you'll have to contend with when you do. As an ex-teenager myself, I know exactly how difficult we can be."

Oh God, has she spotted I like Phoebe? He wondered with horror. *Is she taking the piss a bit?* But Pam stepped aside and gestured for him to climb the stairs. "Vampirella awaits your pleasure. Although you might not recognise her, as The Dark Princess has yet to apply her mask of doom."

A poster of The Damned covered most of Phoebe's shiny black door and from inside he could hear something dark and rumbling.

"If you're out there, c*ome iiiiiinnnn*," Phoebe intoned.

She was sat at a desk in a white shirt, black tie, pleated lace skirt and ripped tights. Her face was free of make up, which was a look Peter hadn't seen in a long time.

"*Au naturel*, I like it. Dressed for work, then?"

"Mm, can't get my head sorted in pyjamas. I need to feel businesslike if I'm doing business. I'm at the Co-op for twelve so all this…" she fluttered her hands over the outfit, "…will be swapped for something more soul destroying, but while I can, I will."

A thumping drum machine stuttered from Phoebe's speaker while *someone* moaned lyrics which seemed to suggest the end of the world.

"What's the music?"

"*What's the music*?" She sniffed. "I am seriously going to have to educate you. It's The Sisters Of Mercy, *Floorshow*. Good, eh?"

"Er…"

"It is, end of argument."

As Peter started to take off his coat and hat Phoebe put up a hand. "Ah, no point, keep them on."

"Why?"

"We're not staying."

"Oh, but it's so welcoming."

"Ha."

A MacBook lay open on her desk, which was stacked higgledy piggledy with books and papers. Pinned to the wall in front were drawings and paintings all with a similar theme; a bare wintry tree whose roots formed symbols and images. Peter saw a dragon, celtic cross, hammer, bones, and what he took to be occult signs. "Did you do these?"

"Yep. They're designs for my book cover."

"Your *book cover*? When did you write a book?"

"Well, I haven't, not yet, it's still very much in the planning stage. When I go to university I intend it to be my thesis, which I'll turn into a full manuscript, sell to a massive publisher, become a millionaire, leave Littel Wade and become a batshit mad old lady who appears on BBC4 history documentaries and about whom everyone says, 'She's still very handsome in her old age.' I've got it all worked out."

She turned to her laptop and prodded a few keys. "I present my *meisterwerk*. Ta-da!"

Peter bent to read what was written there.

"'*Roots Of Reality'?*"

"And the subtitle, Piper."

"'*How Faith and Myth Became Fact And Matter By Phoebe Clarke.'* Wow. That sounds heavy."

"It's not really. To sum up; I think reality's foundations have more basis in fantasy than fact."

Peter must have looked confused.

Phoebe sighed. "All right, I'll give you the overview. Do you believe in God? Any God, take your pick, there are plenty knocking about up there."

"No, I don't believe in any God."

"Why?"

"There's no evidence."

"Really? OK, has there ever been *any* evidence for *any* deity?"

"Is that a trick question?"

"Trick questions are for idiot questioners. Has there?"

"No, obviously."

"Ah, but that's a modern atheist talking. The ancients were surrounded by evidence. That great glowing ball in the sky which makes everything grow when it's strong? Surely that's God, right?"

"Yeah, but now we know it's a star."

She laughed. "Stop being so Milleni-centric. *We* know it's a star, but as far as they knew…yes, *knew*, the sun was a deity, thunder was gods fighting, lightning was their weapon, supernatural beings lived inside volcanoes, rainbows were bridges to Valhalla, souls went to the Moon and waited to be reborn…They knew this stuff was real. They knew it because what else *could* it be?"

Peter felt a strange need to defend modernity. "But they were wrong, though."

"No, they weren't! Our ancestors wondered how the universe worked, so came up with systems they could understand; gods, spirits, giants, elves, fairies, seers, prophecies, messiahs…Those ancients may have thought the stars were souls, but could still navigate by them, yes? So did it even *matter* what they really were? Look, we call the start of everything the Big Bang, they called it Ra, Gaia, Pan-gu…Those creators were as real to them as the Large Hadron Collider is to us, just two different ways of answering the same question; how did we get here?"

"They were still wrong, though."

Phoebe chuckled. "The heretic will not surrender his position. Oh, and by the way, Mr Rationality, even the Big Bang is still just a theory. In fact quite a few astrophysicists hate the term *Big Bang,*'cos they claim it's a simplistic and misleading image. Some prefer the more ambiguous, 'Horrendous Space Kablooie.' which, let's face it, is a way more exciting term and certainly befits the awesome creation of everything."

"Now you're taking the piss. You just made that up."

"I so didn't. Look, nobody's saying those ancients were right, but beliefs based on zero evidence can definitely still have real world effects. 2022 AD is just as affected by legend, fable, folklore, *whatever*, as 2022 *BC.* Isn't social media full of totally fabricated modern myths that have, without doubt, informed the decisions of individuals and sometimes populations? Covid, Ukraine, vaccinations, Qanon, Trump's Big Lie…The internet is a modern Homer, going from virtual village to virtual village telling stories. But when people don't see them as stories, they become facts. We live in an age where one person's fact is totally different from another's. That's bollocks. Facts are facts are facts. So what's the difference between then and now? Who's more *uninformed,* us or them? We've just swapped the great god Zeus for the great god Google. And aren't all conspiracy theories belief systems, too? Y'know, good versus evil, a One True Faith, redemption for believers? YouTube's full of paranoids telling us how they've cleverly seen through the '*Mainstream Media Matrix,'* so know how the *real* world works and are therefore way smarter than the rest of us poor, brainwashed sheeple. But their worldview is based on what are effectively fairy tales. That's what *Roots Of Reality* is about. Do you get it?"

Peter nodded.

"Sure? You don't think I'm suddenly going to sacrifice a chicken to the snow gods?"

"Well, I wouldn't put it past you."

She lightly punched him on the arm then got serious. "Millions have died because of myths. Empires have been formed on the back of them. Look, every village in Britain has a church, erected on nothing more than belief in a totally unproven system of creation. A church is a power station for faith. Put worshippers in one end and it generates a God at the other. Or maybe it's the other way round."

"That's a quote from your book isn't it?"

"That obvious, was I?"

"*And* the stuff about Homer. *And* the bit about the Large Hadron Collider. *And* swapping Zeus for Google. *And* conspiracy theories being belief systems…Oh, and *Milleni-Centric*."

Phoebe held her hands up in surrender. "Guilty. But I do believe real world applications of unprovable myths can still change history, even though we live in a so-called enlightened world."

"Was that a quote, too?"

"Oh fuck off, yes, it was. Stories are *powerful*, Piper, even when we know they're just stories."

She opened her wardrobe and pulled out a huge pair of black buckled boots. "Which brings us very neatly to your mystery book. I thought about taking you through what I've found here in the relative comfort of my room but what with it being such a bracing day a field trip might be better."

"A field trip?"

"Two minutes walk and you'll have some answers. But I'm afraid the answers are only going to lead us to more questions. Shall we?"

*

They walked out of Dawn Street and turned left toward St Nicholas'.

"I'm at the Co-op for mid-day, so no rush, Piper."

Peter's mouth engaged before his mind could think too hard. "I asked about your dad and your mum seemed a bit, well, upset. Is everything OK?"

Phoebe straightened up and pretended not to be bothered. "Yes. No. No, not really." She sighed and her voice caught. "You know he works for *Medicin Sans Frontiers*, right?"

"*Ye-esss…*"

"So every year he goes away for a bit. Sometimes a month, sometimes more."

Peter was aware Bill Clarke had a background in medicine and would often work abroad.

"He's a health promoter and he's just been in Karachi, you know, Pakistan. But anyway, long story short, he was supposed to fly back a couple of days ago and…he didn't."

Her voice cracked again. Peter knew Phoebe was very close to her dad, far closer than he was to his own father. "It's OK, he's fine, but you know, travel is so fucked up there at the best of times and something went wrong with his booking. Apparently he got to the airport and his plane had disappeared. Not off the radar, it was just some screw up with scheduling. So…" she gasped again, a long shuddering exhalation, "…he's not coming back for Christmas. And probably won't be back until about the 28th, which is *shit*. Why does Karachi get my dad and I don't? It's *shit, fucking, fucking shit.*"

She repeatedly kicked the wheel of a nearby car in anger then stopped, stared at Peter and put hands to her mouth. "Oh God, I'm so sorry."

"It's OK, it *is* unfair and it *is* shit."

"But…I feel so stupid." She waved her hands as if in surrender. "'Cos…you know, I didn't mean to…'Cos…"

"*Please* don't worry, it's honestly OK."

"Are you sure?"

"I wouldn't say if I wasn't."

"Thank you." Phoebe squeezed his hand, gave a little shy smile, composed herself, changed the subject and pointed across the road. "OK, your book. Well, Mrs Kerstmann's book. The sleigh's book, maybe George Johnson's book. Or more likely, none of the above. "

"I'm intrigued."

"Mm, so am I. Let's go to one of my favourite places."

"Where's that?"

She waved her hands up and down the ripped tights, black skirt and leather jacket. "The graveyard, of course. I'm a Goth. It's my equivalent of Disneyland Paris, but the occupants are way less rude."

Apart from newer plots at the rear of the church, the graveyard had no sense of order or chronology. Ancient fallen stones lay next to austere carved Victorian angels. Weathered little headpieces, names long erased, stood at angles alongside bumps in the ground whose residents had lost their markers long ago.

"You know, places of rest are also sites of magical thinking," Phoebe said as they picked through the graves. "We put the remains of our loved ones amongst strangers in a place they had no connection with in life.

Then we erect monuments that give a timeframe for their existence to sometimes curious but mainly indifferent passers-by. And *then* we treat that spot as a focal point for our beloved's non-existence." She paused for a moment and studied Peter. "You do see what I'm trying to say, don't you? I'm not being disrespectful, I'm just laying it out. "

"Of course."

"Alright, there's no logic, no science for any of it, but does there have to be? Some things are so *obviously* magic, but we've stopped seeing them as such. Please take a seat Mr Piper." Phoebe indicated a tired old bench.

She reached into her bag and pulled out the sleigh's red leather book. "So as we know, in here there are lots of weird names and words, but no addresses, no dates. On the opposite pages, the names, words, whatever, have a red X next to them. And the spine of the book once had "DORSET" embossed on it. All agreed so far?"

"Agreed."

"Now, you know when something won't get out of your head?"

Like you, Peter thought.

She opened the volume and pointed to one entry.

M Gortoney
Book

"The name Gortoney is very unusual, but I knew I'd seen it before."

She pointed to a tall slab on their right. Carved into its surface were the words;

Mary Gortoney, Sleeping now, in the arms of angels 1834 - 1842

"She was seven, eight years old, " Phoebe whispered. "So bloody sad."

"*Gortoney*," Peter found himself whispering too.

"The same. Well, I assume it's the same. You find a book hidden in a sleigh found in a ditch not a mile from here, and it has *that* name in it?"

"Could be coincidence?"

"Could be," she scoffed. "But let's not stop there." She found another page and name;

W Fillirish
Hoop

"Fillirish?" Phoebc spread her hands wide. "Not exactly Smith or Jones, right? And yet, and yet…" She took Peter's chin with a black-gloved hand and pointed his face to another stone;

William Fillirish 1807 - 1872 Husband of Victoria, Father to Edina & Ada.

"Weird, huh?" As they threaded through the graves, Phoebe selected entries in the book and compared them to carvings. "Names in here match up to names in the graveyard, see? In the book, *T Acorn*, and over there on this stone, see?"

Peter looked over at a simple inscription;

Thomas Acorn 1755 - 1807

"Then…an *A Acree* on the page, over here, *A Acree* on this stone…"

Annie Acree 1899 - 1945

"There's this entry, *P Dawn*, and over there there's this rather pretty memorial…"

They stopped before a small statue of a beautiful woman expressionlessly staring into the distance. She appeared to be sat on a rolling landscape, or waves.

"I love this one," Phoebe said fondly. "For ages I thought she was on hills, but the more I look, the more I think she's sat on a snow drift. But anyway, here in your book, see?" She indicated two words…

P Dawn
Orange

…Then bent to the inscription.

Patience Marryman, nee Dawn, beloved by Francis, with the stars now, iterum, 1774- 1809

"Dawn…" said Peter. "My mum's maiden name was Dawn."

"I didn't know that. Any relation?"

Peter shrugged. "Dunno. *Iterum*, what does that mean?"

"*Again*. I guess, as in 'We will meet again.' But *Dawn's* another name in the book that's here in the graveyard. So what do you think?"

"How many other names match up?"

"I haven't done a full survey, but I've already found quite a few."

"OK, so it's not a ledger of graves, because if it was, there would be dates and full names, which our book doesn't have."

"Yep. Just odd words like *orange*, *book* and *hoop,* and all those red X's."

Peter blew out his cheeks in confusion. "Not a sales ledger either, 'cos as we've said, there are no prices, addresses or dates, so it's absolutely useless as any kind of business record."

"I know." Phoebe put a gentle hand on the statue's head as it stared off into the distance. "I told you I had answers that would only lead to more questions."

"It's weird."

"I *know*," she repeated with relish. "And weird is good, right?"

Peter wasn't sure about that.

22/ KERSTMANN'S YARD, 12:30 p.m.

Peter circled the sleigh and frowned. He'd only just arrived and was already puzzled. "Have you given this another coat?" he asked Mrs Kerstmann.

"*Me* give it another coat? That's what I'm paying you for."

Peter examined the woodwork. "I'm sure it wasn't this bright red last night. The wood looks in better condition, too." He wiped a finger over the runners. "And I'm sure these are smoother, less rusty."

Mrs Kerstmann slapped a palm against her forehead. "Oh, of course, I know why it's brighter, I should have said."

Peter looked round at her expectantly.

"I have these little elves. They only come out at night. Usually to fix shoes, but any odd job that needs finishing, they'll put a tiny hand to."

Peter laughed. "Oh yes, the elves."

She straightened up with some difficulty. "OK,boring explanation. Last night you saw the sleigh by very bright, very artificial light, which bleaches colours out, and doesn't represent how they really are."

Peter looked back at the vehicle and saw the sense in what she said. Mrs K's bright spotlights had washed out everything in the area yesterday afternoon, but in daylight they'd settled into their real hues. She carried on talking, but almost to herself. "Although of course there are no such things as colours in reality, whatever that is. Just the frequencies our eyes can pick up. There's an old Buddhist saying, '*What makes the grass green?*' Any ideas?"

"Chlorophyll?"

"Very good, but the real answer is '*You* do.' Grass is any colour but green. In fact, it reflects what *we* call green back into our eyes. Ask a bee what colour grass is and they'll give you a completely different answer. If bees could talk, that is, and who's to say they don't?"

"So this sleigh isn't red?" Peter hadn't considered the reality of colour before.

"No. It just reflects a frequency of light we call red back into our eyes and our brains do the rest."

"That's interesting."

"The world is interesting." She wiped a hand over the sleigh's body and sighed with delight. "Funny to think what we see here doesn't exist except in our minds, don't you think? That's a concept to bother you for the rest of the day, right?"

"I'll try to be too busy to think about it."

"Good lad, I'm not paying you to philosophise." Mrs Kerstmann started to walk away but then turned back with a minxy smile. "Or maybe I am. Oh, I don't suppose the sleigh's funny little book turned out to be anything interesting, did it? Anything I can sell for a gargantuan profit?"

Peter pulled the book from his rucksack and told her everything he and Phoebe knew, which still wasn't much.

"Phoebe sounds like a girl after my own heart. Curiosity doesn't kill the cat, it makes the cat smarter. That's my motto."

Mrs K. had a lot of mottos.

"Well, keep on investigating, I'd be very interested to know what you find. But sometimes, you know, it's what's you can read between the lines rather than what's on them."

"What do you mean?"

"I have no idea. But it sounds like a plan and occasionally, if something sounds like a plan it's worth pursuing. Right, today's jobs; give the sleigh another coat." She looked about her yard. "Oh, I know, talking of books I have a few boxes of them that I'd like going through and separating into fiction, fact, date, that kind of thing. So plenty to start with, I'd say."

"OK." Peter opened the pot of red paint. "Hold on, I could swear there was more paint in here than this last night. The level is way lower."

"Elves," laughed Mrs K. over her shoulder. "Told you, it's those damned elves."

*

Peter took an hour or so to apply another fire engine red coat to the sleigh. "Oh, Peter?" Mrs Kerstmann called from across the way and waggled some keys at him. "According to the grapevine, some rather interesting items are coming up at Marley's Auction House in Dorchester. Since I do interesting, I should go and take a look. The place could always do with a few more items, couldn't it?" Peter looked at her expecting a wry smile but saw she was deadly serious. "Sleigh's looking exceptionally red now. Come and get out of the cold, do those books I told you about."

She climbed into the cab of her corroded pickup truck. "Might get you working your magic on this old girl, too," she banged her hand against the door. Peter was convinced he saw an exhalation of rust rise from it. "I doubt there'll be any customers, but give me a call if anyone wants anything, my mobile number's on a Post-It stuck to the Victorian desk."

"Wait, you're leaving me in charge?"

"Hardly, 'In charge,' Peter. Just keep an eye on things, call me if someone makes an offer, don't burn the place down. I'll be back by four, five at the latest once I've scoped out any potential bargains. My boxes of books are stacked up next to the mannequin in a Great War uniform. All right?"

"OK."

"Toodle-ooh then."

The truck coughed like an asthmatic smoker then its engine puffed and wheezed into a form of life. There was a further clanking and explosive farting from the exhaust then the machine staggered toward the gate.

She won't make ten metres, Peter thought, but the truck suddenly attained vehicular zen and smoothly slid out of the yard. He watched it go then stepped into her hotchpotch house.

*

The floorboards creaked and stretched under his footfall, which sounded like Mrs Kerstmann's residence was a galleon somewhere on the high seas. Yesterday he'd entered via a different door, so took a moment to orient himself.

OK, so from this *doorway her Victorian desk is over* there. *I would have put money on it being in* that *corner. And the bookcases are...against the left wall. Strange, I had them on the right. And I do* not *remember seeing a chandelier yesterday. No, make that two chandeliers. Amazing what a different entrance can do to your point of view. And* memory, *actually.*

Peter knew the place was busy, *no, chaotic*, but now saw things he really surely should have spotted but missed twenty-four hours ago.

Where did that stuffed bear come from? And is that half a Dalek? *Why didn't I spot that suit of armour? Perhaps I'm looking at the contents of her head. Yes, that's it, I've stepped out of Dorset into Mrs K.'s brain.*

He spotted a dummy in World War One uniform and picked his way over. The ability to walk in a straight line was a rare treat in this house.

It's immaculate, he thought. *Must have come from a film set. Not a fray or rip in it.*

But something told him Mrs Kerstmann didn't *do* fakes or copies. If an object wasn't the genuine article, it would never get past her gate. As promised, stacked beside the mannequin were five cardboard boxes full of books. *OK, so she wanted them sorted by subject, fact, fiction and date, no problem. But once they're arranged, where can I possibly put them?*

There's no room anywhere. Peter spotted a cupboard lurking in one corner and meandered over to it. *If you open the door and there are loads of fur coats in there, do* not *push through them because there could well be a fawn and a White Witch waiting to offer you Turkish Delight. Do* not *take it.*

Peter opened the wardrobe, which was thankfully full of shelves rather than fur coats and Narnia. He grabbed a large book from a box but its cover fell open and various papers dropped to the floor. Stuck inside was a note in swirly Victorian carnival calligraphy which read, "KERSTMANN'S FOR THE INDETERMINATE AND STRANGE, FOR CONCEALED MARVELS AND APOCRYPHAL APOCRYPHA."

Under this legend was an address in equally ornate manuscript; *25, Columbia Road, Hackney, London.*

How long have the Kerstmanns being doing this? He turned the page. Yellowed and cracked tape held a washed-out photograph in the centre. It showed a scrapyard and sign reading; KERSTMANN & SON; YOUR WHITE ELEPHANTS ARE OUR GOLD TREASURES.

Peter flicked on past invoices and receipts, handwritten notes and typed delivery addresses. *Well,* this *is a ledger, at least. One with a bunch of extraneous other cuttings along for the ride.* Yet more old photographs were glued or taped to the following pages, generally views of the Hackney yard, or perhaps other yards elsewhere. It was difficult to tell them apart.

There was a torn flyer; KERSTMANNS! ANTIQUE, VINTAGE, UNWANTED AND ODD. WE PAY CASH. This one had a phone number, CALL DEA 3414.

Blimey, only four digits? That is an old *phone number.*

The other copy suggested; FIND OUR STALL IN KENDALS, DEANSGATE, MANCHESTER.

Hackney? Manchester? What is this, a chain? A franchise? A family business over how many years? Amongst the following pages Peter found two other addresses for Kerstmann Emporia; one in Brighton, another in Edinburgh. But the book's contents didn't seem to have a logical order, so it was difficult to work out any real pattern. *You wait ages for a weird book to arrive, then two come along at once,* he thought ruefully. *But at least I can ask Mrs K about* this *one.* Peter frowned. *Although maybe not. If I ask, that might that look like I've just been rooting through her stuff while she's out. I'm supposed to be putting books in order, not playing about in her family's past.*

He flicked through a little further, stopped, then felt his mouth drop open at another faded photograph of a haphazard yard. This one's sign proudly announced, KERSTMANNS OF HARROGATE.PECULIAR BARGAINS AND WONDERFUL BUYS.

A handwritten annotation read *1922*.

But it wasn't the sign or date that froze Peter.

It was the woman who grinned from the centre, arms wide as if to say, *this is all mine*.

Mrs Kerstmann.

Not *a* Mrs Kerstmann.

The Mrs Kerstmann.

23/ THE UNDERBORE'S HOME, LITTEL WADE, 2:00 p.m.

Gregory Underbore and his mother Florence lived on the outskirts of Littel Wade, if such a remote area could indeed have "outskirts". It may be fairer to say their bungalow seemed to have extricated itself from the rest of the village like a teenager sulking in the corner of a party. It squatted in an acre of balding grass strewn with detritus; plastic barrels, empty plant pots and pieces of motorbike formed dirty islands. A stained and rotted sofa waited for sitters that would never come, like a home furnishing display from hell.

Gregory had just got home from Littel Wade. The mat offered him a worn WELCOME, but that was the only welcome he'd ever get.

Underbore let himself into their dark hallway then stepped into the kitchen to find mother sat at their tiny dining table with a terrifyingly blank face.

Greg's immediate thought was, *This isn't good.*

He knew no expression meant she was too angry to even think about forming one.

Florence had these scary meltdowns every few months.

Something insignificant would annoy her; perhaps he'd left cupboard doors open one too many times, or maybe his room had exceeded her untidiness threshold. Then from these tiny acorns of bitterness huge oaks of bile would grow, and once a screaming fit had begun it would always end with Gregory being accused as the reason father left home.

Dad had moved out in 2012, and since then Florence had compiled an ever-growing list of Greg-related grounds for his absence;

You cried too much.

You were too demanding.

You never did what you were told.

You always tried his patience.

You were too loud.

You were too quiet.

You were a disappointment.

You were too stupid.

You were too clever for your own good.

And so they went on.

He knew the real reason was because *mother was mother* and therefore impossible to predict, tolerate or love.

As Greg steadied himself for the onslaught he saw she was staring down at *something* on the table.

Something eight inches long, thin, straight, and potentially dangerous.

Something he'd recently kept in his camouflage jacket.

Without looking up Florence softly enunciated seven words; "What the fuck is this, Gregory Underbore?"

Whenever she used his full name he knew the sky was about to fall, so stayed silent.

She still didn't look in his direction. "I always go through your pockets before I wash your clothes you know, just in case there's any money or whatever. And my-oh-my I found this. So I ask again, very politely, what the fuck is it?"

"Well, it's..."

At that point mother had surely learned the art of teleportation, because one moment she was sat at the table, the next, instantaneously in front of him spraying spittle.

"Oh I can see what it is. That was clearly a rhetorical question," she squealed, and not for the first time Greg was relieved they lived so far from anyone else. Next door neighbours would have called the police on a weekly basis.

She pushed the object into his face and he cringed from it. "And what did you intend to do with this? Again, a rhetorical question, but I'd like to hear your explanation."

He tried to cower away like a beaten animal but the wall stopped his retreat.

Greg stuttered, "Nu-nu-nu..."

"Nu-nu-nu, nu-nu-nu..." Florence sing-songed, "Who are you? Bananrama? Na na na na, na na na na, hey-ey-ey, goodbye?"

He didn't know what any of that meant. "No, no I'm...I-I-I..."

"You were going to the Piper's house with this? Really?"

"I didn't..."

Florence spun away from her son. "You didn't? Oh, no you really fucking didn't, did you? Shall I tell you what you *didn't?* You *didn't* think for one moment what would have happened if you'd been seen, that's what you *didn't*."

She took a deep breath, pushed the quivering violence away from herself and became still again. In some ways that was worse. Florence sat down and smiled, but it was a grin more like an animatronic human's, pulled tight all the way from uncanny valley. "I do apologise for my fucking swearing," she whispered through gritted teeth. "So, would you explain it to me? As I say, I already know, but it would be so helpful to hear it from you."

"I didn't…I wasn't…"

"Oh, I *didn't*, I *wasn't*, I *wasn't*, I *didn't*," her voice spiralled back into a high pitched tornado. Greg could almost feel his hair blowing away from it.

Greg suddenly realised how unfair this was. "I didn't do anything! You're shouting at me for something I didn't even do!"

Florence shut her eyes and took a deep breath. "Oh, please stop… saying…fucking…*didn't*." When she opened them again Greg recoiled from how empty they'd become. "Go on, say *didn't* one more time and I won't be responsible for my actions." Mother giggled then, a horrible grating sound, worse even than the shouting. "Like you're never responsible for your actions! So you *didn't* go there, but you thought about it!" There was now something metallic about her screeching, like sparks flying from an angle grinder. "And don't you dare raise your voice at me. Don't you dare, you brat. Your father left because you were such a brat, you know that."

Greg did. He'd been told enough times.

Florence's voice suddenly became soft, affable and terrible.

"What reason might you possibly have had for being in Dawn Street? Did you even think about that?"

"It's on the way to Barker's Fields."

"Oh, so you had an alibi, did you? Ah…" she threw up her hands in despair, a gesture that had almost become a tic. Mother turned to face him and her eyes thinned to slits. "So please, son of mine, tell me what you were thinking, being there with this."

Greg whispered his explanation.

"Jesus fucking Christ our Lord and ever-loving Saviour, I can't believe what I'm hearing. Seriously? Really, seriously?"

"I just wanted…"

"Oh, shut up. And if…if…oh, and *if…*" She could barely speak now, whirling in the white heat of hysterical wrath. "If you'd been seen, you'd have to explain, wouldn't you? Then questions would be asked, and answers…" Florence gritted her teeth again, "…would…have…to…be… given."

"Nobody saw."

"And I don't want to see you, either. Get out of my sight. Go and camouflage yourself somewhere. And stay camouflaged, for all I care."

Shaking, Greg turned and left the kitchen, rushed to his bedroom and heard his mother sing song again.

"Me-rr-y fuck-ing Christ-*mas*!"

24/ THE CO-OP, LITTEL WADE, 2:30 p.m.

Phoebe was busy.

Or rather, Phoebe was busy giving the impression she was busy. Under Renee's dictatorship, the appearance of working was just as important as being gainfully employed.

The in-house Supermarket radio blared "Last Christmas" for the umpteenth time. Phoebe hated Co-op Radio. She knew the DJ's tried their best but it was difficult to give much of performance when your playlist was chosen by a room full of infinite monkeys, infinite typewriters and a very *finite* list of Holiday Hits.

Thanks George, thought Phoebe. *Last Christmas was shit, this Christmas will be shit, too.*

Renee appeared round the gluten free section.

"What are you doing Miss Clarke?"

"Er, I'm…Just…going to sweep the floor."

"Very good," Renee purred. "Initiative, I like it. You know…" She pointedly stared at her worker's crimped black hair, "…with a few changes, you could be assistant manager material."

"Really?" Phoebe faked a wide-eyed expression somewhere between hope, surprise, and gratitude.

"Oh yes, I can put a word in for you when the time comes. If you decide to clean up and lose the attitude you occasionally have. '*That crazed girl improvising her music,*' that's you *and* a quote from W.B. Yeats, you know."

I would rather squeeze lemons into my eyes, she thought. *And that's not 'attitude' you passive/aggressive cow, that's me.*

"Well, certainly a lot to think about," Phoebe puffed out her cheeks as if she were actually thinking about it. She glanced down at Renee's aggressively moisturised hands. *No wedding ring. I wonder why on earth that would be? A catch like you, Renee? Single? Whatever next?* "Thanks for the advice." She walked back toward the store front, stopped and stared.

Once again, the primary school caretaker Mr Hamnett stood at the bus stop with his gaze locked on Phoebe.

Oh, for God's sake, she thought. *I'm going to ask him what the hell's going on, what his problem is. This is beyond coincidence now. What, does he have a thing for Goths? Or does he hate us? What's so interesting about me?*

Mr Hamnett put up a hand to his eyes as if surveying a distant horizon, then turned and walked away.

You wait at the bus stop and then leave before one arrives? God, why are the people round here so weird?

Phoebe caught her reflection on the cold cabinet's glass door.

And they think you're *the strange one. What a topsy turvy world this is.*

25/ KERSTMANN'S YARD, 5:00 p.m.

As Mrs Kerstmann's truck turned into her yard at five it surely sensed home was near, because the vehicle began to wheeze in surrender moments after passing through the gates.

Peter couldn't stop thinking about the sepia photograph of his new employer, but taken almost one hundred years ago. So he'd separated the books into categories, stood them on the cupboard shelves, then purposefully left the curious ledger on show to one side.

The idea Mrs K. had lived for over one hundred and fifty years was insanity, of course, but the photo was uncanny. The woman who proudly stood in a long-ago yard wasn't just a doppelgänger but a duplicate. Peter had tried to think rationally but couldn't find an explanation. And while he'd tried to eliminate the impossibility of an immortal scrapyard owner, he just couldn't shake it.

Why? Because everything feels strange right now, he thought. *Like Littel Wade has shifted somehow, which is why the idea Mrs K. is some kind of nicknack collecting Dorian Gray seems like it should at least be* considered. *A storm is coming. No, not a storm, a blizzard. So why do I feel something is coming, hidden inside the snow? And why can't I decide whether that's a good thing or bad?*

Three words flashed into his mind, and somehow he knew the truth of them.

Snow is coming.

Peter was certain of it, just as a dog senses a thunderstorm even before the clouds darken.

But it's not snow. He shook his head. The thought wouldn't focus. *No, it* is *snow, but it's* not. *Whatever is coming is snow, but* isn't. *God, what does that even mean?*

One of the many doors opened to reveal Mrs Kerstmann silhouetted in the frame. "Kettle on please, Peter!" She rubbed her hands together. "Allegedly my truck has a heater, but it's more like the last remnants of warmth from a dying breath. It is brass monkeys out there. Why we're not six feet deep in drifts is a total mystery to me."

Because it's waiting for the right moment, Peter thought, then wondered why such an odd notion should pop into his head.

"How did the book corralling go? Actually, don't answer that quite yet, I have to warm up before I can think about anything but the frostbite which I am certain has already taken hold."

Mrs K. stood arms wide in front of an electric three bar heater like a worshipper. "Were we thronged with customers? Am I a millionaire? Did the Antiques Roadshow come a-knocking and offer me oodles for my unappreciated treasures?"

"Er, in order, no, no and I'm afraid no."

"Fiona Bruce is a bitch, " she sighed.

"Not a single person all afternoon."

"I'm shocked. Why people *don't* want to travel to the back of beyond to root through glorious ephemera two days before Christmas is beyond me. And to add insult to injury, I risked hypothermia for nothing, too."

"The auction?"

"The viewing. The actual bidding takes place tomorrow, not that I'll be there. Absolute waste of time. The usual suspects; medals, militaria, furniture, paintings, oh, seen one, seen them all. There was nothing..."

"...Lovely, hopeful, curious or puzzling?" Peter offered as he brought over a hot mug. She beamed and snapped her fingers at him, pleased.

"Exactly. You've got it. Just because something is from the past, that doesn't mean it's automatically interesting. I mean, look at me. I'm from the past, and what do I have to show for it?"

"You have lots to show for it," Peter gestured about the room.

"Charmer. Ooh, this tea is lovely. Do you know what flavour it is?"

"No. You just have a load of teabags in a jar by the kettle."

"I do. That way I never know what I'm going to get. Every cup is a surprise. Try to stay surprised, Peter, it keeps you young, even if it's only playing Russian Roulette with teabags."

Go on, say something. Peter's mind instructed. *You've got the opening, say something.*

"Er, talking of surprises," he began, shocked how casual it sounded. "About the book arranging."

"Ah yes, how did it go?"

"Right, er..." *Go on, Peter, say it.* "Sorry, but when I was clearing the shelves, this opened and a load of stuff fell out." He picked up the scrap book and watched Mrs Kerstmann's face carefully. Her expression didn't change.

Of course her expression's not going to change, you muppet. Because you've had an impossible thought she's the woman in the photo, which is clearly insane. That's *why her expression hasn't changed.*

"Oh, the Kerstmann Lexicon!" She delightedly clapped her hands. "I knew it was there of course, just haven't thought about it in years. No need to, really."

Mrs K. wandered over and leafed through the book. A proud yet sad smile played across her lips. "Generations of us," she whispered. "But not all were as organised as me, as you can see."

Peter started to laugh, but turned it into a cough when he realised she was deadly serious. "There's a few of these books dotted about the place, and all of them are made of chaos. As you saw, it's tickets, receipts, pictures, all manner of nonsense, no chronology, no order. It offends my highly developed sense of a place for everything and everything in its place. But I can't help it if my ancestors were so…" Mrs K. fluttered her fingers as she searched for the word, "…*Cavalier*. Well, thank you for bringing this back into the light, Peter, I believe I now have my night time reading sorted for a few days."

"There was a photograph," Peter held out his hand and Mrs K. passed him the book with a curious expression. "I wasn't, you know, going through your things. It just fell open, I saw a picture and it…intrigued me."

"Intrigued is a good word, " she mused. "I like intrigued. Which picture?"

Peter flicked through until he came to the photograph of Mrs Kerstmann in another scrapyard, apparently taken in Harrogate, 1922. She expressionlessly studied it, then asked, "And what was so interesting about this particular one?"

"Er…" *Yeah, what is interesting, Peter?* He wondered. *It's just one of her relatives. Nothing special.*

"Well, it's the woman."

The woman who doesn't just look like you, but is *you. I don't know how I'm sure of that, but it's you, isn't it?*

Mrs K. examined the figure. "Mm, but what about her?"

Is she trying to make me say it out loud?

"Well, she really looks like you."

Finally, Mrs Kerstmann gave Peter a wry smile. "Oh, I thought you were going to say something *interesting* about her. Of course she looks like me. She is me, isn't she?"

"What?" Peter hadn't expected that.

"Not what, it's pardon, dear. Look at the sign, a bit of a giveaway; 'KERSTMANNS OF HARROGATE.PECULIAR BARGAINS AND WONDERFUL BUYS.' The clue's in the title. As I just said, we've been doing this for generations and are rather good at it. So of course she's me."

"She's…You? But how old are…"

Mrs K. giggled. “Wait. What, hold on, you thought that’s *me*, me? I’m not sure if I’m flattered or horrified. How old do you think I am, Peter Piper? I’ll tell you. I’m sixty-eight. This picture was taken in 1922, so I hope your maths is up to it.”

“Oh, yes, ha. But she does look like you. I thought for a while that perhaps you were…”

“Older than I look?” Mrs K. did a twirl then went *en pointe*. Peter gasped. “If anything, I’m younger. But if that were me in the photograph, and I’m sure you’ve worked it out, I’d have to be, what, one hundred and sixty? How likely do you think that is?”

“I thought maybe the date on the photograph was wrong.”

No, you didn’t, you liar.

“Uh-uh, it’s correct. We all have an appointment with eternity and eternity does not accept cancellations. No, this is Granny Agnes, my great grandmother.” She studied the picture again and gave a little amused *hfffff*. “I really do look like her, you’re right.” Mrs K. thought for a moment than looked intently into Peter’s eyes. ”Let me explain a pet theory I have. People say they don’t believe in ghosts, but I think we’re surrounded by them.”

“We are?”

“Mm.” She put down the scrapbook and gestured for him to follow. “That’s almost enough for the day, let’s get you paid up.” She nimbly avoided many objects scattered across the floor and made a beeline for her desk. Peter took a little longer to pick his way between them.

“Right, I’m going to throw something your way, which you can either pick up or leave where it lies. You thought Granny Agnes was me. That’s because our uncanny resemblance means we obviously share a shedload of DNA, that’s all. And isn’t that a kind of reincarnation? In appearance I *am* Granny Agnes, alive and kicking once again, aren’t I? To the extent that even an intelligent, rational person like you seriously considered me and her were the same person?”

“No! OK, yes, for a bit. But I knew it was ridiculous. I just…”

“It’s not ridiculous. From our shared appearance alone, in DNA terms, we are almost the same person. But try this; what if genes code more than just physical traits? What if Granny Agnes’ *personality*, the way she talked, her outlook, likes, dislikes, what if they’d also been passed down to me?”

She raised an eyebrow at him in question, opened a draw and pulled out her money box. “Any thoughts on that?”

"So you're saying…if DNA can pass on both appearance and personality, to all intents and purposes you could be a… copy of Granny Agnes?"

"Exactly, well done. I think reincarnation happens all the time, just not in the way psychics and spiritualists say. We all pass on genetic material for our line to be born again and again, that's reproduction. Sometimes lots of ourselves gets shared, like between me and Granny A, sometimes hardly any at all. But that's what I mean when I say ghosts are all around us. People who died generations, centuries, even millennia ago are still walking around, or bits of them, living on in people who don't even know those ancestors once existed." She waved her hand at the door. "*Genetic ghosts*, wandering around out there. I find that comforting, and you should, too. Imagine if Granny Agnes' husband from 1922 could see me now. He would absolutely believe she'd returned from the dead, and she has, I suppose. Then imagine if DNA had also coded her personality and rebuilt it in me. Her husband would effectively be with his wife again, right?"

"I suppose…But you don't have her memories, her experience."

"No, not consciously. But perhaps in some way I do. Who's to say memories can't be passed down through genes, too? Maybe the reason we like some types of people, dislike others, feel at home in places we've never been before…is because they're *genetic memories* which manifest themselves as feelings, hunches, preferences, whatever? Which might explain that occasional, peculiar sense of longing for something or somewhere we never knew. What the Welsh, who know a thing or two about poetry, call *hiraeth*."

Mrs K. dropped into an eerily accurate Welsh accent. "Emotions and memories waiting in our very cells, hmm?"

Peter shrugged. "It makes sense, I guess."

She flashed back into her Dorset brogue. "But you're unsure. That's good. However…lesson over. Food for thought, I hope." She smiled kindly. "And I shall say no more on the subject today. Think for yourself. Theories are wonderful parlour games but can be dangerous and often melt in the presence of facts. Covid proved that. People died of that virus because they denied facts in favour of preferences. Look, register, understand and retain is the best advice I can always give you."

That wasn't idle chat. I've just been told something important, but I don't know what it is, he thought. *No, I don't know what it is* yet.

"Hand out."

Peter put out his hand and Mrs K. counted. "We'll call it £50, since as I say, you're not quite done." She stretched and groaned. "Sometimes it does feel like I'm one hundred and sixty. Yes, one last little job for you. My trip to glamorous Dorchester wasn't quite a wash out. I got talking to a very nice chap from Athelhampton House, you know, the stately home near Puddletown."

Peter did. It was a Tudor home he'd visited a couple of times with mum and dad when younger.

"I always loved the name Puddletown," she said wistfully. "Sounds like somewhere Beatrix Potter invented. But anyway, this lovely fella and I got talking. He was there to see if there was anything he could pick up for Athelhampton. Naturally I went into sales mode and what with it being Christmas, the sleigh came up. Turns out they have festive attractions there every year and a sleigh would be the perfect addition. Bit late for this Christmas, but I got his contacts and said I'd email him some photographs. Would you be a dear and take some pictures?"

"Sure. But instead of just an email, you could share them on social media, too. That way loads of people could see them, like them, re-post and maybe…"

"Urgh, oooh, no, no," Mrs K. held up her hands like a shield. "*Likes*? Why can't people just like things, instead of using *things* to get *likes*?" She sighed. "I prefer reality, Peter. You can't scroll past reality. It rather demands your attention." She reached into her jacket and retrieved a piece of paper. "Here, this is Athelhampton's email. You can send it straight from your phone, yes?"

"Of course."

"I'll stick the spotlights on, so the old girl can make the most of her photo shoot."

Peter looked confused for a moment.

"The sleigh, not me. Alas, neither Man Ray nor Cecil Beaton will ever come calling."

*

Peter took out his phone and approached the sleigh, which squatted in the harsh light like a giant scarab beetle. He couldn't stop thinking about Mrs Kerstmann's theory about departed relatives. He'd had her down as a quirky sort of pensioner, a little *away with the fairies*, as mum said, but she was clearly anything but. Her seemingly endless shelves of books and artefacts weren't just for sale or display. *She learns from them. No, she looks, registers, understands and retains what they have to offer,* he corrected. *She could have just told me that was her Granny,* he thought. *That would have been more than enough explanation. Everyone has relatives they look like, that's what makes them relatives. I just got a bit carried away because Granny Agnes was indistinguishable from Mrs K. Admit it, it's OK, you got carried away because...you* wanted *her to be the same person. Because that's impossible, and if impossible things happen...*

He didn't complete the thought, but circled the sleigh and took out his phone. S*nap, snap, snap* went the camera.

The fire-engine red body and chrome tubing seemed even brighter than earlier, which he put down to yet another change of lighting. Peter climbed up into the sleigh's body and began to document the insides;

Snap, snap, snap...

The hoops where reins were once attached, the beautifully lacquered floor, rear seat and flip top lid.

S*nap, snap, snap.*

The front was dominated by what looked like a curved wooden dashboard, but without dials, meters or gauges.

Snap, snap, snap.

There was a recess underneath. Peter felt along the leading edge and his fingertips brushed against a raised piece of wood. He pushed it and felt a click.

What? Another catch?

A small section dropped down like a car's glove compartment. There was something inside.

You have to be joking.

26/ HIGH STREET, LITTEL WADE, 6:00 p.m.

Peter went into the Co-op, where Phoebe was behind the tills with an expression both bored *and* furious, which he thought only she could pull off.

"Oh, hello, Piper. Welcome to paradise."

He held up a book.

"I just found this in the sleigh. Thought you might want to have a look."

"*Another* book? Give."

Peter handed it over. "Where was it?"

"There was a kind of…I don't know, glove compartment at the front. I hadn't seen it before. It had a little catch. I pressed it and…"

"Whoah, wait, go back. Glove compartment? Do sleighs even have those?"

"This one does, obviously. It just dropped down and this was inside."

Phoebe examined the covers then flicked through the pages. "It's the same as the other one. Red leather binding, 'DORSET' etched into the spine, names, maybe objects and red X's… I'm guessing Mrs K. hadn't seen it before?"

"Nope, it was news to her. She still thinks it's a kind of ledger."

Phoebe frowned. "Still no addresses, dates, prices, deliveries, nothing. So its not much of a ledger. *Again.*" Renee appeared and stared in her direction. "Ah, balls, the Shirk Finder General's coming. Got any plans this evening?"

"My social diary's a bit empty."

"Good. Come over to mine. Bring the one you found yesterday. Let's do a bit of compare and contrast." She handed the book back. "Why do I feel like this is important? It's really weird."

"Same here."

"I finish at eight. Come over at quarter past. I might even treat you to some chips."

"How Christmassy."

"Chips and stuffing then."

"Can't wait."

And he honestly couldn't.

*

Peter wandered on. Something Phoebe had just said kept ricocheting around his mind; *"Still no addresses, dates, prices, deliveries, nothing..."*

Peter frowned. *No dates. There are no dates in these books.*

He stopped at the gates of St Nicholas' church and looked into its dark graveyard. *There are no dates in these books. But...but what?*

Peter shut his eyes and remembered some of the names he'd seen in the first "ledger"; *Gortoney, Fillirish, Acorn, Acree…*

His eyes snapped open.

Yes. The names in the book...

...Are the same as names on the gravestones. And while there are no dates in the book...

He opened his eyes and smiled.

...There are *dates on the gravestones.*

Peter headed into the graveyard with a purpose.

*

"She's up in Elsinore, or her bat cave, or whatever it's called this week," Phoebe's mum pointed upstairs with an expression that said, *rather you than me*.

"It's not a bat cave," squealed a pained voice from the landing. "I've never called it a bat cave, or Elsinore. Only you do."

"She is so easy to wind up,"said Pam Clarke. "You should try it someday, it's really rather fun."

"Do NOT give him ideas," squawked Phoebe. "Come up, Piper, ignore my so-called mother."

"Enjoy yourself with The Wicker Girl," Pam smirked. Peter laughed, climbed the stairs and Phoebe beckoned him inside.

Music blared at blistering volume and she shouted over it. "BAUHAUS! FIRST GEN. GOTH! AMAZING! THIS IS *IN THE FLAT FIELD*! THEIR FIRST ALBUM! MY MISSION TO EDUCATE YOU CONTINUES!"

"IT SOUNDS GOOD," Peter hollered.

"DON'T YOU DARE DAMN THESE *GODS* WITH FAINT PRAISE!" She turned down the tumult. "Did you bring the books?"

He pulled them from his rucksack. "Better than that, I had a brain wave on the way home."

"Careful now, don't damage yourself."

Peter placed the first book down on her bed. "The names in here don't have any dates. But the graveyard does. Plenty of dates. I made notes."

Phoebe grinned as she realised his point. "Oh, that's genius."

"Now, obviously we can't pin down exactly when these entries were written, but the gravestones can give us a broad idea." He indicated a name. "In the book, *M Gortoney*. And in the graveyard there's *Mary Gortoney,* 1834 - 1842, so the book's entry must have been written within that year range, right?"

"Makes sense."

He flicked through and found another name.

"*W Fillirish*. In St Nicholas' we have *William Fillirish*, 1807-1872. So those dates plus Gortoney's put the time scale covered in this book to sixty-five years."

"Right, good."

"Sixty five years of entries. Anything funny about that?"

Phoebe stared at Peter quizzically. "Er, no. Should there be?"

"Possibly. In the book; *A Acree*. In the churchyard, *Annie Acree 1899 - 1945*." Peter raised his eyebrows at Phoebe. "*1945*. Does that tell you anything?"

"Please, just tell me."

"It's better to spot it for yourself. We have *T Acorn,* and on a gravestone, *Thomas Acorn 1755 - 1807*."

"Yes? Well? What?"

"So from those four entries alone, the dates in this book go from 1755 right up to *1945*. Which is how long?"

Phoebe squinted in thought then whistled. "One hundred and ninety years."

"Ah-ha. Not even taking any of the other entries into consideration, at *least* one hundred and ninety years."

She sat down heavily next to him on the bed. "I've seen documents that cover decades, but this…two centuries? Why?"

"Well, that's the big question, isn't it? But you're missing something equally big."

"Equally big? What?" What am I missing?"

Peter began to turn the pages and tapped one entry after another. "What do you think the average lifespan was in, say, 1872?"

"Must have been about forty?"

"Correct, between thirty to forty years. That's the average. OK, so what's wrong with all this?"

When Phoebe realised what he was alluding to she put her hands to her mouth in shock.

27/ NUMBER NINE DAWN STREET, 8:30 p.m.

Anthony Piper sat at the kitchen table and stared into his dark, tiny back garden. He was due to start driving at nine, but couldn't seem to get out of the chair and as he gazed into the garden its darkness glared right back.

This afternoon he'd once again woken to an empty house. Julie had Blu-Tacked a terse note to the bedroom mirror: "THINGS TO DO; OVEN NEEDS CLEANING ASAP. CHRISTMAS TURKEYS DO NOT LIKE DIRTY OVENS. CAN YOU FIND THE RADIATOR KEY, IT'S FREEZING. BUY CRACKERS. SLEEP WELL X" There was also a fresh message from Peter by the kitchen sink. *"Hi, I'm at Mrs K's again. Should be back by six-ish. Might go to Phoebe's tonight that OK?"*

Anthony had spent the rest of the day in front of the TV while a variety of festive entertainment attempted to grab his attention. But it was just white noise that *whoooooshed* passed time before he pretended to be a taxi driver again.

Eventually, and against his better judgement, he stood on a foot stool and retrieved a white folder from the top of the bookshelf. He'd hidden it up there some months before, and a handwritten sticker on the front read; HOUSE, BANKING AND IMPORTANT DOCS. That made the contents sound bland, which Tony knew they weren't, not by a long way. The folder was full of photographs and papers, which he shuffled into different orders, none of which were acceptable. Thirty minutes later he placed the folder back on top of the bookshelf, away from prying eyes. Then he returned to the kitchen table and stared into his dark back garden, as he'd done on so many silent afternoons. While his face remained expressionless, Tony's mind whirled; *It's my fault it's all my fault it's my fault it's all my fault my fault, my fault.*

28/ PHOEBE'S HOUSE, 8:40 p.m.

"*Pheeeeooo*," Phoebe whistled in amazement as she turned the pages back and forth. "Tie up your laces and put smiles on your faces, it's all in the *same handwriting*."

"Yep, and how weird is that?" Peter whispered for dramatic effect. "Nearly two centuries of entries in the same hand? What, the writer lived for over two hundred years? Maybe more?"

"Whoo."

"Thought that would interest you," Peter said smugly.

"Just a bit," she muttered. "What about the book you found today?"

He laid that one next to the first then opened it with a flourish.

"Ta-dah," Peter said, drolly.

Phoebe tapped her black nails on the pages. "This one has exactly the same handwriting too. Bloody hell."

"Yep, and the same format. Names and objects on the left side, names with a red X on the right."

"Do any of these names match gravestones in the church?"

"Well, I made a note of some of the more unusual ones and had a quick search about the churchyard earlier." Peter flicked through the latest book and pointed to a right-side entry with a red X. "Here, this says *M Fernsby dolly X*." He pulled up a photo on his phone. "Take a look."

It showed a small headstone inscribed, *Margaret Fernsby 1927 - 1957 Beloved Daughter.*.

Peter found another entry; "This says *J Loughty Guitar*. And see…" He selected another photo of a monument, with the inscription *James Loughty 1959 - 1973. Singing On In Heaven.*

"He was just fourteen? Wait, are these books records of children's deaths? That's grim."

"I thought that, but remember William Fillirish died at 65, Annie Accree was 46 and Thomas Acorn passed on at 52. Hardly kids, right?

"Hardly. So the books aren't a ledger of child mortality. Oh, hold on, that's interesting," Phoebe examined *J Loughty's* entry then the photo of his gravestone. "The book says *guitar* next to his name and the grave has *'Singing On In Heaven'*. So James Loughty was musical."

"That would make sense."

"All right, your new dates bring the books' age range to easily over two hundred years, and yet the handwriting appears to be the same throughout. So what's the most likely explanation?"

"Family tradition? A writing style passed on?"

"Bingo, baby," she laughed and fired up her laptop. "Weird shit like this is why I love history. See, there are precedents for fonts that remain unchanged for decades, even centuries, and they're all about tradition."

Phoebe *click-clacked* at her keyboard. On the screen were letters from A-Z, wrapped in beautiful curls, colours and tiny, intricate images. "You know these, right?"

"Yeah. They're old book letters."

"*Old book letters*," she scoffed. "Medieval illuminated manuscript, thank you very much. Some scribe took months, maybe years to write these *old book letters*, so a bit of respect, please. "

She Googled another page which showed books with densely packed pages of complex writing. "These are Bibles and liturgical services from way before mechanical printing. Teams of scribes all wrote in exactly the same way, so you couldn't tell where one monk took over from another. Islamic and Judaic holy writing has the same uniformity, and a single mistake meant the entire page has to be scrapped, even if it had taken days. That's your penance for not focusing on God's words. Medieval scribes would have killed for cut and paste."

Peter stared at Phoebe and hoped the wonder he felt wasn't showing too obviously on his face. "How do you know this stuff?"

"Well, you always remember subjects you love, right? But my point is this; the writers of those manuscripts used a unified style so their own personalities wouldn't end up on the page. And that applied to secular documents too."

Phoebe brought up images of faded parchments and papers. "These are legal and business documents from the 16th, 17th century." She clicked on one after another. "Different writers, different parts of Britain, different decades, even. But look how similar they are. Most people were illiterate back then so if you learned to write, you used a standardised font. *This* one…" She pointed at a swirling style that appeared on all the documents, "This particular handwriting represented trustworthiness, continuity, officialdom. It was used for centuries. I could find you examples of business ledgers from even the *nineteen fifties* where entries remained almost identical despite the book-keeper changing. So you see, there are totally rational explanations for everything."

Peter looked from Phoebe's screen to the sleigh's books. "So…These *are* ledgers of some kind, written over centuries by a business who used a constant, traditional style of writing?"

She clicked her fingers. "Scadoosh. Spot on." She picked up the first book and waved it in Peter's direction. "These have kept a record of *something* for more than two centuries. Question is…what and why?"

*

What and why.

Both excellent questions, but if we must pick one word that's fuelled our curiosity over millennia, it is *why*.

The other determiners; *who, what, where, when*, well, they query *identity, specifics, position,* and *time*.

But only *why* asks the *purpose* of it all.

A long time ago in our story (1533 to be exact), we saw how Thomas Cromwell named Little Wade, and I promised we'd meet him twice more. So now the time has come to discover why Little Wade became *Littel Wade*.

Hold on tight, we're about to fly back to Tudor England.

Why?

Because we can, of course.

INTERLUDE

CHRISTMAS DAY, 1533

THE PALACE OF PLACENTIA, EAST GREENWICH, 7:30 p.m.

Thomas Cromwell sighed deeply as The Palace Of Placentia, Henry VIII's birthplace, appeared round a bend in the Thames. His route here had meandered south east of the city, past Limehouse, Rotherhithe,and Deptford, where buildings gave way to snow-dressed fields and woods. Now Placentia dominated both the riverside and Cromwell's thoughts.

Tonight's journey had been as cold as his trip to Dorset three days earlier, when he'd been sent on a pointless expedition to find possible locations for a garrison. True, among other titles he *was* Henry's Surveyor Of The Woods, but that hardly made him an expert in fortification. Following a humiliating fall through ice, Cromwell had effectively given up and declared the immediate area favourable for further investigation.

Thomas shivered, remembered, and hoped he'd made the best of a bad job.

*

"Coachman," he'd instructed the stick-thin, toadying driver. "I shall remain in the carriage to prepare a preliminary report for his majesty." That was a lie since he had no intention of doing so. Snow had begun to wheel and tumble once more, light was fading and the temperature plummeting. Therefore Thomas would stay fur-wrapped inside the vehicle and sleep his way through the injustice of it all. "While I write, I wish you to ride with the guards and further investigate the nearby locality."

"Yes, sir," the coachman had said. "And what should me and the guards look for?"

"Areas of strategic importance," Cromwell had replied, airily. "Commit the lie of the land to memory, all of you!" He'd raised his voice to include the two soldiers standing idly nearby. "Examine what you can with the remaining light and then you shall ride out again in the morn for any further clarification of the landscape in view of suitable fortification as the king has ordered." Thomas hoped the more extravagant language would sound like he knew what he was talking about. The coachman and soldiers simply looked confused, which, to be fair, had been their standard expression throughout the entire trip. "So we, er, 'ave a look about?" offered the driver.

"Yes, yes, *have a look about,* then I shall provide you with an old chart of this area. Inscribe your new additions on it and on our return to London you will work with the king's cartographers to re-draw the map in respect of a possible fortified construction. Is that clear?"

There were a few confused nods which implied it wasn't. Cromwell didn't care, since he just wanted to drift off to dream of roaring fires and rich feasts. "Then leave me to my important work whilst you go about yours!" He gave a dismissive wave, pulled the coach door shut and wondered, not for the first time, why Henry had sent him on such a fool's errand.

*

As Thomas left London he saw evidence of Advent everywhere, as smells of cooking and sounds of laughing shared the air with snowflakes. People had fasted for weeks but now the starving was over, festivities were in full flow, and Placentia was the centre of it all.

Cromwell had always admired this palace's powerful austerity, but today was a different story as the king welcomed hundreds, sometimes thousands of guests for Christmas. So this was the last place Thomas wished to be, surrounded by an orgy of excess and vulgarity.

On the shore, drunken crowds ebbed and flowed about the palace walls and light blazed from many windows. On the river joyous shouts and clouds of bonfire smoke rolled across the Thames' calm, icy waters.

There was revelry everywhere except in Cromwell's mind, which whirled with possibilities, few of them good.

His boat pulled alongside a small jetty lit by flaming torches. As Thomas approached, guards stood back and the hollering throng silenced and parted.The chancellor was pleased to see he still wielded both power and fear over his populace.

The hubbub intensified as he entered the palace under a kissing bough; verdant holly, bay, apples and evergreens weaved around a wooden frame suspended from the ceiling. Cromwell ignored the decoration much as he also blanked out be-ribboned mummers and masked players who cavorted around him. Oh, The Master Of The Revels had earned his keep this season.

But despite Thomas' carefully cultivated disdain, he enjoyed carousing as much as anyone. Fine wines and foods were never far from his table, he kept an exotic menagerie and had once invested an *insane* one thousand pounds on a silly costume just to amuse Henry. But the king's invitation to this festive celebration had arrived with a worrying request; he also wished to discuss fortifications, landscapes and maps.

Work, on *Christmas Day?*

That was completely out of character. Earlier, the sovereign had attended Matins at Chapel Royal followed by a solemn feast. Cromwell imagined his majesty fidgeting through the service, impatient to get to Placentia because for the next twelve days, merrymaking would become an endurance sport here. *Fun* was a competition Henry would always win, but now the king wanted to forgo even a second of his precious roistering to hear a report on *Dorset*?

One word kept bouncing around Thomas' head; that most important of questions, *why?*

Thomas entered Placentia's smoky, flickering great hall, where lines of servants marched out with seemingly endless platters of roast peacock, swan, roast beef, prawn patties…a cornucopia most of the king's subjects couldn't begin to imagine, let alone taste. Thomas saw at least three stuffed boars' heads amongst the feast; a rare expense only found on the wealthiest tables, which these definitely were. Since Henry first popularised turkey as part of the Christmas feast, columns of the birds were *walked* to the capital from farms as far afield as Norfolk. Therefore in December it wasn't unusual to get stuck behind a long parade of poultry, which, by the looks of things, had all trooped straight into this palace's ovens. The traditional Yule Log crackled and spat in a huge hearth, illuminating carol singers and twirling dancers.

I hate other people's parties, was Thomas' appraisal *AND I hate Christmas parties even more. AND I hate a Christmas party where the king wishes to talk business most of all.*

At that moment Henry spotted his chancellor. "Cromwell!" he stood and shouted from the top table. Conversation died and heads turned his way. "Welcome, friend, welcome!" Thomas bowed deeply then realised he was dripping with sweat, and not just because intense cold had become stifling heat. "Your majesty, I wish you Advent greetings."

Henry wore a peculiar crown made of twigs and deer horns, a green felt tunic, plus bright red doublet and hose. The king did so *love* dressing up and often forced lords and earls to wear odd costumes for his amusement. Cromwell prayed that one such demeaning outfit wasn't waiting somewhere for him to sport tonight. "Greetings to you, too, Thomas! Look! I am King Of The Forest!" Henry laughed and spun so all could see his ensemble. A few of the more obsequious applauded, *And probably not for the first time tonight*, Cromwell thought.

Minor diversion over, the guests returned to quaffing and chomping. Henry beckoned for Thomas to join him. "Christmas pie?" he asked. A gigantic wheel of pastry dominated the table. It had clearly been greedily attacked from many directions but the meal's sheer size made it appear virtually untouched. The dish was made of thirteen ingredients in honour of Christ and His apostles, but along with the suffocating heat, the sight of dribbling fat and sweating suet made Cromwell feel quite nauseous.

"No thank you, your majesty."

"You are a damned fool, chancellor." Henry spooned himself another large helping.

"You wish to talk of Dorset, sire?"

The king laughed. "To business so soon? No idle chitter chatter? No gossip?"

"I do not appreciate gossip."

Henry waggled a finger in Thomas' face. "Don't talk shit, Cromwell. You gossip more than the ladies in waiting and *their* tongues wag more than a two tailed dog in particularly fine temper."

Thomas gave a thin smile.

Henry gestured to the other nearby guests. "My chancellor is too busy for revels!" As they burst into laughter, Cromwell spotted who was amused and memorised their faces for future reference and revenge.

"Very well, if we must, let us bore ourselves with business before we return to the important matter of merriment." The king gestured to a servant. "Fetch the map. The one I spoke of earlier." The servant bowed, Henry patted an empty chair. "Sit, sit." There was something gleefully furtive about his manner that Thomas didn't like one bit.

It was as if Henry had a surprise in store and not a good one.

The servant returned with a rolled up parchment.

"Ah! Your map, Thomas! Excellent! So…" The king gestured for the guests to still their conversation. Thomas didn't like that much, either. "Tell me, no, tell *us* of your trip to Dorset."

"Well, er, I did as you instructed. I went to the area you wished me to investigate for the purposes of a garrison, and, I believe, found a place which may be suitable."

"Good! Excellent fellow. And on your return, you had this map made, is that so?"

Something is wrong, Cromwell thought. I*'m being led somewhere but only the king knows the destination.*

"Yes, sire."

"I wish to be clear; *you* had this map drawn up, as I requested?"

"That is correct, yes."

It wasn't, of course. Thomas had returned to the warm hearths of Austin Friars with no intention of thinking about dank and dark Dorset for a long time. So he'd charged the coachman to work with the king's map-makers and draw up what they'd found. The result now lay rolled before him.

I should have checked this before Henry saw it, he internally wailed. *And I shouldn't have taken sole credit just now. I have set myself a trap. Oh, that has quickly become very obvious.*

Eyes glittering, the king pushed aside plates, unrolled the parchment and weighed its four corners down with wine glasses.

"I see your recommendation…it is *your* recommendation?"

Cromwell swallowed. He couldn't admit to bolting back home and leaving a coachman in charge. "Indeed, sire."

"Indeed sire! So you believe a place called…" Henry made a play of squinting at the map. "…*Little Wade* is suitable. I have not heard of it. Pray tell why the place has such a peculiar name."

"Oh, yes, sire, that is a joke, I suppose."

"I do love jokes," Henry fixed Cromwell with a gaze that suggested he didn't, not really. "Go on."

"Ah…In order to reach the area…there was a frozen dip in the road. I attempted to cross, since I follow your instructions no matter where they take me…"

"Loyalty, very good, yes."

"And alas, the ice broke and I was forced to do, well, a little wade to reach it. I felt the name appropriate, your majesty."

"Little Wade!" The king bellowed and laughed. "Oh, that is very good. Very good, Thomas. I knew you had a sense of humour somewhere under that stony complexion. Little Wade! Little…Wade."

The way Henry repeated the words un-nerved Cromwell. "And may I just ask, for the sake of your map…It *is* your map, yes?"

Thomas nodded his head in the same way one might do when putting it on a chopping block.

"The spelling of your new village? Might I clarify that, so that all here will know it should they ever find themselves lost in Dorset? The spelling?"

Cromwell cleared his throat. "Well, it is spelled in the traditional way."

"Which *iiiiiiiis*?"

"L.I.T.T.L.E. W.A.D.E"

" So he *can* spell it properly!" Henry yelled. "But I can only assume you must have been tired from your travels when working with my map-makers. We all make mistakes when exhausted, do we not?"

"Er…"

With a flourish, the king pointed his spoon at an area of the map. "Because here it is spelled L.I.T.T.E.L. W.A.D.E. *L.I.T.T.E.L*!"

The guests began to chuckle. "L.I.T.T.E.L!" Henry repeated. The chuckles become laughs. "Should I be sending my chief minister back to school? *L.I.T.T.E.L!*" The laughs became guffaws.

That stupid coachman, Cromwell thought. *He obviously couldn't spell but was acting on my authority so the map-makers were too scared to contradict him. I have tumbled into a hole of my own digging and don't believe I can dig myself out again.* He attempted to laugh along with the crowd but knew his face couldn't support good humour. "Obviously there has been a tiny mistake…" he began.

"Of course! Just two letters the wrong way round! A *little* error…" The king emphasised the word with relish.

"And I will have it corrected immediately." Thomas made to pick up the map but Henry laid a large hairy hand over it.

"No, no! You have named it *Littel*, so *Littel* it should stay. I would not dream of denying you a place forevermore on all maps of my fine kingdom. In fact…" He turned to the servant, who instantly handed him a freshly inked quill, almost as if these mocking moments had been planned in detail beforehand. "I shall make it official." The king bent to the map and carefully wrote, *WORK OF THOMAS CROMWELL 1533*, in one corner. He stood back, satisfied. "A most happy Christmas, Thomas. This is my gift to you. A place in our landscape's history."

Cromwell bowed once more, but only to hide his pained expression from the court.

"No, wait…" Henry paused, then added with perfect comic timing, "… this is my *little* gift to you. Or perhaps my *Littel* one."

The great hall filled with laughter once more and the king spread his arms to receive it. Thomas gave a rictus grin to the assembled revellers and thought, *Curse that place and all who live there. Curse Little Wade.* He bowed to the king again, thinking, *no, curse* Littel *Wade.*

*

A footnote; Thomas' suspicions about the king's lack of faith in him were correct, since on the 28th July 1540, he was publicly beheaded. I'm sure as Cromwell felt his head and neck separate, the honour of naming a misspelled village in Dorset was of great succour.

We have one more meeting with our Tudor acquaintance to come. It will explain much more.

BOOK THREE
23rd DECEMBER 2022

29/ LITTEL WADE, 7:45 a.m.

One morning, two teenagers, two dreams.

Gregory Underbore awoke freezing cold after kicking off his duvet during a nightmare he'd had many times in the last three years.

In it, he picked his way through Marryman Forest stalking a prey which moved as quietly as himself. He held a crossbow and a knife, so clearly whatever he hunted was extremely dangerous.

In dreams everything becomes a ramped up version of its real counterpart, so one is never *mildly perturbed* in a nightmare, it is either overwhelming terror or nothing. So it was with sleeping Gregory Underbore as he pushed through branches and bushes. One moment, alive to the chase, the next, possessed by paralysing dread, aware hunter had become hunted.

Greg tried to throw away the weapons but discovered they were glued to his hands. He loudly moaned in both dream and reality until the duvet was kicked aside, December cold reached for his body and sleep retreated.

Two dreams, two teenagers.

Same event.

*

Across Littel Wade, Peter also woke thrashing like a drowner.

His dream had come again. Twice in two nights was unusual but not unexpected. This time it had begun with that odd revision of Littel Wade, redesigned like a Christmas card scene. As always, the bells of St Nicholas' chimed at seven p.m. That was the cue for snow to fall; tiny dots at first, then fluffy pom-poms which rebuilt the village in their own image. Houses and shops fluttered as their brickwork transformed itself into icy waterfalls.

These scenes were the best part of the dream. Littel Wade in snow motion always remained wondrous. Then once more out of the blizzard a blurred body began to form. But as it walked toward him, the dream jump cut and *smasssshed* Peter against a wall. It felt as if he were in a speeding car that had been violently arrested by a tree trunk. He listened with horror to the reptilian hissing from the other side and knew the creatures that writhed there intended to do each other great harm.

Then with no warning the dream spliced into its third act. Peter lay in bed and heard something roar just outside his window. After an eternity the desperate fury began to recede, replaced by far-away rumbling and finally the ticking of his bedside clock.

Once all three sections had played out, he woke, grasped at his covers and tried to re-inhabit reality. But real life was just as unwelcome as the dream and unlike those dark nocturnal theatrics, he couldn't wake up from it.

23rd December. He thought. *The 23rd. One day to go. OK, OK, OK. Think about anything else,* he commanded himself. *Think about Phoebe. Think about the books. Think about last night. For God's sake, think about anything else.*

So he shut his eyes once again and remembered what else had happened in his friend's room yesterday evening.

*

As Peter had studied the latest book with Phoebe's brass magnifying glass, she'd studied *him* with a wry smile.

"You're really getting into this, aren't you?"

He grinned back. "Ah-ha, I want to know what these are as much as you do."

"That's because we're currently in the part of a historical investigation I like to call the Flirting Stage."

Peter felt his cheeks redden. "The what? The *flirting*?"

She giggled. "Not us, Piper, the books. You know when you meet someone and find them incredibly interesting, exciting and slightly sexy?"

Yep, he mentally agreed.

"But then, after a while, you discover what you thought was interesting, exciting and slightly sexy about them was actually only what you were projecting? And in reality they were quite dull but only looked thrilling at first?"

"That's quite a specific set of circumstances."

"But you know what I mean."

Peter did. He'd once developed a long distance crush on a girl at school who'd seemed perfect girlfriend material. Unfortunately he'd constructed an entire personality for her that didn't match reality. What had seemed like sparky, quirky individuality had turned out to be shallow attention seeking.

"Yes, I do."

"We all do. So that's what I mean about the *Flirting Stage*. These sleigh books appear to be interesting, exciting and yeah, why not, slightly sexy. But prepare to be disappointed. I speak from experience."

Peter examined the pages again with Phoebe's magnifying glass. After a couple of minutes he waved a hand in her peripheral vision. "Woah, wait. Look at this. Recognise any names?"

Phoebe read the entries, frowned, then her lips formed an O of surprise. "*J Farr Comic X.* Wait, *J Farr*? Our Mr Farr from The Candy Box?"

"I believe his Christian name is Julian, so, yeah, why not?"

She gazed up at the ceiling in thought. "Why are some names and words on the *left* hand page and why are others on the *right* with a big red X? There's a pattern here, and it goes back over two hundred years. So what is it?"

"Perhaps we should ask Mr Farr what his entry means, what the red X means."

Phoebe sat down on the bed. She looked serious. "I don't think that would be a good idea."

"Why not?"

"For starters, red Xs never mean anything good. Second, people on the right hand pages have clearly been placed away from those on the left. History tells us that separating people out into groups then marking one out with a symbol never normally ends well."

"Oh, bloody hell, look at this." Peter pointed at more names spread over the right hand pages, all with red Xs next to them.

F Spencer Gun X

J Bramell Brush X

N Marsh Soldier X

"F Spencer? Is that our fishy Mr Fred Spencer?" She whispered. "And our fruit and veg lady, Joyce Bramell, isn't it?"

"And Mr Marsh's name is definitely Norman."

Our Butcher, our Frier, our Fruit and Veg seller. Sounds like a rhyme. A really bad non-rhyme."

"And look who's here," Peter gestured at another entry.

G Hamnett Poems X

"Mr Hamnett the caretaker? What does it mean?"

Phoebe rubbed her eyes with both hands and smudged the make up. Peter thought that looked just as good. "Over two hundred years worth of names from all over Dorset generally and Littel Wade specifically," she said. "But yeah, '*what does it mean?*' is pretty much the only question, isn't it?"

*

Peter lay in bed and thought about books, names, words and red Xs. While Phoebe had remained fired up and full of possibilities, by ten thirty, fatigue had fogged his brain and he'd left.

She would have talked into the early hours, he thought. *And I'd have gladly listened, but I know this much. If someone's talking and you're yawning, then it really doesn't play too well.*

His phone chirpily announced an incoming text. Unlike most of his generation, Peter's relationship with the smartphone was one of convenience rather than addiction. He didn't receive many notifications, so whenever the Nokia demanded his attention it was always something of a novelty. The row of texts on display were from the same few contacts; college friends, mum, dad and spam. This morning's was one of only a handful he'd ever received from Phoebe.

Peter smiled. Her message began with several Dancing Girl emojis in a row. *She's obviously excited about something. That or she's* literally *wearing a red dress and high kicking. Both are possible.*

WAKE UP PIPER! WAAAAAAKE UUUUUUUP! I'M AT CO-OP FOR ELEVEN. That was followed by a poo emoji. BUT FANCY ANOTHER FIELD TRIP? OF COURSE YOU DO. 9:30? I'VE HAD A THOUGHT WHICH MAKES ME EITHER A GENIUS OR INSANE. SO BRING ANY ANTI-PSYCHOTIC DRUGS YOU MAY HAVE. SEE YOU AT THE BUS STOP. I WILL PROVIDE REFRESHMENTS AND A SELECTION OF CHUTNEYS AND JAMS. I LIED ABOUT THE JAMS. MAYBE NOT THE CHUTNEYS THOUGH.

He turned out of bed, padded over to his wardrobe and pulled on a dressing gown. A snowflake patterned scarf hung from the top shelf, made by mum when she'd suddenly taken up knitting before deciding she was, "*Too young to act so old,*" and dropped the hobby.

As Peter pulled the scarf out it dragged a few more items in its wake; gloves, pants, and socks all tumbled to the floor along with a small box, deliberately obscured deep on the shelf. Peter stared at that last object as if it might bite. The box was not much bigger than his mobile phone and wrapped in silver paper. He tentatively bent down and retrieved it.

Couldn't stay hidden, could you? He thought. *Had to jump out now after so long. Why today?*

He occasionally saw flashes of the silver wrapping from within the wardrobe, but forced himself to ignore them. It felt like the box was desperately trying to get his attention whenever it twinkled like that.

Just open the bloody thing. Get it over with. Open it, go on, right now. What's the worst that could happen?

Peter's fingernails scraped against the sellotape, but he already knew the answer to his question. *The worst that could happen is nothing. Better to just imagine than to know. I've filled this box so many times and the reality of what's inside might kill me.*

He shook the object, but knew no sound ever came from within.

But it might save you, he added. *Do you want to acknowledge that possibility?*

Peter carefully placed the box back on the top shelf, covered it with clothing and shut the door. There would be no sparkles or flashes for a long while if he could help it.

He took a deep breath, pulled an expression that suggested everything was *just fine* and headed downstairs.

*

"Mum, what on *earth* are you doing?" He stood at the kitchen door and stared at his mother, busy blowing up balloons while dressed in police uniform.

Cheeks puffed out and wide-eyed like Louis Armstrong, mum waved a hand at him to *just hold on a second, please*. She pinched the neck of her current inflatable, tied it, then leaned on the work surface, out of breath.

"I don't even smoke but clearly have the lungs of a twenty-a-day," she eventually managed. "What does it look like I'm doing?"

"Well, it looks like you're blowing up balloons but that can't be right, because it would be insane."

Mum clicked her fingers and pointed at him like a game show host. "I'm not insane, but I am on balloon duty. Ten points, well spotted. You could have a great career in the force one day with observational skills like that."

She'd already inflated five; three green, two red. They gently bounced about her feet like odd shaped slow motion puppies. Peter pointedly looked down at the party decorations and said, "Two days before Christmas is not a good time to start a nervous breakdown."

"When is a good time, do you think? Cup of tea? Toast?"

"Yes, please, both. And why are you blowing up balloons?"

"Good question. Breakfast first."

Peter watched as Julie waded through her little flock of balloons then switched on the kettle and toaster. "Mum?" He said. "Are you *ever* unhappy?"

She turned, eyebrow arched. "Odd question this early. Why do you ask?"

"It's just…" Now he'd actually said it out loud, Peter didn't know where to go next. "Nothing seems to get to you."

"Oh, things get to me," she smiled. "Otherwise I'd be a robot. But it's just a case of knowing what's truly important. And, it turns out, that isn't much."

"But there are loads of things that are important."

"No. Knowing the difference between what you can change and what you can't is the key. Life's full of things that only seem to be important until you step back a bit. I sobbed my heart out when I got chucked by my first boyfriend. It was like the end of the world, but it turned out he was a total walking *arse* and getting chucked was one of the best things that happened to me." She frowned. "Is this about something else? Anything you want to get off your chest?"

"No. Just asking."

Julie looked her son deep in his eyes. "There's nothing you can't tell me. Nothing. You know that."

Peter thought for a moment before answering. "Of course I do."

"Hm. OK. Look, I'm not saying you should wander about thinking everything is lovely, but life is short, so why waste time being miserable? If you *can* be happy, then *be* happy, and I'm happy because, well…" She kicked a balloon. "It's more fun, for starters."

He kicked another then changed the subject."Is dad back?"

She gazed at the ceiling. "Ah-ha. We passed on the stairs, as per usual. He looked knackered, but then again, who wouldn't with those hours?"

"What's your shift?"

"I'm hoping nine to six, maybe seven today. Might be late tomorrow but I'm trying to get out of that, what with it being Christmas Eve and everything."

"What are the chances you can bunk off?"

Mum shot him a look as she poured his tea. "I represent the Dorset Police, which one does not bunk off from, rather, one tries to change shifts to something less awful. At present, I'm not having much luck in that department, but I'd rather work late and be back for Christmas Day morning, if that's the only option. Oh, here we go..." She held up one finger in anticipation. "And a-one, and a-two and a...three!"

The toast popped up in perfect time. Peter gave a sarcastic *whoop*.

"Come on, a bit of enthusiasm, that was good."

"I'm distracted."

"Ah, I knew it. What by?" She raised both eyebrows in anticipation.

"Well, I'm distracted by the red and green oxygen filled elephants in the room, if I'm honest."

"Oh, you mean the red and green *carbon dioxide* filled elephants in the room. Actually, I need a coffee..." She filled a pot and set it on the hob.

He batted a balloon at her head. "So why are you blowing these up?"

"Er, it's Christmas? And we don't have half enough decorations in this house. Hence balloons. I'm just making an effort."

"Nobody has balloons at Christmas."

"Ah, but these are *red and green* ones, traditional festive colours, see? I picked them up last night at the petrol station."

Peter couldn't help but laugh. "But balloons are for birthdays!"

Julie cackled then spread her arms wide in triumph. "Exactly! Ha, you fell into my trap! They are for birthdays, and I think you'll find Christmas is definitely one of those. Or does Jesus not deserve balloons? The Nativity would have been very different if the Three Kings had brought decorations rather than gold and whatnot. It would have really livened up the shed."

"Stable. You're not even religious."

"I'm hedging my bets," she retorted primly. "Maybe we can get one of those big glittery banners to hang over the fireplace too, HAPPY BIRTHDAY JESUS, you know?"

"You are so weird."

"But you love me, right?"

He picked up a red one and launched it in her direction, but despite air being their natural habitat, balloons are ungainly in flight and rarely go in a predictable direction. In a sudden kamikaze dive it shifted course, landed on the lit gas hob then exploded. Benji began to bark in the hallway.

Mum looked at Peter, he gaped at mum and they both winced in anticipation. For a few moments there was only silence.

"I think we got away with it," Julie mouthed/whispered, but then a furious banging came from above as if a poltergeist was having a particularly fraught haunting.

"For *fuuuuuck's* sake," dad shouted. Although muffled, his anger was clearly white hot.

"Sorry, love. Accident? Balloons?" Mum called upwards then gritted her teeth in anticipation of a further verbal assault, which wasn't far behind.

"*Balloons*?" Dad hollered. In his fury and dulled by flooring, the rest of Tony's sentence was reduced to semi-words and yells. "Fucking…Oooh… Oons…Fucking…Ooons? Keep…oiseown…fucking…NO SLEEP. Ucksake! Ucksake! Balloons."

"Sorry," Julie tried again.

"Fuck off," thundered one last yell.

Benji gave a few more indignant barks before silence thankfully returned.

"Jesus," Mum whispered, shaken. "I know he's tired, but come on. That was a bit OTT."

Peter looked at the ceiling as if it might crack and tumble down on them both. Julie carefully gathered up her balloons and pushed them into a corner. "I was only trying to brighten things up a little." She sounded genuinely hurt. "Glad I'm off to work now, it'll give him a chance to calm down. God, he's so angry right now. Sorry you'll have to deal with him, Peter, but it was only a bloody balloon." She sighed. "My lift will be here any moment. Try to be quiet."

Peter watched his mother pull on her police bowler-style hat, and before his head could stop his heart, it asked a question; "Are you and dad OK?"

Julie looked at him in surprise and turned the phrase over like she'd heard it for the very first time. "Are… me and dad…*OK*?"

"I mean, he sounded…I mean, I've never…He doesn't normally swear like that…and it sounded like he really meant it…he seems a bit…"

"Mm, he does seem a bit, yes." The earlier brightness in her expression had melted and now she also looked very tired. "I think it's work. It's work, and fatigue, and…" She swept her hands at the window and Peter knew she meant the entire world, "…and all that. We're all *a bit* these days. And we really have to try not to be. Because before you know it, a bit can become a lot." She shook her head. "Sixth form philosophy this early in the morning, what am I like?" Julie peered down the hallway. "I think my lift's here."

There was a *beep-beep* of a car horn from outside followed by another bout of swearing from above, “Tell your *friend* to stop fucking bibbing!”

“Alright, alright!” she shouted upward, then gave Peter a hug and looked him in the eyes fondly. “I’ll have a chat with dad. Honest, don’t worry, I think it’s just…, you know…a bit. But I don’t want that kind of shouting to happen again. Not before Christmas, not at any time.”

“Shall I put the balloons up?”

She stifled a laugh. “I don’t think balloon fun would be a good idea just yet, do you? How about later? Perhaps Mr Got-*Into*-Bed-The-Wrong-Side-This-Morning might even help.”

“I wouldn’t hold your breath.”

Julie sniggered. “Perhaps holding my breath would have been a good idea in the first place. No breath, no balloons.” She kissed her index finger and placed it on his cheek. “Be good.”

“I will.”

“I know.” Mum smiled at her son. “You always are.”

30/ LITTEL WADE HIGH STREET, 9:30 a.m.

Phoebe sat at the bus stop and shouted at Peter as he approached. "*Hel-looo*! I'm here!"

"I can see," he yelled back. Peter was dressed in a duffle, gloves and his blue snowflake scarf. Phoebe, in contrast, wore a frock coat, PVC trousers, huge buckled boots and a floppy velvet hat. "Wow, Piper, you're really rocking that Paddington look."

"Well, *you* could have made an effort."

"Sometime I just need to dress down a bit. I hope you haven't made any marmalade sandwiches, because…" She held up a paper bag. "I picked us up some sausage rolls as a winter warmer." Phoebe looked at the sky. "Cold enough for snow, Piper, but the clouds are just not making the effort. Let's see what we can do about that."

Peter sat down on the bench. "What *we* can do about that?"

"I'll postpone the answer to that question for a bit if I may. Here…" She handed him a sausage roll.

"Thanks. You said there would be chutneys."

"I lied."

They munched their rolls quietly for a while as Littel Wade passed by, then Peter asked, "Heard anything about your dad?"

She sighed. "Still in Karachi. He called this morning. Shitty line, I could barely hear him, but…yeah, he's still there."

"I'm sorry about that."

Phoebe put her hand in his, squeezed and smiled. "It's OK, you didn't cancel the flights." She turned and frowned."You didn't cancel the flights did you?"

"Innocent."

"Good. So…Guess what time I got to bed."

Peter shrugged. "The question in itself implies late. Three? Four?"

Phoebe looked disappointed."Three-thirty. I was hoping you'd say something reasonable like midnight so I could surprise you." She pulled out the two sleigh books and a laptop from her rucksack. "I started researching and before I knew it, the witching hour was upon me. As I said in my text, I'm either a genius, insane, or somewhere in between."

"I'm going for the second option."

She punched him lightly on the arm. "You haven't heard what I have to say, so less of the cheek. All right, I now have a few theories about your books. Well, maybe not theories as such but educated hunches. And I'd like to try an experiment, too."

"An experiment?"

"Think of it as a field test for my thesis. You know what I said about how myths and legends have real world consequences?"

"Yes, but I'm going to need a bit more information to understand it, really."

"Oh, don't worry, you will. Right, let's start at the beginning." Phoebe pointed up the high street. "You know the legend of how Littel Wade got its name, right? Please tell me you know that."

"The thing about Henry The Eighth wading across a road, or something?"

"*The thing about Henry The Eighth wading across a road or something?*" She shook her head. "You will never be a historian. It was allegedly Thomas Cromwell who did the wading, actually. Henry's attack dog, Hilary Mantel's boyfriend."

"What?"

"Don't worry. So the story goes that Cromwell was sent to Dorset on a reconnaissance mission to find a suitable spot for fortification." She opened a notebook and consulted some scribbled entries. "Cromwell had so many roles within Henry's government, but crucially for our purposes, he was Surveyor Of The Woods…So getting sent to Dorset in the winter of 1533 to scope out possible castle positions was well within his purview. The legend says when he got here, he found a dip in the road somewhere up there…" Phoebe looked towards the village sign, which depicted a soldier and farmer shaking hands with the latin motto *Ad Meliora,* "…and his carriage got stuck so he was forced to wade through a deep icy puddle. Cromwell was so pissed off he named the area Little Wade for a laugh, then it's believed some dumb scribe spelled it *Littel* and it stuck. Oh, do you know what *Ad Meliora* means?"

"Nope."

"You go past it every day and never wondered? Blimey. It means *on towards better things*, which is ironic."

"Why?"

"I'll get to that, too. So apart from the protagonist, *Henry The Eighth wading across the road* is essentially correct, but only according to legend of course. That particular story is only briefly mentioned in one of Lord Lisle's papers after Cromwell's beheading in 1540, and mainly serves to make Thomas seem vindictive and like he couldn't spell, which means it could have been propaganda designed to undermine his reputation. Henry was keen on that kind of thing, so we have to treat the whole wading and naming thing with suspicion."

You love this stuff, Peter thought, slightly awed. *And because of that, I love it too.*

"So are you following me so far?"

"Yep, road, puddle, wade, propaganda, Thomas Cromwell was possibly a bit of an arse."

"Pretty much the thrust of things, yes. But do you know the other part of the story? The bit that heads into magic?"

"No."

"Good, because this is where it gets really interesting. I have this old book called *Folklore, Myths And Legends Of Britain.* It claims Cromwell was so angry about being made to look an idiot he put a curse on Littel Wade, meaning no-one would ever smile here."

Peter pulled a big toothy grin. "He got that wrong, see?"

Phoebe smiled back. "Fair enough, but let's face it, our village isn't exactly laugh-a-minute, so there may be something in it."

"You don't seriously believe curses are real?"

"What is *real* is neither here nor there, as I will demonstrate. So that's the background." She opened her laptop and punched up a map of Britain. "Have you ever heard of Ley Lines?"

"Aren't they like druid roads, or something?"

"That's almost as good as *Henry The Eighth wading across a road or something*. Not quite. Here…" She hit another key and red lines slashed over the map, cleaving Britain in every direction. "These are just a few. The theory says these are *spiritual* roads that link ancient monuments. They're channels of positive energy the druids followed to construct their henges, stone circles and monoliths. In other words, positive things happen on Ley Lines. Have you ever been to Stonehenge?"

"When I was about ten. Mum and dad dragged me there."

"You had to be dragged? You heathen. How did it make you feel? Seriously, think."

Peter thought for a moment. "Awed, I guess. Kind of calm, but buzzy. Like Stonehenge was a…" he tried to find the right word, "…a battery. It kind of hummed. Does that make any sense?"

"Totally. That's the feeling most people have when they visit those sites. Buzzing, a feeling of withheld power. I say *most* people. Anyone with no interest in the spiritual side of things just sees a bunch of stones and feels nothing. That's important. Now how about this; there are no Ley Lines passing through Littel Wade. One's aligned with the Cerne Abbas giant, but that's to be expected. Our village, however, is not so blessed. Alright, come on."

She stood and held out a hand for Peter. "Next stop, the post office." Phoebe marched away. "You'll need to keep up, Piper. Both physically and mentally."

*

They walked past a few shops, silent side roads and sullen houses. As they passed the chemist, Gregory Underbore stepped out, barged straight into Peter and dropped some pieces of card. Greg stared about wildly as if he'd suddenly found himself in a war zone with no idea how he'd got there, then his mouth opened and closed like a particularly stupid goldfish.

Is he drunk? High? Peter wondered. He knew Gregory's reputation as an erratic loner but this behaviour was something else.

"Sorry," Greg spluttered.

"It's OK, Greg. Just an accident."

"What do you mean?"

Jesus, he must be off his face, He looks haunted, Peter thought with surprise. *No, not haunted,* hunted, *like something is in pursuit.*

"I mean don't worry. It's fine."

"I'm sorry," Underbore muttered again, then without looking back he ran up the High Street.Both followed Greg's stumbling progress through Littel Wade until he was just a flailing stick man in the distance.

"I literally have no idea what that was about," Phoebe shook her head. "Do you?"

"Nope. I think he'd been sniffing glue or something."

"I think the *or something* you refer to is that he's extremely weird."

Peter had to agree with her on that point.

Phoebe picked up one of the cards. "PLAYSTATION 4 AND SIX GAMES FOR SALE," she held it out for Peter to see. "Look, all in strident capitals. How very *Gregory*. Looks like he's trying to grab that lucrative two-days-before-Christmas market."

"Should we give them back to him? He's probably sticking them in windows all over the village."

"We should but I really can't be arsed. I think he's got even stranger in the last couple of years. Probably late onset puberty."

"Mm, there's something very creepy about someone wearing camouflage who isn't actually a soldier."

"Oh come on, Piper, didn't you know? In his mind, he *is* a soldier. My mum once caught him shooting at pigeons with an air rifle. Gregory is a small mammal killing machine. I think he’s training on voles and whatnot until he can join the army.”

“Jesus.”

“OK, enough of Corporal Underbore. To the post office, Piper, and don’t spare the horses.”

31/ LITTEL WADE HIGH STREET, 9:45 a.m.

"OK, this is as good a spot as any. I'd like you to take a good look about."

"What am I looking for?"

"Just take it all in, Piper. Try and see what I see."

Peter studied Littel Wade High Street. The buildings were so familiar as to be almost invisible. Here, if somebody suffered a mental breakdown and painted their door a different colour, it would become the subject of much pained village discussion for days afterward.

"What's missing?"

Peter thought for a moment."Excitement?"

"Your facetiousness has a grain of truth. It's only two days 'til Christmas, but you'd never know, hm? Hardly any decorations, right?"

It was true. As you already know, Littel Wade stubbornly resisted the festive touch.

"All right, Piper, have we ever had a village Christmas tree?"

"Not that I remember."

"Not that anyone remembers. Almost everywhere has a Christmas tree, even if it's just a sad little sapling with a few coloured lights. But not here. We have no community spirit whatsoever. Do you know when the last Littel Wade village fete was? Rhetorical question; 1974. *Forty-seven years ago*. Before that the local curmudgeons managed one in 1945, but I couldn't find evidence of any others. No fetes, no football team, no am-dram group, no societies, no book clubs, no pub bands…See what I'm saying?"

"No excitement."

"Exactly. Nothing fun happens here. People seem resistant to it, like fun's a waste of time. Littel Wade has never been…" Phoebe waggled jazz hands, "…*Christmassy*. That's one of my favourite adjectives by the way. Lovely onomatopoeia, too, like footsteps through snow. *Christ-mass-sssy*. As in, 'I'm feeling *so* Christmassy, this year' or more likely, 'I'm just *not* feeling Christmassy' right? But Littel Wade seems to have zero *Christmassy* in its very brickwork, hmm?"

She looked up and down the high street. "So try this; if there are Ley Lines, spiritual roads of positive energy, what if there are anti Ley Lines? Negative paths of energy that suck away life force? For every action there is an equal and opposite reaction, so doesn't that make sense? What if Littel Wade is slap-bang on an *inverse* Ley Line, where nothing good can ever happen?"

Phoebe grinned and Peter felt himself swept along with her excitement. It was difficult not to.

"Close your eyes," she commanded. "You said Stonehenge felt like a battery, pumping out power. What does Littel Wade feel like?" Peter did as he was asked, relaxed and let *whatever-it-was* flow through him. Still with his eyes closed he said, "Like I'm being…sapped. As if energy's being pulled from me." Peter was surprised he'd never articulated it like that before.

"An anti Ley Line?"

"Yes, I guess, like an invisible power cable drawing everything away."

"OK. So does everything I said now seem plausible? About stone circles, the curse of Thomas Cromwell, the negative Ley Lines?"

Peter nodded. Now the reason for Littel Wade's dolorousness became clear. It had taken sixteen years but he finally knew what the village really was; a black hole that sucked the vitality from its inhabitants.

"Yes. Yes. I see it now. I *feel* it now. Littel Wade's a plughole. Anything good just drains away."

She nodded. "Aha, it all makes total sense now, doesn't it?"

"Yes, God, yes."

Then Phoebe sighed so deeply it sounded like a broken promise. "Ah, but what a shame most of what I just told you was total bullshit."

"*What*?"

"Yep, utter New Age, hippy bullshit. I lied. Come on. All will be explained."

*

They reached their tiny post office and sat down on a bench outside.

"Did you say you just told me a load of *bullshit*?"

"I did. Sorry about that, but it was for your own good."

Once again Phoebe pulled out her books, notes and laptop. "I just constructed an alternate history for you, made from a mash up of facts, myth, legend, theories, real and pseudo science…and I did it with total conviction. I told you a story that *seemed* to explain why our village is a vacuum. But although it appeared to be a coherent narrative, I'd weaved that particular cloth out of bollocks. Let me explain, I'll go back through each part. Cromwell's wading legend *only* appears in the Lisle papers, which does suggest some post-beheading mischievousness. I've found just one mention of "*Cromwell's Curse On Littel Wade"* in my folklore encyclopaedia, nothing anywhere else. The theory of Ley Lines has no basis in history. There is literally no proof whatsoever pagans followed spiritual roads to link their monuments. You can connect anything if you put your mind to it."

"But you said the Cerne Abbas Giant has a Ley Line through it, and that's from pre-history."

"No, it's not. That's just another bit of wishful thinking by some antiquarians. Experts have nailed Mr Willy to around medieval times, long after Britain's stone circles were raised. And Ley Lines were first postulated in 1924…" she checked her notebook. "…by Alfred Watkins, who got quite pissy when no serious historian or archeologist agreed with him,mainly because his so-called research involved dowsing and numerology, neither of which have credibility with anyone half sane. So Ley Lines didn't exist until crazy old Alfred dreamed them up in the twenties."

Peter stared at his friend. "So why did you tell me all that? What was the point?"

"The point was, for a moment, you really did feel the presence of an *anti* Ley Line, right? You did. Be honest, for a few seconds, you knew exactly why Littel Wade is so shit. Because I'd given you a *reason* to believe it."

Peter nodded. "But again, why?"

She tapped his forehead and smiled. "The power of belief, Piper, belief, faith, whatever you want to call it. This is how myths take hold. What was it Churchill said…" She consulted her papers again."'*In wartime, truth is so precious that she should always be attended by a bodyguard of lies*'. But the reverse also holds true. If you sprinkle just enough truth into a crowd of lies, then those lies start to look real."

Peter found himself stuck on repeat. "Yes, I get it, but why?"

Phoebe pulled out the sleigh books."Because of these. Sometimes in order to find truth, you have to surround it with lies."

"That makes no sense."

"It will. But let's go back to one provable fact for a moment. Littel Wade has no fetes, societies, sports teams, bands, anything social that every other village, town or city enjoys. That's truth, along with our almost total lack of Christmas decorations. Covid cancelled Christmas in 2020, but that didn't matter here. Littel Wade pretty much cancels it every year. The question is *why*. An anti Ley Line seems plausible until you pull aside the curtain and see utter dogshit. A curse only works if you live in 1533, and although these days Britain feels like that sometimes, we don't. But…somewhere between fact and myth there's a kind of twilight zone where the impossible is possible. So, first let me give you a reasonable, historical explanation for the sleigh's books, and from there…" she smiled, "…from there, let's head way out into the Twilight Zone, where things may get a little bumpy. You can handle bumpy, Piper?"

Peter was happy to go anywhere she suggested.

32/ THE POST OFFICE, LITTEL WADE, 9:50 a.m.

"OK, now let me tell you some solid facts." Phoebe looked round at Littel Wade's tiny post office, surprisingly empty despite the calendar's proximity to Christmas. She flicked through her notes again. "Did you know the Royal Mail was started by our old friend Henry VIII?"

Peter frowned, surprised. "No. That long ago? Really?"

"Yeah, he set up a position called Master Of The Posts. Then James VI set up a Royal Mail service between London and Edinburgh. Charles I finally let the public use his Royal Mail in 1635. Our post office was built in 1882, and on this spot before that there was a coaching inn, The Blue Boar. Mail was bought to the inn on stage coaches, then delivered locally. With me so far?"

"Yep."

"Weird question I know, but have you ever wondered why we have addresses?"

"So we know where people live?"

"True, but back then it was to let the *Postal Service* know where people lived. And in somewhere tiny like Littel Wade, people wouldn't have even needed full addresses. A letter to you would have been addressed *P Piper, Littel Wade, Dorset* and whoever ran the coaching inn would have known exactly where you lived anyway."

Where are you going with this? Peter wondered.

Phoebe pulled out one of the sleigh books and paced up and down in front of the bench. Her big buckled leather boots *clunk-clunk-clunked* as she marched.

"This is important; where was the sleigh found?"

"On George Johnson's land."

"Right, George Johnson, our much missed postmaster. I looked into it; the Johnson family ran Littel Wade's postal service for *generations*."

She flicked through the book.

"So these entries *are* deliveries. Deliveries and…cancellations. They don't need addresses because the innkeeper knew where all the locals lived. They don't have prices, because the goods were purchased somewhere else. I think entries on the *left* pages are items that were delivered. The ones on the *right* have a red X, so I reckon they're goods that *never* got delivered. A red X traditionally means negative, right?"

"So why weren't they delivered?"

Phoebe held up a finger. *Hold on.*

"These two books sat in your sleigh for years, maybe stored away by a distant member of George Johnson's postal family when they were using that very sleigh to make their winter deliveries."

After all Phoebe's intriguing talk of curses, spiritual roads and stone circles, Peter found himself disappointed. The explanation was so prosaic, so mundane, so…*boring*. His despondency must have been obvious.

"What's with the long face?"

He shrugged and gestured helplessly at the grey and listless village around them. "So the books are just deliveries and cancellations? That's it? I was hoping it might be something more…"

"More what? Magical?" She sat down again. "Exciting? Something more Ley-Liney, legendary?"

"Well, yes. When you told me all that magic stuff, I honestly thought it was something that would have made Littel Wade…" He grasped for the right word, "…Mythic, if you like. But then you tell me that's all bullshit and the truth is just like this village. Just dull. *Nothing*. I was hoping for more than a bunch of lists." Peter stared back toward St Nicholas'. "The graves, dates, weird handwriting…For a day or two, I thought…"

"You thought there was more to all this…shit?" She looked around the High Street again. "That maybe…underneath all the boredom, Littel Wade actually had something special?"

He pouted and nodded.

"Drop the lip work, you look like Trump. *We-ell…*" Phoebe smiled. "Well, well, well…" The way she said the words made Peter frown. They'd sounded mischievous.

"Well? What do you mean, *well, well, well*?"

She smirked and raised one cheeky eyebrow. "*We-ellll*, I said I'd start with a reasonable historical explanation…in fact, a dull one, to use your somewhat dismissive description. But remember, after that I said we'd head out into the Twilight Zone."

Phoebe reached into her bag once again. "So stop sulking. Shall we go for a walk on the wild side? Ready for things to get bumpy like I promised?"

Peter was always ready for anything she suggested.

33/ LITTEL WADE, 9:55 a.m.

The village went about its business.

Mr Farr skulked in the Candy Box, peered out of his dirty window and vacantly opened a Toblerone. From his tinny old transistor radio an over-excited local DJ announced, "It's the classic *Merry Christmas Everyone* from Slade! Am I too early for a party? No!" Mr Farr clicked off the radio and then the only sound in the shop was his rather noisy chewing.

*

Mr Spencer leaned on the Fish & Chip Shop counter and sipped a cup of bitter coffee. Mr Spencer preferred it bitter since he felt sugar to be an indulgence.

*

Mrs Bramell had arranged a small and battered Nativity group in her shop window, but like The Candy Box's solitary tinsel, it was her only nod to the incoming festival. Baby Jesus lay in his manager surrounded by carrots and cauliflowers. Over the years some of the figures had disappeared; Mary was absent, which suggested she'd scarpered after giving birth to the Son Of God and left newly single parent Joseph to deal with an influx of two Wise Men, one shepherd, a headless sheep and the Angel Gabriel, who'd fallen flat on his face. The holy messenger therefore looked like he'd started on the Babycham early and badly misjudged his capacity for alcohol. The surrounding carrots and cauliflowers also made Bethlehem appear full of genetically modified super sized vegetables. At least the guests wouldn't go hungry, even if Jesus would be denied his mother's milk.

*

Mr Hamnett lurked outside the Co-op again, and pretended to wait for a bus. He peered inside, wrung his hands and at points started to cross the road, but always pulled himself back. This made him look like someone standing on a high window ledge who hadn't quite committed to jumping just yet.

*

In the butcher's shop, Mr Marsh hacked away at part of a dead pig. Behind him, a card featuring a laughing Santa Claus asked shoppers if they wanted to join his CHRISTMAS CLUB. Mr Marsh didn't look like he wanted to join any club, let alone a festive one.

*

Gregory Underbore lay on his old bed, stared at the cracked plaster ceiling and thought.

Something eight inches long, thin, straight, and potentially dangerous lay on his bedside table.

An envelope.

Next to it was a single sheet of paper.

Mother had found a similar envelope in his jacket pocket yesterday afternoon and furiously confronted him about it. She'd destroyed both the envelope and letter inside, but Gregory could recreate its contents easily.

If he dared.

Eventually he made a decision, grabbed a paper and pen then began to write.

It didn't take long.

Mum passed his closed bedroom door, muttering under her breath about some injustice or other, Greg quickly hid the letter under his duvet, but she moved on. He'd bought a whole pack of envelopes in Dorchester, which had been secreted under the mattress. Mum never changed his bedding, so they were safe there. Gregory pulled one out and slipped his message inside. He didn't lick it shut, since DNA could be matched by saliva. Greg didn't think it would ever come to that, and but didn't want to run the risk.

In more block capitals, he wrote;

THE PIPERS

Gregory Underbore sat on his bed, stared into the middle distance and shivered.

34/ THE MARRYMAN FOREST, 11:15 a.m.

After their strange tour of Littel Wade, as Phoebe headed back to work Peter had wandered toward Marryman Forest for his last afternoon's dogsbodying for Mrs Kerstmann.

But just before leaving she'd retrieved another document from her bag then formally passed it to him. "Our little walk and talk was just laying the ground for this," she'd said, seriously. "It was the last thing I wrote before I dropped off. It's a bit rough round the edges, but hey-ho, it's not my thesis." She'd gazed about the High Street and bit her lip. "Or maybe it is. All the stuff about Ley Lines, magical thinking, curses, coaching inns…I had to explain all that to re-wire your brain just a little, so you could read this without prejudice." She'd tapped the paper in Peter's hand. "*This* is the Twilight Zone, so take it somewhere and have a look. And afterward, if you come running through the village dressed as Matthew Hopkin and insisting someone find a ducking stool for me, then fine."

"Did you make up George Johnson's history too?" Peter had asked.

"No, no. That was real. But then again, when it comes to myth, science and magic, the big question…the only question, is this…" Phoebe had turned away and kicked at some bracken,"…what is real anyway? Hmm?"

*

Now alone in Marryman Forest, Peter mentally took a deep breath and started to read the "Twilight Zone" document Phoebe had given him. He could hear her voice and it made him smile. But as his eyes took in the words and he processed their meaning, he began to frown.

*

22/12/21
Too Bloody Early In The Morning!

Hi Peter,

I'm not even sure if I will give you this. It seems to make sense at three in the morning, but then again, weird stuff normally does. So if you're reading these words, I've taken the plunge and therefore cordially invite you to my other explanation for the books you found.

By this point, if I've stuck to my plan, you've probably been given a potted history of Littel Wade with some dubious facts about Ley Lines, curses and more thrown in. That was mainly to get your mind into a different way of looking at the world, because you're going to need it.

As I hope I've already pointed out at some point today, there are really only two kinds of thinking; logically and magically. Both kinds have changed the world. Logic requires proof. Magic requires faith.

Temples, churches, marriages, shrines, stories, legends, theatre, wars, genocides, miracles, political decisions, borders, wedding rings, decorated trees, haunted houses, Harry Potter and more have all changed our reality direct from their beginnings in magical thinking.

I know I've skated about these ideas with you, but I'm setting the scene again, as it were. OK?

*

OK, thought Peter. *But what kind of stage set are you asking me to accept.? This isn't the Wicked Queen's castle in panto. This is a whole other universe.* He pushed on.

*

Alright, you may not believe in Gods, but we can agree religions are definitely real. Billions of people follow complex rules of behaviour to find favour with a deity who ignores them. The writer Alan Moore nailed it. He said, "The one place Gods inarguably exist is in our minds, where they are real beyond refute, in all their grandeur and monstrosity." Good, huh? And it's that bulletproof faith that moves mountains.

Blows them up, too. Faith is defined as a conviction something exists with no evidence but what is in your heart, and that can never be measured empirically. Hold that thought, it's important.

To your books, then.

First, let's look at a logical explanation. They were passed down through George Johnson's long running postal family, and are simply ledgers of goods delivered or not delivered to children. And those goods were possibly Christmas gifts.

That makes sense, right? If the books are records of Christmas deliveries, of course they'd be kept in a sleigh, the only vehicle able to travel through long-ago, snow-bound Dorset in winter.

That's a good, logical explanation.

It's also very dull.

So what happens if we consider the books magically? What if we think like the children whose names fill their pages?

I'll park that for a moment, if I may. Because first I need to explain why Father Christmas is a god.

*

Oh. I didn't expect that. Maybe she's talking metaphorically. Probably not, though. I know Phoebe, he thought. *She's fond of going off-road. But just how far off are we headed?*

A crow cackled somewhere from within the tree line. Scrunching up his face in concentration, Peter dived in once more.

*

Santa Claus, Father Christmas, Kris Kringle, whatever you call him, isn't just some fictional folk character. I think he is way more than that.

Hang on tight, Peter, I'm going out on a limb, you're coming with me and this particular branch is, well, a little cracky.

Here we go.

Father Christmas and his rules, myths and legends are, to all intents and purposes, a secular religion.

Yep, I just said it. Keep hanging on.

It's a secular religion that billions of children believe in and quite a few adults, too. Nobody calls it a religion of course, but if you're a child, it has exactly the same power, mystery and, yes, magic.

You may now lock me up and throw away the key, but before you do, hear me out, calm down and try not to panic too much. I'm only poking at the edges of reality, here.

Let me list what all religions have in common, and add Santa into that mix. He fits just nicely.

1/ AN OMNIPRESENT DEITY, OR DEITIES.

Like every other god, Father Christmas sees you when you're sleeping and knows when you're awake. He also knows when you've been bad or good. All children accept Santa knows what they're doing, all year round. Parents capitalise on this of course, but remember what Alan Moore said; "The one place Gods inarguably exist is in our minds." Children simply know Father Christmas exists and is everywhere. It's irrefutable.

Omnipresence; Tick.

2/ AN OMNIBENEVOLENT / IMMORTAL DEITY.

No god is truly omnibenevolent. They've all had jealous hissy fits, fucked up revenge sprees, and made weird needy threats, like, "If you really adored me you'd kill everyone you love!" So Santa's withholding presents for being naughty seems the most benevolent punishment of the lot. As regards being eternal, Father Christmas is, was, and always will be aged somewhere in his 70s. Even back when he was Wotan, or

Odin, he was a sprightly pensioner. Kids know this, too. Santa is eternal and he is good, as long as you are good in return. Fair deal.

Omnibenevolent / Immortal; Tick.

3/ OFFERINGS.

Religious practices often involve offerings, which have evolved over time from handing over your first born to giving gold, frankincense, myrrh, food, statues and nowadays, mainly money. Santa, however, is happy with mince pies, a carrot and a tot of brandy. They might not seem much but deep inside we see these little things as what they are; offerings.

So, offerings; Tick.

4/ ATTENDANT, LESSER (BUT STILL MAGICAL) CHARACTERS IN THE CANON.

Angels, devas, saints, golems, demons, asparas, malachim, elves, reindeer, Frosty The Snowman, Lutins, Krampus, Jack Frost, Mrs Claus...I rest my case.

Attendant magical beings; Tick.

5/ HOLY SITES / PLACE OF PILGRIMAGE.

Despite being omnipresent, paradoxically every god is associated with one or more numinous areas. For Catholics it's the Vatican, for Muslims, Mecca and Jerusalem, which is also a holy site for Christians and Jews. Father Christmas' holiest of holies is The North Pole, but if that's too general, then Santa Claus Village in Rovaniemi is his Vatican, but much less commercial and tacky. There are billions of kids who dream of making that pilgrimage, but never do. Then, to be deadly serious, extremely ill children are flown there every year. I need not point out the analogies between that and the many holy places from where hope, health, and happiness are believed to flow. Lourdes and Lapland, anyone? And like Santa, doesn't Mary, Mother Of Jesus, hang around a grotto? Just saying.

"Holy" sites; Tick.

6/ MIRACLES

Gods would be pretty unimpressive if they had exactly the same skills as us, so they don't. Every god is a creator, magicking up something from nothing, and all children know that's what Santa does every twelve months. He makes the toys, billions of them, in his workshop. Impossible, yes, but that's the definition of a miracle. Then he delivers every single one across the entire planet in one night without a single mistake. And he does it via flying reindeer, invisibly going down tiny chimneys, changing his size and mass, eating millions of mince pies and drinking lakes of brandy. There are organised religions thousands of years old (and branches of physics) that subscribe to stuff way weirder and not half as much fun.

Miracles; Oh, tick.

6/ PROMISE OF ETERNAL LIFE.

At first this seems a bit tricky but hang in there.

All religions offer hope you can live on after death at the side of your chosen God. That's the kickback for all the effort one puts in pleasing him/it/they/her.

But when you're tiny, concepts of life and death have no real meaning. You simply can't perceive just how massive they are. Even when confronted with the death of a pet or relative, those ideas remain outside a kid's understanding, nebulous. For adults, aware of their own guaranteed mortality, eternal life is your heart's greatest desire; the Biggest Present Under The Tree, top of most of humanity's wish list.

But as a child, when you don't understand what immortality really means, your heart's true desires are simpler but just as important.

Gods offer adult humanity their greatest wish.

Santa does the same for kids.

The gifts may be different, but the prospect of a wonderful, miraculous, all consuming yearning fulfilled is identical.

Your greatest desire, received; tick.

7 / PRAYERS.

All religions have forms of prayer. And what are these prayers, mainly? Wishes, right? "God, please help me with my driving test," "God, smite mine enemies," "God, please give me money / make me well / let West Ham win," etc. A child's Christmas list is a form of prayer. Some people even burn their list on the fire and so send it directly to The North Pole in the form of ashes. This is exactly the role of the thurible in church, which makes prayers ascend through smoke to the heavens.

Just like praying, wishes are a two way deal. "Please give me this, and in return I will do that." Santa's pretty easy to keep happy, though. No big rules or regulations; just be nice. That's the deal you make with Father Christmas; "If I am nice, will you give me what I want?" And that's crucial when we come to your books.

Prayers; Tick.

OK, so listing the similarities between Santa and deities may be a bit of fun but remember it's totally serious when you're a child. Father Christmas' existence is as important to kids as any gods' is to their believers.

For hundreds of years, billions of children have had unarguable faith in Father Christmas. He ticks all the boxes of a religion without being one, and therefore has all the power that goes with it. Without even realising, children have had faith. And what happens when that faith cracks, or even breaks?

Littel Wade happens, that's what.

*

Peter looked up at small patches of white cloud in between broken frames of branches. If he squinted, it resembled an impossible jigsaw whose pieces changed every time the wind passed through. *She's making no sense, and yet total sense,* he thought. *You just have to squint at reality a little, blur it a tad, see what shapes it makes when you adjust the focus.* So Peter read on, and mentally squinted at reality as Phoebe had done.

*

I hope I've made a convincing argument that Father Christmas has many, if not all facets of a religion. Of course unlike other religions, his loses its power as one gets older. By the age of ten most kids have committed apostasy as regards to Santa, and put him in that box we all have marked, "Childish Things."

But we don't throw that particular box away, do we? It sits at the back of one of our mental cupboards and what's inside affects us for the rest of our lives, even if we don't realise it.

So now I've set the scene, let me try an idea; a mixture of logical and magical thinking that might explain why our village seems rather short on smiles. AND what you and I can do about it.

Logical thinking; using a formalised business font, the books are ledgers of Christmas gifts, some delivered, many not, by the Johnson family over generations.

Magical thinking; as far as the children involved knew, our books really were Father Christmas's Lists Of Gifts, separated into two groups; the nice kids who got what they wanted, and the naughty ones with a red cross next to their name who didn't.

Let me be clear; I'm absolutely NOT saying your books belonged to "Santa Claus." But I am saying that doesn't matter, because the children believed they did. And when it comes to faith, belief is all that matters. Proof is unnecessary.

So...over hundreds of years, there were so many little boys and girls in Littel Wade with red crosses by their names who never got their heart's greatest desires. Remember, when you're that young, Father Christmas is as real as any god, complete with his own set of recognisable religious systems.

And then he turns his back on you.

Or, worse still, you suspect he doesn't even exist.

When something that powerful simply evaporates, it can have massive effects.

Because the harsh realisation of Father Christmas' non-existence may be the first time a child has questioned their parents, maybe even reality itself. Because if Santa Claus, the bringer of all wonder in your little life suddenly doesn't exist, all bets are off.

Those kids grew up, but disappointment, rejection, oh, lets' be dramatic and say the death of magic stayed with them. They might not have even realised, but remember, what we lock away in that box marked "Childish Things" does not stay quiet. It rattles and taps, reminds us of who we once were and because of that, who we still are.

You'll find attached to this document another piece of paper; it's a list of toys and gifts mentioned in your latest sleigh book. When you go to Mrs Kerstmann's, would you see if she has any we can get hold of? Because I think we can give some of our old villagers the presents they never got all those years ago. And that might be the first step to making Littel Wade a slightly happier place.

I have no proof for that, but if you've got this far, I hope you'll agree proof isn't everything. Faith, on the other hand, can be.

So how do you fancy a shot at being one of Santa's Little Helpers?

35/ THE MARRYMAN FOREST, 11:30 a.m.

Mulling over the contents of Phoebe's strange document, Peter wandered further south through the forest. He thought, *she's either a genius or totally crackers*, then remembered she'd texted almost exactly that statement this morning;

I'VE HAD A THOUGHT WHICH MAKES ME EITHER A GENIUS OR INSANE.

People can be both, he thought. *But Santa's Lists and undelivered gifts?…That explanation only makes sense if we think magically. And if we do, we're both pulling on our straight jackets and taking a trip to Crazy City.* He smiled ruefully. *Which you know damn well you are very happy to go with Phoebe. Let's be honest, you'll follow anywhere she leads. What's so great about reality anyway? Reality's been shitty to me, so fuck it.*

Peter *had* been heading toward Kerstmann's Yard for the last few hours of work, but now discovered his mind had subconsciously brought him here to a familiar spot. Just as some animals can sense direction through magnetoreception, Peter always knew this lay-by's location through some kind of emotional compass.

This was the first time he'd approached it from the surrounding woodland, since there'd been no point before. But yet, unbidden, his feet had carried him back to this place.

Why? There's nothing here. Just the forest, as it always was, always will be.

Peter turned towards Kerstmann's, but then something flickered in his peripheral vision. Just as the sleigh had announced its presence with a tiny glimmer, something in that tree line did the same. *It's nothing,* he thought. *A nail. A sign. A piece of glass. An empty drinks can.* The winter sun strobed on an object half way up an old blasted sycamore. Intrigued, Peter approached the tree and saw a shaft protruding from the bark. He grasped it and pulled.

A crossbow bolt.

Still shiny. This isn't some Tudor poacher. This is recent.

He turned it over, felt the edges.

So what? It's a forest. There are animals, and where there are animals, there'll always be hunters. It means nothing.

But Peter wasn't convinced by his own indifference. He pocketed the bolt, examined the injured sycamore then rubbed his finger around the hole in its trunk.

If that hit you, *tree, at least it means* something *got away.*

For some reason, that thought echoed around his mind as he headed back towards Mrs K's yard.

36/ THE CO-OP, LITTEL WADE, 11:36 a.m.

Phoebe stared at Renee, who glared right back. The store manager was saying *something* but Phoebe tuned it out. Occasional words got through but they meant little more to her than road noise.

*"Grumblegamble*late*whirrrgrurk*everytime*pannarjammerflammerflim mer*norespect*harglebarglehrrrrt*hestateofyou*brimplefrimblesplurgle*onawa rning*prapplesnapplemurdyblah...*"

Phoebe twirled a lock of hair around her forefinger. If she'd been chewing bubblegum this would have been the perfect moment to inflate a pink balloon in Renee's face, but alas, her mouth was empty.

"You're six minutes late!" The boss thundered, beehive shaking with the outrage of it all. "Anything to say?"

"Er, is it, I'm sorry?"

"You have to ask if 'I'm sorry,' is the correct response?" Renee shrieked. "Oh you think you're so clever. You're not, you know. *I'm* clever, you, my girl, are not. *'But listen, I am warning you,'* that's Anna Ahkmatova. Wonderful poet, not that you'd know."

When someone needs to tell you they're clever, Phoebe thought, *that's the first indication they are* catastrophically *stupid. She'll be telling me she's a very stable genius next.*

Phoebe bit her lip contritely. "I see. I promise not to be late again. I wouldn't want to jeopardise my career." *I've gone into giga-sarcasm now*, she inwardly giggled. *Sarcasm so dense it's a black hole of scorn.*

Oblivious, Renee gave a satisfied nod, then strode off as if she had something important to do, which she hadn't.

"Jesus Christ," Phoebe sighed, turned to look out of the front window then snarled the same words. *"Oh, Jesus Christ.*"

Mr Hamnett was at the bus stop staring directly at her. He held his hands in front of his crotch as if wringing an imaginary cap.

You pervert, she thought. *You weirdo pervert. OK, enough is enough. Now is now. I'm not putting up with this shit any more.*

Eyes blazing, Phoebe marched out of the shop toward her stalker who quickly turned and walked away.

"OY. STOP. Uh-uh, no, you stay right where you are. You stay put. You've been there enough times already, so a few more minutes won't hurt."

He stopped and looked down at the ground like an aged naughty schoolboy. Phoebe went right up into his personal space, darkly kohl'd eyes flashing. "Here I am, then. I'm right here. So what do you want, huh?

I'm eighteen. And even if I was twice that age, you'd still be a weirdo pervert."

Hamnett shook his head wildly. "No, no, no. I'm sorry, I didn't mean to…"

"Didn't mean what? You can't just perv me out on a weekly basis then say, 'I didn't mean to,' because it doesn't wash. Like you, clearly, it doesn't wash."

Hamnett held up his hands in surrender. "Please, I…"

"*Please*? So how about this? How about this as a plan? How about you stay away from me, *please,* for like, oh, I don't know, forever? Or I go to the police? How about that?"

"It's not what you think."

"And you're the school caretaker. Jesus Christ on a lilo, the school caretaker? Please don't say you do this to kids even younger than me."

"Please, it's really not what you think."

"So what is it, then? Like Dumbo, I'm all ears."

Slowly, stammering at points, Mr Hamnett told her. After a few sentences, Phoebe smiled. A few more later, she'd started to titter, and by the time he was done, she was bent double, tears streaming down her cheeks, laughing and holding up a hand for him to stop before she wet herself.

37/ KERSTMANN'S YARD, 12:20 p.m.

Mrs Kerstmann peered at Peter over the rims of her glasses, raised an amused eyebrow and tapped a piece of paper on the desk in front of her. It was the list of toys and gifts Phoebe had given Peter.

"This is a very eclectic, some might say very chaotic inventory, Mr Piper."

"Yes, but, you know…" was the best he could offer.

"Yes, but I don't know. You *say* these are Christmas presents but it's the 23rd and Mary is busy buying candles for Jesus' birthday cake. A little late in the day, don't you think?"

Peter grasped for any kind of response but could only find a cliche."Better late than never?"

She huffed. "Better early than late is what's better. And for a Christmas gift list this is vague bordering on pointless. What ever would Santa Claus make of this?"

"My friend Phoebe wrote it."

"Don't blame someone else. You are complicit since you brought it to me." She looked down at the paper once more. "So you want to know if I have any of these items? The answer of course is yes. But as I say, a little more detail would have been most welcome."

Mrs K. began to read. "For example; '*Comic, brackets, Superman, question mark, close brackets. 1940s, question mark.*' And this means what…?"

"Do you have any 1940s Superman comics?"

She thought for a moment. "Naturally. There are at least four I can think of in the comic section, bottom shelf of the bureau by the various bar stools." She read on. "Gun? You want to give someone a *gun* for Christmas? Not very festive, is it? I have a few guns dotted about, all deactivated of course, not my thing at all. Any pointers on that score?"

"A toy gun I think."

"Thank heavens. But again, what era of entry-level weapon are you after?"

"Probably '40s, '50s."

"The plot thickens. May I ask who these gifts are for? The occupants of a Home For The Perpetually Childish?" But before Peter could answer she'd read on. "*Wood Horse'?* As in gymnastic equipment beloved by World War Two escapees? Or perhaps the Rocking or Hobby kind equally adored by little girls and boys from a sadly bygone age?"

Peter wished Phoebe had been more specific, but knew exactly why she'd kept things so vague.

"Moving on, it says here, simply, 'Poems'? Have you any idea how many poems there's ever been, and are being written even as we speak?" Mrs K. shook her head in despair. "Love sonnets? Musings on life? Or perhaps Stick-Ones-Head-In-The-Oven-Or-Weigh-Oneself-Down-With-Rocks kinds of poems? Any guidance you wish to give me?"

"An old book? Just poems, I suppose."

She *tut-tutted.* "Well, next time I bump into Wordsworth or Rumi, I shall be sure to ask them if they're still *just* writing poems." Her stern expression broke and she laughed. "I won't ask too many questions. This feels like something meaningful, despite its nebulous content. Whatever that meaning is, I shall leave with you and your friend Phoebe." She read a few more entries. "'*Soldiers*'? '*Brush*'? '*Dan Dare*'? '*C/work Car*?" Curiouser and ever curiouser. Well, if you wish, I'll poke about and find a few examples of all these items, then you can choose whichever one is most suitable."

I wish I knew that myself, thought Peter.

"Well, leave me with it." As she stood, either her body or her chair creaked. Mrs K didn't seem to know which, either. She looked about for the source of the noise. "When one cannot tell the difference between one's hips and one's furniture than surely old age is imminent, don't you think?"

Old age imminent? Thought Peter. *Surely you got on that particular bus a long time ago.*

"Why you want these particular gifts is of no interest to me. They are Christmas presents, and that's all that counts. There's no such thing as a bad Christmas present in my book, so whoever these are intended for will be delighted, I'm sure."

She took out a twenty pound note, offered it to Peter, then shook her head and withdrew the money. "That would have been your pay for today, but nothing in this world comes for free, so I'm going to charge you £20 for all the items on your list. I'm not a charity."

"£20 sounds very reasonable."

"Then perhaps I am a charity after all. Give, give, give, that's me."

Mrs K. pulled open one of her doors and took a deep breath. "Ah, good. Snow Air," she sighed, pleased, and Peter heard the capitals she'd given the words. "You can feel it trying to make icicles in your ventricles. Snow Air isn't happy until it is full of flakes and will therefore try to build them anywhere it touches."

Peter joined her and looked up at a gleaming white sky. She nudged him in the ribs. "Go on, breathe it in. In summer we must endure Sun Air which rudely cooks everything. Sun Air is no fun for lungs. But Snow Air…" she took another deep breath. "Snow Air is vital, Peter. Enjoy it as one would a fine wine. This may be one vintage we might not be able to lay down for the future." Peter inhaled, felt tiny flowers of cold bloom in his chest and smiled.

Snow Air, he thought. *Yeah, that's it. Whenever I breathe Snow Air I feel like I'm home again. Winter is home.*

"Now, I'm shutting up shop tomorrow for Christmas. Should be back by the 27th. I'm off to see my boy, as is right and proper." Peter hoped she might elaborate on the *"...& SON"* on her yard's sign, but she moved on. "So…your last job is to get the place as spick as possible and as span as time allows. Then in return for your tidying talents, I shall find you the gifts you wish to give others. Deal?"

"Deal."

"Quick smart, then. This yard won't tidy itself."

Peter ventured out and looked around the premises. His shoulders sunk. *Tidy* was an impossible dream since Mrs K's business resembled the debris field around a sunken liner.

Start at the edges and work your way in, he remembered her saying a few days ago. *That's a plan. I'll start at the edges.*

As Peter made his way toward the sleigh he noticed how the chrome seemed to glitter more vibrantly and its paint glowed brighter than yesterday.

Peter gazed up at the December sky. *OK, the weather's been overcast until now. This is the first time I've seen proper sunlight on the sleigh. No wonder it looks so good. Bright wintery days make everything High Definition.*

But another part of him whispered, *No, it's returned to day one. I'm looking at this sleigh on the day it was built.* But he ignored that little voice which was surely making mischief. *Ah, I'm looking at* everything *magically now. Phoebe's totally got under my skin.*

Which, he realised with delight, was exactly what he wanted.

38/ THE CO-OP, LITTEL WADE, 12:30 p.m.

Over the shop loudspeakers, Jona Lewie was still trying to *Stop The Cavalry*, but had been doing it for decades with no luck. As Jona's brass band faded out the Co-op DJ brightly announced Yorkshire puddings were on a buy-one-get-one-free offer, "So the whole family can have extra helpings this Christmas." Phoebe muttered that *he* could have an extra helping of *fuck off* this festive season, which seemed to do the trick as the show segued into, "Fairytale Of New York".

As the opening notes twinkled Phoebe thought, *Kirsty MacColl is with everybody every Christmas except her own family. How must that feel? Hearing the one you love so close wherever you go, but unable to see them, hold them?* For a moment her eyes glazed with tears which she angrily blinked away. *Stop. At least dad's coming back. Late, but he's coming home. Some people aren't so lucky. The ones they love are permanently delayed.*

She couldn't bear to think about that for too long, so instead flashed back to her recent confrontation with Mr Hamnett. The memory quickly returned a smile to her face.

Renee strode past with an *I'm very busy so do not speak to me* expression and Phoebe resisted the temptation to bray like a donkey.

It's too beautiful, she thought. *It's just too beautiful. No, no wait a minute. It's more than that. Bloody hell, it fits. The entry in the book fits perfectly.* She shook her head. *Does* everything *fit? Are the entries relevant to the past* and *the present? Or are you OD'ing on magical thinking again? It's easily done, when you start tumbling down that particular rabbit hole.* Then she pictured Mr Hamnett's face and laughed out loud.

*

Fifty minutes ago, Phoebe had marched across the road to where Mr Hamnett stood and locked eyes with him.

"Please, it's really not what you think," he'd almost whined.

"So what is it, then? Like Dumbo, I'm all ears."

"I'm not looking at you."

Phoebe had frowned. "Oh really? Really? 'Cos where I'm often sitting, which is…," She pointed across the road to the tills, "…*there*, I can see over to *here* just fine, thanks to the miracle of glass, which has some degree of transparency. I'm not sure if you know that."

Mr Hamnett held up his hands, either in surrender or to try and stop the freight train of Phoebe's fury. Neither option was viable.

"So for months now, I've had the dubious pleasure of seeing you here, gawping at me like Charlie Bucket finding the last golden ticket. Months, it's been." She thought back along the time line. "Yeah, I remember now. You started your little voyeur trip back in April. Yes, that was it. Because not only was I having to deal with a brand new and frankly horrific manager, I was being eyed up by Mr Peeping Paedo here. Not the best combination of events."

"If I can just explain," Mr Hamnett tried again, but Phoebe was on a roll.

"You're bloody lucky I haven't called the police on you."

Something pinged in Phoebe's mind. It was a far-off thought, but that little ping got her attention. "So let me remind you of the plan. You never, never, ever stand here again creeping the Kentucky Fried *Fuck* out of me. If you do…"

Phoebe ground to a halt as that ping became more strident. She thought for a moment and then shook her head."April," she said, quietly. "You started staring in April, didn't you?"

"Yes." He chewed his lip, embarrassed, and broke eye contact.

"April. Oh God. It was April. How could I have been so thick? You weren't staring at me at all, were you?"

"That's what I'm trying to say. I'm so sorry you thought that. I would never…I'm not a, you know, one of those…"

Phoebe put a hand to her mouth to stifle a laugh.

"Oh bloody hell, no. Really?"

"I'm very shy, you see. I was hoping she'd notice me. I've come in and tried to talk to her, but I could never find the words. Other people are good with words, but not me."

"No way," Phoebe couldn't help herself and laughed out loud."Sorry."

Mr Hamnett ploughed on. "You thought I was looking in your direction, but it was only when *she* was there. I'm trying to find the words."

"Renee?" Phoebe spluttered, and wasn't surprised to discover tears had started to tumble down her cheeks.

"Mm, yes. When she moved here, I just thought she was…wonderful. So glamorous. Not like anyone else in Littel Wade. You know what I mean, don't you? She's like a movie star."

Phoebe guffawed, bent double and waved a hand at Mr Hamnett to stop, but he was lost in the reverie.

"I suppose it is a bit funny," he shrugged. "Someone like me possibly having a chance with someone like her. I don't even smoke."

For some reason, that set Phoebe off again, and she machine-gunned a combination of laughs and coughs. "You don't even smoke?" She managed. "What…does…that…have to do with anything?"

"I could have offered her a light. Or given her a cigarette if she'd run out. That would have been a good excuse to talk to her, wouldn't it?"

Phoebe straightened up. "I think I'm going to get hiccups. Oh Mr Hamnett, that's actually really cute. Sorry, I don't mean to sound patronising, please don't think that, but it is very cute." She looked at the empty Co-op, satisfied herself that Renee was unaware of her absence, turned back to Mr Hamnett and another thought, combined with a memory, flashed in her mind.

"Poetry," she said, quietly.

"Sorry?"

Phoebe threw herself back several years to the hard, cold wooden floor of Littel Wade Primary School, on the last day of term before Christmas, with Mr Hamnett in his ropey Santa Claus costume. After he dished out presents to the littlest kids, Santa would always read three poems; "A Visit From St Nicholas," "Little Tree," and "Stopping By Woods On A Snowy Evening," which remained her favourite poem of all time. For that, she had to thank the shabby St Nick.

"Nothing. I've never said thank you for being Father Christmas when we were tiny."

"You knew it was me?" He sounded genuinely surprised.

"Not at the time, Mr Hamnett."

"Oh, thank heavens. That wouldn't have done at all."

"We worked it out later, though."

He waved a hand to dismiss the confession. "Later is fine. But I would have been most upset to think you children knew it was me."

God, that's cute, too, thought Phoebe, with a new found respect for the caretaker. She remembered something else, too; an entry in the sleigh book.

If we're right, when he was little Mr Hamnett wanted a poetry book. Renee loves poetry, too. Phoebe thought. *So I think me and Piper can help Ted out, here.* "You really should try and talk to her," she said.

He nodded, but without much conviction. "I'm very shy."

"No you're not. You're not shy at all. You're Santa Claus. And if you can fool a bunch of kids that you're Saint Nick and help them love poems, then you *can* talk to Renee. Hey, look, it's Christmas, maybe even give her a gift, huh? Nothing ventured and all that."

He nodded, slightly more confidently.

"What should I give her?"

"Oh, I'm sure something appropriate will come to mind." Phoebe started to walk across the road, but turned, walked backwards, searched her memory then spoke. "Oh, and *the woods are lovely, dark and deep, but I have promises to keep and miles to go before I sleep...*"

"*...And miles to go before I sleep.*" Mr Hamnett answered.

Phoebe winked and headed back to the shop, a skip in her step. If Peter had understood her document and done as she asked, they were in for a busy night.

39/ PHOEBE'S BEDROOM, DAWN STREET, 8:30 p.m.

Phoebe sat with Peter on the edge of her bed and looked down at a little collection of wrapped gifts, items listed in the sleigh book he'd sourced from Mrs Kerstmann that afternoon.

"This is madness," Phoebe sighed and smiled. "And either totally pointless or a brilliant example of magical thinking having real world consequences. We'll see what the results are tomorrow morning, if any."

Phoebe consulted her list and checked it against the presents."Alrighty-ho-ho-ho. Your book listed names and what we assume are gifts. If I'm right, many years ago, the kids with a red X *didn't* get what they wanted, but will this year. So in no particular order, several decades after he asked, Mr Spencer is finally getting the toy gun he wanted…"

Mrs Kerstmann had supplied Peter with a silver cowboy cap gun, complete with a roll of caps. Amazingly, decades after leaving the factory, it still worked and was now wrapped in red and white striped paper, with a label that simply said, *"Fred"* in the best copperplate Phoebe could manage. She pointed at another gift.

"Mrs Bramell will finally get her brush…Which might explain why her hair is such a birds-nest mess, right? One ancient Christmas ago, Santa never delivered it, and she gave up on her locks."

Peter laughed. "Now you're reaching."

"Am I, though? Alright, once upon a time, Marsh the butcher wanted soldiers…"

Peter picked up a small wrapped box, rattled it and from inside came a tinny clattering. "They're from the '50s, so probably covered in lead paint and therefore deadly."

"I can't see Mr Marsh sucking on a tiny soldier." Phoebe grimaced. "God, that sounded disgracefully wrong."

"It really did."

Peter picked up an A4 sized package and turned it over in his hand. "The entry in the book just said *J Farr Comic*. Why did you say it had to be Superman?"

"Glad you finally asked. It's because I pay attention. There's a faded old Superman poster up in The Candy Box. And since Mr Farr has owned that sweet shop since the cretaceous period, it's obviously his. So I'm taking a chance little Julian once wanted a Superman comic. Good work getting one from the '40s. That would be his vintage."

"We have to thank Mrs Kerstmann, really. That woman has everything."

Phoebe consulted her list again.

"Mrs Newman at the laundrette once wanted a wooden horse…"

Peter grabbed a long gift with a bulbous end. "Hobby horse."

"It will have to do, since the sleigh book is somewhat lacking in detail. Moving on, once upon a time the younger Mr Nelson our newsagent wished for Dan Dare…"

"One Eagle annual, 1955, with Christmas themed Dan Dare adventure called *Operation Plum Pudding*."

"How appropriate. A *C/work* car for angry Brian Davies at the Garage…again, very appropriate. And a spinning top for the tiny girl grumpy Mrs Belton at the Post Office once was."

She gazed about the gifts once again and looked a little sad. "There were so many kids with red Xs by their names. I wish we could have given all their adult selves what they once wanted."

"That's assuming your theory is correct."

She shrugged. "Fair point."

Peter picked up one last gift. "And what about this for Mr Hamnett?"

Phoebe took the package from him and held it up. "'*Paynes' Select Poetry For Children.*' 1948 edition, good work Mrs K. The book said *Hamnett poems*. And as we Littel Wade Primary alumni know, Mr Hamnett is rather fond of verse."

"Oh yeah. Father Christmas' Poetry Corner."

"The same. But this book isn't actually for Mr Hamnett. I'm hoping he'll pass it on to someone else."

"Who?"

"Well…" Phoebe grinned. "It turns out our old caretaker has a bit of the old unrequited love thing going on. And, better still, we can help. Pay attention, now. Are you sitting comfortably?"

"Well, vaguely."

"Then I'll begin." Phoebe told Peter about the events at the bus stop earlier. By the time she'd finished he was laughing fit to burst, too.

"Ted and Renee, that's priceless. And kind-of sweet in a weird way, bless him. So, we've got the gifts, I guess we should…" Peter stopped talking because Phoebe was looking him up and down with a serious expression.

"What? What's wrong?"

"Oh Peter, you know we have something important to do, so I think you'd better get those clothes off."

*

A few doors down, Anthony Piper sat alone at the kitchen table again with his folder of HOUSE, BANKING AND IMPORTANT DOCS.

Tony blankly went from one pile of documents to another, tapped at a laptop and clicked on websites he'd already visited over the last few months.

Somehow I have to make all this fit, he thought, and not for the first time. *All these documents have to equal what I find on the websites, but I just can't do it. I can't balance the equation and I have to, I have to, I* have *to for us, because...*

He had the radiator on full, but it was little more than furniture against the zero-degree temperature outside. A chill passed through Tony's body and he rubbed his hands together.

Was it always this bloody cold? He wondered. *I don't remember shivering indoors before...all this. There's no snow this year, but somehow it's colder. These insane heating bills don't help. Or maybe the house is the same and* I'm *colder. We're losing more heat every day we stay here.*

He looked at his reflection in the window. The double glazing had blurred and doubled Tony's appearance to coal-black eyes, a jagged mouth and white skin. *Look at me, I'm a snowman.* He tittered, but the laugh cracked like ice underfoot. *Give me a scarf and a floppy hat, then I'll walk in the air clean out of here to the North Pole. It's probably warmer there.*

He stuck two fingers up at himself, stared back down at the papers and angrily stabbed at a calculator. *It doesn't matter how I put the numbers in, I find figures in one place then lose them in another. Numbers don't lie, that's the problem.*

Tony stared up at his cracked, patchy ceiling. *But* you *lie,* he thought. *You lied, and you hide, and all this*...He crumpled a few sheets in his hand. *All this is the result.*

Anthony slammed the laptop shut, unable to look at the same endless numbers and pictures which offered no answers.

*

Peter felt his heart accelerate. "Sorry, *what*?"

Phoebe pointedly looked down at his trousers. "I said you'd better get your clothes off. What part of that don't you understand?"

"Get...my...?"

She sighed. "We're going out to deliver presents the recipients *possibly* wanted when they were children but never received. In order for this experiment to succeed, no-one must realise we're responsible. Magic only works when it's unexplained. These gifts…" she gestured round at the packages, "…are going to turn up decades later as if by magic, straight from the North Pole. Haven't you been listening? This…" Phoebe picked one up and waved it in Peter's face, "…must seem impossible and therefore make reality wobble. Come *on*, Piper, we're using magical thinking to create real world consequences. So what's the problem?"

"Get my clothes off?" he squeaked as if his voice had never broken.

Phoebe went quiet and bit her lip. "Ah. Yes. I see how that could have been misconstrued.Sorry, my fault. Mind you…"She waggled an admonishing finger at him. "Typical male. A girl says, 'get your clothes off' and he immediately thinks just one thing."

"Well, it's not a phrase with many options."

She sighed. "It *so* is. OK, I'll spell it out. This is an operation undercover of darkness. We're gift-Ninjas, no-one must see us. But you turn up in…" She pulled a classic Sid Vicious sneer, "…light grey trousers, white jumper, white trainers and a khaki coat? Not exactly Special Ops, is it, unless the SAS have started shopping at Primark, which is actually possible given the cuts to defence spending."

Phoebe rummaged in her wardrobe. "Lucky for you, black is my favourite colour. Well, technically my favourite shade." She threw out black jeans, jumper, beret, long overcoat and boots. "They should all fit. The boots are too big for me, which is their entire point."

Peter gaped at the outfit. "I'm going to look like a…" he gazed about the posters again, "…a Sister Of Mercy?"

"That, my friend, is a good thing. I might even stick some eyeliner on you. Hell, in that gear, I could even fancy you a little."

Peter didn't need much more convincing. He started to pull off his jumper.

"Jesus, Piper, not here!" Phoebe pushed him toward the door. "The bathroom, you bloody perv, the bathroom!"

*

A few minutes later, Phoebe checked out his change of image and nodded.

"Ah, the children of the night, such sweet music they make," she purred like Bela Lugosi. "So. Ready?"

"I think so."

Phoebe had packed the gifts into a black duffel which she held up. “Here we go, then. *Now* is *now* and this is a bag full of magical thinking. So let’s get delivering.”

40/ PETER'S HOUSE, 10:30 p.m.

After an hour or so creeping about Littel Wade depositing random gifts based on a scientifically and historically dubious proposition, Phoebe and Peter parted company. He wandered home the few doors up Dawn Street, and wondered what they'd achieved, if anything.

*

Dad was working but mum sat at the kitchen table with a cup of tea, staring blankly out at the Dorset night. Then she turned and beamed at her son. "Oh, *here* he is! I've been waiting.Hello, lovely late-comer." Julie still wore her uniform and gave an exaggerated comedy salute which Peter returned with a smile. "It's rare you get in after me. So what's been keeping my boy so busy tonight?"

"Er, I was out."

"Oh, *really*," she laughed. "I guessed that, since you just came in, which normally happens after one's been out. Have you eaten? Want me to rustle up something of no nutritional value whatsoever?"

Peter sat down."No thank you. I ate at Phoebe's."

She smirked knowingly and raised a questioning eyebrow. "Oh, at *Phoebe's*, were you?"

Peter sighed. "You know I was, and I know what you're getting at."

"Of course you do, so that saves us both a lot of time, then. Come on, you've been in each other's pockets for days now. What's the deal with you and her?"

Ah, that's mum; always straight to the point with the questions I really should be asking myself, he thought.

"There's no deal," Peter wondered why he'd lied, since there was exactly zero point in doing so.

"Of course there isn't. Pretty girl, why should there possibly be a deal?" Julie looked him up and down slowly. "And you're wearing goth black, which is her favourite colour. Or shade. Or whatever. Total coincidence, I'm sure."

Peter felt his cheeks redden so changed the subject. "It's so cold out there, but still no snow."

Mum gazed into their little garden. "No, and that's a shame. Can you believe it's the twenty-third and not one flake of the white stuff? I tell you, the moment it starts snowing I am straight out in it,whenever, wherever."

"Same here."

Julie turned back to her son and smiled again."Oh, I see, very clever, trying to make me talk about something else, eh? I'm not your ventriloquist doll and you're not off the hook that easy. Sorry to say, your private life is of great interest to me. You and Phoebe, then. Can you at least say what you're up to?"

Ah, tricky question, mum.

"Um, not yet."

"Not yet?" She whistled. "So either you know but don't want to say, or… you don't have the faintest clue, correct? The plot thickens. Go on, give me a hint."

Peter wondered how to articulate what they'd been doing without sounding insane. Because in the cold light of the kitchen's fluorescent tube and outside Phoebe's orbit, their secret gift-giving exercise did seem extremely strange.

"It's nothing bad."

"Well, I already knew that. Remember, I know all, dear, and since you're my son it's genetically impossible for you to be up to no good. But try me."

OK, if I could tell anyone else about this, it's mum. Dad wouldn't understand. He'd think it was a waste of time. But let's have a go, say it out loud, he thought. *But perhaps tone things down a bit, see how that sounds.*

"We've…" He took a deep breath and finally said it. "We've been out delivering Christmas presents to some of the older villagers."

Julie clapped her hands. "Really? Wow, bravo. Good for you, that's great." She thought for a moment. "But why? What suddenly turned you both into Mr and Mrs Claus?"

There she goes again, typical police officer, asking the right questions while guessing I don't have the right answers. But you know that's exactly why she's asking them.

"It just seemed right, I suppose. A nice thing to do."

"Hm. Which it is…" She looked deep into his eyes and waved her hands like a spooky stage hypnotist. "But you forget as your mum I can read your every thought and I'm guessing there's more to it than that, isn't there?"

How on earth do I explain? He wondered. "Yes, well, er, but…It's… you see…it's complicated. I think. Er…"

"Ah, he flounders." Julie put her forefinger on his lips. "Ssh, don't panic. You and Phoebe haven't worked it out yourselves yet, am I right? You want some motherly advice, is that it?"

Peter nodded.

"Well, that's what I'm always here for, at your beck and call. Oh, whistle, and I'll come to you my lad." Julie laughed, then pondered for a moment. "OK…Sometimes you find out *why* you're doing something by getting off your backside and actually doing it. Like…er…blowing up festive balloons," she tittered. "So I'm sure whatever this is will make sense when the time is right. And then you can explain *alllll* the details to me. Promise?"

"Promise." She solemnly shook his hand to seal the deal and yawned. "I'd best get off."

"Oh, don't go. This early?"

Julie looked at the clock. "Ah, but early or late depends how tired you are. Sorry, I'm tired, Peter and it's already way too late." She stood and kissed him on the forehead. "We can't all be on teenage hours, you know. I'll be gone by the time you wake up, whatever ungodly hour you deign that to be."

"I know."

Julie stretched, yawned again and headed toward the kitchen door. "Nighty-night, then, sweetie. Look at us, ships in the night. Love you."

"I love you too," he blew a kiss her way which she mimed catching, then held to her heart like an over-acting silent movie actress. "To sleep, perchance to dream," Mum spun and waved over her shoulder. "*And* it's only two sleeps to Christmas! Hope your presents bring a few smiles!" She disappeared into the dark of the hallway giggling and singing *Santa Claus Is Coming To Town*.

Smiles and what else? Peter wondered. *Because this is about more than just smiles, isn't it?*

Isn't it?

BOOK FOUR
24th DECEMBER 2022

41/ LITTEL WADE, 8:00 a.m.

Mrs Joyce Bramell lived above The Fruit & Veg Shop so her morning routine and commute involved tea, toast, pulling on a tabard, going downstairs and opening up.

Today, however, was different. As Joyce unlocked the door she stopped in her tracks and looked down at a little wrapped package on the step. She gingerly picked it up then rattled the parcel by her ear. No sound came from within.

She carried the strange item inside at arms length, like it might go off at any moment. Once at her counter she saw a gift tag was attached on which was written; *Joyce.*

"Joyce?" Mrs Bramell whispered as if attempting to translate an ancient language. Eventually she tore open the gift to reveal a wooden brush with inlaid mother-of-pearl handle.

"Pretty," she murmured. Joyce slowly raised the brush to her dry hair and pulled it through the bracken. Then she stared at the ceiling as a distant memory flared.

"Brush," she said, thoughtfully. "*Brush*? Hm."

Something about a brush.

Something from long before the days of tea, toast and tabard.

Something from before everything else, when the world was still so very big and her view of it hadn't become so very small.

Joyce glanced over at her shop window Nativity scene. The Angel Gabriel remained flat on his face. Mary still hadn't managed to make the occasion, lost in a box somewhere. Joseph looked down into the crib as just two Wise Men offered up gold and myrrh. A headless sheep knelt at one side, perhaps baby Jesus' first miracle; the Lord had bestowed life to an animal despite its lack of a rather important piece of anatomy.

Hallelujah.

Mrs Bramell frowned.

"That won't do," she said, and got busy.

*

With minor variations, that scene took place on various doorsteps across Littel Wade on the morning of Christmas Eve.

42/ PHOEBE'S HOUSE, DAWN STREET, 8:00 a.m.

Phoebe opened her eyes. As always during those first moments in the arrival lounge between sleep and wakefulness, her mind took a second to adjust from dream to reality. That particular line had been blurred last night when she'd spent a surreal hour with Peter creeping around Littel Wade anonymously leaving presents on certain villagers' doorsteps. Although they'd committed no crime, both gift-givers had still felt slightly jumpy. Phoebe thought that was because if they'd been caught and forced to explain the real reason for their festive *largesse*, well…

Oh you see officer, it's all very simple; Peter found some books in a sleigh and so of course *we came to the magical conclusion they're ledgers of kids who never got the Christmas presents they wanted. Yes, officer, you're right, in many ways, the books* are *Santa Claus' Naughty & Nice Lists, but you don't have to say it so sarcastically. Well, I do admit skulking about under cover of darkness does look like we're on a burgling spree, but you're not thinking* magically *officer. We're just delivering presents, but decades late! What's that? I'm allowed one phone call, you say? No, I don't have a lawyer.*

Phoebe shook her head, relieved that scenario hadn't come to pass. *But what* has *come to pass?* She wondered. *Have a few Littel Wadians woken up today and found some wonder in their lives again? Or are they simply confused, looking at random objects dumped on their doorsteps and wondering which of their neighbours is either taking the piss or having a breakdown?*

There was only one way to find out, of course.

Phoebe pulled back the edge of the blackout curtain. *Please, please, please, please,* rattled through her head as she risked a look outside.

Ah, shit. Typical.

Her lawn hadn't been re-carpeted in white, the gutters remained icicle free and there were no snowy sills on the windows. As always, Littel Wade continued to resist the festive season.

But what did you expect? Phoebe thought. *That giving out a few secret gifts would somehow recalibrate the bloody* weather? *We don't even know if we've changed* anything, *but we certainly haven't magicked up snow.* Still, part of her had expected to wake up and see *Magical Thinking Stage One; Snowfall*, and was now a tad sulky it hadn't happened.

Oh grow up. It's not the lack of snow that's the problem and you know it. Dad's not home for Christmas Day and won't be. It's one degree centigrade out there in Littel Wade, while he's probably dealing with forty degrees in Karachi, and the rest. Cheers, climate disaster.

She grabbed her phone intending to surprise her father with a call, but stopped.

What are you thinking? First things first.

Phoebe texted Peter;

Thanks for last night. How are you?

She lay back and stared at the solid white cloud above, willing tiny dots of white to tumble from it, but none came. Then, a swooshing sound; incoming.

Fine thanks.

OK, I won't push it, Phoebe sighed, then texted;

Now the hurly burly's done, when do you want to meet up? See if anything's happened with our gifts?

Swoosh; outgoing.

Swoosh; incoming.

Yes, let's see what's what in the village. I wonder if your theory has worked? I hope so. What time?

Swoosh; outgoing.

Got work first thing, bah, humbug. Only a half day though, so hooray. Shall we say three? Give me time to get home, get my warpaint on, summon up the spirits of both Christmas and Bauhaus?

No delay this time. A Tears-Streaming-Down-Laughing-Face emoji appeared, followed by;

Three it is. I may even wear black, as your acolyte.

She smiled at the emoji then wrote;

Acolyte. I like that. It is as it should be.

Swoosh; the message flew a few doors up the road.

43/ PETER'S HOUSE, 9:00 a.m.

Peter lay in bed and stared at his ceiling. Through the fog of half-sleep earlier he'd heard dad return home without any attempt to regulate any noise. There'd been a slamming of doors, stomping of stairs, and now the snoring of a shattered and angry man.

Peter picked up his mobile, re-read the text exchange with Phoebe, muttered, "*Acolyte*? Too much?" then flicked through the rest of his messages.

From; Mum.

Hi! Again, there's good news and bad news. I'd call, but you're probably lying in, as per. Good news; I'm NOT working Christmas Day!

At that point, mum had inserted *way* too many firework and party-face emojis.

That's Xmas DAY. I've wangled a split shift, a few hours this morning, heading into town for some last minute stuff, then back at work 10pm to 2am. That's the bad news. And the other bad news was dad was in another foul mood this morning. No idea why, so give him a wide berth today until you can judge the lie of the land. Needless to say I will NOT be buying (and exploding) festive balloons again! Love you, XXXXXXXXXXXX

"Oh mum, *festive balloons*." Peter lay back and stared at the geography of his ceiling once again.

Three o clock couldn't come soon enough.

44/ THE CO-OP, LITTEL WADE, MID-DAY.

Phoebe gritted her teeth as George Michael moaned about his previous year's mis-placed holiday romance, *again*. She liked Wham, but "Last Christmas," at least four times a day was dangerously close to sonic water torture.

"Ahem-hem, mid-day break!" she called over to her team leader. "I'm owed my mid-day!"

"It's Christmas Eve! Can't you wait until it's calmed down a bit?" whined the leader. "We're all hands on deck, here."

"If anything, it's going to get worse," Phoebe replied. "Come on. Legally, I'm owed two fifteen minutes. I might as well take one now."

"All right," sighed the team leader, who grabbed a box of mixed nuts and stoically threw themselves back into the fray.

"One day they shall sings songs of your bravery," Phoebe shouted after them, grabbed her bag from the stock room and left the store.

*

Ten seconds later she sat at the bus stop munching on a sandwich and watching the Co-op descend further into festive carnage. She pulled out her phone and texted Peter.

It's me. But you knew that. Hope you're OK and still on for three. I haven't seen any evidence our trip out has changed much, but I'm hardly expecting a variety of Scrooges to appear at windows flicking their half-crowns at urchins. That sounded wrong. Let's explore later, see what we can see.

She thought for a second then added;

Oh and please do wear black. It suits you. I'll be at the church for three, OK?

Phoebe pulled out one of the sleigh books. She'd examined every page, convinced something was hiding but still couldn't quite work out what.

No dates. No addresses except a faded "Dorset" on the spine. There's absolutely nothing else to see, so why do I still get the feeling I'm not looking at it right?

Phoebe saw Mr Hamnett striding purposefully in her direction but with his gaze locked on the Co-op. For the first time in living memory, he was wearing what must have been His Very Best Suit, which translated to; His Other Suit. Unlike Ted's tired and crumpled everyday wear, this outfit was clean and pressed. His shoes and eyes shone and he wore a bright red cravat. All this was surprising enough but what really caught Phoebe's attention was the wrapped package he held, the same one she and Piper had left on his doorstep last night. The paper was slightly torn which suggested he'd opened, thought about, then re-wrapped it.

My God, it's happening. It's really happening. Oh, bravo, Mr Hamnett. You've put two and two together to make wonderful. This is it. This is your moment. Good luck, Ted, oh, the very best of British luck.

She watched Ted determinedly walk into the Co-op then collar a befuddled worker, who scurried off to the storeroom.

You're going for it. We gave you the gift, you've grown the balls and joined the dots. Exactly as we hoped. Oh Renee, please don't ruin his Christmas Eve. Please.

Renee appeared at Ted's side, and Phoebe leaned forward to watch. At first her store manager looked confused, as if Mr Hamnett had dressed up to come and complain. But then he shrugged, held out the gift, and went into what was surely a well-practiced speech. For a second, Renee looked like a shy schoolgirl as she carefully opened the package and at that moment Phoebe fell in love with her…just a little.

With lips forming an "O" of surprise, Renee leafed through *"Payne's Select Poetry For Children*". Ted didn't take his eyes off her face as she laughed, then read out a verse. Renee smiled up at her benefactor and lightly tapped him on the chest in thanks. Phoebe wasn't sure, but they both seemed to be blushing.

You took the plunge, Ted, and didn't sink. Phoebe put her hands to her mouth in delight. *Our gift changed something. Mr Hamnett got the poetry book we* believe *he wanted but never received. It's given him confidence. So what else have we changed? Or am I just seeing what I* want *to see rather than what I* should *see?*

She looked down at the book on her lap.

So what should I be seeing here?

Phoebe picked up her phone again and texted.

Piper! First evidence is in. I just saw Mr Hamnett give Renee the poetry book, just as we hoped. She likes it. She's smiling and blushing, which is an event of Halley's Comet rarity. Can't wait to see you at three and find out what else is happening in our village.

45/ PETER'S HOME, 1:00 p.m.

Dad's still-snoozing presence was occasionally announced with a panicked intake of breath like a drowner surfacing.

Peter had learned to filter out dad's slumbering broadcasts, just as someone who lives under a flight path no longer registers the roar of engines. He spent the morning in a holding pattern of his own, creeping around the silent house. He'd pulled that little silver wrapped box from his wardrobe then realised his fingers were scraping at the sellotape. Peter pulled them away as if the box were hot.

By 1 a.m. his stomach had started to sulk, so made himself a Cup-a-Soup and shuffled into the living room. Peter glanced about the tiny space, which had never really changed. Mum's quirky (and often tacky) holiday memorabilia sat on the TV. Dad's crime novels and technical manuals lined the bookshelf. Photos of Tony and Julie smiled from a variety of locations. Benji slept in his favourite chair.

All *was* as it *was* and probably always would be.

Except it wasn't.

Something was different.

Something slim and white stuck out from the top of the bookshelf. This was *verboten,* because years ago mum had pronounced, *"Bookshelves are for books. The* tops *of bookshelves are for dusting. I do not want to see any clutter up there, OK?"*

Clearly mum wasn't responsible so that meant dad had squirrelled away…what?

Peter stood on a footstool and pulled out the object, a folder marked HOUSE, BANKING AND IMPORTANT DOCS in his father's handwriting.

What are you hiding from? He mentally asked the file. *Because, yeah, that's what it looks like. You've been hidden up there from prying eyes. Why's that, then? Who hides their bank statements?*

Part of him didn't want to look but opened it anyway, flicked through and found one letter from an estate agent dated *9/5/22;*

Thank you for your recent enquiry. We enclose a list of properties as per your family's requirements and budget. Please contact us at your earliest convenience to view them, but as you're aware the market is fast moving and it is possible some have already been earmarked. Your best bet is to check our website regularly.

I hope to hear from you soon and anything we can assist you with, of course, we will.

Your faithfully,

Darren Jacobs (He/Him)

Senior Salesperson, MTG Homes & Properties (Dorchester)

Peter sat for a while as the letter's contents sunk in. *So we're moving, are we?* Are *we?* Eyebrow raised, he flicked through properties in the document. *But if we are, what's the reason for hiding this folder?*

Papers in hand, he sat back and listened to dad fight his way through another dream upstairs.

46/ LITTEL WADE HIGH STREET, 3:00 p.m.

Phoebe was sitting on the bench by St Nicholas' church, back in her day-wear of black leather and studs. She waved and held up a paper bag. "Afternoon! Sausage roll?"

"Thanks," Peter took the pastry and sat down.

Phoebe looked at the solid white cloud above Littel Wade. "Pah, still no snow. That sky's like some boyfriends I've had, you know? It keeps promising something wonderful, but never quite gets round to delivering." She turned to Peter and smiled. "You're wearing black! I thought you only texted that to suck up to me." Sure enough under a black jacket he wore a black jumper, jeans and pumps. "It's good," she nodded approvingly. "There are very few things or indeed people that can't be vastly improved by the liberal application of black."

Peter gave a sarcastic curtsey.

"You sure you want to do this?" Phoebe asked with a mouthful of sausage roll.

"Oh God, yes." He gazed up the High Street. "So did our magical thinking work? Have any of our Scrooges asked for the biggest turkey in the shop?"

"Ha, well, not quite. I wasn't expecting full Dickens, just some evidence of change, however small. If this was my thesis I'd have to provide proper control groups, pre-and-post experiment interviews, some empirical data to measure Christmassy…"

"Can you measure *Christmassy*? Isn't it just a feeling?"

"Exactly. There's my problem. That's why all this…" She reached into her bag and produced the list of gifts and recipients, "…can't really stand up as a genuine experiment I can put up for peer review. It's more to see if magical thinking can be researched in the real world. And…" she stood, "…If nothing else, it's been fun, hasn't it?" She offered Peter her hand and pulled him up. "So let me take you on another tour of Littel Wade, *after* our deliveries. I think you'll be rather pleased with the results."

They stopped opposite Mr Farr's Candy Box.

"OK as we both know, Mr F. hasn't exactly been Mr Joy To The World. But last night we anonymously delivered him an old comic…" She twirled a flourish with her hands, "…and so Piper, I give you…Result A."

The sweetshop looked dark and unwelcoming as always. "I'm not seeing…Oh. Wait. That's new."

A Christmas wreath was pinned to the door.

"When have you ever seen The Candy Box with Christmas decorations, hm?"

"Never."

"Right. And it gets better, come on."

As they crossed the road Peter saw a hand-drawn sign below the wreath; "FREE SWEET BAGS FOR XMAS. JUST ASK!"

Phoebe grinned. "Ah-ha. He's got pretty little paper bags of chews and whatnot lined up on his counter, all twisted shut at the top. He's giving them away. *Giving them away*. Now I ask you, is that what we'd consider normal behaviour from him?"

"Hardly."

"Can we prove it's down to him finally getting a comic his younger self once wanted? Nope, not unless we ask. And we can't do that because…?" Phoebe circled her finger in the air, waiting for a response.

"Because if we ask, we reveal who gave him the present and take away the magic."

She clicked her fingers, *snap*. "Spot on. Remember, magic ceases to be so once it's explained. But do you think, or rather *feel* we're somehow responsible?"

Peter looked back at the wreath and searched inside himself. "I do. Yes. I've got no proof, but yes. That's what I feel."

"Believing without proof is faith, Piper. OK, next stop, Result B…"

*

"It's not quite as spectacular as The Candy Box but it's definitely something." They'd stopped opposite The Fish And Chip Shop.

"In the scowly stakes, Mr Spencer was possibly in a dead heat with Mr Farr. On a scale of one to ten, Piper, a few days ago how was his frying festive spirit?"

"Zero."

"Not exactly in the one to ten scale as requested, but I'll let it pass. But now see what you can see."

Mr Spencer sat behind his fryers reading a newspaper.

"Er…Nope…"

"Come *on*. What's that on his head?"

"Jesus Christ."

"No, it isn't. And just this once I shall allow such blasphemy this close to Christmas on account of you being in shock."

Fred Spencer had a Santa hat perched on the back of his head like some people might wear a beret.

"Ooh, that's dangerously jovial for Mr Spencer," Peter said.

"Indeed it is. That hat demonstrates a remarkable sense of devil-may-care and a lack of taking oneself too seriously, both traits our fishy friend has never shown before."

Peter frowned. "It's not a *huge* change, though."

Phoebe slapped him on the arm. "Oy. For you, maybe. But for Mr Spencer, it's seismic. This is a man for whom wearing coloured socks would be tantamount to going out in full drag. Mr Spencer doesn't *do* light-hearted. And I put it to you, Mr Piper, that a Santa hat, worn jauntily on the back of a head, is definitely light-hearted. What were you expecting? Cartwheels?"

"It would have been nice."

She hit him on the arm again, harder. "Everyone's a bloody critic," she snarled. "Onward, cynic. Result C."

*

Their next stop was THE FRUIT AND VEG SHOP.

Phoebe pointed at the window. "OK, cut to the chase. Mrs Bramell always has a Nativity scene and it's always, forgive the pun, Godawful. But now, pardon the pun again, there's been an epiphany."

Peter had seen Joyce's half-hearted Nativity scenes for as long as he could remember, but this was like she'd seen the light.

The tiny participants at Jesus' birth no longer shared the manger with gigantic carrots and monstrous potatoes. Mary was back after being lost in a box somewhere, staring beatifically down at her and God's only son. The formerly two wise men had finally been joined by a bright and shiny third, clearly a very recent purchase. Angel Gabriel was now upright rather than floundering face down like a paralytic at a party, and next to Joseph stood a drummer boy in anachronistic Napoleonic era uniform. He had nothing to offer the newborn king but his *pa-rup-a-pum-pum*.

"Wow," mouthed Peter as they passed.

Phoebe nodded sagely. "Told you. We'd become so inured to Mrs Bramell's Nativity horrorshow even I didn't spot its upgrade for a bit." She thought for a moment. "I never got the drummer boy thing, though.

Think about it, you're heavily pregnant and a tad confused because the father is, well, *God,* which is one hell of a one night stand. You've had to schlep across boiling Judea to attend a stupid census, there's no rooms available so you end up in a bloody cowshed where, *just for a laugh*, you go into labour. No gas and air, so you're in dreadful pain and compromised because said shed is suddenly full of stinky shepherds and random animals eyeballing you, plus, *apparently*, three blokes with gifts that frankly are of no use whatsoever right now. 'Thanks for the myrrh lads, but I could do with some pethidine.' Then a kid gatecrashes with a fucking *drum* and starts bashing away at it in your ear. That's really going to tip anyone over the edge, let alone a new mother. If I was Our Lady, I would have jumped up from the hay and stuck his drumsticks up his arse."

Peter waited for Phoebe to finish her broadside, then whistled. "That is obviously something that's bothered you for some time."

"It has," she conceded. "And don't even get me started on how the Magi didn't *actually* tip up to Bethlehem 'til January the sixth, hence, Epiphany."

"Really? That late?"

"Well, no, not according to the Bible, which never gives specific dates as we'd know them. But the church does love its festivals, so January sixth was chosen. However…biblical chronological fuck ups, unnecessary and unwanted drumming aside, it seems that Mrs Bramell now has a sense of festive aesthetics she never cared for before."

"It does seem that way."

"Sorry about the rant."

"Accepted."

"Result D, then."

*

Phoebe pointed at one lonely sprig of mistletoe hung above the door of Mr Nelson's Newsagents. "Subtle, but present. We gifted him an old annual yesterday, today he's made this romantic concession to the season."

"Subtle is the word," Peter agreed.

"Ahem," she coughed and tapped her white cheek. "I do believe there's a tradition to be observed." Peter gave her a chaste kiss and felt his own cheek redden.

"Ooh, quite the gentleman, aren't you, sir?" she curtseyed.

"Hold on, though," Peter stepped back. "That mistletoe could have been there for weeks and we never spotted it."

Phoebe shot him an impatient look which clearly signalled, *I'm ahead of you, Piper*, and pulled out her phone.

"Nope. Yesterday afternoon I took photos of all our delivery addresses so we'd have something to compare and contrast with today. This may be a flaky experiment but we should at least try to do it properly." She flicked through shots of the various places they'd visited last night. "This time yesterday The Candy Box had no wreath nor free sweets. Mr Spencer wasn't sporting a Santa Hat. Mrs Bramell's Nativity was still a building site." Phoebe zoomed in on a photo of the newsagent's."See? No mistletoe above the door. And as we proceed, you'll see that *every single person* we anonymously gifted now has some kind of nod to Christmas, however tiny, where there was none before."

"But what does it mean?"

"I'll defer that if I may." Phoebe glanced back up at the mistletoe. "Oh, go on, then," she pouted her black lips. Peter just stared. "I'm not going to stand here like a Kardashian, Piper. Now or never." He kissed her and felt himself blush once more. She strode on and called out over her shoulder, "That was just because it's Christmas, Piper. So don't think we're getting a room."

*

A visitor to Littel Wade wouldn't have slapped their thigh pantomime style and bellowed, "My, but this is the most prettiest decorated village in Christendom!" Only Peter and Phoebe recognised the tiny festive changes that had taken place since last night.

She pointed at The Anchor pub's bay window. "Ahoy, love's young dream." Renee and Mr Hamnett were framed there; she with a white wine, he with a pint, both giggling like shy teenagers. "Fast movers, aren't they?"

Peter goggled at the two sixty-somethings in full flirt mode. "I can't believe…"

"Believe what? Old people don't fancy each other? Wrinklies can do speed dating? Renee is human? But our poetry book made that happen." She followed Peter's gaze and smiled fondly at the tableau. "Or rather, Mr Hamnett's poetry book did. It's what he once wanted as a kid and now look; that gift gave him the confidence to make the unrequited, requited."

Peter couldn't take his eyes off the couple.

"*Renee and Ted*," he whispered with a hint of awe.

"OK, stop gawping, Piper. It'll happen to all of us eventually." She winked. "Even me and you. Come on, only three tiny miracles left."

*

Mrs Newman's laundrette now had a poster of Father Christmas in the window. Faded, yes, torn a little, but still present when he hadn't been a day ago.

In Mr Marsh's butcher's window, a few crackers were laid out with the sausages and joints. The toy soldiers they'd delivered to him last night also stood around the meats, which made his display look like an art installation about the futility of war.

In the garage lot, Mr Davies had wound tinsel around the cars' ariels. "That's not the best bit," Phoebe said as they passed. Brian had his head in a bonnet as usual, then stood and stretched.

"*Et voila*, Piper. Check out the knitwear." Mr Davies wore a jumper featuring the smiling face of Father Christmas and the words I'M ON THE GOOD LIST.

"Ugh. Where did he even get that?" Peter asked.

"Fucked if I know," she shrugged. "Why, do you want one?"

"I've never seen him in anything but overalls."

"Well, isn't it just your lucky day?"

"It's not a look I'll quickly forget."

"Same here. I think I may be waking up screaming for months. But you have to admit, it's a definite change. Onward."

Phoebe and Peter sat down on the bench outside the post office. "Our tour is nearly over," she said. "We dropped off a spinning top here for sulky old Mrs Belton last night, so…see anything different about this place?"

Peter looked about for any festive additions. "Er…no."

"That's because it was a trick question. Try *listening*."

"Oh," he realised what she was referring to and smiled widely. "That is unusual."

"I'd say."

The crushing silence in Littel Wade Post Office always made a monastery seem like a party at a drop forge. Total quiet was enforced with slitted eyes and pursed lips from the manager Mrs Belton, who resented customers *asking for things* and shattering her perfect stillness.

But not today.

"She's got music on," Peter gasped. "Actual music. In the post office."

"Yep. Not the radio either, a CD. Look, the case is on her counter."

Sure enough there was a NOW THAT'S WHAT I CALL CHRISTMAS in full view. The Beach Boys' *Little Saint Nick* blared from a speaker somewhere.

"I'm shocked."

"Join the club, Piper, join the club."

A Royal Mail driver jumped out of his van, went inside then reappeared with a sack. He was quickly followed by Mrs Belton herself. "Oh, *Da-a-ve*," she called after him.

Peter's eyebrows nearly shot off his forehead. The normally dour, cardiganned-and-bloused Mrs B. was wearing a brightly coloured sweater of shimmering sequinned flowers.

"Is that *make up*?" he whispered.

"Oh yes," Phoebe hissed back. "She's discovered eyeshadow and lipstick at sixty-three. Better late than never, eh?"

She almost skipped up to the driver. "*Da-a-ve*, I totally forgot. Can I order more stamps? I don't normally allow them to get this low, but naughty old me, tut-tut, slap-wrist I'm nearly out."

"Righto Mrs Belton," said Dave, who was half her age.

"Oh, call me Susan, please," she trilled.

"Oh my God she's flirting," gagged Peter.

"What *have* we done?" asked Phoebe.

"How many books do you want to order?" Dave asked and slowly backed away from her.

"Best have a hundred firsts, fifty seconds."

"Righto, Mrs…Susan."

"Merry Christmas," she waved and disappeared back inside..

Phoebe and Peter sat in stunned silence for a while.

"That was different," Phoebe said eventually. "Come on, let's walk and talk." She stared after the departing van then bit her lip, a sure sign of deep thought.

"What is it?" asked Peter.

"Nothing. Something. I'll let you know when I know." Phoebe watched the vehicle head south, out of Littel Wade. "Something…" she repeated. "But what?"

47/ LITTEL WADE HIGH STREET, 4:00 p.m.

The sky had blackened. In the U.K. sunset is at 3:55 p.m. on December twenty fourth, and thick cloud over Littel Wade hastened darkness yet further. Street lamps flickered on, jaundice-yellow.

"So what happens now?" asked Peter.

"Happens? Nothing, I guess. This wasn't a proper experiment by a long way. I'd get laughed out of university if I tried to pretend it was. We skipped steps, failed to carry out adequate controls, held no interviews, gathered no empirical evidence…If I offered up what we did for peer review, things wouldn't end well, put it that way."

"But we have seen actual differences."

"But are they differences? Or coincidences,conjecture,and assumption, all of which are enemies of fact." Phoebe waved her hand in the air. "But I do have something which is potentially persuasive."

She lit up her phone and selected the camera. "Alright, I took these yesterday afternoon 'cos I wanted a record of any changes." The photos showed shops, homes and buildings around Littel Wade. Phoebe scrolled through them. "Everywhere we left a gift last night is showing some kind of festive difference today, no matter how tiny. But now compare that to where we *didn't* go." Phoebe swiped through more snaps of properties. "Take a look, before and after. All the locations that *never* got a gift are exactly the same. No changes, no decorations, no festive additions. The only places that became *more* Christmassy in the last twenty-four hours are the ones we delivered to. Interesting, don't you think?"

"That has to be some kind of proof, doesn't it?"

"Well, 'some kind of proof' is the correct description, since it's not actual proof magical thinking has real world consequences. But I'll ask you again, what do you feel? Not think, *feel.* Did our little bit of Christmassing have a real effect on the people we chose?"

Peter nodded. "Yes, I believe so."

She returned the nod, satisfied. "Were your books lists of gifts some kids never got? Well, we thought so, and that belief made those gifts a reality. You see, Piper, we were the real experiment. We allowed magical thinking to guide us into acting magically. And when you think about it that way, this experiment was one hundred percent successful."

"We were the real subjects?"

"Uh-huh. Subjects *and* researchers. That's a first, I think. Totally unacceptable, of course.The subjects of an experiment can't also run it, but let's face facts, we were investigating magic, so bending the rules was almost compulsory."

They reached St Nicholas church and sat down. "We did a good thing, I think," Phoebe hugged herself, either for warmth or in congratulation, Peter couldn't tell.

An Amazon delivery van went past and she watched it go, lost in thought.

"What?" Peter asked.

Phoebe held up a finger; *one minute, please.* She scrunched her eyes, tipped her head side-to-side and rolled an idea about in there.

"Bloody hell. That's it."

"What?"

"I know what they really are. The books."

48/ ST NICHOLAS' CHURCH, LITTEL WADE, 4:15 p.m.

Phoebe flicked through the last book Peter had found. "Something about what Mrs Belton said. I remember now. Yeah, That's it."

"What's what?"

"She asked for an order of stamps."

Peter didn't know where Phoebe was going. "Stamps?"

"Mm, but the important word in that sentence was *order*. We thought these books were lists of *deliveries*, right?" Her porcelain face seemed to shine with excitement. "But that explanation always annoyed me because it didn't make sense. You can't have a ledger of deliveries without addresses, that's ridiculous."

"So…?"

She held up the book. "This is a list of orders, Piper. Not deliveries, *orders.* Alright, let's imagine we run a…Toy factory; *Piper and Clarke's Made-To-Order Toys*. We make the toys then someone else distributes them, yes?"

"A-ha."

"So as the supplier, we only have to know what toys to make and how many. So we work to a list of orders; *one toy gun, three bouncy balls, two spinning tops*…See what I mean?"

Peter studied the entries. "So these are all items to be made?"

"Correct. Orders fulfilled, and…*orders cancelled.* The cancelled ones have a red cross next to them. That explains why there are no addresses in our books, which means somewhere out there…" she waved her hand vaguely at the world beyond their bench, "…are other books full of delivery addresses. But these ones you found in the sleigh are just lists of items to be manufactured or sourced."

Peter thought for a moment. "So…the sleigh took orders to a factory somewhere, then picked up the goods for delivery?"

Phoebe shrugged. "Yeah, why not? The question is, what kind of factory and where?" She tapped the pages. "I mean, how weird can you get? It's been operating for hundreds of years, making and storing comics, clockwork cars, brushes, oranges, wooden horses, blah blah blah. Random as hell, if you ask me."

"So one answer leads to another riddle, doesn't it?"

"No, not if you think magically. Because if you believe these books are Father Christmas' naughty and nice lists, then they make perfect sense."

"But they're not, because Santa doesn't exist."

"Exactly. But it works as a *magical* explanation, and isn't that what all this has been about? Sprinkling a bit of magic on something dreadfully prosaic? You know Sherlock Holmes' maxim?"

"Er…"

"'*Once you have eliminated all which is impossible, then whatever remains, however improbable, must be the truth.*' But for our books, I'm going to suggest we invert that." She considered her words for a moment. "OK, once you eliminate the *improbable*, then whatever remains, however *impossible*, must be the truth. So lets eliminate the *improbable* idea there's a centuries old factory that makes totally random goods for very little profit, and accept the *impossible* thought that somewhere in the North Pole there's a bunch of elves with tiny hammers working on a once-a-year mass delivery."

"You're joking, I hope."

"I am, but again, why not? Does it really hurt to believe in something that doesn't exist, even if it's just for one day a year? People around the world have faith in way stranger things. So you can have your cake and eat it; the books are both a boring list of orders *and* proof of something amazing. It is possible to keep two totally opposite ideas in your head, you know."

"It is?"

"Yep. One of my favourite Scott Fitzgerald quotes is…let me get it right…'*A first-rate intelligence is the ability to hold two opposed ideas in your mind at the same time and still have the ability to function.*' I live my life by that rule. I know what's true, but also accept what's false is often way more fun."

Peter nodded. "I like that worldview"

"You should. What are you doing tonight? You can come to mine if you like, you know."

"I should be at home, really."

Phoebe nodded. "Of course." She opened the book again and thought for a moment. "Ah, sod it, in for a penny, in for a pound."

"What do you mean?"

"Don't be scared, but I wonder what would happen if I totally accept these are Santa's gift orders. What if I leave rationality at the door and jump in, 100%? Faith moves mountains, so…" She shut her eyes and laid a hand on the book as if she were swearing an oath in court. "I believe,

OK? I really, really believe. And that's the truth, the whole truth and nothing but, so help me whatever deity may or may not run the universe."

"What are you doing?"

"Same as always; I'm thinking magically. So to that end, I'm going to place an order, of course. Why not?"

She delved into a zippered pocket, found an eyeliner pencil then wrote in the book with her tongue sticking out in concentration

She shut the covers with a satisfied thump. "Nothing to lose, I suppose." Phoebe stood. "I'd best get off."

At that moment her phone rang. "Hi Mum. You OK?" Phoebe's eyes widened. "…What? No! Really?…How? Oh my God…really?…*Really*? That's…Oh my God, that's…Oh my God!"

Peter stared at his friend and raised his eyebrows, *what is it*?

Phoebe spun on the spot. "Yes, yes, I'm just round the corner. On my way. That's brilliant. Bye, see you in a minute, bye."

She put both hands to her face, open mouthed in happy shock. "That was my mum. Dad's actually managed to get himself a flight. Last minute cancellation thingy. He's back tomorrow morning! He's coming back for Christmas!"

She did a silly spinning dance, which quickly slowed then stopped entirely like a clockwork toy running down. "Ah. Oh, sorry, I'm *such* a twat." Phoebe hung her head.

"No, you're not."

"But…Sure?"

"Positive. It's brilliant news and you are *not* a twat."

She gave him an embarrassed little smile, but that also quickly disappeared. "Whoah, no. No, no, no, *nooo*. Coincidence. It's only coincidence."

"Sorry, what's coincidence?"

"Just magical thinking," she spluttered and waved her hands in the air. "Coincidence, that's all. It's nothing."

She held up a finger as if she were telling herself off. "Get a grip, Clarke. Get. A. Grip. It's nothing. I'd better go back, see mum, get the house sorted, all that stuff. Piper, call, please call if you need me, promise?"

"I promise. But what…what's going on?"

Phoebe shook her head and started to walk away. "*Nothing's* going on. It's all just magical thinking, like I said."

"What is?"

"Look in the book, but it's nothing. Coincidence, that's all. Sometimes you just have to err on the side of reality more than fantasy, or you go insane. Call me."

She crossed the road without looking back.

Peter opened the book and flicked through. There, written in thick black eyeliner amongst the other "*orders*" was a new one;

PHOEBE CLARKE MY DAD

49/ PETER'S HOUSE, 4:20 p.m.

"Hello? Anyone home?" The darkness gave Peter his answer. He knew where mum was, but had expected dad to be here at least.

"Are you still in bed?" he shout/whispered up the stairs to silence. There was a small envelope on the mat, addressed in pen to THE PIPERS. Peter picked it up, walked to the kitchen then threw both envelope and sleigh book onto the table.

He switched on the kettle then stared out at the still, black December afternoon. From his blanket in the corner Benji barely managed a grunt in greeting.

You should go back and see Phoebe, Peter thought. *Don't just sit around here for the rest of the evening, doing nothing. She said to call. I should just go. No-one's here, so what's the point?*

He sat down with a cup of tea and opened the book to Phoebe's eyelinered entry;

PHOEBE CLARKE MY DAD

Peter raised his eyebrows. *Yeah, like she said, it's nothing. Phoebe wrote that, then finds out her dad's coming home. So what? We're desperate to find connections where there are none. The universe does its thing, not ours. Prayers don't work. Wishes don't work. Enchanted wells and burnt offerings don't work. There's no magical causality apart from what we attach to events.*

He tapped the pages thoughtfully.

But we did *change things today. Only a little, but it happened. We acted on the book, and whoever got our gifts shifted their worldview. I believe that. Phoebe believes that. So what's next?*

Peter looked at the envelope.

THE PIPERS

There were no other markings. *Weird. If it's a Christmas card from a friend, why not use our Christian names? THE PIPERS is a too formal for festive, isn't it?*

Something stopped him from opening it. Peter had an odd feeling that if he did, things would change. This strange foreboding was irrational but then again, he had thrown rationality to the winds over the last few days.

No. Not now. Whatever it is can wait.

He pushed the envelope away with one hand, but traitorously his other pulled it back and then together they tore it open. Peter watched this happen with amazement, as if his body had suddenly taken to making independent decisions. He slipped out a folded sheet of A4 and as he smoothed it down, the colour drained from his already pale face.

There was just one word; in capitals, no full stop.

SORRY

What? He thought. *Sorry? No name, no explanation,* sorry*? Hand delivered, sorry?* Sorry*?*

The word looked like it had been written in a child's uncertain hand. Peter crumpled the page. *What the fuck?*

He strode to the front door and glared up and down Dawn Street in case the author waited in shadows, but nothing moved and no-one watched. Face dark with fury, Peter turned back inside, sat down and stared at the mysterious paper once more.

SORRY

"Sorry…" he whispered. Peter turned the word over in his mind. It was familiar, yes, but also…recent.

He shut his eyes and tried to work out where and when *sorry* had been said, and by whom.

SORRY

Sorry. Sorry. Sorry. I'm sorry.

His eyes snapped open. "*Underbore*," he whispered. "Greg Underbore."

Two days ago, Gregory had barged straight into Peter. It was nothing, a stupid case of not looking where he was going, but Underbore had made it into a big deal. Greg had apologised far too many times, avoided Peter's gaze, stuttered, stumbled, gasped…*You only walked into me, no-one was hurt, but you acted like…What* did *you act like? And what else was said?*

At the time Peter had thought the collision was yet another vignette of Underbore weirdness. It had been nothing, but now felt like everything.

He said sorry, then what did I say? And why was it important?

Peter closed his eyes again and tried to recreate the scene. Greg had collided with him, dropped his cards then gone into an apologetic frenzy. Piper now recalled Underbore's cards were written in shaky, naive capitals, just like this odd note.

…And I said...I said, 'It was just an accident.'

Peter pictured Gregory's haunted face. He'd looked like he wanted to run and never stop.

I said, 'It was just an accident,' and *then he said...oh Jesus, he said, 'What do you mean?'*

Peter shook his head. *Wait, he needed the statement, 'It was just an accident'* clarified*? That phrase is what it is. Unless of course it means something else to* you, *Underbore.*

He stood and this time let his body make an independent decision. Without thought he climbed the stairs and almost sleepwalked to his room. Once there he waited for his subconscious to make its next move. Eventually, Peter opened his wardrobe and pulled out the jacket he'd worn yesterday morning. Then his hand scuttled from pocket to pocket until it closed on something.

Peter turned the object over in the pale glow of his bedside lamp.

It was the shiny crossbow bolt he'd retrieved from a tree in Marryman Forest. As he examined the bolt, Phoebe's description of Greg rose up; "*Greg Underbore is a small mammal killing machine. I think he's training on voles and whatnot until he can join the army.*"

Peter felt the tip of the quarrel. *I think this is yours, Gregory. And if I'm right, then what are you apologising for? What are you* sorry *for? Oh God, what are you sorry for?*

Without further thought, he pulled on the jacket.

I'm not sure I want to know, but I'm going to find out.

50 / THE UNDERBORE'S HOUSE, 4;40 p.m.

Out at the Underbore's it was even darker, if that were possible. Littel Wade's street lamps were sparsely located anyway, but here at the village edges they're non-existent. During his ride over, Peter's mind had been stuck on repeat, turning with the pedals; *This is insane. You don't know it was Gregory. This is insane. You don't know it was Gregory.*

But part of him was convinced Greg had crept up to his letterbox earlier to deliver a note which read, simply; SORRY.

He left his bike in the Underbore's excuse of a garden. A dull glow washed out from under their bungalow's living room curtains.

He knocked.

Against the stillness, the *k-bap-bap* sounded incredibly loud.

There was no answer, which was a relief. That meant Peter could just go home, bunker down and sit out the rest of the so-called Festive Season. *So that's that then*, he thought. *Oh well, questions and answers for another time but not, thankfully, for today.*

However his fist wasn't convinced and rapped on the door three more times, louder than before.

"Oh fucking hell," Gregory's voice moaned from within. "Not interested, whoever you are. Fuck off."

So what do you do now? Peter thought. *You get on your bike and leave, that's what. Just leave.*

But once again, his fist vetoed that idea and banged again.

"Fucking HELL," shrieked Greg."I swear to God…" There came a petulant fusillade of Underbore's angry feet stomping up the hall. "I'm missing telly 'cos of youse," He yelled. "This had better be…" The front door swung open and Gregory went from fury to stunned silence as he stared at his visitor, who stared right back.

"Hello, Greg," Peter had never felt so calm, so ice-sharp.

Underbore's mouth opened and closed like a ventriloquist doll whose operator had forgotten their act. Eventually he managed to gasp, "Piper."

"Mm-mm," Peter felt himself channel Phoebe's cool superiority. "Merry Christmas and all that. No carol singing though, sorry."

Gregory looked past Peter's shoulder. "My mum, my mum, she'll be…" he babbled, "My mum will be back any minute."

"Oh, your mum will be back will she? *Your mum* will be back? Great, then we can all have a nice chat, you know, about this?"

He slowly took out the sheet of A4 and fed off how uncomfortable Underbore suddenly looked. At that moment he knew beyond any doubt this squirming teenager was responsible. Greg rallied for a second and peered at the word as if he'd never seen it before. "Sorry? What's that about? What's going on, Piper?"

"Please. Acting's not your strong suit, is it? This is yours, yes? You posted it earlier? I recognised the handwriting, such as it is, from your little advert."

"You've gone mental, Piper. You've finally gone mental." Greg tried to shut the door but Peter blocked it. He'd never been this confrontational before, but at this moment righteousness was his superpower. "Come on Greg. A Christmas card I'd understand, sort-of, although one from you would be odd. A piece of paper that says SORRY, though?"

"My mum really will be back soon, and if she sees you here…"

"I really couldn't give one single fuck," Peter hissed. "So, want to enlighten me?"

One could almost see the colourful Fisher-Price plastic cogs of Gregory's brain turn. "Just, you know, sorry, because of, well, because of…This time of year, you know. Sorry."

"Very compassionate. Didn't think to sign it, though?"

"Please, Piper…"

"OK, how about this…" He held up the shiny crossbow bolt. Underbore's eyes widened in disbelief, which again was all the confirmation Peter needed.

"I found this in a tree trunk in part of the Marryman Forest I think you know rather well. I do, too. I *really* do, don't I, Greg?"

Gregory's face crumpled and he began to cry. Peter scowled. "Grow up. So what happened? What happened that you put a bit of paper through our door that says SORRY? What's been eating you up, Greg? And what does this…" he turned the bolt in Underbore's face, "…have to do with it? With us?"

"I…I'll tell you, but can we go somewhere else? I really don't want my mum…"

Peter froze. An awful, poisonous thought rolled across his mind like mustard gas. "Wait. Your mum wouldn't care about someone visiting on Christmas Eve, would she? After all, I'm just Peter. Except…You care that she'll see me. *Me*, Greg. Oh God, whatever happened…whatever you did, your mum knows, doesn't she? She knows, too. She knows and never said?"

Greg started blubbing again. "If anyone found out, I'd be arrested. They'd take me away. Dad left her, she couldn't deal with me going, too. She didn't want me to send that note, but I had to, I had to. I had to say sorry. I had to."

"She knew, she actually *knew*," Peter whispered in amazement then realised *he* didn't know, not really. "OK, Underbore, let's walk and talk. You've already been silent for three years, I can't afford your mum turning up and you clamming up again. So tell me exactly what happened, every detail, every second, and what happened next. Then *I'll* decide what happens next."

"Yes, yes, OK, yes." Gregory looked like he might vomit. "Yes. I'll tell you, Peter. I'll tell you."

Peter picked up his bike and they walked together toward Littel Wade as Greg gasped, cried and whimpered while Peter listened, ashen faced, eyes overflowing with tears. Eventually Underbore could say no more and Piper didn't want him to, so they parted without any further words.

*

On returning home, Peter discovered number nine was dark and dad's car was still absent from their drive. With the same conviction that Underbore had written the SORRY note, he now knew where his father was. Perhaps he'd always known.

So let's ride with Peter, past his silent birthplace, past Phoebe's bright and expectant house, past church, homes and shops of villagers who wondered where strange gifts had arrived from this morning, past the sign which read *Ad Meliora*, "*On toward better things,*" past trees, round darkened curves, past Kerstmann & Son's Yard with its, "*Curious, Puzzling, Old, Unwanted, Lovely & Hopeful Artefacts Passing Through,*" past watchful Roe and crying Tawny, to a lay-by near the A352.

51 / A LAY-BY NEAR LITTEL WADE, 24th DECEMBER 2022, 5:15 p.m.

As Peter had suspected and deep down always known, his dad's Vauxhall was sitting in the same lay-by he often visited himself. The lights were on, windows fogged, and exhaust fumes curled around the vehicle like dry ice. The only sound was its gently grumbling engine.

"Dad?" he tapped on the glass and saw the silhouette of his father inside. "Dad?"

After a few moments the window slid down and Anthony Piper looked out, face wet with tears. "Peter. How did you know I was…?"

"Because I come here too. But I think you knew that, didn't you?"

Tony nodded, then quickly moved something off his lap. But Peter saw it; a coiled yellow and green striped hosepipe, now curled at dad's feet like a snake.

"What are you doing with a hosepipe?" The question was rhetorical. Peter knew what the pipe was for, and recoiled from it.

"I didn't…" Tony cried. "I wouldn't. I've kept it in the boot for so long. I just…I had awful thoughts. So many times, I had terrible thoughts that I could make all this…" he gestured to a spot in the tree line, "…go away. But I couldn't. I wouldn't do it, because of you. You know that, don't you?"

"Oh dad. Oh, dad."

"I wouldn't have done anything, I swear. I just thought about it. I thought about it so much, but I'd never do anything. I love you."

"I love you, too."

"I keep coming here. I can't help myself. I don't want to, but it's like, it's like…" He stared up at the roof of his car as if there were any answers there "…it's like a magnet. A horrible, *horrible* magnet. I come here and sometimes get the hose out, but I'd never do anything. It's like when you look over a cliff edge and part of you wonders how it would feel to just… jump. So I come here and I wonder how it would feel to…Jump. But that's all." The words poured from dad in a torrent, held back for so long, now bursting through the dam he'd built himself. "I can't bear it, Peter. I can't. And neither can you, I know that. Sometimes I want to talk, but talking is too painful, isn't it?"

Peter nodded. "Yes. I know. I know how you feel. I feel it too, all the time."

Anthony wiped his face with both hands, pulling his skin downward like clay, re-moulding his mouth into a scowl.

This was all too much for Peter to take in. He felt as if he might hyperventilate, or start screaming. *One step at a time,* he thought, taking deep breaths, *deal with everything one step at a time or you will explode. Dad has sat here for the last three years with a* hosepipe *in his car? I can't take that in. I can't take any of this in. It's too much. First Underbore, now dad, let alone Christmas Eve.* Peter subconsciously put a fist to his mouth and bit down, unaware he was stifling a scream. *A fucking hosepipe, he actually has a hosepipe.*

"I wouldn't have done it," his father repeated, and Peter knew that was the truth. But the fact he'd even contemplated such an act would have to be addressed, and by therapists, not a sixteen year old. For now he changed the subject. There was no other choice, since that way lay madness.

"Dad, I saw your file. About the houses. About us moving."

Tony's shoulders began to shudder again. "I didn't want you to see that. I was only looking. I hate this place. I hate Littel Wade. I thought if we got out, got away…" He waved helplessly at the tree-line again, "… Then things might be better. But they'll never be better, will they? They'll never get better."

"Let's just go home," Peter reached into the car and squeezed his father's shoulder. "Let's go home. We have to talk. About what happened on Christmas Eve."

Tony looked up at his son, eyes wide. "We know what happened already." His gaze snapped back to the trees. "We already know *how*. But *you* don't know why, not really." His shoulders slumped, he wailed and banged the steering wheel. "It was my fault!"

How could it possibly be your fault? Peter wondered, but wasn't sure he wanted to know the answer.

"No, dad, no, it was nobody's fault."

Anthony Piper pointed accusingly at the tree-line, then at himself. "It was! It was my fault! She was only here because of me! Because of me, mum died! Only because of me!"

Peter stepped back from the car, and held up his hands to ward off his father's words. "No, no, it couldn't be. Dad? What are you *saying*?"

You see, Julie Piper was dead, and had been since Christmas Eve, 2019.

*

Remember what Mrs Kerstmann said; "Some truths can hide in plain sight if you don't look at them *just so*. Seemingly irrelevant facts become extremely important once you know their context, but unless you look, register, understand and retain they will *remain* irrelevant."

Let me help you look at Anthony and Peter's truth *just so*.

Julie Piper died on December the twenty-fourth, three years earlier.

Peter had copied mum's voicemails and kept her texts on his phone, and would occasionally read or listen to them if he had the strength, just to imagine her still there at the other end, somewhere, somehow.

You've seen those texts and heard her messages, but they were just digital back ups of moments long passed.

Each year on December mornings leading up to the anniversary of her death, Peter would sit in the kitchen remembering the last few days he'd seen her alive. You've been privy to those memories;

Julie pirouetting in her police uniform.

Shouting, "*I love you*!" through a loudhailer at her son.

Wrapping tinsel around her neck like a feather boa.

Blowing up balloons and making his sleeping dad crazy when one had exploded.

All times lost he replayed every December twentieth to twenty-fourth since 2019, when his world had ended.

The scenes you witnessed were the same ones Peter saw, but only within his memory.

Sometimes he would picture having conversations with mum as if she were still present, to imagine what her opinion might have been of certain situations. You were privy to one such make-believe chat on the night Peter and Phoebe delivered their gifts around Littel Wade.

Anthony Piper also hoarded souvenirs of Julie. When she was alive he'd mostly worked nights at the hotel, so would discover little communications she'd taped up for him to find when he returned home. Back then reading those notes made him laugh; now they broke his heart. But he never had the strength to take them down, so there they remained, slowly yellowing, curling, and getting further from her hand with every passing day. You read them as recent. He read them as relics.

Julie Piper was dead, and Peter thought he'd known what had happened to his mother. But then Gregory Underbore turned that thought on its head, and now his father had done it again.

*

It took a while for Tony to calm down enough to make the short drive back to Dawn Street. Father and son drove in silence, but each had so much to say.

52/ NUMBER NINE, DAWN STREET, 6:00 p.m.

At a house party further up the street, a booming yet muffled Chris De Burgh claimed Jesus was a spaceman whose message for humanity was simply, *"La, la la la la la la la la,"* repeated.

Peter and Anthony Piper seemed unaware of the noise. They sat in silence at the kitchen table just like so many times over the last three years. Tony sipped from a tumbler of whisky, while Peter stared out of the window at their dark and tiny box garden. He didn't want to either lead or force the conversation, and waited for dad to begin whenever he was ready.

What's going on? Peter thought again. *Dad had a hosepipe in his car? He actually sat in that hateful lay-by and wondered what it would be like to let his car fill with fumes and drift away? He actually* contemplated *that?*

Tony's eyes were fixed on the montage of family photos. As Chris De Burgh faded out, the tick and tock of the kitchen clock faded up.

Tick, mum & dad on their wedding day.

Tock, Peter as a baby.

Tick, Peter as a toddler.

Tock, Peter starting school.

Tick, a picture of Peter and his grandparents.

Tock, mum in her police uniform.

Dad's shoulders quivered again and he took a long gulp of whisky. "She loved that uniform," he whispered.

Peter followed his gaze to the frame. "I know."

"And she loved you in your school uniform, too," Tony tipped his tumbler at the photograph. "Must have had thing for uniforms," he coughed out a dry and bitter laugh. "Well, that's what I thought, anyway. Ah, fucking hell." Dad hung his head and took a sharp intake of breath, which made him judder. "I was so stupid."

"Dad, what are you talking about?" Peter gently asked but Tony changed the subject. "You know when we met? Me and mum?"

Peter nodded, but dad talked on anyway.

"That was when I worked at Dorchester South on the trains, you know, before I got that Front Of House job at the hotel? Mum was a passenger. I took her ticket…"

Then you took her number, Peter completed the phrase, which had become a Piper catchphrase over the years. *I know this, so what does it have to do with anything?*

Anthony still didn't look at his son. "Then I took her number. She wrote it on a ticket stub and you know what she said? 'I'm easily persuaded by a man in uniform.' In uniform! You should have seen mine. An awful South West Trains grey thing. But still, she said, 'I'm easily persuaded by a man in uniform' and so I got her number, I got her, and then we got you." He finally glanced over at Peter just for a moment. "That phrase never left me. 'I'm easily persuaded by a man in uniform.' And so when she started the police job…" He angrily swallowed another large whisky and topped up the glass. "Not at first, you know? I wasn't jealous at first, no. But I started fixating on things. How much overtime she was taking on. How many nights she worked. And most of all, how she'd always get a lift to work with the same officer. *Every time*. You clocked that, didn't you?"

Peter tried to keep his expression neutral, but moments and memories started to ping back into his mind; snarky comments from dad to mum when she'd left for work, sulks and shouting that were totally out of character, muttered asides, barbed comments. One scene leaped into his head; the morning of twenty-second December, 2019. You've already seen Peter's memory of this moment.

*

There'd been a *beep-beep-beep* of a car horn outside and dad had said… what? Peter squeezed details from the past. Dad had muttered…

"Must be nice getting a lift every day."

To which mum had replied, "What do you mean by that?"

"Just what I said. Must be nice having company. Talking about work, having a laugh."

She'd frowned. "It's just a lift, why are you being so shirty?"

"I'm not being shirty, I'm just saying you get a lot of lifts."

"What, do you want me to get the bus? Or shall I use Peter's bicycle?"

"You could drive yourself."

"Or I *could* take up the kind offer of a lift, which I do."

"Very kind offers," Tony had sneered. "Very *kind*."

*

What had seemed at the time like the little moments of stress every married couple have had now been revealed as far more seismic events.

As Tony had stomped upstairs Peter had asked mum if she still loved dad, to which she'd replied, “Of course I do. The stupid, moaning, paranoid bloody idiot. Of course I love him.”

So she knew he was jealous, he thought. *But how does that possibly make him responsible for what happened?*

Peter now recalled the last message he’d received from mum, on December twenty-fourth 2019. She’d texted to say how her shifts had been, well, shifted, so would be home for Christmas Day. Then she’d ended it with;

…And the other bad news was dad was in another foul mood. No idea why, so give him a wide berth today until you can judge the lie of the land. Needless to say I will NOT be buying (and exploding) festive balloons again! Love you, XXXXXXXXXXXX

The clues had been in plain sight all the time, but Peter hadn’t seen them, or perhaps he’d *chosen* to make facts invisible, subconsciously hoping ignorance wasn’t just bliss but also somehow a negation of truth.

“It’s OK, dad. Everyone gets a bit jealous once in a while. That doesn’t mean…”

Tony snarled and dismissed the thought with a wave. “I haven’t told you what I did, though, have I? I should have told you ages ago, but I’m a coward.” He took another deep, shuddering breath. “OK, OK. I was convinced she was sleeping with that officer, totally convinced. So I thought I’d get there first before she could confess. I wanted to make her feel how *I* felt, see? The best defence is offence and all that?” He took another drink, almost gagged, and some of the whisky ran down his chin.

“Dad, you're a bit drunk. Wouldn’t it be best to save this for when…”

“NOW!” He shouted. “No, now. Because if not now, not ever. That’s how it works, isn’t it? If you don’t say it or do it *now*, then you might never get a chance to say or do it again.” He stilled, then after a few moments began to quietly speak and as he did, Peter realised dad had rehearsed these words many times before in his mind.

“You’d gone to bed. It was one in the morning. Mum was on a split shift, so had come back to freshen up. I heard her police car pull up outside, so I sat at the table and waited. I’d been drinking, ready to have it out.”

Anthony Piper went back to Christmas Eve 2019 once again.

*

"You waited up!" Julie Piper walked into the kitchen, pulled off her stab vest and bowler hat then hung them up. She noted the empty bottle of wine on the sideboard next to her husband and the half-finished one in front of him. "Blimey, love, Christmas has started early. No wait, it *is* The Big Day. Happy Christmas, darling." She bent to kiss him but he didn't respond and she raised an eyebrow in surprise."Don't have too much, love, or you'll be knocked sick for the big day and that will *not* do."

She turned to fill the kettle. "Oh, you can say hello if you're not too plastered. That's kind-of traditional when someone, particularly your loving wife, enters a room."

"Loving wife," he sneered. Julie turned back slowly to face him. "Sorry? What was that?"

"*Loving wife*," he locked eyes with her and took a long, defiant drink of wine as if daring Julie to stop him.

"OK, so what's this about?" She looked simultaneously confused, afraid, and a little angry. "Or should we wait till morning when you're relatively sober and talk about it then?"

"You don't know?" He raised his voice. "You don't know?"

Julie made the flat palmed mime for *keep it down*. "Well, clearly I don't," she whispered. "And whatever's on your mind, either keep it for another day or at the very least try not to wake Peter up."

"Oooooo Kaaaaaay," he hissed, "is this better? Or perhaps Peter should know."

"Know what?" She hissed back, "Actually, *you* know what? I don't have to take this weirdness, not any time, especially not Christmas Day when I have another five hours of shift at least. So, enjoy your festive tipple and bitterness, or whatever this is, and I'll see you when you've calmed down."

*

"It was ridiculous," Tony shook his head. "It was pathetic. I was pathetic. You were asleep and we were down here whispering threats at each other so we didn't wake you up."

"My dream," said Peter, unaware he'd spoken out loud. *Oh God, that's part of my dream. Two reptiles in the kitchen, fighting each other.*

"Your what?"

"Nothing. What happened next? What happened, dad?"

Anthony quivered a little, either from rage or fear. Peter suspected the latter and waited for dad to reconnect.

Their argument got into my head and my sleeping mind...reinterpreted it. Mixed the sounds about, turned whispers into hisses, changed my parents into snakes. I still knew it was bad though. My subconscious realised it was a terrible thing, so always made it the worst part of my dream. So what was the rest of that dream about?

"I fucked up," Tony eventually whispered. "I fucked up so badly. I couldn't leave it. I was drunk, Peter, you have to know that. I would have never..."

"Dad, please. I have to know. What happened?"

Do I have to know though? Peter thought with dread. *What happened was bad enough. I couldn't cope with it being worse.*

"I lashed out," he sighed, and his eyes began to run again. "That was all it was. Lashing out." Anthony went to take another drink, then looked at the tumbler, surprised it was already empty. He poured another large measure, drank, and span back to 2019.

*

Shaking with rage and confusion, Julie Piper pulled the stab vest back on, grabbed her hat and hissed, "Finish your wine, pass out and hopefully you won't remember any of this so we can have a normal Christmas Day. But *I* won't forget and eventually we *will* be talking about whatever's going through your head right now."

Tony pulled a moue and raised his eyebrows in mock fear. "Oh, we're going to talk about it eventually, are we? Why not now? What are you running from?" He snapped his fingers at her. "No, wait, who are you running *to*? Going back to your friend? Got a gift for him?"

"What? What are you talking about, Tony?" She walked toward the kitchen door. "Actually, I don't care. See you in the morning."

Upstairs, Peter rolled in his bed and moaned. The whispers and hisses downstairs percolated into his dreams. This violent, sibilant soundtrack suggested vague images which his subconscious formed into fighting lizards.

Tony waved at his departing wife, then twisted the wave into a raised middle finger. Julie gasped at the gesture.

"Bye then, bye," he smirked. "But I've seen, you know. I've clocked it. The same policeman, most mornings. 'Ooh, my carriage awaits,' you giggle like a schoolgirl."

Julie took a couple of steps backward and raised a shocked hand to her forehead. "What are you saying?" she still managed to whisper.

"You like a uniform, oh, you love a uniform. So how much do you love *his* uniform, your *friend*, your *whoever-the-fuck-he-is*."

"Wait, what? Wait, you think…you actually think I…?"

"Long shifts, such long shifts," Tony waved his hands airily. "Always having to do an extra night here and there. 'No way round it darling, nobody to cover.' How stupid do you think I am? How blind do you think I am?"

Julie shook her head furiously. "Stop. Stop this now. I don't know how you've taken two plus two to make five million, but please stop. Why didn't you just ask me, talk to me?"

Anthony Piper laughed. "So you could deny it, just like you're doing now? But you know, two can play that game. I've had a couple of offers myself."

Julie's jaw dropped. "What did you say?"

"You heard. I've had offers to go for drinks and, you know. Got a few numbers in my phone. Might take them up. Might already have done. If it's good enough for you, it's good enough for me."

Anthony noted with satisfaction that his wife's confusion and fury had been overtaken by tears. "You haven't…" Julie managed.

He took another large gulp of wine and simply stared in reply.

"Oh, Christ," she looked around and tried to centre herself, as if the room had become totally unfamiliar, which in some ways, it had. "Tony. Please. Calm down. I swear…" Julie tried to take her husband's hand, but he pushed it away. "There's nothing. Nothing. It's all in your head."

"You would say that."

Julie Piper's hands grasped in the air, trying to hang onto something, anything, since her seemingly solid ground had just become sand.

"Listen. Please. Sergeant Mellor is married," she said through gritted teeth then aggressively held up her own wedding ring in front of Tony's wavering gaze. "Do you need it spelled out? He lives in Holnest, so I'm on his route to Dorchester. That's it. He picks me up because he's nice. That's it."

Anthony held up his own wedding ring. "So what? Bit of metal, so what? My customers see this on my finger and they still come on to me."

"Oh, there's no fucking point, whatever this is, you're wrong," Julie's eyes were both blazing and streaming. "His personal life's none of your business, but Sergeant Mellor…OK, Phil, yes, he has a name, *Phil's* been married to Jake for five years now. Jake. Get it? Jake. Go on Facebook, take a look, Phillip Mellor and Jake Tibbs, in Holnest. So even if I was interested, which I'm not, he wouldn't be."

Silence filled the room as Tony's drink-compromised mind tried to take in what his wife had said.

"He's gay, if you need it any easier, which you clearly do."

Anthony stared ahead blankly, all fury gone. "I didn't…I didn't… know…"

"No, you didn't, did you? Because you never asked. You just built up this…shit…in your mind, then got drunk enough to throw *that* shit in my face. But tell me, since you mention it, did you do anything with your rides?"

"I was just…" He angrily pushed the wine glass away as if that were the guilty party. "No, I was just trying to…"

Julie looked down at her husband, piteously. "Just trying to what?"

"Please," he stood, wavered, tried to grab the table, missed, staggered backward into the wall and crumpled to the floor. "Please, I was just…"

She rushed down the hallway toward her police car. Anthony struggled to his feet then clattered after her.

"Please, Julie!" He shouted, the first time either of them had raised their voices.

"No," she screamed back, all attempts to stay quiet forgotten. "No, no."

This exchange took place below Peter's window and his dreaming mind aurally morphed it into a roaring which literally shook the glass. As Julie climbed into her vehicle sobbing, Peter's dream remixed the sound into something unknown, shifting from human to a rumble, a growl, and finally a bird screeching into the distance.

"Fuck off, Tony," she howled. "I'll be back in the morning. We'll talk after Christmas."

Except she wasn't, and they never did.

*

The last sounds Anthony Piper heard from his wife were crying, then the acceleration of her car into oblivion.

53/ NUMBER NINE, DAWN STREET, DECEMBER 24th, 2022. 6:25 p.m.

Up the road, Paul McCartney was *Simply Having A Wonderful Christmastime.* Occasional whoops and laughter also floated down the street. In Peter's kitchen the sound was as meaningless as a tumble drier. Anthony sat face down to the table, head in hands, fringe hanging like a barrier. Peter looked at the glass of whisky. *I could just knock that back, grab the bottle and keep going,* he thought. *But you can't drown sorrows. They should have built the Titanic from sorrows. They're unsinkable.*

He tried to take dad's hand, but Tony kept it fixed to his forehead. He'd talked himself dry, his throat and eyes were arid. "They were her last moments with me and I pushed her away because I was jealous of something that didn't exist."

"Dad…"

"She drove off crying. That's my final memory of her. I can't stand it. The last time I saw her…beautiful…face, she was crying and looking at me like…she didn't know me any more."

"Dad, please. You made a mistake. But that's all it was. You were jealous…"

Peter knew he was talking his father down from the ledge but had nobody to do the same for him. "…People get jealous all the time. But you didn't do it. You did not kill mum. Things happen. People fall out…"

Tony raised his face to Peter's. "Yes, and they make up. They get a chance to put it right, to explain. But mum died thinking I'd…thinking I'd…And you know what? Part of me thinks she may have done it on purpose. Just, you know, a stupid impulse, she just thought, 'Ah fuck it,' turned the wheel and…"

"No dad, no. Please don't think that."

I do not want to ask the next question, Peter thought. *Because it's one of the most awful questions I will ever ask, and if the answer is* yes, *then I don't know what I will do. I can't take any more tonight, and if dad says* yes, *then I might just fold myself away and never come back. This is too much, too much, too much.*

But he asked, of course.

"Dad, was there anyone else? Any other women you met in the cab? Did you…did you ever…?"

Tony shook his head so hard his hair flew out in all directions like a wet dog shaking after the rain. "No! No, I swear, Peter, on your life, on mum's life…" His face crumbled again. "I never did a thing. No women ever came on to me, and if they had, nothing would have happened. I lied. I just wanted to see her reaction, see if it forced mum to admit what she was up to. But that was all in my head. It was spiteful. And she drove off, thinking…" Anthony put his head back into his hands again. "Thinking I'd cheated on her. I never did, and I never would. I love her, Peter, I love her and because of that, I was jealous." He closed his eyes. "How stupid. Because I loved her, I was jealous. How does *that* work? So you see, she wasn't concentrating. She was all over the place, and those roads, those fucking roads, they punish mistakes. Except the mistake was mine, and now I'm punished every day. Like I deserve."

Peter stood, went over to his coat and reached into the pocket."Dad. You made a mistake, but you are not responsible. You have to believe me."

"I am."

"No, you are not. Mum could have been on that road without you saying any of that and it still could have happened." He held up Gregory Underbore's bolt. Tony stared at the object, totally puzzled.

"What's that?"

Peter felt his eyes tear up again. "A crossbow bolt. That's why mum died." He offered it to his father who recoiled, even though he had no idea of its provenance.

"There was a note on our mat when I got home earlier." Peter retrieved the folded sheet from his trouser pocket and handed it over. Tony read the single word. "*Sorry*? But who…?"

"It was in an envelope addressed to THE PIPERS, written in capitals."

Anthony's gaze jumped between bolt and paper. He'd been adrift before, but was now totally lost.

"I recognised the handwriting from an advert card. It's Gregory Underbore's."

"Gregory Underbore? But why does it say sorry? And why…?" Dad gestured to the quarrel.

"So I went to his place, showed him the note and this bolt. I was right. They're both his. Greg told me what happened that night, and why he's sorry."

"But I…"

"Dad, this isn't easy, but you have to hear. Because it will help. Only by the tiniest amount, but it will help."

Tony nodded, but looked scared.

Through the confession of Gregory Underbore, Peter jumped back to early Christmas morning 2019, specifically to a hateful bend in a road bordering Marryman Forest. We were here together at the start of this story, so let us visit again, but from a different angle. Come with me, and we'll let the light of the Cold Moon show us what else happened that night.

*

It was exactly 1:36 A.M. Gregory Underbore knew this from the faint glow of his glow-in-the-dark military watch. Dressed in camouflage gear, he crept between birch trees and gorse. The frozen ground was full of traps for an unwary hunter; the cracks and snaps of fallen branches, frosted leaves and icy puddles were loud enough in daytime, but at two a.m. even Greg's shallow breathing was a cacophony.

He held a crossbow at his side

Not only was he too young to own it, but the weapon had been converted to a lethal draw weight. These two facts weren't Gregory's only transgressions tonight. Hunting is forbidden in Britain except on private land with the owner's permission, which he obviously didn't have.

There was a distant shuffling as *something* picked its way through the undergrowth, illuminated by a shimmering December Cold Moon.

Greg's eyes widened as he realised with joy the grey patch was a female Roe deer. She daintily nipped at leaves and occasionally raised her head to check the surroundings. Gregory had never killed a deer since they are protected by law. His heart quickened with the prospect of such an illicit thrill.

Greg raised his crossbow and aimed for a head shot which would ensure a quick, merciful death. After that, he'd take a photo; the only trophy possible. It was freezing cold, easily minus eight or more. The roads were thick with black ice and the forest braced itself for snow, so a shaky hand would be disastrous.

Underbore focused on three elements; sight, trigger and the doe's head. Everything stopped.

At that moment, a tawny owl called out; *K-wick.*

The deer looked up, span, and rushed away. Greg fired but the bolt missed by a heartbeat and he heard it slam into a tree.

At that moment, light scattered through branches and bushes as a vehicle took a sharp bend just past the tree-line. Headlights splashed across Greg's face and he instinctively raised a hand to shield both his night-adapted eyes and guilty features. Then he saw the panicked Roe run, jump and zig zag into the path of a car.

Whoever was at the wheel also behaved instinctively and desperately turned from the deer, but the road's tight curves were unforgiving in warm daylight, let alone coated in black ice on a bitter December night. Like the Roe, the vehicle also zig-zagged, but unlike the animal it couldn't slip between tree trunks and foliage.

It slammed headlong into a group of trees then buckled against a thick oak whose sturdy branches smashed through the windscreen and grasped into the car itself.

Gregory froze, unable to comprehend the horror which had just unfolded in less than three seconds.

From screech of tyres to dull *crump* of impact, tearing of metal and splitting of glass, all that now remained of the cacophony was a dumb grinding of terminally injured machinery under the car's bonnet.

Underbore stepped forward, since the ingrained need to help another human took precedence over self preservation. But then two realisations stopped him and he snapped his hands out as if to ward off danger.

First, he saw the dying vehicle was a *police car*. Its engine coughed before settling into weak throbbing. Then Gregory registered the driver. At first he couldn't see if they were male or female, since their head was tipped forward.The airbag had deployed but now hung pitifully from the steering wheel, having failed in its one purpose. A thick branch had smashed through the windscreen and thrust into the driver's upper torso.

As Greg took a few steps nearer he saw with horror the driver was Peter Piper's mother.

She tried and failed to raise her head from the wheel, then he heard air rasp and grate from deep in her throat.

Julie Piper's face was…*crumpled*…on one side, as if dented.

Her left eye turned in Gregory's direction, focussed, lost depth, re-focussed.

"H…" she exhaled. "H…H…Help me." Her speech was gossamer as a gentle wind; intimations of words. Blood bubbled about her lips.

"Help…" Julie managed again, and Underbore could hear even that one syllable was unbearably painful.

Help her, help her, take out your phone and call for help, part of his mind screamed.

You did this, another part said. *You did this and you will pay. You will pay.*

Then another, terrible thought rose.

Nobody knows you are here. Nobody.

Julie's left eye swivelled and shimmied in its socket.

She's dead. She's already dead and it was an accident, it was just an accident and you can't help her now. Go. Just go.

Distantly Gregory realised he'd wet himself.

Julie Piper's breathing slowed yet further. She fixed him with one last pleading gaze; *Help me. Please help me. Please. Please.*

"I'll get help," Underbore lied, then vomited down himself.

The engine gave one last rasp, Julie hacked one last gasp then silence returned to the forest, implacable in its judgement. Gregory spun and crashed through the woods but couldn't stop fearfully glancing behind him, unable to believe what he'd seen, what he'd done, unable to tell anyone, unable to breathe.

54/ PETER'S HOUSE, CHRISTMAS MORNING, *2019*. 6:30 a.m.

Woken by knocking, Anthony Piper stirred from a drunk's toxic sleep. Somewhere inside his still intoxicated mind he thought, *My head. Jesus, my head.*

A squeal of pain shot through him then his second, worse, thought was, *Earlier. Oh no, I said those things. I actually said them out loud to Julie. Oh no.*

He recalled flashes of their exchange, but not details.

He'd told her of his suspicions (*My certainties*, his mind accused).

He remembered tears. His, or hers?

There was anger, oh yes, lots of anger on both sides. Righteous on his part, confused on hers.

Then he'd...*Oh God, I told her there'd been other women.* Anthony moaned a little. The almost apologetic knock sounded again. *I told her that. Why did I say it?* And she said...He moaned again, louder. *The guy's gay. That officer is gay. And I knew she was telling the truth. I just knew. She'd left only a few minutes after arriving.* He pictured her face as she'd climbed into her vehicle. Julie had looked furious, but also, so, so sad.

I'm in trouble.

Another knock.

He opened the curtains, saw a police car in the road. It was empty, which suggested Julie had driven herself rather than getting a lift, and that meant...*She's back, and she's come in* that, *which means she's not staying. She's here to have it out with me, then drive back to work. Julie has no intention of spending any time with me today. Christmas day. Oh shit, shitshitshit.*

Anthony shut his eyes, tried to centre himself then made his way downstairs, preparing for what would surely be the worst few minutes of his marriage.

He had no idea.

As he descended, Tony Piper was in the last seconds of his old life. He didn't know that, of course.

We all have before and after moments we can pin down in retrospect, pivots on which things turn for good or bad, airlocks between what *was* and what will now *always be*.

Once he opened the door there would be no going back. Eventually Tony came to believe if he could have stayed halfway down those stairs forever, convinced the worst thing about to happen was a furious row, then he would have, frozen in liminal bliss.

Time doesn't work like that.

Anthony took a deep breath, formed what he hoped was the most contrite expression he'd ever pull, and opened the door.

Julie Piper *should* have been stood there with an expression so blank as to be terrifying. That was what Anthony expected. Instead, he opened the door onto a new and unacceptable reality; two policemen.

That was confusing, and for a moment Tony thought, *What, she's sent her mates to come and get her things? To pass on a message? This is worse than I thought if she can't even face me.* But deep down another part of his mind panicked and gasped, *Nonononono, there's only one reason* two *policemen turn up on your doorstep wearing expressions like that, Julie's done this for other people, she's told me all about it, how this is the worst job in the whole of the force.*

He grabbed the doorframe, suddenly dizzier and more nauseous than any hangover had or would ever make him.

"Mr Piper…" one began.

"No." Tony managed. "No. It's not…You can't…"

"May we come in?"

It's Christmas morning, he thought, wildly. *This can't be happening on Christmas morning. It's not allowed. It's not allowed. It's not allowed.*

"No, you can't."

One of the officers glanced at the other and Tony realised with horror they had tears in their eyes. He vehemently shook his head. "No, you can't come in. Whatever it is, it can wait. It's Christmas. Julie's back soon and we have to get everything ready."

"Mr Piper. I'm sorry. We're sorry, we're so sorry." A pause followed that felt eternal."Julie's dead."

And there it was. Two words that can never be taken back, negotiated with or changed.

Anthony's knees buckled so the officers gently lowered him to the hallway floor. "She's coming back," he wailed. "It's Christmas and she's coming back. Julie's coming back. Julie's coming back for Christmas."

The officers' barely controlled composure also cracked and they too began to sob. Nobody saw Peter at the top of the stairs, looking down on a scene which made no sense in his logical mind, but complete sense in his emotional one. "Dad?" he managed. "Dad, what's happened?"

But Peter knew and he too collapsed against the wall. Silently he watched as his father grasped at the officers, silently tears began to tumble down his face, silently he hung his head and knew this moment would always be waiting to play out again every time he shut his eyes.

*

The death of any loved one is inevitable but always unbearable. Whatever their age, however expected or unexpected it may be, their passing rends reality in two. But the end of one you love at Christmas is particularly cruel. Since the festive season begins so early, its symbols lose their joyful meanings and simply become markers of bereavement, signposts the worst time on earth is coming around again and there's *nothing you can do to stop it.*

Every shop plays the same songs on repeat. Office parties spill into the streets, virtually all TV shows are reminders that *'tis the season to be jolly* when in fact it's a hateful time and why can't other people realise their enjoyment only twists the knife of your loss ever deeper?

And with a sudden death you are thrown into Post Traumatic Stress Disorder in seconds. Nothing makes sense. You stare at the kettle as if it is an alien artefact. Speech happens, but it sounds like somebody else has decided the order of words and you are merely repeating them. The world continues, but not one you recognise, or even wish to know. It is simply somewhere you move through, amazed that nobody else on this planet has realised it has ended. Mornings are intolerable, bedtimes insufferable. Eating fulfils a biological need and nothing more. Dressing, shopping, washing, talking, watching, hearing, speaking…they are all equally meaningless, performed rather than experienced. And a sudden death at Christmas is worst of all, since you can never ignore December twenty-fifth, wipe it from the calendar, close the curtains and go to bed until the date has passed.

Christmas is a jolly marching band parading through your life every day for two months of the year. It follows wherever you go and everyone else smiles and laughs as it passes. You try to shake off that marching band, but it always knows where you are and where you will be.

Like Jona Lewie sang, you cannot stop the cavalry.

Julie's crumpled car had been spotted by a motorist around five that morning. On any day except Christmas she would have been found earlier, not that it made a difference. Julie had died on the spot and initial thoughts were that Officer Piper had lost control on black ice. RTA officers knew that nine out of ten drivers in such crashes walked away. She'd been unlucky; a perfect storm of speed, road condition and natural obstructions conspired to end her life in moments. Tony never told the police about their argument that morning. He tried not to confront it himself, let alone welcome others into the likelihood Julie had been out of control of her emotions rather than her vehicle. So that knowledge had sat inside him, cancerous, destructive, and manifesting itself physically as a hosepipe coiled with eternal possibilities.

*

Presents sat under the tree for a few more days as father and son sleepwalked through the dreadful protocols of shutting the door on Julie's life. Eventually and with no prior agreement, they removed the wrapped boxes and hid them under the stairs. The tree was silently dismantled, decorations removed and returned to their dark lonely loft.

One day in April 2020, locked down like the rest of the planet, Peter and Tony finally unwrapped the gifts with no ceremony, anticipation or enjoyment whatsoever. Lockdown suited the remaining Pipers just fine, as that had been their natural condition since December twenty-fifth. The silence, sadness and confusion in the world outside matched the very same states of being inside number nine.

Only one box remained unopened.

Julie had pointed it out to Peter a few days before Christmas; a small gift wrapped in silver paper. "I'm pleased with that one," she'd said to her son, who'd rattled the box by his ear. "Ooh, no, no noisy clues or spoilers from that. I had it done specially for you. And for dad, yes, but mainly you." She'd balanced it in the middle of the tree, where Christmas lights caught and sparkled against the silver. Julie had smiled, proudly. "Save that one for very last. I want to see your face when you open it."

But on that locked-down April day, Peter took mum's special gift from the tree and placed it behind clothes in his wardrobe. He was scared to tear off the wrapping in case she'd simply exaggerated the contents. He wanted to keep the idea of a meaningful mystery present intact rather than reveal a bland reality, so since then it had hidden in darkness.

He'd occasionally taken out the box and wondered about its contents, but fear of disappointment always prevented him taking the irrevocable step of ripping it open. So back behind the clothing it went, to occasionally catch both the light and his attention.

And there it stayed.

55/ PETER'S HOUSE, 24th DECEMBER 2022, 6:50 p.m.

The street's festive music had mercifully stopped for now.

"She was…alive?" Tony whispered.

"Greg said so."

"Oh God, oh God, she was still alive?" From disbelief, Anthony's expression hardened. "And he didn't call for help? He *ran away*? He fucking *ran away*?"

Peter nodded.

Dad slapped the table in rage and the glasses shook in agreement. He stood and ground his jaw. "I'm going to kill him. I'm going to kill him."

Peter gently took his father's hand. "I know. I want to kill him, too. When he told me, I was this close to punching his face, then hitting, and hitting and *hitting* until there was nothing left."

Anthony literally quivered with rage. "I'm going there to his shitty house and I'm doing that. Then I'm fucking dragging his scum mother to the police. Let's both do it. He fucking killed mum. I want to kill him, kill him, *kill him.*"

"No," Peter said quietly.

Dad looked down at his son incredulously. "Why? Why not?"

"Because that wasn't what mum would have wanted. She believed in the law. We'll let the law deal with the Underbores because that's what mum would have done. If we do something stupid she would be *so* disappointed."

Tony's shoulder's slumped as he saw the truth of his son's argument.

"The police, dad. That's what she *was*. That's what she *did*. If we mess up, we let her down."

Dad sat back down heavily and gestured at Greg Underbore's crossbow bolt squatting between them like a cursed object."A deer?" He whispered. "A fucking deer ran out, because of this? And so mum swerved, and…" He started to sob again.

"Yes, that's what happened. It was an accident, a million to one chance Greg fired at the moment she came round the corner. If he hadn't put the SORRY note through, I wouldn't have found out. It's eaten him up."

"Oh, *poor Greg*." Tony's expression hardened then collapsed again. "But she wouldn't have been there unless…"

"Yes, you had an argument, but in the end what took mum was a stupid, stupid, accident."

"A deer. And it got away?"

"Greg says so."

Tony nodded, satisfied. "I'm glad something got away." Peter studied his dad's face for any trace of sarcasm and found none. Anthony looked down at his empty tumbler then across at the equally empty whisky bottle. "This is all too much. I've lived with one version of what happened and now I have to…" He looked up to the ceiling and searched for the right words.

"Recalibrate it?" Peter offered.

"Yes. That's a nicely emotionless word. Recalibrate. I like that. It takes out the heartbreak, makes things more mechanical. Yes, we must… recalibrate everything."

"But at least we have something solid to work with. Something to understand."

"Mm." Anthony stood. "The Underbores will pay, though."

"Yes. They will."

"I'm sorry, Peter, but I really need just a few more drops of the hard stuff tonight, and we seem to be out. I'll go to the Co-op. Want anything?"

"Just you."

Finally, Tony smiled. "That you'll always have. Ah, so much to take in, isn't there?"

"We'll never take it in will we?"

"No, but I don't want to, not really. I think if the rawness disappears that would feel like a betrayal." He squeezed his son's shoulder, then thought better and gave Peter a tight, never-let-you-go hug. "I'll just get changed, nip out, come straight back. OK?"

"OK."

As Dad left the room, Peter picked up the bolt, turned it over in his hand then looked out into their dark, tiny garden.

No, you're looking in the wrong place, a voice whispered in his head. And that was peculiar, because it wasn't his own.

Not outside, look in here.

The words were simultaneously next to him and yet far apart, away, elsewhere. He turned and considered his kitchen. There was nothing different about it.

It's just my mind, he thought. *It's had a lot to deal with over the last few days, huh, over the last few hours. My head's having a bit of a judder.*

Despite that, his gaze slid round the kitchen trying to work out what he'd missed.

No, no, the voice faded in again.

There.

The second sleigh book lay on the sideboard where he'd left it a lifetime ago. Peter idly began to leaf through.

Thank you, Phoebe Clarke, he smiled. *You made this Christmas almost bearable for the first time in three years. Whether this is just an order book or something magic is irrelevant. It worked on me, took me somewhere else for a few days.*

Then Peter realised everything had suddenly become silent, like God had pushed a MUTE button on the planet.

There was no noise from the party down the road, not even a background rumble of conversation. He looked at the normally ticking and tocking kitchen clock, but even though its hands moved they made no sound. Puzzled, Peter clicked his fingers and that produced no audible response either.

Have I gone deaf? He wondered.

No, your ears are fine, concentrate, waved that voice at the edge of his perception. He continued to turn the pages, then reached Phoebe's entry in eyeliner;

PHOEBE CLARKE MY DAD

Dad was upstairs but accompanied by no creaking of floorboards nor rushing of water. As far as Peter knew, he was alone in a perfectly stilled universe. He traced Phoebe's words.

What did she say? He thought back to a few short hours earlier when the world seemed only fractionally saner. *She took the book, and said,* "Ah, sod it, in for a penny, in for a pound."

Then I asked her what she meant, and she replied...

"I wonder what would happen if I totally accept these are Santa's gift orders?"

So she reached into her pockets, found an eyeliner and I asked...

"What are you doing?"

And she said...

"Same as always; thinking magically."

Thinking magically.

Peter fetched a pen and sat down before the book. *Phoebe writes MY DAD in here and the next thing you know, he's coming back from Karachi. So as she said, in for a penny...*

He held his biro over the page. *This makes no sense. But then again, neither does a suddenly tickless clock that has ticked my whole life. Neither does a sleigh that somehow has reversed its own ageing process. Neither do books of names going back hundreds of years, nor pointless accidents on dark roads caused by infinitesimal chances. Order is not the universe's natural state. Perhaps there is a place between science and magic, theology and physics.* He gazed around his infinitely silent kitchen one more time. *And perhaps right this second I am in that place. And I may never come here again.*

With no further thought, he wrote his name, PETER PIPER, and next to that, just two words. Then as he shut the book and looked into his garden, sound returned. The kitchen clock faded up; *tick-Tick-TICK* and from down the road, St Nicholas' bell tolled seven.

56/ PETER'S HOUSE, DECMBER 24th 2022, 7:00 p.m.

It started with tiny white full stops against a black page. Peter registered their movement first as they swirled and danced, twirled and fell, rapidly grew in size.

Ah, hello, snow. Peter smiled. *It's finally snowing.* The bells of St Nicholas' continued to chime. *And it's seven o'clock, of* course *it is.*

The flakes became thumb-tack sized, then, as if time had lost a few seconds, leaped to the width of a ten pence piece. Peter watched in wonder as more jostled to ground. In the distancc an *oooOOOOH!* grew steadily louder as sound returned to the nearby party, then laughter tinkled out front as people rushed into the street.

The snowflakes bloomed again to fifty-pence sized and already Peter's brown and patchy lawn was coated with a thin layer of white that grew thicker with each passing second.

In years past when this world still had his mother in it, Peter would have joined those revellers spinning in the fall, but something kept him in his seat.

Do not look away, his mind commanded. *Do not blink, do not be distracted. The snow is just prelude.* Peter didn't know where these thoughts came from, but knew they were true.

Scatter
Flitter
Flutter
Fall.

It was now a benign blizzard out there, more whiteness than darkness, churning and turning. Peter laughed out loud and felt his eyes prick with happy tears, the first for a very long time. He reached up, touched salt water on his face and laughed again. "Hello, snow," he waved at the flakes. "Oh, it's good to see you. It's *so* good to see you." Peter knew Phoebe was doing the same, laughing and probably pulling on a hat and coat ready to come and knock at number nine.

But something will hold you back, won't it, Phoebe? He knew. *You'll dither for a little while, just enough time for…for what?*

Within the rolling flakes something started to form by the back fence where darkness still held sway. An area of…no, not solidity, but certainly greater density. It was like seeing a shape emerge from deep water.

"Dad?" Peter tried to call, but his throat was suddenly dry. "Dad?"

"Mmm-mm?" came from upstairs.

"You need to come. You need to come quickly."

"What?"

Peter tried to raise his voice. "You need to come *so* quickly, dad."

Inside that blizzard the shape formed into snowy patterns; cylinders, a sphere, curves, lines.

My dream, my God, my dream. Peter put his hands to his mouth. *It's seven p.m. and there are houses made of snowflakes, rolling and falling. Littel Wade is full of people laughing in the street. And there was a doorway, no, a person. A snow person.* This *snow person.*

The form continued to grow and gain clarity. It now resembled an animated pencil drawing on paper which crumpled and folded by itself. But those tumbling dots of snow were blurred and difficult to follow.

As Anthony Piper entered the kitchen, Peter pointed out of the window.

"What is it? What…?" Dad followed his son's finger and stared. "What is t*hat*?"

Optical illusion, guided intelligence or hysteria, Peter didn't know. But whatever-it-was, it was *happening*.

The shape became a figure that bent and warped as the snow flittered and lost cohesion. More detail emerged from the whirling; a face, blank as a showroom mannequin at first, then drawn with two glinting, playful eyes, a nose, a mouth. This person wore a domed hat; specks of snow arranged themselves against the dark to create a black and white patterned band around its rim. Hair appeared, curling in constant movement like the locks of a mermaid under water. There was no colour, only shades created by more or less flakes in any specific area.

"Oh my God," Anthony croaked. "Can you see that? Am I seeing things?"

"If you are, I am," Peter whispered in reply.

Bright buttons grew and fizzed along the front of a well cut jacket. A skirt was drawn by a torrent of flakes all jostling for position.

The snow person began to move.

Peter had once made a flicker book animation and this looked just like that, jerking and jumping between frames.This figure's left arm shuddered, raised to the head and gave a formal salute.

And there…

Like static on a badly tuned TV screen, Julie Piper's face appeared. It rolled and glitched, but she winked and smiled. Then as her snowy lips formed three little words, the snow could hold its structure no more. The figure, if indeed there had ever been one, became blizzard once more.

Peter remembered to breathe.

"I saw…" Dad gasped. "I saw…did you see? Did you *see*?"

"Yes."

"But it can't…It can't have been."

"No it can't. Because that would be impossible."

Anthony Piper sat down heavily next to his son. "Did you see what it… what *she* said?"

Peter nodded and felt those happy tears begin to fall again. "I saw."

"Oh God."

"Maybe. Or maybe not God, maybe something else. Who knows. Perhaps just love?"

"Yes. Love. That's it."

Outside, Slade loudly wished everybody a Merry Christmas.

For the first December twenty-fourth in three years, Anthony and Peter Piper slept dreamlessly.

57/ PETER'S HOUSE, CHRISTMAS DAY 2022

Peter woke to find snowfall had continued overnight and still lazily fell this morning. The view from his window was like a Littel Wade cake so thickly iced it was now surely more sugar than sponge. For many, snow on December twenty-fifth is the best gift possible, but unlike other wished-for presents, it's never guaranteed. He glanced down at the spot in his garden where the blizzard had formed odd shapes last night (*Odd shapes!* His mind gasped, accusingly, *Odd shapes, you call them! You know exactly what, no, who it was*) but of course, no trace remained of whatever may or may not have stood there. Already the images of those strange, wonderful moments had started to white-out in Peter's memory, wheel and spin like snow itself.

But I saw her, he thought. *I know I did, and dad saw her too. She was there. I don't care about rational explanations. Sometimes only magical ones will do. I wrote MY MUM in the sleigh book and she was there. Only for seconds, and how much effort must it must have taken to come from wherever she is now to here, but mum came back to us. The books* create *your wishes. That's what I believe, and I don't care who thinks otherwise.*

Christmas Day at Number Nine Dawn Street would never again be a truly happy occasion but in 2022 it would have a serenity, at least.

Today, traditions which had been pushed aside tentatively made their way back into the Piper home. Neither father nor son decided this should be so, they just happened.

Peter discovered a present at the foot of his bed, what mum had always called the *amuse bouche* gift. The last time one had appeared was in 2018, when Peter found a hand-knitted, snow patterned scarf with no idea it marked the end of an era. Things often only assume their importance in retrospect. Today's return of the *amuse bouche* gift was a collection of Ray Bradbury short stories with a tag which simply read, LOVE DAD X.

In turn, Anthony Piper found his son in the kitchen preparing scrambled eggs for breakfast. In days far gone, this tradition would have been accompanied by smoked salmon, but for obvious reasons none had been purchased, so Peter made do with a tin from the back of a cupboard. The radio was on (another unusual occurrence but par for the course on Christmases gone by) and Cliff Richard joyously proclaimed this was the Saviour's Day.

Tony gave Peter a hug. "I really missed salmon and eggs on Christmas morning."

"Me too. It seems OK to have them, though, doesn't it?"

Dad knew what his son was trying to say and gave him another squeeze. "Yes, of course it's OK. I think we're allowed." And Peter knew what dad meant by that, too.

Presents were opened at eleven; always were, always would be. Mum had instigated the tradition before Peter was born and her logic was, "Open them at breakfast and there's nothing to look forward to. Open them after Supper and it's too late. Eleven is just right." And so it was.

As you know, no gifts were opened in 2019. There were just a handful in 2020, but filled with guilt and sadness. 2021 welcomed a few more, yet their presence didn't seem right, either. Today, however, Peter and Tony felt that somehow they had permission to enjoy the simple acts of giving and receiving.

But there was one present that stayed hidden in Peter's wardrobe; a silver box mum had been proud of and eager for him to unwrap.

Yes, I'll open it today. The thought wasn't entirely surprising. *But not with all the rest of these. It deserves more ceremony. Mum's special gift should be opened all by itself, not here, not now, with the socks, books, gift cards and shirts.*

Dad and son spent the next couple of hours cutting, chopping, boiling and stuffing like millions of others across Britain; many with loved ones, many alone, some welcoming new additions, some mourning much missed faces.

Their huge turkey dominated the oven but that was traditional, too. "Since turkey is really only eaten once a year," mum had decreed, "Surely *once* counts for as many times as you can possibly manage." So the bird would be re-purposed over the coming days into stews, sandwiches, curries, and eventually, bones to be picked over. On this day, however, it was roasted, as was right and proper.

Michael Bublé soundtracked their meal, the first time he'd been played in the house for three years. Bublé was always mum's chosen musical accompaniment for Christmas dinner, his crooning as much of the meal as cranberry sauce. Again, neither Peter nor Tony consciously decided this was the time to welcome Michael back to the table; he was simply just present again.

The upsetting, confusing and strangely joyous events of the last twenty-four hours had been conspicuously absent from discussion. There was much to say but no idea where to start, so instead Peter avoided the past and instead focussed on the future.

"Dad. How far did you get with thinking about us moving?"

Tony's hand faltered for a moment over a roast potato before spearing it. "Just thinking," he answered without looking at his son. "No more than that. Making enquiries, sounding it out, getting prices. Just thinking," he repeated.

"I don't think I'd like to leave here just yet," Peter said, quietly.

"I wouldn't have just shut up shop without asking you. But I couldn't stand walking around this place. I still can't really. It's…unforgiving. Every corner hurts. She's everywhere."

"But isn't that the point, dad? She *is* everywhere.I find that comforting. Every time I sit in this kitchen, I remember her. It feels like mum's just in the other room, or even…" He fixed his father with a pointed gaze, "… just watching, smiling in the garden."

Tony looked at the snow which flickered and fell out there. He smiled for a moment and Peter knew why.

"I'm just saying let's not rush into moving because the memories are painful right now. Because if we do, we'll never get this place back and mum won't be anywhere in a new house except in our minds. I look at the sink and she's there. I come down the stairs and she's waiting at the bottom. She's in the walls here, dad. And she wouldn't be if we moved somewhere else."

Tony nodded. "I'll think about it, as I said. But give me time, OK? It's still so raw."

"It always will be."

Soon enough, the once heaving plates were empty. As Anthony cleared away, Peter went upstairs to his wardrobe and picked up the small silver box mum had once carefully placed in the centre of their Christmas tree.

He still felt a little scared. *If this is nothing, and I've built it up to be something, I don't know what I'll do*, he thought. *I've invested so much thought in this gift. What if mum didn't? What if...*Peter stopped himself. *Yes, what if. And what if books of names are magic? What if a blizzard can become a body? What if wishes can become gifts because two people believed they should? And what if this...*He scratched at the wrapping like he'd done so many times before. *What if* this *is part of all* that*?*

*

"I had no idea." Dad looked down at the wrapped gift on the table between them. "I don't even remember this one," he shook his head. "But why would I? I've tried to block out that entire time. Some things I've forgotten more successfully than others, it appears. Like this." Tony finally picked up the gift and rattled it.

"No point,"said Peter. "It's silent."

"So it is. Why didn't you just open it before?"

"It didn't feel like the right time."

"And now it does." Not a question; a statement. Peter nodded. "…And dad, I wanted to keep possibilities open. If you don't know what's in a box, then *anything* can be inside, right?"

"Why not? Schrödinger's Gift," dad smiled. "And you say she was proud? Excited to see you open it?"

"I'm pretty sure I haven't created false memories, no. She was…You know how she used to get a bit giddy?"

Anthony laughed a little. "Giddy, yeah. I do." He sat up straight as if there were important business to do, which of course there was. "So go on, then. Let's see mum's last…" His voice caught but he managed to push through the heartbreak. "Let's see mum's last present."

Peter reached forward. There was no point dragging it out any more.

As Phoebe said, now is now, he thought. *Those three words make more sense with every passing moment.*

Peter ripped off the silver wrapping, aware he was irreversibly destroying folds his mother had fashioned with love three years before. But that's the paradox of a Christmas gift; something must to be destroyed in order for something else to be revealed.

He now held a smooth black plastic box. Tony nodded, *yes,* and his son opened it. Inside was a square of black velvet which Peter placed on the table then carefully lifted its four corners.

"Oh," whispered dad. "That's lovely. That's lovely, isn't it Peter?"

Sitting on the material was a small rectangular locket attached to a silver necklace.

Peter turned it in his hand. "I should open the locket, shouldn't I?"

"Well, if you don't, I will."

But neither of them moved for a few moments and each knew what the other was thinking; *I hope she put something in the locket and didn't leave it empty for* us *to fill. I hope she made that decision for us. I hope this is more than just an accessory. I hope, oh God, I hope, I hope.*

Peter found a tiny clasp and gently pulled at it with his fingernail. The rectangle unfolded into three small frames, each filled with a tiny photograph.

In the right hand frame, Anthony's smiling face.

In the middle, Peter himself, aged twelve.

In the left, Julie, wearing her police hat and uniform, cheekily winking and smiling at the camera, while saluting with her left hand.

Peter saluted back, then father and son wept. They smiled, even laughed, but then cried as they always would and always should on December twenty-fifth.

On the stereo, Michael Bublé pointed out it was *beginning to look a lot like Christmas*.

Peter finally had to agree.

58/ 27th DECEMBER 2022, PETER'S HOUSE, 8:45 a.m.

Peter woke and pulled back the curtains. Snow had continued to fitfully fall over Christmas and Boxing Day, so Littel Wade remained crusted in white. Flakes were spinning in the air this morning, too. He had an idea, reached for his phone and texted Phoebe.

Hi how was it?

He assumed there wouldn't be an answer for a few hours, and was surprised when moments later came a *swoosh*; incoming.

Good thank you. How was yours?

She'd followed the message with a fingers crossed emoji. Peter texted back.

Much better thank you.

He thought for a second then added;

Peaceful.

Swoosh.

I'm pleased. Want to do anything today? 27th is always a bit meh isn't it?

Swoosh. Peter considered for a moment, then thought, *stuff it, why not?*

Would you like to come for a walk in the snow? I haven't really been out in it.

Swoosh.

OOOH. Yes please.

Swoosh. Peter smiled and thought, *in for a penny.*

I think we should go and see Mrs Kerstmann, tell her what we did. She was part of it, after all. It was her sleigh, her books, I guess. And she provided the gifts. I suspect she'd get it.

Swoosh.

Yes, I do too. Don't know why, but I do. That's a good idea. See you on the bench at say eleven?

Swoosh. Peter went to text one reply, but then changed his mind and wrote;

That's a date.

He laid back and his smile became even wider. But then the phone *swooshed* again, announcing three surprising words and one capital letter;

I missed you X

Peter's eyes went wide and he read the message a few more times to take it in. As he did, the phone *swooshed* once more.

Only a bit, mind.

Careful now. You don't know what that really means. So Peter trusted in brevity and replied.

You too X

Swoosh.

Bloody hell, he thought, head spinning. *Oh bloody hell, Phoebe, what are you saying? I hope it's what I'm hoping for.*
He lay back again, praying for time to hurry up and be eleven.

*

As planned, Phoebe was at the bench as St Nicholas' bell tolled the hour. As Peter approached, she waved and span in the snow, which had fallen thicker as the morning progressed.

"Did we do this, do you think?" She laughed.

"What, the snow?"

Phoebe gave him a hug. "Yeah, why not? We have the power of GODS now, GODS!" She gave a long, Bela Lugosi laugh. Peter silently watched, eyebrow raised, until her diabolical cackle stuttered to a halt. "You're supposed to join in with a horror laugh," she pouted. "It's a law, or something."

"Actually, I'd like to address the elephant in the room," he said, pointedly looking at the black top hat she wore.

"Oh, this old thing," Phoebe waved him away. "No, it really is an old thing. Christmas present from mum and dad. They know me so well."

"What is it?"

She fixed him with a balelful, kohl'd stare. "I hope that was a question of specifics rather than generality otherwise I have seriously misjudged your IQ. In generic terms, it's a top hat. But you knew that, didn't you?"

"Yes, I did. I have seen them occasionally, you know, on Victorian serial killers."

Phoebe punched him in the arm and he pretended it hurt. "*Specifically*, it's vintage. G.A. Dunn and Co. Late 19th century. Not cheap, but as I say, mum and dad indulge me sometimes. I love it."

As she span again her frock coat fluttered outwards into the flakes. "It's a bit more steampunk than goth, but there is a crossover between the two, so who cares? Come on then, you tell me yours and I'll tell you mine." She offered her arm to Peter which he gladly took and they strode up Littel Wade High Street.

*

Peter told Phoebe about recent events, but left a few holes. For example, his father's pilgrimages with a hosepipe to the site of mum's accident would stay between him, dad, and whatever counsellor they'd confide in. Likewise, Anthony's plans to sell the house weren't mentioned.

For now, Peter also kept his mother's impossible appearance inside the Christmas Eve blizzard to himself. He'd tell Phoebe about that eventually, since she was the only one he trusted to have a valid opinion on how those strange snowbound moments meshed with reality.

But he did reveal Gregory Underbore's involvement in the awful events of 2019.

"That *shit*," was her succinct appraisal. "You're going to the police, of course?"

"We already did. '*Wheels are in motion*,' as they say. I don't know what will happen, but it's all we can do, really. Dredging up that night all over again is going to be awful but we're, well, not *moving on* as such, but…getting a grip on things, I suppose."

"The fucker left the scene of an accident and neither him or his mum reported it," Sally shook her head in disbelief.

"Yes, but…he also tried to say sorry. And if he hadn't, we'd be no nearer to knowing what happened, and dad…well, who knows what dad may have done?"

She flashed him a look which asked, *what do you mean by that?* But Phoebe saw Peter's fixed expression and went no further.

He changed the subject to the gift mum had left on the tree three years before. Peter pulled the locket from his neck and unfolded it. Phoebe peered at the three tiny photographs then sniffed a little, but not from the cold.

"That's beautiful," she said. "It must be comforting."

"Yeah. Every time I hold it, I think of her carefully putting these photos in here."

"She was lovely, your mum. Lovely and funny. I was really fond of her."

"I know. She was fond of you, too."

"Really?"

"Mm. 'Why can't you be more like Phoebe?' she'd say."

"*Really*?"

"Yep. 'She's always smiling, polite, smart, pretty…'"

"Too right. Especially the pretty bit. I hope you agreed."

Peter risked a shy sidewards look at her. "Of course."

She returned the glance, satisfied. "Good."

They passed shops and homes that had received their gifts three days before. "It's not just the snow, is it?" Phoebe mused. "The place does feel a quantum amount happier. I swear there are more decorations, too. I truly think a bit of magical thinking goes a long way. Now I just have to prove it for my thesis, which is a whole other kettle of sorcery entirely."

"Sometimes things are best left unproven," Peter offered, and thought, *I wouldn't want my mum appearing in the snow explained. I want to keep it as something that existed in* its *own way, not ours.*

"Hear, hear," she said, and pointed up the road. "To Kerstmann's!"

*

Eventually Littel Wade gave way to snowy B-roads and forests, but on their arrival at Mrs K.'s, the lights were off, van missing and gate locked.

Peter peered through the chain-link and spotted a gap in the jumble of items that made up Mrs Kerstmann's "stock".

"Wait. The sleigh's gone."

"Oh, that's a shame. I really wanted to see it in person, as it were."

"But I don't understand. She hadn't sold it last time I was here. Unless someone picked it up on Christmas Eve."

Something about that statement bothered Peter, then he realised what it was. "But she wasn't here on Christmas Eve. She was shutting up to go and see her son." He thought back. "Yeah, Mrs K. said she'd be back by today. So where is she?"

Phoebe had already wandered off to the yard's padlocked gate.

"Hey!" she called. "There's something for you. Look."

Fastened to the fence was a zippered plastic cover, which contained an envelope, addressed to;

PETER PIPER ESQ.

Inside was a single sheet of paper, which Peter read out loud as Phoebe looked over his shoulder.

"Dear Peter,

I wanted to thank you for all the hard work you did over Christmas. I would have done this in person, but alas, my travels will be a smidgen longer this time and I shan't be back in Littel Wade for a while. As you know, I have many yards in many places, and there's always one problem or another which requires my attention. This year it was here, next, who knows? But my son and I are kept busy, for which we are thankful. It's not the devil who finds work for idle hands to do, but ourselves.

Speaking of which, <u>you</u> were busy this year, yes? I never found out exactly why you and lovely Phoebe Clarke wanted those gifts, and who they were for…"

"*Lovely* Phoebe Clarke," Phoebe said. "Today is truly compliment day."

Peter *humph'd* and read on.

"…but am I right in thinking they had something to do with those curious books you found in my sleigh? Well, I say *my* sleigh, but as you'll have probably noticed, it has flown off to pastures new. Or rather pastures familiar. But you did a wonderful job on it, and so the old girl (not me!) will now have many more happy years in her. Did you and Phoebe work out what the books were, and who they belonged to? Intriguing! If not, I can only offer my usual advice; look, register, understand and retain. And of all those, as I may have pointed out, the ability to *look* properly is perhaps the most important. So, I hope to see you and re-acquaint myself with Phoebe sooner rather than later, but like leaves in the wind, I am rather buffeted by forces that take me where I need not necessarily wish to go, but go I must. Take care, Peter Piper.

Yours, Mrs Kerstmann.

P.S. Don't forget now, *look*, register, understand and retain."

"Keen on that, isn't she?" said Phoebe.

"It's her mantra, I think."

"Well *my* mantra is *fuck, I'm cold.* Jesus, I've just realised I'm freezing and we're at least a mile and half from anything half-resembling warmth. Shall we head on back?"

But Peter offered no reply and re-read the letter. Phoebe watched his face. "You're thinking, aren't you?" she said eventually. "What about?"

"Why did she mention 'look, register, understand and retain' twice? And why emphasise 'look'?"

"It's her mantra, as you said."

"No, *look*." Peter shook his head. "Oh God, look, Phoebe, look."

She did as he asked and studied the letter. "What at?"

"Everything."

Phoebe frowned and started to read once again. "Ah, nope."

"No, not the words. How they're *written*."

She gasped.

"It looks like the same handwriting as in the books."

"Seems that way, doesn't it? Coincidence?"

"She was telling us to look. Did she mean look at her *handwriting*? And if it is the same, what does that even mean?"

"I don't know."

Phoebe looked up at the sky, toward the dots of white that wheeled and fell there. "Let's not ask too many questions. Sometimes, like snow, it's best to let things be what they are, and accept them as magic, rather than prosaic." She turned back to face him. "So, what now, Peter?"

"Well…" He stopped and smiled. "Wait. You never call me Peter. It's always Piper."

"Not any more." She bent forward and kissed him on his cold lips. "Shall we?"

"Shall we what?"

Phoebe gestured back toward Littel Wade. "Life doesn't live itself. Fancy sharing whatever life is with me?"

He kissed her back. "Yes."

"Correct response," she laughed. "At least we have one answer we can agree on."

They walked together into the snow, which welcomed them into itself.

EPILOGUE

DECEMBER 21st 1533

DECEMBER 21st, 1533, SOMEWHERE IN DORSET, ENGLAND

"This is ridiculous. Now where am I? Exactly?"

Thomas Cromwell, Henry VIII's Chancellor Of The Exchequer, Surveyor Of The Woods and more, glowered out of his carriage window. Resentment had been his default expression over the last couple of days as London receded and Dorset rolled toward him.

Snow lay crisp, deep and uneven wherever he looked. The heavily forested route had been cold, pot-holed and uneventful, as expected when leaving civilisation. Cromwell banged on the roof.

"*Coach-mannnn*," he bellowed again. "I asked where I am."

The driver explained a wrong turn had taken them away from Dorchester, not toward it. That was not an answer Cromwell wished to hear, but since the king had demanded Thomas' presence there, he would get to the city, then deal with the driver later with as much prejudice as he could muster.

Eventually, the carriage reached a deep hole in what was laughably referred to as a "road'. In a literally vain attempt to show leadership, Cromwell attempted to walk across its iced surface.

"The ice holds!" He beckoned to his three gawping companions. "Come, let us…" At that point, the ice decided not to hold any more. Cromwell fell through, flailed, but had no choice than to head forward. Now a frozen, shivering mess, Thomas looked toward some nearby huts, from which what appeared to be an ambulatory bundle of rags approached.

Despite his sodden garments, the chancellor attempted to sound authoritative. "You there. I am Thomas Cromwell and represent the king. What is the name of this place?"

The rags shrugged. He could now see they covered a woman of indeterminate age.

"Name? No *name*, sir." She seemed amused by the very idea. "So what brings you here? I see that this is a foreign land to you, just as a smile is a foreign language to your face. It does not hurt to smile, sir."

"It does if smiling results in your head being removed from your neck."

The woman laughed. "Oh, sir, you do have a fine sense of humour."

"Oh I do. If this place does not have a name, then what is yours?"

The woman told him her name but he could barely make it out, lost in Dorset's rolling vowels and tapping consonants.

But had Thomas Cromwell listened just a little harder, he would have heard; "Kerstmann, sir. It is Kerstmann."

The Snow Trilogy

The Littel Tale Of Wintering is part of The Snow Trilogy, along with *The General Theory Of Haunting* and *The Gentle Art Of Forgetting.*
*A*lthough the three stories can be read independently and in any order you choose, they are connected.
Seemingly minor references in one become major themes in another.
Ideas set up in one story are given further explanations elsewhere.
Themes recur in all three, but in different contexts.
If you still have questions after one book, I hope you'll find the answers in another.

The Gentle Art Of Forgetting.

Jane Dawn wakes in a hut surrounded by a snow covered forest with no memory of who she was, where she is and how she got there. From this mysterious beginning, this story of love, loss, memory and mortality explains her curious life. You'll jump between Jane's new, snowbound existence back to her childhood and then travel from the '70s up to one day in 2003, when the threads are drawn together to reveal exactly what has happened to Jane and why.

The General Theory Of Haunting.

Six work colleagues have battled their way through dense snowfall to reach a New Year's Eve party at a remote mansion in Dorset. Isolated with no phone signal or internet, the guests' secrets and personal demons begin to surface. But the hall itself also has a secret built into its walls. A grand and terrible purpose, kept hidden for over two hundred years. One by one, the party-goers begin to experience *events* that may or may not be other visitors. As their personalities and relationships fall apart, the hall has one final, dreadful role to play…

ALSO BY RICHARD EASTER

Don't You Want Me?

London,1981. As race riots erupt, Charles and Diana prepare to marry & New Romantics dance, an identity-shifting serial killer is operating in plain sight.
Detective Inspector Anna Leeding suspects certain accidents and suicides are planned, and strange blue charcoal messages may be the key to something deadlier.
But Leeding also has secrets of her own in a story of revenge where no-one is what they seem. So, come back to '81.
It was a hell of a year.

Cover Stories

Eight classic songs are "remixed" here as short stories, including tracks by Bowie, The Beatles, The Stones, Hendrix and more. Find out why Major Tom got lost in space, who Prudence went out to play with, why The Stones' devil needed sympathy and much else besides. It's a compilation album with paragraphs and to be read EXTREMELY LOUD.

Richard Easter has been a professional writer mainly working in TV and radio since 1988. He lives in Manchester with his wife, daughter, and a varying amount of cats depending on their relative ages.

Along with her husband, **Jane Dawn** is a professional psychologist and occasional landscape gardener. She's also a part-time writer who first originated the story of *The Littel Tale Of Wintering* (then called *The Sleigh*) in the late '90s. It has gone through various iterations since, but she teamed up with Richard Easter in 2022 to create this, the definitive version.

With love

To my new friend

Ann

HIDDEN TREASURES

CEREDIGION

Edited by Lucy Jeacock

First published in Great Britain in 2002 by
YOUNG WRITERS
Remus House,
Coltsfoot Drive,
Peterborough, PE2 9JX
Telephone (01733) 890066

HB ISBN 0 75433 820 7
SB ISBN 0 75433 821 5

FOREWORD

This year, the Young Writers' Hidden Treasures competition proudly presents a showcase of the best poetic talent from over 72,000 up-and-coming writers nationwide.

Young Writers was established in 1991 and we are still successful, even in today's technologically-led world, in promoting and encouraging the reading and writing of poetry.

The thought, effort, imagination and hard work put into each poem impressed us all, and once again, the task of selecting poems was a difficult one, but nevertheless, an enjoyable experience.

We hope you are as pleased as we are with the final selection and that you and your family continue to be entertained with *Hidden Treasures Ceredigion* for many years to come.

CONTENTS

The Poems

Leaving School

Now I am eleven,
It's time to move on.
Bigger classes,
Lots more friends,
Going for lunch
Where the queue never ends.
So many teachers
And projects to do,
Uniform so perfect,
Tie so straight.
Catching the bus,
I just can't wait!
Saying goodbye
And thank you so much,
Don't forget to keep in touch.

Sarah Roberts (11)
Cilcennin Community Primary School

GOING SHOOTING

Put on my old clothes,
Make sure I wrap up warm,
Put on my wellington boots,
I'm ready to go on the shoot.

Check the gun
And look for the sun.
The birds fly past,
I can fire at last.
Too late, it's gone,
I missed that one.

I walk across the field,
Listening and looking,
My eyes searching
For the woodcock and snipe.

I stop, then I aim and shoot.
Its wings drop, it falls to the ground.
I walk over and pick it up.
'Poor thing.' At last I have my supper.

Daniel Jones (10)
Cilcennin Community Primary School

FOOD OF THE DAY

Start the day off
With egg and bacon,
Plenty of bread
For the day ahead.

Then in the afternoon,
Lunch with a crunch,
With crisps and a
Big ham sandwich.

For dinner, something posh,
That costs a lot of dosh.
Red wine and a roast,
Then someone says, 'You sure do boast.'

At night, a midnight feast.
A fat boy
Eats like mad,
Another boy sees you like a beast.

David Smithers (10)
Cilcennin Community Primary School

DORA

Dora is a dog,
A very fat little dog.
She sleeps in the Rayburn,
It's her haven.

Football is her game,
But makes her a real pain.
Merlin is her buddy,
But she bites his leg.

Daniel Sawyer (9)
Cilcennin Community Primary School

DANCING

Dancing is my favourite hobby,
On the stage I perform.
First an orphan,
Then a clown,
In and out and upside down.
Changing quick for my next scene,
Girls together, we are a team.
Disco, tap and ballet too
Are the lessons I like to do.
When I am dancing at my best,
My teacher puts me to the test.
Toes pointed,
Back straight to the tune,
Don't be late.

Stacey Roberts (8)
Cilcennin Community Primary School

THE GAME

I go in the stadium,
Look for my seat.
The crowds are noisy,
We wait for the players.
We look at the tunnel,
The players run out,
The crowd erupts,
'Derby . . . chchch. Derby . . . chchch.'
They wave to the crowd,
They're looking at me,
They take their positions.

The whistle goes,
The players are off,
They take a shot and they miss.
The crowd all go 'Boo.'
Shouting and screaming,
Louder and louder.

The game goes on,
They take a shot and score a goal.
The whistle goes,
It's half-time.
The players play on,
A corner, a throw-in, a foul,
Another goal is scored.
The crowd are shouting.
The final whistle blow.
One-all,
Time to go home.

Ryan Jones (8)
Cilcennin Community Primary School

FOOTBALL

I like playing football,
It's my favourite sport.
Eleven players in each team
And it's Liverpool I support.
Our players are Michael Owen,
Patrick Berger and the rest
And with such good players,
It makes Liverpool the best.

Jack Weston (8)
Cilcennin Community Primary School

THOMAS

My cat Thomas
Always bites and fights,
Tickle his tummy,
He won't bite at all.
He bites his mummy
On her tummy.

Thomas is as black as night,
But has a little white,
But it's all right,
You can't see him at night.

Benjamin Sawyer (7)
Cilcennin Community Primary School

FOOTBALL

One of our players hit the post,
A brilliant goal it was almost.
The keeper dived to save the ball,
But all he did was hit the floor.

The crowd all shouted, booed and hissed
Because our star player Jones had missed.
The final score was 7-3,
We'd won the match so we went for tea.

Kieron Boyes (7)
Cilcennin Community Primary School

Christmas, Christmas, Christmas

I just cannot wait until Christmas,
I jump around and shout 'Hooray!'
Open presents from family who miss us,
Ooh, it's such a lovely day.
Chocolates, clothes and teddies,
And all the lovely 'readies!'

Kinkari Bateson (8)
Coed-Y-Bryn Community School

My Dog

My dog is tall and fluffy,
Her favourite game is footie.
Her name is Tuppy,
She is a puppy.
When my pals come round,
She goes nutty.

Jemma Rayner (9)
Coed-Y-Bryn Community School

Christmas Fun

Presents under
The Christmas tree,
While in the oven,
There is a turkey.

Food and gifts,
With puds and potatoes,
Gravy and stuffing
And lots of vegetables.

People hanging up
Holly and mistletoe,
While children are playing
Out in the snow.

In the snow
Where people go,
Having fun
On their sleds.

Time flies past,
On Christmas Eve
Children waiting
For Santa Claus.

The meaning of Christmas
Is Jesus' birth,
When the son of God
Came to Earth.

Tom Bluett (11)
Coed-Y-Bryn Community School

CHRISTMAS

Christmas is
A time for caring,
For singing carols,
For remembering good things,
For gathering around the fire.

Christmas is
For playing with new games,
For calling friends,
For making snowmen.

Christmas is
Celebrating,
Remembering,
Happiness.

Ceri Davies (8)
Coed-Y-Bryn Community School

Hobbies

If you are bored and have nothing to do,
You should play with your computer, or PC,
Or go out with a friend, or even two.
Take them somewhere nice, maybe a zoo.

Go to see a film, or a museum,
That might keep you awake.
If you have a garden, play tag or hopscotch,
Or even go fishing by a river or a lake.

If your bedroom is untidy
And you want to make it clean,
You can tidy it up, to get to your bed,
Then your brother goes and wrecks it all, that's mean!

Get your Scalextrix out and race against your parents,
Or play with your action figures or dolls.
Or if you're the sporty type,
Play a big of football and score some fab goals!

Get your paints out and paint a view
Or draw a picture and write about it.
Colour them in with crayons, pastels,
Wax crayons, or full-of-life felt tips.

Play with your dog,
Throw a squeaky toy or even a bone.
Well, it shows you it's good to have a hobby,
Especially when you're alone.

Harley Watson (11)
Coed-Y-Bryn Community School

Army, Army

Army, army, shoot the salami,
Army, army, you think like a Barbie,
Army, army, go to a party,
Army, army, you dance like a smarty,
Army, army, you make me laugh,
Army, army, go and have a bath.

Chloe Renolds (8)
Coed-Y-Bryn Community School

Foot And Mouth

Animals dying,
People sighing,
Children crying
And there is nothing I can do,
Except watch the flames
As the cases become
Hundreds, thousands.

Children know
How it's affecting their lives,
Seeing these animals dying
Before their eyes,
But the circle goes on and on,
Gets wider and wider
As it fees on death and despair.

Hannah Wagg (11)
Coed-Y-Bryn Community School

I Saw A Movement In The Trees

I saw a movement in the trees,
I wasn't sure if it was a breeze,
But when I turned around to see,
There was an animal there, sat on my knee.
But what puzzled me so much was that the bird was blue,
Quite like my shoe.
So sorry that I have to go,
So I need to say goodbye, OK?

Laura Reed (10)
Llanilar Community Primary School

Full Moon Fever

I've got full moon fever,
It was an accident though,
I looked at the full moon for a split second.
I looked like a *horrible* wolf!
A wolf with fangs and hate the
Size of the galaxy!
The only cure is to look at the full moon again,
At the exact place, at the exact time,
And you will turn back.
But it only happens once a month,
Such a pity it is if you turn into a wolf!

Nathan Reed (10)
Llanilar Community Primary School

THE PHOENIX

There is a phoenix in my bedroom,
It must have come through my window.
It won't eat worms, it won't eat seeds,
It is so quiet.
Its golden feathers, so bright and pretty,
If you don't believe me, come and see.

Sian Hedley (10)
Llanilar Community Primary School

My Friend The Frog

I saw something rustling in the leaves,
It looked like a frog,
But I'm sure no one will believe
If I told them it jumped down,
Soared through the air,
Then dropped onto the ground.

It looked at me with longing eyes,
So I took it home,
But I didn't manage to disguise
His slimy skin and webbed feet.
My mother stood up and just yelled, 'Out!'
And threw us out on the street.

Its skin was metallic,
Rainbow coloured,
Its hunger was manic,
I scurried around, frantic.

I found a mushroom,
I found a pear,
I found a doubloon,
I didn't care.
I couldn't find anything good to eat
On the market,
On the street.
I only had two pounds to spare.

Andy Wheeler (10)
Llanilar Community Primary School

Wake Me Up

The monster in my closet
Is very, very nice.
The monster in my closet
Needs yummy rice.
He needs it to eat with
His yummy human curry.
Aaargh! Wake me up, Mummy!

Lisa Garrad (10)
Llanilar Community Primary School

Rugby

Rugby, rugby, what is it for?
A little bit of mud and a little bit of war.
As the ball spins everywhere,
Quinell jumps through the air.
The crowd goes silent,
What for?
To see the 300-pounder
Fall onto the floor.

Sion Summers (11)
Llanilar Community Primary School

The Fat Bird

Deep down in the garden lay a bird,
Fat and ugly, without any feathers.
Two months later lay two big eggs,
Out pops a chick, out pops another.

Ricky Evans (10)
Llanilar Community Primary School

THE LEPRECHAUN

One day in the heart of Ireland,
I met some green guy wearing some shorts.
I said, 'Who are you?'
'I am the leprechaun,' he said.
'Here is a pot of gold,
You have reached the end of the rainbow.'
'I'm not on a quest,' I said,
And then he said, 'Go somewhere else instead.'

Aimie Garrad (10)
Llanilar Community Primary School

DRACULA

I saw a monster,
He had huge teeth.
He was very tall and think,
He had a black cape.
He said, ‘Come here.’
I went closer and closer.
I was suddenly surrounded by them,
And then I realised that was
Dracula!
I woke up.
Phew, it was only a dream.

Luke Morgan (10)
Llanilar Community Primary School

Untitled

Guess what? I've got Harry Potter living in my shed.
I think he used to live in a castle, because he is
Building one out of some old breeze blocks and a sand pit.
I think he misses his friends, because he has made models
Of two people, out of clay and wire.
Oh yes, I think he misses his owl, because he keeps on
Tying letters onto the plastic flamingo that lives by the pond
And he keeps on blasting my sister with his wand, because
She is a Goth and she is evil, like you know who, and I said,
'Who is you know who?' and he said he could not tell me.
I asked, 'What will you do?'
'Put the imperial curse on you.'
I asked, 'Why, is he lonely?'
And he said, 'No, he just wants me dead.'

Seren Hinde (10)
Llanilar Community Primary School

I Won The Lottery

I won the lottery,
I went on holiday to Florida,
I bought a big, big house
With a big, big garden.
In the house there was a gym and a cinema.
Two pools, one inside and one outside.
We have all our animals
And I have everything I want.

Sinead Meddins (10)
Llanilar Community Primary School

WALKING

I was walking, I stopped and looked,
There was a butterfly on the floor, lying there still.
I picked it up, but it wouldn't move.
I thought it might be thirsty, I gave it some water,
But he did nothing and then I said, 'I think I know what's wrong.'
He was lonely and then his wings fluttered, he was awake and
He would flutter his wings every time a person came round.
I was right. He was lonely, but not anymore.

Lowri James (9)
Llanilar Community Primary School

The Dog

I was walking along
On the path in the forest.
I saw a dog, he growled.
I think he wanted something to eat,
So I went out of the forest
And went to town.
I bought something for the dog to eat
Then I went back into the forest.
It went dark and there was the dog
So I put the food down on the floor.
I went home, so every day then,
I went with some food for the dog to eat.

Sara Tudor (8)
Llanilar Community Primary School

UNTITLED

I am a caterpillar and I like to wiggle,
And when I meet my friends, I giggle.
I have a friend called Snaky,
And he likes to shake me.
I can fit into small places
And I make funny faces.
I have lots of legs
And I come from eggs.

Joe Hedley (9)
Llanilar Community Primary School

A Ghost Called Ann-Marie

There is a ghost called Ann-Marie
In Llechryd School with you and me.
She holds her head under her arm,
But remember, she might not do much harm.
She might cuddle, she might kiss,
Please remember to make her miss.
You might shiver head to toe,
So make sure she'll just go.
Don't play her ghostly game,
You don't want to end up being the same.
Floating through the class and hall,
Trying to chase a ghostly ball.
So Ann-Marie, I'll say goodbye,
You can't catch me, so don't even try.

Sarah Sommerville (8)
Llechryd CP School

REPTILES

Cold-blooded animals,
Snakes slithering about,
Crocodiles in the water,
Iguanas on the rocks,
Turtles in the water,
Boas in the trees,
Cobras in the grass,
Rattlesnakes in the deserts,
Alligators hiding in mud,
Scales on snakes,
Shells on terrapins.
These are some
Of my favourite animals.

Branwen Lewis (8)
Llechryd CP School

My Dog Snoopy

Black hair,
Blue eyes,
Fluffy ears,
Long legs,
Rough, pink tongue.

Chasing his tail,
Chewing his toys,
Gobbling his dinner,
Barking at his reflection,
That's my dog, Snoopy.

Samantha Francis (7)
Llechryd CP School

A HAUNTED HOUSE

Vampires moan,
Mummies groan,
Ghosts go *whoo-whoo*,
Owls cry tu-whit tu-whoo,
Staircase creaks,
Cobwebs all over the place,
This is a haunted house.
Cobwebs all over the place,
Staircase creaks,
Owls cry tu-whit tu-whoo,
Gosts go *whoo-whoo*,
Mummies groan,
Vampires moan.

Angharad Rees (9)
Llechryd CP School

JUNGLE

Jungle, jungle, jungle,
Swinging through the jungle,
Monkeys fight,
Tigers bite,
Spiders crawl,
Parrots screech,
Birds sing,
Insects crawl.
Steamy forest,
Leaves fall,
Flowers blossom,
I love it all.

Hannah Curran (9)
Llechryd CP School

To The Snowdrop

White and brave,
Strong and bendy,
Smelling lovely,
Nice and bright.
They come out in winter.
I love snowdrops,
Silent and still in the night.

Hannah Sommerville (8)
Llechryd CP School

The Ocean

I wish, I wish
That I could see
What wonderful things
Live under the sea.
Maybe sharks,
Hunting for their prey,
Maybe shipwrecks,
Old and grey.
Maybe an electric eel
Looking at me,
I wish, I wish
I could dive,
Deep, deep into the sea.

George Evans (8)
Llechryd CP School

TROUBLE AT THE STATION

The sun goes down,
The moon comes up,
At the station, the police go home.
A ghostly lady goes inside,
She moves things,
Breaks things and writes 'Beware.'
She breaks the phones,
Lets the prisoners out,
Knocks over the chairs,
Tears the curtains.
The moon goes down,
The sun comes up,
The police wake up and say,
'What a mess!
Send for the ghost detective!'

Amy Robinson (8)
Llechryd CP School

FOOTBALL

Football is fun,
Learning skills with a ball,
Dribbling and shooting,
Fun for us all.
Kicking and passing,
A goal is our aim,
Team works together,
We're all the same.
Trying to win
Is important we know,
But if we don't win,
We still give it a go.
Football is fun,
Learning skills with a ball,
Dribbling and shooting,
Fun for us all.

Bethan Curran (10)
Llechryd CP School

W4

If I built a motorway,
It would be for worms,
With stalls selling cakes,
It helps their squirms,
And hygiene sprays,
Get rid of germs,
Ten lanes wide,
Flowers on the side,
With a super food station,
Worms will squirm,
Right across the nation.

Aled James (10)
Llechryd CP School

BIRDS

I looked out of the window to see the birds,
To describe their beauty, I just don't have the words.
Their colours are so fine and fair
As they swoop and dive through the air.

But if the poor bird gets caught by a cat,
By the morning, it will be dead on the mat.
Wait a week and the flesh will turn green,
Watching the maggots can be quite serene.

As we sit here, by and by,
Each maggot turns into a fly.

Ruth Sommerville (10)
Llechryd CP School

FOOTBALL

Kicking,
Dribbling,
Heading,
Scoring,
Diving,
Saving,
Throwing,
Passing,
Winning,
Losing,
Celebrating,
Planning,
Football.

Alvin Johnson (10)
Llechryd CP School

My Sister Sara

She is as cute as a lion with make-up,
She is as light as a mouse on a cloud,
She is as quick as a cheetah on a jumbo jet,
She is as happy as a monkey being tickled,
She is as great as a sister can be -
My sister Sara.

Megan Williams (9)
Llechryd CP School

MISS LEWIS

Miss Lewis,
Miss Lewis,
She helps me all day.
Miss Lewis,
Miss Lewis,
She's maths-mad I'd say.
Miss Lewis,
Miss Lewis,
She's there for us all,
Miss Lewis,
Miss Lewis,
In class or in hall.
Miss Lewis,
Miss Lewis,
I will try my best,
Miss Lewis,
Miss Lewis,
The best in the west.

Kerry Thomas (10)
Llechryd CP School

My Uncle's Farm

Grass growing,
Mower mowing,
Tractor ploughing,
Seed sowing,
Muck spreading,
Combine harvesting,
Mart selling,
Fly spraying,
Sheep shearing,
Silage bagging,
Cattle grazing,
Chickens laying,
Cows milking.
What a busy place,
My uncle's farm.

Barry Sullivan (11)
Llechryd CP School

My Dog Tina

Brown,
Funny,
Playful,
Chewy,
Waggy,
Sleepy,
My dog,
Tina.

Sophie Yates (10)
Llechryd CP School

MONKEYS

Monkeys swinging through the trees,
Jumping swiftly from branch to branch,
Searching for fruit and other food,
Grooming each other's fur for fleas.
Caught on film for us all to see,
Grooming each other's fur for fleas,
Searching for fruit and other food,
Jumping swiftly from branch to branch,
Monkeys swinging through the trees.

Kelly Maskell (10)
Llechryd CP School

DIWALI

D ancing
I n the night,
W omen painting patterns,
A ll welcoming Lakshmi,
L amps light up the place,
I ndia's Diwali.

Antoni Castaglioni (11)
Llechryd CP School

The Penguin Highway - P25

Penguins have no roads,
So how do they travel?
One minute now, son,
They travel on the P25.
It has baby centres for their tots,
And pubs for the husbands.
Penguins use the P25
To go to Wales and Ireland.
Do the penguins walk?
Well of course not, son,
They use icicles
Or motorised icebergs.
Does anyone see them?
Of course not, son,
They travel at night
Under starlight,
Along the P25.

John Williams (10)
Llechryd CP School

The Spook House

Dirty cobwebs hanging down,
Laughter cackling from deep down.
Pictures with moving eyes
Would give you a big surprise.
A ghostly figure floating high,
You might hear a spooky cry.
The spook house creaks and groans,
Shivers, shakes, sighs and moans.
Would you like to visit soon,
Underneath the silver moon?

Amy Carter (8)
Llechryd CP School

My Pet Cat

My pet cat is
As furry as a sheepskin rug,
As fast as a jaguar speeding by,
As fierce as a tiger in the jungle,
As clever as a scientist experimenting,
As gentle as a teddy bear dreaming,
As ginger as a jar of marmalade,
That's my pet cat, Sardine.

Lewis Rees (9)
Llechryd CP School

The Horse

Galloping, galloping, galloping free,
Up and down the lane with me.
Over hills and under trees,
Galloping, galloping, galloping free.
Out in the open, never stop,
Keep on moving and don't go clop,
Run, run, until you drop.
Through the forest, in the lake,
Running free with my friend Flake.
Out in the field, round the bend,
The fun never stops when I'm with my friend.
We can go and come when we please,
As long as we're together through the breeze.
But when we go home and put him to bed,
There's plenty of time tomorrow
To go out instead.

Haidee Harvey-Brown (10)
Pennant CP School

CAT

The cat sat on the mat.
The rat went under the mat.
The cat ran after the rat.

Carys Lewis (7)
Pennant CP School

Wizards

Wizards, wizards,
They're everywhere,
So you'd better watch out
Or you're in for a scare.

Some wizards are good,
Some wizards are bad,
I once saw a wizard
That looked like my dad.

They have magical creatures
And magic wands too,
Some people say wizards
Should be locked in a zoo.

I once saw a hippogriff,
Half-eagle, half-horse,
It pounced off the ground
And was set on its course.

Wizards are not all that bad,
Some even help you too,
But you'd better watch out
Or they'll be after you.

Caio Jones (9)
Pennant CP School

CAT

The big cat
Swallowed the rat,
Along came a bat
And frightened
The cat,
Who landed on
The mat
With a big
Miaaaaooow!

Hayley Evans (7)
Pennant CP School

My Horse

There is a horse
Who has
Black teeth,
Like a bin bag.
She is as thin
As a rag
And she looks
Like a rake.
Her feet are
As long as
A tree trunk.
Her mane is
As wavy as
The waves.
Her tail is
As messy as
A bin full of rubbish,
But I love her!

Dafydd Jones (9)
Pennant CP School

MY BROTHER

My brother is annoying,
He bugs me all the time,
He's such an annoying brother,
He can't commit a crime.
He gets me into trouble all the time,
He's such an annoying brother,
I just want to scare him
With a big, black spider!

Ben Evans (8)
Pennant CP School

THE CAT

The cat sat on the mat,
The rat went under the mat,
The cat chased the rat,
Under the mat.
The cat jumped on the rat
And ate it!

Jennifer Moffit (7)
Pennant CP School

My Dream

When I was sleeping in my bed,
I heard a clatter in my head.
It was the image of flying cars
And floating, metal bars.

Some were big,
Some were small,
How strange it seemed as
They fought the law of gravity.

There even were rockets
That could fit in your pockets.
One did a whiz
And nearly hit me in the head,
So I ducked,
And fell out of bed.

Gwyn Evans (10)
Ysgol Ciliau Parc

Animals

I love animals,
They are really cute,
Some are fluffy,
Some even wear a suit.

Take snails for instance,
They wear their house on their back,
But if someone stamps on them,
Their shells go *crack!*

Horses run through the wind,
They go as fast as lightning.
Their manes blow as well,
It looks really swell.

Dogs bark at night,
They run down the road,
They give you such a fright,
They do not even follow the code!

Cats run smoothly across the ground,
You cannot hear them,
But when there is food around
They make such a sound.

Hamsters sometimes bite,
Or go to sleep on your hand.
They are so very cute,
Like a big, round fruit.

I love animals,
They mean a lot to me,
I love them will all my heart
And will do so for eternity.

Carys Price Jones (10)
Ysgol Ciliau Parc

My Alien Brother

My brother's an alien, I saw him last night,
He was shedding his skin, it gave me a fright!
He had stringy blue hair
And his legs green and bare.
He had a purple tail,
At its end was a nail.
He had grown about six feet,
Boy, my brother's really neat!

Suddenly, there was a flash of green, white and blue,
Then it went quiet. Atchoo! Atchoo! Atchoo!
My mum and dad were waking up,
To get some water in a cup.
I jumped into my brother's room,
I shut the door with a *boom!*
I slowly turned around in stealth,
But my brother was back to his normal self!

Aaron Hughes (11)
Ysgol Ciliau Parc

ANCIENT EGYPTIANS

Ancient Egyptians were very fascinating,
With lots of secret treasures.
I like to study them a lot,
Rich men enjoyed great pleasures.

The Egyptians were good farmers,
They farmed along the Nile,
But some were really vicious,
Some were even vile.

They built a load of great pyramids
Full of mummified bodies,
Disgusting they were, revolting in fact,
Unlike a cute bunch of teddies.

Many of the Egyptians were slaves,
Ruled by great pharaohs.
There were lots of battles and wars, too,
Many had to hide in burrows.

Hieroglyphics was their written language,
With symbols and many a body part,
It's a tricky job to work it out,
In fact, it's quite an art.

There was a pharaoh called Tutankhamun,
He led a very great tribe,
But unfortunately he died at eighteen,
It's quite hard to describe.

Lungs, liver, stomach and brain
All stuffed into separate jars,
Quite disgusting, don't you think?
Like dissecting men from Mars.

So there you have it, my horrorsome tale,
As my favourite subject, it will never fail.

Harri Davies (10)
Ysgol Ciliau Parc

My Cat Truffles

My cat Truffles is so fluffy,
I don't know why she is so lovely.
She runs so fast,
I never see her fly past.
She is so big,
Not like a fig.
She is quiet plump,
More like a lump
Always on the hunt,
Ready for a stunt,
She never looks away,
Or she might miss the day.
Then she comes in to be fed
And gets ready for her bed.

Anton Barnett (11)
Ysgol Ciliau Parc

My Sister Chloe

My sister Chloe keeps me up all night,
If you get near her she'll start a fight!

My sister picks her nose all day
And loves to play in the sand and clay.

She snatches the phone from the wall
And demands to answer any call.

This morning as it was a school day,
She wanted me to stay home and play.

My little sister flies a kite,
Would I change her? Too right!

Karis Thompson (9)
Ysgol Ciliau Parc

The Farm

The farm is noisy,
The cows are nosy.

The pigs are sleeping,
The chickens are laying.

The dogs are howling,
The cats are miaowing.

The sheep are grazing,
The ducks are sneezing.

The farm is great,
Next time, I'll take a mate!

Richard Dowdeswell (10)
Ysgol Ciliau Parc

The Lord Of The Rings

A circle of gold
Was found one day,
A ring that was special
In every way.

A story of old, tells the terrible truths
Of the dark side and danger of wizards and spooks.

A hobbit who was brave and faced all his fears,
Took the ring of gold to the dark side and disappeared.
Who knows what happened next?
The tale has not yet ended,
Good luck to the one who holds the ring,
May it be a happy ending.

Ryan Dabner (10)
Ysgol Ciliau Parc

My Cat Candy

My cat Candy
Drank the brandy.

My cat Candy chased a mouse
Up and down, around the house.

My cat Candy is so brown,
She got her colour underground.

My cat Candy is so sweet,
She really is so very neat.

My cat Candy is the best,
So much better than the rest.

Emily Mellars (10)
Ysgol Ciliau Parc

I Wish

I wish I could fly
To a faraway land,
Like Spain or even a place where no one has been.
I would call it St Maddy's.
I would rule St Maddy's with care,
It would be the best place to live on Earth.
Who would say no to living there?
There would never be a rainy day,
The sun would shine brightly every day.
I would have cakes and ice cream every day,
People would worship me,
I would be their queen.
What would your wish be?

Madeleine Bates (9)
Ysgol Ciliau Parc

My Cat

My cat isn't at all bad,
He's a playful cat and a loving cat.
At night he leaps on my bed,
Cuddling like a ball on my cosy duvet,
But at midnight he jumps off,
Wanting to go out into the dark night
Where his delicious prey is waiting for the cruel cat.
The purring panther sees his prey,
He scans the helpless mouse with his glistening eyes,
His mouth full of white daggers, ready to attack.

My cat has a good sense of smell.
He runs wildly into the kitchen,
Twisting and turning around my ankles like a spinning top.
I give him a plate of red salmon
And in a flash, the plate is spotlessly clean.
But really, my cat is a sweet cat.
Yes, that's my golden cat.

Marged Howells (10)
Ysgol Gymraeg Aberystwyth

MONEY

Greedy old Mr Thomson
Was a millionaire,
He looked down fiercely at the poor
With his nose right in the air.

He bought everything he wanted,
A palace and a bar,
And drove around the city
In his big, red, flashy car.

But unhappy Mr Thomson
Thought that money grew on trees,
And he soon grew into debt,
With bills up to his knees.

Old Mr Thomson,
No longer rich and fat,
A smelly old tramp
Lying on the street with his cat.

A foolish tramp,
Sprawled with litter on the street,
Gazing at people as they go by,
And begging for a penny at their feet.

Hannah James (11)
Ysgol Gymraeg Aberystwyth

MONEY

M ighty rich at last,
O h after all that's past,
N othing came for a year or two,
E ach day I looked at you,
Y et nothing came my way.

A t last I've got my money,
T oday my life has changed.

L ife is lovely now,
A ll posh and no worries,
S o lovely, full of money,
T oday I'm feeling glad.

Anna Lewis (10)
Ysgol Gymraeg Aberystwyth

MONEY

When I won the lottery,
I was so, so happy,
I was very lucky
To have that much money!

I thought of buying a mansion,
A car or a plane
And at the same time,
Driving everyone insane!

But then I suddenly realised,
I was turning into a snob,
Having that much money
Really made me unlucky!

Nia Richards (11)
Ysgol Gymraeg Aberystwyth

My Cats

M y cat is very mischievous
A t any time of day,
T roublesome and tiny and very tatty,
T ickly and touchable at times,
I gnorant, but incredible.

P ositive and posing she purrs,
I diotically she plays,
X mas she was born,
I mpressively she jumps and
E legantly lands.

S lyly she walks,
I ntelligently she stalks,
O ld but wise,
N osy and nice,
I ll and sick at times, poor thing.

Menna Passmore (9)
Ysgol Gymraeg Aberystwyth

Cats

Black, bad, boisterous cat,
Teeth like daggers, claws like knives,
Growls when he's angry, pounces on his prey,
I hate the cat, he's a killer.

He stares at me and arches his back,
Displays his white daggers in the crimson cave,
His eyes are visible in the darkest nights
And his shadow appears everywhere.

He kills the birds and eats the fish,
But when the crime's discovered, he's not there.
His meals come from a rubbish dump
And he steals cats' food for a tasty snack.

Sali Hopkins (10)
Ysgol Gymraeg Aberystwyth

Cats

Stray cats are sad and smelly,
Others are tatty and tall,
Some cats are beautiful, but bony,
They always stand by the door,
Sometimes purring for more.

Some cats are ragged, racing rascals
And some are ugly, unhappy and fat,
Cuddly, cute, crazy and wild,
They are not my kind of cat.

Angry, active and annoying,
Mad cats which can't be caught,
But the attractive and homely,
Quiet queens are my sort.

Catrin Lloyd (10)
Ysgol Gymraeg Aberystwyth

Cats

I hate monstrous, massive, growling cats,
With yellow eyes and evil ears, who look like bats.

I don't like fat, fierce, filthy cats
Who kill thousands and millions of tiny rats.

I don't want a naughty, noisy, silly cat
Who always curls up and sleeps on a mat.

I wouldn't ever even touch a smelly, slimy cat
Who is hideous, horrible, ugly, crazy, old and fat.

I want a nice, friendly, fluffy cat,
Who doesn't eat a single rat.

Rhianwen Daniel (10)
Ysgol Gymraeg Aberystwyth

My Cat

My cat stalks its prey,
Small mice, too scared to move.
His dagger-like teeth are long
And his back is black and smooth.
In the dark his emerald-green eyes glow
And his tail is as beautiful as a dolphin.

My cat sleeps on laundry baskets
And old clothes.
He scans the room for food
And sniffs dirt with his nose.
Sometimes he jumps around,
As happy as the sun.
He scratches the door,
As if knocking to come in.

Harry Williams (10)
Ysgol Gymraeg Aberystwyth

CATS

An adult cat catches food,
A baby cat is always in a mood.
A charm cat never bites,
A dreadful cat stays out of light,
The evil cat's eyes glow in the dark,
A friendly cat always comes and stays.
A good cat comes to my doorstep,
A healthy cat always comes back for more
And an invisible cat comes and eats it all.
A jealous cat is always sad
And the kind cat is mad.
A laughing cat is always lazy
And I could call the master cat Maisy.
A nervous cat hides in boxes
And the old cat tries and gives them a swipe
A perfect, poorly cat catches the birds,
Then the racing cat comes and licks his nose.
If the unselfish cat can show her paws,
The tame cat always likes to be tickled.
The ugly cat comes to be cuddled,
The vicious cat has stolen buns
And when Xmas comes,
They all like to share in the fun.

Catrin Mair Dewhurst (10)
Ysgol Gymraeg Aberystwyth

THE ALLEY CAT

The nasty, mean alley cat hunts at night.
It is a long, sleek, black cat,
It looks like a fierce, wild panther.
In the night, its yellow eyes flash like two candles.
It hears a noise and hides behind a dustbin.
It jumps and kills the little mouse
And lies on a soft bed of leaves to eat its prey.

In the day it is a warm, cuddly figure that sleeps on your lap.
It licks its paw gently
With its small, pink tongue
That looks like strawberry jam.
It adores every plate of fish it can see,
You would never think
That this lovely cat
Was a fierce alley cat at night.

Tomi Turner (10)
Ysgol Gymraeg Aberystwyth

Money

If I won the lottery,
I would be very glad,
I'd go on a shopping spree
And drive my mum mad.

My face would be on every front page,
'Sioned, The Lottery Winner,'
I'd hold a big cheque for fifteen million pounds,
Everybody would say, 'She's not a beginner.'

I'd buy a mansion and a limousine too,
A solid gold mobile - one each week,
Cooks and waiters who would obey me,
My life wouldn't be bleak!

I'd give money to charity,
I have it all planned,
Listen to this -
It's only fantasy land.

Sioned Thomas (10)
Ysgol Gymraeg Aberystwyth

MONEY

When I get some money,
I just spend, spend, spend,
Tammy, New Look or Woolworths,
It's all gone in the end!

Some people aren't true friends,
They just act,
They're jealous for one reason,
Your bank account is packed!

I'm like a seventy-two year old woman,
All fussy with my clothes,
I like the latest fashion,
But how I get the money, no one knows!

Some people win the lottery,
Or Who Wants To Be A Millionaire?
As long as I've got real friends,
About money, I don't care.

Carys Dodd (11)
Ysgol Gymraeg Aberystwyth

Money!

She sat on the street corner,
Looking all pale and bleak,
Outside the bank,
She was a tramp,
To the busy bees, who would grovel and shout.

All day she sat
And would constantly pat
Buster the dog, who was as big
As a witch's pot,
And would sit at his mistress's feet,
Collecting money.

One day she bought
A most expensive sort
Of ticket.
The next day she found
A suitcase shoved into her hand
With £25,000 inside.

When she got over the shock,
She put £5,000 in a box,
A gift to charity,
Then she spent another on friends.

The rest of the money she kept
Very safely in a bank in Kent
And spent it wisely.
But when it came to money,
She didn't really care, that much!

Genna Fitch (10)
Ysgol Gymraeg Aberystwyth

MONEY

He was a snob,
Because he had as much
Money as he needed,
But he still thought
That he was poor like
The old tramp on the street
Even though he had
Won the lottery ten times in a row.

He lived in a huge manor,
A castle in the green countryside,
And inside
All the furniture was expensive,
Modern and expansive.
He had ten maids,
Two cooks and a butler,
But he still thought that he was poor
Even though he had
One hundred thousand pounds in every
Bank account he owned.

Then, one awful morning
One of his colleagues from the bank
Where he was manager
Called him on his flashy silver mobile
While he was driving his speedy convertible
Like a shiny black beetle running through the grass,
Told him the awful news
The bank had sank.

Anne Llwyd (10)
Ysgol Gymraeg Aberystwyth

Money

No money, no home,
He sits on the step,
Lonely and quiet,
Like a deserted island.
In his sack, he begs
The people that pass
To give him a penny or two.

His hat is always empty,
He must be nearly eighty.
His back is like a question mark.
Crinkly skin like autumn leaves.
He's always there
On the same old spot,
Not eating but always hungry.

A penny drops,
The smile on his face,
The wrinkles disappear.
His face glows up like the sun,
But then his face dies.
It's back to the street again.

Ffion Evans (10)
Ysgol Gymraeg Aberystwyth

MONEY

Old Mr Tinker
Living in the street
Every day now,
With nothing to eat.

He found a case of money,
Lying lonely there,
Delighted he jumped on the bus,
Now he could pay the bus fare.

He bought a new scarf
To keep out the cold,
He threw his walking stick
And walked coolly down the road.

The girls adored him,
He went on dates,
No wonder he had
Lots of mates.

But all he did was
Spend and spend,
He drove everyone
Round the bend.

So now old Mr Tinker
Is living in the street,
Huddled together,
Warming his feet.

Carys Davies (10)
Ysgol Gymraeg Aberystwyth

MONEY

Two greedy snobs,
Out while it's sunny,
Out for a reason -
To get some money.

Pointing out faults
As they walk to the bank,
The rubbish on the road
And that old leaking tank.

But first Mr Grancher
Dropped into Spar,
To get a lottery ticket,
So he could buy a new car.

Mrs Grancher on the other hand,
Bought some new things,
A blouse and a skirt
And two gold rings.

But the snobs weren't quite happy
With the life they had,
They didn't mix with other people,
In fact, they were quite sad.

Sarah Trotter (11)
Ysgol Gymraeg Aberystwyth

MONEY

Puffing cigars
In their big, posh cars,
Counting money,
All the very wealthy.
Big property, others in poverty -
Weak and poor,
Cold and sore,
Counting pennies,
Hugging their teddies,
Living in slums,
Feeding on crumbs,
Shivering cold,
Trying to be bold.
Oh, it's a different world!

Tomos Hywel (11)
Ysgol Gymraeg Aberystwyth

MONEY

P ay day for the rich, nothing for me,
O ver there they walk with their mobiles, and me,
V ery cold and hungry, with one blanket to keep me warm.
E ach day like a pile of books,
R eady to fall flat on the floor,
T rying not to give up,
Y et nothing comes my way.

Deian Thomas (11)
Ysgol Gymraeg Aberystwyth

FARMING

Pigs like rolling in mud,
They'll also eat a spud.
Horses run round the field,
To the cows, they're a shield.

Friesian cows are black and white,
Sometimes they watch the kite.
Sheep are sheared in summer,
We don't use a strimmer.

Samantha Boshier (8)
Ysgol Gymunedol Llanarth Community School

FARMING

There was once a horse called Tazzle
And he always went on the razzle.
Down the field he went one day,
He really isn't worth his pay.

Mark Jones (8)
Ysgol Gymunedol Llanarth Community School

Farming

There was a fat cow
That lived with a pig,
They both played in mud
And then ate a spud.

Stephen Clasby (8)
Ysgol Gymunedol Llanarth Community School

FARMING

On the farm I'd like to go,
To see the farmer go.
Every day I eat some meat,
The sheep have had a lot to eat.

Curtis Burt (8)
Ysgol Gymunedol Llanarth Community School

FARMING

Farm animals I like.
Cows, sheep and horses too.
They are getting fatter,
The farmer feeds them so.

The quad is leading them
To the field, where they eat.
Fields are getting greener,
They have a lot of wheat.

Aimee Davies (8)
Ysgol Gymunedol Llanarth Community School

FARMING

I like tractors very much,
But if you are young, you must not touch.
Do not touch ferocious cows,
They can be nasty if they have calves.

Andrew Pool (8)
Ysgol Gymunedol Llanarth Community School

FARMING

Farmers are very happy
To see their animals grow.
Sometimes they are snappy
When they see the big, bad crow.

Liam Choules (8)
Ysgol Gymunedol Llanarth Community School

Farming

Fun on the farm
Is fun every day,
Looking at the animals
Doing the things they do.

The cows say moo,
The sheep and lambs say baa,
While the cows are getting milked,
The pigs are getting cleaned.

Jacqueline Jobling (8)
Ysgol Gymunedol Llanarth Community School

FARMING

The lambs are frolicking about
On the soft fields.
There is lots of machinery on the farm.
The farm is very muddy.
The cockerel sings in the morning,
To wake the farmer for work.
He gets up because the sheep and cows
Are calling for their food.
The cows are ready to be milked
And the farmer is ready for breakfast.
The farmer's life is full of care,
He has no time to stand or stare.

Dylan Morgans (8)
Ysgol Gymunedol Llanarth Community School

FARMING

Early morning, early morning,
The farmer is milking the cows,
As the sun has not risen.
But he does not moan at all.

Rhys Mcloughlin (I8)
Ysgol Gymunedol Llanarth Community School

FARMING

Early morning, sheep are sleeping,
The farmer comes to see them.
The cockerel sings and the cows are eating,
Everybody is happy.

Sarah Beard (8)
Ysgol Gymunedol Llanarth Community School

FARMING

Farmers work hard in spring,
When the birds begin to sing.
Now lambs are born every day,
They jump around and play.

A farmer's work is never done,
He is often up until one.
Still the cockerel wakes him up
Before he even has a cup.

Tomas Miles (8)
Ysgol Gymunedol Llanarth Community School

FARMING

I like sheep very much,
Pigs, cows, dogs and the such.
I like watching them all play
And working hard all day.

Gavin Jones (8)
Ysgol Gymunedol Llanarth Community School

My Dog

I've got a nice, big dog,
He runs about with me
And when we're tired of playing,
We go home for our tea.

Anthony Worrall-Grant (9)
Ysgol Gymunedol Llanarth Community School

The Little Hen

'Cluck, cluck, cluck,'
Said the hen one day,
'Cluck, cluck, cluck,
Come out to play.
The sun is warm
Up in the sky,
Let's flutter our wings
And fly up high.'

Carian Stevens (9)
Ysgol Gymunedol Llanarth Community School

Henry The Horse

Henry the horse
Is big and strong,
He pulls a cart
All day long.

He's tired at night,
Is Henry the horse,
Sleeps on the hay
And snores and snores.

Melissa Carne (8)
Ysgol Gymunedol Llanarth Community School

A Pig With A Problem

I am a pig,
So very big,
In fact
I'm quite gigantic.
My sty is now
Too small for me,
I can't turn round
To eat my tea!

Claire Crees (9)
Ysgol Gymunedol Llanarth Community School

Guess Who?

I'm cute from
Head to toe,
And my home
Is a hole in the wall.

To say hello,
I come out at night,
But have to be careful
And keep out of sight.

Can you guess
Who I am?
Can you guess?
I'm sure you can!

Sean Thomas (9)
Ysgol Gymunedol Llanarth Community School

Cows

Cows give us milk
To pour on cornflakes.
Mum always uses it
When she bakes.

From milk we make cheese
That's good for our bones,
We also get cream
To make ice cream cones.

My favourite animals
Are cows I must say,
I hope I will have one
Of my own, one day.

Victoria Barber (9)
Ysgol Gymunedol Llanarth Community School

Dusty The Donkey

Dusty the donkey
With a coat of grey,
Clippetty-clop,
He eats all day.
Stops here and there
To eat his hay,
Clipetty-clop,
He goes on his way.

Levi Davies (9)
Ysgol Gymunedol Llanarth Community School

A Pig's World

I'm a pig
With a curly tail,
I live in a sty
And I like to sit
Watching the world go by.
Looking, listening,
All day long,
I'm a pig
All pink and strong.

Jacob Farr (9)
Ysgol Gymunedol Llanarth Community School

The Little Lamb

The little lamb,
Her name is Fleece,
Warm and cuddly,
She lives in peace.
Curly and tight,
Marble-like eyes,
So black and bright,
Button, wet nose.
She prances high,
Up and down,
High in the sky.

Heulwen Williams (9)
Ysgol Gymunedol Llanarth Community School

My Dogs

Jack, my dog,
Has loads of spots.
Jack, my dog,
I love him lots.
He's big,
He's black,
A Labrador
Who loves to sleep
By the kitchen door.

Ben, my dog,
He's lovely too.
Ben, my dog,
He hides my shoe.
He's golden and shiny,
A grand retriever.
Throw him a twig or two,
He won't retrieve it for you!

Bethanie Nicholson (10)
Ysgol Gymunedol Llanarth Community School

Rosie The Pig

Rose the pig was fat,
She even wore a hat!
Off she went to the market place,
With flashy make-up on her face,
Pinkish-red and white,
She really looked a sight
Tottering down the busy street
With fancy booties on her feet!

Shane Bolwell (10)
Ysgol Gymunedol Llanarth Community School

THE GUINEA PIG

I'm cuddly,
I'm fluffy
And I live in a cage.

I'm hairy,
I'm scary,
Do you know my age?

I sleep in a bed
Which is soft and warm,
Safe in my cage
Where I come to no harm.

Ruhena Awal (10)
Ysgol Gymunedol Llanarth Community School

I Like Cows

Farmer milks his cows
To give us milk and cream,
And cheese as well
To keep us well.
I like the farmer's cows.

Laura May (10)
Ysgol Gymunedol Llanarth Community School

Denis, My Goat

Denis, Denis,
Such a menace!
Why so mischievous
Every day?
Pulling down our neighbour's washing,
Why can't you be
Like the other goats?

Denis, Denis,
Such a menace!
Why so naughty
Every day?
Rummaging in our neighbour's bins,
Why can't you be
Like the other goats?

I know I'm naughty,
I cannot stop.
I love to run and leap and hop.
I'll try and listen
To you each day,
But whether I'm good,
I cannot say.

Catryn Boland (10)
Ysgol Gymunedol Llanarth Community School

LAMBS

I like to watch the little lambs
Kick their legs up high,
And when they're looking for their mums,
I can hear them cry.

Their mums hear them from far away
And come to their side,
They give them milk to fill their tums,
Then the lambs run off to hide.

Amanda Beard (10)
Ysgol Gymunedol Llanarth Community School

TOWZER THE SCHNAUZER

Towzer the schnauzer is cute and cuddly,
When you touch him, he feels very fluffy.
When you wake him out of bed,
All he thinks about is being fed!

When it's food time, you don't want to know,
Because I'll tell you this, it's not a good show.
When he's chasing rabbits all day,
He runs in a very funny way!

At the end of the day,
When he's finished his play,
He climbs into bed,
Even when he's wet.
So goodnight, Towzer,
Goodnight.

James Bromley (10)
Ysgol Gymunedol Llanarth Community School

THOMAS HENRY!

Thomas Henry, such a lazy cat,
Thomas tell me,
Why are you so fat?
What do you eat that makes you so?
You need to exercise and go, go, go!

Go chase the chickens around the farm,
But please don't do them any harm.
Tyson the dog would love to play,
All you need do is get in his way!

Or go and pester Monty, the fish,
But we all know tuna's your favourite dish.

Oh Thomas,
Oh dear,
The best in the world,
Beside the fire he'll remain curled.

Carys Hunt (10)
Ysgol Gymunedol Llanarth Community School

Sly Old Fox Gets What He Deserves

Sly old fox
In the midnight darkness,
Hunting for his supper
Of delicious chickens.

Slowly, silently
He creeps along,
Quietly the chickens sleep
In the warmth of the hay.

Until the silence is disturbed
By the sly old fox.
Panic everywhere,
Feathers flying,
Chickens clucking.

But suddenly the rooster appears
And nips the fox,
Who screeches and disappears
In the darkness of the night.

Sharalouise Clive (10)
Ysgol Gymunedol Llanarth Community School

RABBITS

I'm a little rabbit,
All white and fluffy.
My tail is like a
Ball of cotton wool.
When danger is near,
I warn the other little rabbits,
By wagging my fluffy tail
And we all run away.

Kierron James (9)
Ysgol Gymunedol Llanarth Community School

The Moon

The moon is a ball, so shiny and bright,
It lights up the ceiling of the dark, dark night.
I looked out of my window and there was my moon,
I wish I could visit it very soon.

I took out the cat, as I said bye-bye,
This thing dropped down from the twinkling sky.
I thought it was a brick from far,
But the moon had kicked down a star.

As I try and find my moon-friend each day,
I'm told by the clouds it's floated away.
My moon, my balloon, so lovely and bright,
I'm glad that I see it every night.

There was a half-moon in the sky last night,
It was half a ball and half as bright.
I wonder if there are creatures on the moon?
I wonder if I'll see them soon?

Coral Kennerley (8)
Ysgol Gynradd Wirfoddol Myfenydd

Fish

I think fish are fast swimmers.
Some have got small fins
And some have big fins.
Some people try to catch them,
Sometimes they do,
Sometimes they don't.
I caught one once, but it wriggled away.
If I caught the biggest fish in the world,
It would really make my day.

Andrew Fricker-Power (8)
Ysgol Gynradd Wirfoddol Myfenydd

My Best Friend Is A Heron

My best friend is a heron.
On my way to school,
When I go over the bridge,
He's always there
Looking for food.

He's funny,
Everyone says so,
Just because
He's busy fishing
For food
All morning.

If I was a heron,
I'd do the same thing
And then
I would
Feel the same
As him.
At least I'd be able to fish a bit better!

Sometimes
He's not there.
Usually in the
Afternoon,
Because he's
Gone home,
Just like I'll do!

Joey Sinclair (8)
Ysgol Gynradd Wirfoddol Myfenydd

Monsters

I've never seen a monster,
I don't know if they exist,
Everyone seems to be a fan of them,
I think they got lost in a mist.

Every night I dream of these creatures
Coming up to me,
But when I wake up in the morning,
There's nothing for me to see.

At night I am too scared to sleep,
In case they come into my room,
But all of a sudden,
I hear a loud boom.

I look beneath the bedclothes
But there is nothing there,
Until I suddenly realise
Someone had messed up my hair.

Elinor Morgan (8)
Ysgol Gynradd Wirfoddol Myfenydd

THREE LITTLE KITTENS

Three little kittens
Have lost their mittens
And don't know where to find them.
Mother came, 'Where are your mittens?'
'They're lost, they're lost, they're lost.'
'No milk for you and you and you.'
'Miaow, miaow, miaow.'

Three little kittens
Have found their mittens,
'Look here, look here, look here.
Mother, Mother, we have found our mittens.'
'You clever kittens,
You have found your mittens,
More milk for you and you and you.'
'Purr, purr, purr.'

Gwenllian Rees-Evans (8)
Ysgol Gynradd Wirfoddol Myfenydd

BIRDS

Woodpecker's knocking on the tree,
Robin fluttering through the leaves,
Stork nesting on chimney high,
Red kite circling in the sky,
While waiting for his prey,
And that prey will die.

I wonder what it's like to be a bird?
Flying through the open sky,
Swooping, diving and soaring high.
The wind dashing through my feathers
In all kinds of weather.
I think I would love
Being a bird.

Steffan Woodruff (9)
Ysgol Gynradd Wirfoddol Myfenydd

My Two Dogs

My two dogs
Are lovely and soft,
Gentle and playful.
They will play with me
If I give them a treat,
Or stroke their necks or bellies.

They will play
And make me happy.
If I feel sad or grumpy,
They will wag their tails
And come to you
If you call them,
And hug you
In their funny little way.
My friends . . .
My two dogs.

Kara Knowler-Davies (9)
Ysgol Gynradd Wirfoddol Myfenydd

COLLIES

Collies are fluffy,
Fluffier than a fur coat.
A candyfloss on four legs,
That's collies!
They make such good pets.
Their noses are pointy!
Their teeth are sharp like sharks'.
They are not boring at all!
I love collies,
Oh yes!

Steffan Evans (9)
Ysgol Gynradd Wirfoddol Myfenydd

Raindrops

Raindrops falling from the sky,
From clouds that are grey, like elephants.
The sun has gone away to sleep!
People with umbrellas, cold and cheesed off,
Raindrops soaking our houses,
While I feel blue under the black sky.

Eleanor Farley (8)
Ysgol Gynradd Wirfoddol Myfenydd

HALLOWE'EN

Howling through the dark, creepy night,
A lot of spooky noises surround me!
Light is faintly shining on the windowpane,
Louder noises creeping outside our house.
Oh! I'm getting scared!
We all stay in our beds and pull our quilts over our heads.
'Eek! Eek!' Is it a ghost or is it a witch?
Even the loud noises get louder in the night's darkness!
Night is a spooky time of day.

Help! Help! Ghosts and witches
Are here, they screech and howl!
Louder and louder as the strange light shines,
Little girl, I am no more!
'Oh no! Oh no!' I scream as a witch points her finger.
When I looked, I was riding a broomstick!
Everywhere I went, people would hear cackling,
Everybody ran into their houses!
Now I am a *witch!*

Marisa Morgan (8)
Ysgol Gynradd Wirfoddol Myfenydd

The Day I Survived

I saw a huge, scary castle,
With windows blacked out from inside.
The large flags that hung from the wall
Looked like floating ghosts,
Waiting to jump on anyone who dared to enter.

I lurked inside
And soon I was also a captured prisoner,
Locked in this slimy building.
The spiders on the wall
Stood as large as tarantulas,
Spinning webs as big as nets.

I hear noises as loud as if
They are on a ghetto-blaster
Playing in the air.
The wind whistles loudly
As I shiver in the cold.

I start to dread
That I'd ever entered this deafening slammer,
Undercover in the woods.
My teeth start to chitter-chatter,
I freeze in shock.

I see a large shadow on the wall,
Could it be a giant monster,
Or is it a tiny, killer ant?
Aaaahhh! It's . . . it's . . .
Only a little fluffy kitten!

Ffion Lewis (10)
Ysgol Gynradd Wirfoddol Myfenydd

THE GHOST MANSION

As I enter the big, ghoulish, unearthly mansion,
I close the creaky door behind me.
The dust and cobwebs are like blankets of glittery cotton
And the untouched wood is starting to rot.

Something falls, causing a ghostly echo.
As I flinch, my heart races,
I feel as if I'm not alone.
A spine-chilling breeze fills the house.

The stairs quietly creak under my feet,
Hairy spiders run for cover,
Sunlight streams through a small hole
In the ancient, grimy, rotting wood.

I trip over something hard and cold,
As I turn around to look,
I'm frozen with fear, for lying there
Is a pale, gruesome, human *skull!*

Nicholas Morgan (11)
Ysgol Gynradd Wirfoddol Myfenydd

CHURCH AT NIGHT

In a damp church at night,
Nothing to see - just darkness.
The windows are like monster heads,
Staring at me, revealing their sharp teeth.

The lava-red devil is ringing
The loud bell covered in stringy cobwebs.
I look into the old, cracked mirror,
I quiver in my shoes.

A talking ghost whispers,
Candyman is in the bloody mirror.
My heart is about to jump out of my mouth,
But nothing happens.
Without warning, a slimy snake slithers up my leg,
I scream the church roof off.

The wind starts to howl,
A 'Z' of lightning appears in the sky,
Striking the weather vane,
Shaking the church as if there was an earthquake.
I ask myself, 'When will it be morning?'

Siôn Jones (11)
Ysgol Gynradd Wirfoddol Myfenydd

My Wild Imagination

Going into my dark cave of a bedroom at night,
My brain starts imagining things.
All alone at night in my solid, sweaty bed.

Killer clowns from outer space
Walk like rusty robots.
Poltergeist with gleaming red eyes
Start throwing blood-sucking needles.

The wind changes rapidly,
North to south, east to west,
It's cold, cold as ice.

I shiver violently.
I want to escape from this madness now!
But I can't.
The monsters are as scary as nothing.
I scream and they go away,
I am left alone, on my own.

Silk Younger (10)
Ysgol Gynradd Wirfoddol Myfenydd

My Bedroom At Night

When the sunlight disappears,
I get goosebumps and fear.
Shadows form on my wall,
I imagine they all call.

When I hear a creak downstairs,
I wonder what is there.
I dare not get out of bed,
Imagine all those ghosts, dead.

When the curtains start to shake,
It feels like an earthquake.
I wonder if it is a ghost
From the nearby coast?

When the sunlight comes up again,
I feel safe in my homely den.
I hear my mum shout,
'Come on, get up and about.'

Harriet Farley (11)
Ysgol Gynradd Wirfoddol Myfenydd

UNDER THE SEA

One hot summer's day,
I went on a glass-bottom boat.
I saw beautiful dolphins
That looked like rubber,
A vicious shark with very sharp teeth,
A gigantic splashing whale,
Colourful fish suddenly started dancing,
Pretty sea horses dodging the slimy seaweed.
Oh! I'd love to go under the sea.

Kelly Miller (9)
Ysgol Gynradd Wirfoddol Myfenydd

Under The Sea

Under the sea is lovely,
Full of different animals and fish,
Some small, some big,
Swift and as colourful as a rainbow.
Shiny crabs sliding with their gigantic claws,
Fat whales as black as night,
Fast dolphins as blue as the sea itself,
Long, thin, slippery seaweed,
Smooth, skinny shells,
Electric eels as fast as the speed of light,
A massive octopus waving his lanky arms about.
I love it under the sea.

Marie Wilmot (9)
Ysgol Gynradd Wirfoddol Myfenydd

THE THREE LITTLE PIGS

Once upon a time,
When the clock started to chime,
It chimed six,
Get out, you three little pigs.

The first one got some straw,
His house was very poor,
But the wolf blew it down,
He looked like a clown.

Then he went to look for twigs.
'I want some pigs.'
They both ran to the house,
When they saw a mouse.
'Do you want to come for a walk?'
'Sorry, I can't talk.'

They ran to the house of bricks,
Then they heard some kicks.
They opened the door
And the pigs hit him on the head
And he fell on the floor.

They put his head in a bin,
They did that with a pin.
They made some chops
And had them for the rest of the week!

Zoe Kennerley (10)
Ysgol Gynradd Wirfoddol Myfenydd

I'M SCARED

I'm scared of hairy spiders,
I'm scared of snakes,
I'm scared of poisonous stuff,
And I'm also scared of volcanoes
And earthquakes too.
I'm scared of scorpions and
I'm scared that the red devil
Is coming through my door,
Every inch of the wall
And I think its coming
Through my window.
My eyes are filled with terror.
Nightmares every night,
I'm sweating like a pig,
Fear going through me.
The morning comes,
I'm not afraid.

Trefor Hughes (10)
Ysgol Gynradd Wirfoddol Myfenydd

Alien's Visit To Earth

Ready, steady, go!
Off the UFO spins,
In one little flash,
Its windows like tiny slices of bread.

Down the UFO lands,
Onto the enormous ground,
Lights flashing away,
Out the slimy alien stomps.

Slipper-slapper,
Yuck!
So gungy,
So unbelievable,
So amazing,
So disgusting.

All the horrid people run
As fast as they can,
Shouting and screaming,
Then . . .
Not a person in sight!

Christian Lewis (11)
Ysgol Gynradd Wirfoddol Myfenydd

Dreams

I'd love to live in warm, sunny Spain,
From people in Wales that are sometimes insane.
I'd stare at the flowers that are so bright,
And enjoy the beautiful sight.

I'd love to go to the casino
And play a good game of bingo.
I'd win every time
And be at my prime.

I'd love to sunbathe on the beach
And eat a lovely, juicy peach.
I'd lie down until I'd have a tan,
And I'd be as hot as a frying pan.

I'd love to swim in the deep, blue sea
And ride on my favourite dolphin, called Lee.
I'd love to see the different kinds of fish
And that would be my best wish.

I wouldn't look forward to going back to Wales,
But at least I could tell them all my tales.
My luggage would weigh a ton,
But all my stories would be fun.

Carys Flynn (11)
Ysgol Gynradd Wirfoddol Myfenydd

Worm

I am a worm,
I live underground
Without making a single sound.
I've got a friend, Bug,
He's only a slug.
We eat apple pie,
Sometimes on the sly.

Daniel Evans (10)
Ysgol Y Dderi

The Bat's Plea

Please don't be frightened of me,
I am a night-time creature
Of wise and graceful joy;
Feel free to come, to visit me
In my den of wisdom.

I feel happy when I am sad,
And sad when I'm happy.
Please come and visit me
In my den of wisdom.

I teach my children
And my children teach me.
I feed them by breast
And they need my company.

I fly and swoop and duck,
Under, over and over, under,
And my life
Is a bit like this.

Carys Dalton (10)
Ysgol Y Dderi

Dolphins

Out to sea on a very clear day,
The waves are calm and it's peaceful today,
But below the surface there is something happening,
The dolphins are playing, feeding and chattering.

Everyone here having games and fun,
Enjoying a day in the warm summer sun.
Smiley faces and bright, beady eyes,
They play in the sea under bright blue skies.

Spinning and gliding all day long,
Clicking and squeaking, what a happy song.
The water glistening, sparkly, shiny blue,
So inviting, would you like a swim too?

Lowri Jones (11)
Ysgol Y Dderi

MOUSE

I am smaller than a bird,
Bigger than a moth,
I can fit in small holes
And eat quite a lot.
I can swing, using my tail,
This helps me eat a lot.

I live under the floorboards
And up in the attic.
I scream when you're near,
To scare you away.
When you're far,
I eat your leftovers.

I have friends
And relatives all around the world.
My mum in America,
My dad in Australia,
And my gran next door.
As you probably know,
Yes, I'm a mouse.

Callum Patterson (10)
Ysgol Y Dderi

I Found A Dragon In My Bed

I found a dragon in my bed,
It had a very big head.
It wouldn't eat any cheese,
So I tried ham instead.
It looked down at the ham with scorn,
Then the guardsman blew a horn.
I thought, 'Oh no, the warning horn.
It has blown from the north.'
It meant disaster, I knew it would.
I started towards the cellar door,
But then I remembered the dragon, poor.
I went to pick him up,
But suddenly, with a small 'phut,'
The dragon grew massive
And flew off down the passage.

Martin Theodorou (11)
Ysgol Y Dderi

A Bug's Life

I'm a little bug
And I live in a rug.
I am very small,
So I'm not very tall.
I crawl underground,
Without making a single sound.
My feet get sore,
When I walk past the door.
I like to eat food
When I'm in the mood.
On my head is a hat
That makes me look like a prat.
Anything comes my way,
I will make them pay.
My name is Sam,
That is who I am.

Guto Jones (11)
Ysgol Y Dderi

COLOURFUL CREATURE

I went for a walk along the sandy beach
And I saw a lovely, colourful creature
Swimming in the blue sea.
The creature saw me bending down,
I looked at its head,
It was wearing a golden crown.

It tickled my fingers when I touched its green head,
The creature rolled over and pretended he was dead.
I laughed and laughed until I cried,
I walked away, but I never forgot,
This fish was so wonderful,
It meant a lot.

Owen Williams (11)
Ysgol Y Dderi